THE ACCIDENTAL DEBUTANTE

JANE DUNN

B

Boldwood

First published in Great Britain in 2025 by Boldwood Books Ltd.

Copyright © Jane Dunn, 2025

Cover Design by Alice Moore Design

Cover Images: Shutterstock and Alamy

The moral right of Jane Dunn to be identified as the author of this work has been asserted in accordance with the Copyright, Designs and Patents Act 1988.

Every effort has been made to obtain the necessary permissions with reference to copyright material, both illustrative and quoted. We apologise for any omissions in this respect and will be pleased to make the appropriate acknowledgements in any future edition.

A CIP catalogue record for this book is available from the British Library.

Paperback ISBN 978-1-83533-561-1

Large Print ISBN 978-1-83533-560-4

Hardback ISBN 978-1-83533-559-8

Ebook ISBN 978-1-83533-562-8

Kindle ISBN 978-1-83533-563-5

Audio CD ISBN 978-1-83533-554-3

MP3 CD ISBN 978-1-83533-555-0

Digital audio download ISBN 978-1-83533-558-1

This book is printed on certified sustainable paper. Boldwood Books is dedicated to putting sustainability at the heart of our business. For more information please visit https://www.boldwoodbooks.com/about-us/sustainability/

Boldwood Books Ltd, 23 Bowerdean Street, London, SW6 3TN

www.boldwoodbooks.com

To Love
The first time ever I saw your face
I thought the sun rose in your eyes
And the moon and the stars were the gifts you gave
To the dark and the empty skies.

— EWAN MACCOLL, WRITTEN FOR HIS
FUTURE WIFE, PEGGY SEEGER

CONTENTS

AUTHOR NOTE

All my five novels exist entire unto themselves. *The Marriage Season, An Unsuitable Heiress, A Scandalous Match* and *A Lady's Fortune* all have new characters in new situations. This fifth, *The Accidental Debutante,* is also a stand-alone, but it follows the story of some of the characters from *An Unsuitable Heiress.* However, you do not need to have read that book to completely understand and enjoy this one.

1

THE WINGED VENUS TAKES FLIGHT

Spring 1817

It was midnight and the crowd at Astley's Amphitheatre was feverish with expectation. Outside, the night was cold and blustery; inside, the steamy air smelt of ale and onions and hot human bodies. Prebbles Flying Circus reached the climax of their show when the horses thundered into the ring and were ridden round the amphitheatre at speed in a flurry of flying hooves and swirling dust. All eyes were on their star rider, Clorinda the Winged Venus, dressed in narrow silk pantaloons and a tight braided gold jacket with small padded wings on her shoulders. A mask half-obscured her face and a feathered cap emphasised the luxuriance of flaxen hair that cascaded to her waist. Astride her horse, Percy, she rode without a saddle and was fearless and supreme in her horsemanship.

As she galloped round the perimeter of the arena, Eliza Gray savoured the familiar sight of the audience's faces whirling before her, smiling, grimacing, shouting, flushed and shiny with liquor. This was her last sight of something she had known nearly all her life and she was filled with sadness, combined with the thrill and trepidation of an adventure about to begin. Percy galloped alongside another rider and as their speed was matched, she stood to spring off her horse and onto the other animal in one graceful leap, their paces never slowing. After a circuit, Eliza leapt back again onto her own mount and immediately reined Percy in to a steady canter before balancing like a dancer on one leg, her arms outstretched. In a fluent movement that seemed to defy gravity, Eliza then executed a backflip and landed as light as a bird on his rump while Percy maintained his metronomic gait, as trusty as the sun.

The crowd went wild. Ale splattered down on the heads of those in the pit as the audience in the boxes threw up their hands and cheered in delight. Eliza then performed a controlled handstand on her horse's back as he sped round the amphitheatre, and a roar went up that echoed through the surrounding streets. Even the boatmen on the mighty Thames heard and smiled, as they navigated their large-sailed barges downriver through the stone pillars of Westminster Bridge. Astley's was a favourite place of entertainment where everyone from the poor to the haut ton gathered.

Eliza rode up alongside her fellow equestrian, Rose Bowman, who was dressed as a highwaywoman, slung about with pistols and wearing a tricorn hat. They brought the show to an end, the horses and their riders left in clouds of dust and the crowd, as they always did, roared for more.

Eliza rode Percy through to the stables where the usual young bloods congregated, waiting for her and the other circus girls, hoping for favours. But she barely glanced at them, determined to take her horse to his stall and rub him down before he had his supper of hay. The stable boys were busy with the other horses, but Eliza knew she would not see Percy again and this clutched at her heart. As he munched, she put her arms around his neck and kissed his cheek, meeting his lustrous eyes one last time. 'Thank you, old friend,' she muttered, breathing in the smell of him. 'I will never forget you.'

Mrs Prebble had emerged into the yard to see off the hangers-on. She said in a loud voice that invited no demur, 'Go home, gentlemen! The show is over.' A fierce, no-nonsense woman, she was as wide as she was high and nobody chose to cross her. Prebbles Flying Circus was contracted by Astley's for the Season and she ran the show with iron discipline.

Once the yard was clear, Eliza emerged from Percy's stable. Gazing back at him, eating, unaware of the turmoil in her heart, tears sprang to her eyes as she ran up the outside steps to the quarters she shared with Rose. Her friend was already asleep when Eliza tiptoed into the dark room. Earlier in the day she had packed her small valise with all her worldly goods and stowed it under her bed. Tonight was the night Eliza had determined to run away. She longed to find her lost parents and live a more regular life, with love, a home and her own family, something she had never known beyond the bluff camaraderie of the circus people with whom she had spent her girlhood.

Glancing out of the window, she was grateful the wind had swept the night sky of clouds; the full moon would light her way across the river to St James's Place. The circus girls had talked about Mistress Burridge who lived at No. 3 and would find work for runaway girls, asking no questions. But she knew she would have to disguise her youth and looks as much as possible to walk the streets alone at night.

Eliza's training with Prebbles had not just been as an acrobatic dancer and rider but as an actress too. She had decided the best way to pass unmolested was to look as if she were an old washerwoman. Aware of Rose's regular breathing and not wishing to wake her, she sat at the window and pulled the thin curtain back a fraction to let in the moonlight. Sitting on her bed, she etched wrinkles across her forehead with her stick of grey theatrical make-up. She added soot to the front of her fair hair then slipped on her cloak to cover her workaday dress, pulling the hood over her head.

Looking down at Rose, her breath caught. They had grown almost as close as sisters in their years of harsh training, sharing the pains and small triumphs along the way. But Eliza knew her friend did not wish to accompany her on this risky adventure; she too wanted a broader life but had never had the restless desire to discover who she was. Instead, Eliza had to go on alone. Afraid of losing her courage, she hurriedly pulled the ring with the blue stone from her finger. Rose had little jewellery of her own and had always loved this ring. Eliza gently lifted the sleeping girl's hand and slipped it onto the middle finger where she knew it would fit. She placed her farewell letter beside the pillow, and another letter for Mrs Prebble, thanking her for rescuing her from the streets of Bath all those years ago.

She grasped a small cloth toy fox from under her own pillow and stuffed it into the pocket of her cloak. Her valise was tied in a sheet for disguise and she slung it over her shoulder to tiptoe down the stairs. The clock on the great church of St Margaret's struck twice, its muffled sound floating across the water.

Pulling her cloak close, Eliza slipped into the chilly night and turned towards the river. The crowds had long departed, weaving home along Westminster Bridge Road, full of good humour and ale. There were still a few carts, some gentlemen's curricles and the occasional chaise bowling home after a party or ball. She had pulled her hood so low she could barely see, but knew that crossing the bridge would bring her to Westminster Palace. She'd marked it with a red cross on the quick sketch she'd made, copied from a map the Prebbles kept in the locked office.

Halfway across the bridge, the northerly wind off the Thames was so persistent and bitter that Eliza found it hard to walk. People passed like wraiths bundled in cloaks and sacks against the chill. It took all her energy to make it to the northern bank where she eventually reached Parliament Street. Eliza had been warned to avoid the Park and Birdcage Walk, areas frequented at night by predatory men and half-feral dogs and children, but even The Mall with its numerous trees seemed dark and threatening when you were cold and alone.

With growing anxiety about what lay ahead, Eliza's adventure suddenly seemed less exciting and bold, and more likely foolhardy and fraught with danger. Her tired mind began to question whether Mistress Burridge would be the helpmeet she had hoped; perhaps the work she would help her find would not be as an assistant in a draper's shop or a maid in a grand house, but as a worker in a bawdy house. She realised how bleak was her world, without family, and now without work or a home. How wild and hare-brained this escapade suddenly seemed. She shivered with more than the cold.

Eliza had taught herself to read from the novels Mrs Prebble had borrowed from the lending library. She had learned of the variety of lives lived outside the narrow confines of the circus, but had become aware too of how lacking in education and experience she was. She plodded on, growing increasingly exhausted, afraid she had made a terrible mistake. The moon lent its light to show her the way but her scribbled map was hard to decipher and putting down her burden, she came to a stop, peering at the dark buildings, glimpsing a few fleeting shadows travelling in the opposite direction.

Eliza had absolutely no idea where she was. Her spirit

quailed. Before her she glimpsed a long strip of dark wasteland, desolate and wintry in the moonlight. In her fevered imagination, it was as if no one had passed through since the beginning of the world. She shuddered as the distant clank of metal on stone brought her back to the present. Hope flared again and she turned towards the sounds of life. The night was suddenly full of noises: a distant cry, the hoot of an owl, dogs barking, the occasional clop of horses' hooves and a carter's oath. Ahead of her was the hum and faint rattle of metal wheels on cobbles on what must be a main thoroughfare. Eliza shouldered her baggage once more and set off to meet her future.

Turning the corner into a wider street lined with grand houses, she was buffeted by a sudden gust of wind and stumbled into the road just as a speeding curricle appeared from nowhere. A great cry of warning rent the air. She fell to her knees as the horses, panicked at the sight of her and being reined in hard by the driver, trampled over her. The curricle wheels clanked to a halt just before crushing her leg. Eliza's head hit the cobbled road with a sickening thump and everything went black.

* * *

His lordship, Raven Purfoy – more formally Earl Purfoy of Hartfield Castle in the county of Herefordshire – was in a good mood. White's was his favourite club for a reason: it was filled with aristocrats like himself, mainly of a Tory political persuasion, with more wealth than 90 per cent of the general population put together. Landowners all, they were convivial gamesters, and gossip of fortunes lost or gained entertained the ebbing hours. He had had a good night, winning at his favourite occupation, playing hazard with well-lubricated friends, but it was past two o'clock in the morning and he was tired and over-toped on brandy. He pocketed his winnings, rose from the table, saluted his friends and set off in search of Taz, his groom.

Lord Purfoy carried his drink better than most, but those who knew him well would recognise that his customary drawl was more marked, his dark eyes more glittering, his pallor heightened by points of colour on his cheekbones. As he strolled into the chill night he glanced around. He knew his tiger, Taz, cared more for his horses than for anything, as in fact did he. Taz would not allow them to idle in the cold as other grooms did, waiting on the whim of their masters. Lord Purfoy put two fingers to his lips and gave a piercing whistle and, within a minute, his smart navy blue curricle, pulled by a pair of the finest greys, trotted into St James's. Taz jumped down and his sharp black eyes glanced disapprovingly at his master. 'M'lord, ye're too foxed to 'andle them prancers. I'll keep the reins.'

'Impudent fellow! My friends are right. I allow you far too much licence,' Purfoy muttered as he walked round to climb into the driver's seat.

'Sir, neither you nor I wish these prime 'uns injured.' Taz had ultimate authority when it came to the welfare of the horses. He had been picked off the streets by Lord Purfoy who had noticed that this wizened jockey-like figure had a miraculous way with animals. However, Raven Purfoy's admiration for him was not returned. Taz only had eyes for the horses, although as humans went, he thought his master was as good as they could get. But he offered no forelock-tugging respect; in fact his lordship's friend, Mr Shilton, a stickler for propriety, complained bitterly at the liberties allowed to a mere servant, given by his master the respect due to a friend.

Lord Purfoy was irascible. 'I'm driving my own beasts, damn you! I still have my wits, you know.' He hauled himself into the driving seat and Taz reluctantly conceded and leapt up to his perch behind. In Raven Purfoy's uncharacteristically slack hands, the horses set off at a pace too fast for the road and heading south down St James's Street, in the opposite direction from home. Taz was about to climb over the back of the seat to take the reins himself when an old woman, bundled up in a cloak, was suddenly before them, blown by the wind it seemed, and staggering under the weight of her baggage. Too late, Lord Purfoy pulled the horses up hard and the woman, with a cry and in a flurry of cloth, tumbled under their hooves. The shock of the accident sobered him up.

'Damnation! Where did she come from? Taz, check the horses!'

* * *

Eliza emerged from the blackness to find herself lying on the street, her head thrumming with pain and with a stranger's fingers trying to open the top fastening on her cloak. In a panic, she struggled. 'Git yer 'ands off me!' she said as loudly as she could, but just this effort drained her of energy and she closed her eyes, dizziness overcoming her.

When she opened her eyes again, she gazed straight into the handsomest face she had ever seen. The stranger was leaning over her, his breath smelling of brandy, his eyes dark and intense. His hat and gloves were tossed on the cobbles where he kneeled and his black hair was dishevelled, a wavy lock flopping forward onto his forehead. His fingers had been moving along her jaw and down her neck, in search of a pulse. 'Thank God!' he said with emotion in his voice.

Eliza could not remember being shown any tenderness in her life and the intimate touch of his hand, the concern in his eyes, was electrifying. Even though it was the touch of a stranger, in this instant the exultant recognition of *something* intensified her senses. She felt her spirit flow out to meet his. As he turned to address the small man behind him, Eliza noticed his high cheek-bones and fine aristocratic nose, his noble authority and calm, and was reminded poignantly of her beautiful black stallion left behind at the circus. Percy was the only living being she loved with all her heart and trusted with her life, and she felt the sharp pang of his loss constrict her chest.

Eliza heard the stranger's voice continue in an unruffled way. 'She lives, which is a mercy, but I have to check for injuries.' His fingers gingerly probed the back of her skull through her coils of hair and when he withdrew them, she noticed they were dark with blood. In the shadows she saw him start and look at her more intently. 'Does anything hurt?'

Having heard him speak, she knew she had to talk in the 'proper' way she had learned as a child and answered carefully. 'Only my head. But I've known worse.'

'What's your name?'

'Eliza.'

'Eliza what?'

Fear clutched at her heart. If she told him the truth of where she had come from, she would be escorted back to the circus. In a moment of clarity, Eliza realised she had to pretend she could not recall anything, apart from her given name.

The gentleman, watching her hold her head, waited and she answered haltingly, with a catch in her voice, 'I can't remember.'

He responded in his sardonic way, 'I shall call you Miss Mysterious until you do.' Eliza struggled to sit and he extended a hand, so warm to her frozen touch. 'Do you recollect where you may have come from, or where you were going?'

'I don't know,' she muttered, aware of how many lies she now had to tell. Looking up, she asked, 'What is *your* name, sir?'

Lord Purfoy hesitated. 'Purfoy. Lord Purfoy,' he said, his languor returned, 'and this is Taz, my tiger.'

Eliza was shocked. She had never been this close to a member of the nobility before. Callow young scions of noble families gathered after the show in the hopes of wheedling a kiss, but she always gave them short shrift. This man was so much more distinguished and she turned her head away, embarrassed by the social gulf between them.

Then she glanced across at Taz to see a face that was comfortingly familiar to her. There were circus folk who worked with the animals who had the same dark weathered skin and bright, questing eyes that missed nothing. Eliza felt entirely at home in this man's company. His manner towards her too seemed to soften. 'Ye a lucky lass not to be more out of sorts. That 'ead'll need seeing to but no limbs are broken, thank the devil!' He spat into the gutter.

Taz had collected her valise from the road and picked up Mr Fox. Eliza had not realised he had flown out of her pocket in the collision and her heart turned over at the thought she might have lost him. She grasped the small creature and pressed it to her cheek, the only connection with her old life, so distant in time and now no more than a fragment of a dream.

She saw Taz show his master her map which he'd found crumpled on the road, and watched the two men frown as the smaller stuffed it into his pocket.

Lord Purfoy asked her, 'Do you have any memory of your family?'

Eliza shook her head. 'Mr Fox is the only family I have.' When his lordship looked nonplussed, Taz explained it was the toy he had retrieved from the road and Eliza interrupted firmly, 'He's *not* a toy, he's my family and been with me all my life.' She realised how much she had revealed in that comment but consoled herself that she was only concealing her recent past. Her loss of memory was only half a lie as she had little idea of what had come before the circus, and had never known her true identity. Neither man, however, seemed to have realised this slip-up in her story, so exercised were they with the present conundrum of where she might belong.

'Is there anywhere you'd like me to deliver you?' Lord Purfoy sounded concerned.

Eliza was uncertain and said in a hesitant voice, 'I did have a map with an address and the name of a lady who might give me work.'

Lord Purfoy ignored this and said to Taz, 'I can only think that Mrs Wolfe would be the person to know best how to proceed.' He offered his hand to help Eliza to her feet. 'Miss Mysterious, let's get you off the street.' She stood unsteadily. 'I will have to take you somewhere safe until your memory returns.'

Taz helped her up into the curricle as Raven Purfoy sprang into the driving seat, miraculously returned to cold sobriety by the crisis. He gazed with some anxiety at the young woman beside him, her head drooping. 'Taz, sit up here and make sure Miss Mysterious does not slip off the seat.'

Taz barely took up any space, so diminutive and lean was his frame, but he put his arm around Eliza's shoulder to hold her upright. Everything about him seemed reassuringly familiar. 'You smell of horses,' she murmured.

'That I do. The best prancers in London.' Taz's voice was proud and emphatic.

'I think it the sweetest smell in the world.' Eliza's response was quiet but both men heard and exchanged surprised glances. Neither had ever met any woman who would agree with her. Taz felt a certain respect for a female who obviously loved horses too, and Raven Purfoy looked closely at this grimy girl sitting beside him, suspecting there was much more to her than met the eye.

They were bowling through the dark streets and Eliza was doubtful about where they were headed, but in the sinewy grasp of this small man, she felt secure. The horses too were the most perfectly matched pair she had ever seen, their elegant heads held with grace and their fast trot, synchronised and swift. Eliza decided these men understood and loved their prancers. In her experience, such men were inherently good. She noticed that Lord Purfoy seemed entirely in control of his pair of greys, holding the reins lightly in his gloved hands.

He turned to look at her and said, 'So, Miss Mysterious, what induced you to scamper about the streets well past midnight, throwing yourself in harm's way? Rather foolhardy, don't you think?' Before she could answer, his fine-boned face was enlivened with a knowing smile. 'Oh, I forgot! Since being cracked in the crown, you can't remember!' His mischievous look made Eliza wonder if he believed her story at all.

She did not think all the blame lay with her and answered with some indignation, 'Sir, if you'd been driving less recklessly, I wouldn't now be sitting here with a bloodied head.'

Eliza felt Taz's chuckle deep in his chest. They were so closely packed on the front seat built for two that she was aware of the warmth of the bodies of very different men squeezed on either side of her.

Lord Purfoy did not care to have his driving skills questioned and responded sharply, 'Pert miss! If I hadn't run you over, you'd by now be in the toils of Mistress Burridge and her sort. You have me to thank for evading that fate!'

'How do you know I was on my way to Mistress Burridge? She was to help me find a position as a maid.'

'That may have been your idea, but I fear such innocent employment is not Burridge's forte.'

Eliza's growing sense of ease evaporated as once more a sense of foreboding took hold. 'Well, where are you taking me? I'll need to find employment in order to live.'

'I have friends whose town mansion is in Brook Street, where Mrs Wolfe presides over the household. She is a sensible woman who will give you shelter until your head heals and your memory returns.'

Eliza's nervousness was not allayed; surely this was very presumptuous of him? They were approaching Grosvenor Square and she looked up anxiously. 'How do you know Mrs Wolfe will be happy to give me lodging when you haven't asked her?'

His lordship looked smug as he drew his horses up in front of a grand porticoed house, the windows dark. 'The Wolfes are old friends of mine and I know they'd do anything for me, as I would for them.'

'But at this impious hour?'

Taz had leapt to the ground to take the horses' heads and Lord Purfoy climbed down from his seat and walked round to help Eliza. He dismissed her worries with an airy, 'This is a household cursed with a brawling brat. I doubt they ever sleep!' He took her hand and watched her closely as she reeled a little, unsteady on her feet. 'Take my arm,' he said brusquely as he led her up the steps and knocked gently. They waited. He knocked again, more insistently, and the large black door opened just a crack to reveal a bleary-eyed kitchen boy. 'Please tell Gibbons that Lord Purfoy is here on an urgent matter.' They entered to stand in the grand hallway with only a lit candlestick to illuminate the cathedral darkness. In the shadows, its serpentine sweep of staircase rose to the left from the black and white marble floor, and a painting of a handsome gentleman in court clothes of the previous century dominated the opposite wall.

Eliza had never set foot anywhere so imposing in her life and for the second time that night, her spirit quailed at the thought of what a wild plan her dash for freedom was proving to be. She had always thought she would make her own way in the world and not impose on others, and here she was about to be a huge imposition on a stranger. She glanced sideways at Lord Purfoy who seemed to be much more sanguine than she.

A genial elderly gentleman emerged from the kitchen stair-case just as a tall man walked out from an upstairs room, wearing a brocade dressing gown, and descended the stairs. 'Raven! What the devil! Do you know the hour, man?' Alick Wolfe's words were full of exasperation but his eyes were friendly, and when they alighted on Eliza, they widened at her outlandish appearance. 'Who's the young lady? And why injured?' With his face full of concern, he came forward to look at her wound.

'This is Miss Mysterious, a young woman whom I ran over on the street.'

His friend suppressed a smirk as he said under his breath, 'Surely not, Rav? You, the great Corinthian, most skilled driver of us all?'

Lord Purfoy cast him a quelling look. 'She seems to have lost her memory and can only recall her first name, Eliza.'

Mr Wolfe took her hand. 'I am pleased to meet you, Miss Eliza. My name is Alick Wolfe; Mrs Wolfe is asleep upstairs.' He then looked at his friend. 'I see your dilemma, Rav. You cannot nurse the young lady at your house. I'm sure Cory will be more than happy to offer her sanctuary until her memory is restored.' Eliza met his humorous brown eyes and knew here was someone she could trust.

Gibbons had just received her valise from Taz and came forward. 'Shall I get Polly to make up the Chinese bedroom for the young lady?' he asked his master. 'And Polly can then clean the wound.'

Held in the hand of this benign household, Eliza felt safe for the first time and the tension ebbed from her body. She was overtaken by exhaustion, and sudden hunger too, but dared not ask for any more indulgence. Before following Gibbons and her luggage upstairs, she turned to the two friends and said, her voice faltering, 'Thank you, Mr Wolfe, and you, my lord. This is more kindness than I could ever expect.' She sank into the low curtsey she had been taught to give at the end of her performance and was disconcerted by the surprised amusement in the men's eyes.

'Come Rav, let me get you a drink. You look hollowed out.' Alick led his friend into the library where the embers had burned low. As they sat either side of the fireplace, he asked, 'Well?'

Lord Purfoy stretched his long legs out and sighed. 'I was driving too fast and foxed. Taz tried to stop me but I thought my wits were sharp enough. It seems Taz was right.' He then sat forward, his eyes looking haunted in the firelight. 'I was deadly afraid I'd killed her, Al.' His expressive hands were clasped so hard together his fingers had turned white. 'The sight of her, apparently lifeless in the road, brought back memories I'd long struggled to forget.'

Alick touched his arm in concern. 'Rav, why so distressed? She's fine.'

'I know. When she opened her eyes, I was overwhelmed with relief that this time, Fate was kind.'

Alick steered his friend's thoughts back to the present. 'So, who is she? And what's the chit doing out so late? Running away?' Alick Wolfe's eyes were troubled.

'That's what I presume. She had in her hand a rough sketch

of a map with a starting point from south of the river and it seems
Mistress Burridge's abode in St James's Place as a destination.'
Both men frowned, their eyes meeting. 'She hoped that lady
would find her employment as a maid in a noble house. We, of
course, know better. So obviously I could not deliver an innocent
to that door.' Lord Purfoy gazed into the embers so intensely it
seemed he was willing them to break into flames once more.

'No, certainly, Rav. But do we know she's innocent? I'm
welcoming her into the heart of my family, after all.'

'She's not as disreputable as she looks. Taz – who knows
everything, as I have learned to my cost over the years – surmised
from her map that she may have run away from the circus at
Astley's.'

'Dammit, Rav, the circus! It attracts all kinds of scapegraces
and scandal!'

His lordship shook his head. 'There's something about her
that is different. She can talk like she's gutter-born but also knows
how to talk like a lady. She loves horses, so that's halfway to being
a Trojan, don't you think?' He smiled. 'Taz says she's used to
horses; she certainly approved of the smell of him!' Both men
laughed heartily and quaffed their brandy, and as the liquor
warmed his spirit, Raven Purfoy's composure was restored.

Alick looked at his friend with a keen eye. 'I can see that
having run her down, you couldn't leave her on the roadside.'

'Aye, there's the rub. As Taz pointed out, she's my responsibility until we really know who she is and where's she's from.' He
stood up to leave. 'I really am grateful, Al. I knew I could count
on you, and especially on your redoubtable wife.'

'Well it's lucky you live next door. I don't have far to go to
complain, should this all turn out to be a very bad idea indeed!'

* * *

Eliza was given a candle and followed Gibbons and his lamp up the wide staircase past the first-floor drawing room, dark with shadows, and what must be the master bedroom, its door slightly ajar, and on to the second floor. In the dimness she could make out the ancestral portraits hanging on the walls, their eyes watching her in the flickering flame. She felt such an imposter. How could she lie to these generous people? But equally she knew she could not return to her old life having tasted even this small, if rather alarming, sip of freedom. Gibbons led her into a room that seemed palatial in the swooping arc of his lamp. The walls had a ghostly tracery of twining vines and birds and the high, canopied bed dominated the centre of the room. A young maid was turning back the sheet and a steaming jug of water waited for her on the dressing table.

'This is Polly and she will help deal with your wound. I hope you sleep well, miss.' Gibbons bowed and left the room. Eliza sat down in the chair by the looking glass and saw her reflection for the first time. She gasped in shock. What a disgrace she was, her face grimy, her flaxen hair grey with dirt, and dark red at the crown with dried blood. Her clothes had always been workaday but now they were stained with the mud and dust of the road. She looked like a beggar-girl and felt ashamed. What had Mr Wolfe and Lord Purfoy thought of her? She was amazed to be given this beautiful room and not just a cot above the horses in the mews.

Polly straightened the quilt and came to stand beside her. Eliza was embarrassed to be offered the services of a maid who had been woken from her bed, and gazed uncertainly into the young woman's sleepy blue eyes. But Polly's charming, scrubbed face and friendly manner put Eliza at her ease, grateful for her care examining her head. 'Lawks, miss! What a mess. Lucky it's not bleeding any more.' With a damp cloth she began to dab delicately at the dried blood in the surrounding hair, careful not to disturb the healing wound.

'Thank you, Polly. Can you tell me how large the cut is?'

'Only about an inch, miss, but there's no accounting for heads; they bleed like stuck pigs!'

'Do you have a cloth I can use to wash my face and hands?'

Polly handed over another linen towel and Eliza dipped it into the jug of water. 'Oh, what a relief to get this dirt off my skin.' She was just trying to clean the soot from the front of her hair when there was a knock at the door.

Polly opened it to find Gibbons with a tray and a plate of bread and ham and a couple of sweet pastries. 'I thought the young lady might be hungry,' he said as he handed it over. Eliza could have wept with gratitude.

Polly was sleepy and stifled a yawn. 'I think your head is now as cleaned of blood and dirt as possible, miss. Do you need help undressing?'

'Thank you, Polly, for all your care. I'm sure it's time for you to return to bed. I can manage to undress myself.' Eliza had never had the luxury of a maid and seldom wore stays as she was often in the loosest of clothes. For performing she wore pantaloons or tights, and bound her breasts beneath her tight jackets so she could execute her riding feats unimpeded by her costume. Polly looked relieved and bade goodnight, turning towards the stairs to the maids' quarters at the top of the house.

Having eaten every morsel of food offered to her, Eliza carefully hung up her dress and chemise, washed her stockings in the remains of the water and hung them to dry on the windowsill. She only had one other set of clean clothes which she unfolded from her portmanteau, ready for the morrow. Slipping into a simple calico nightgown, she placed Mr Fox on the bedside table as a talisman to watch over her as she clambered into the high bed and fell into an immediate dreamless sleep.

* * *

Just after dawn, the house in Brook Street began to come alive. Servants cleaned out the grates, swept the hearths and straightened cushions while others prepared breakfast. As it became more truly morning, pitchers of hot water were carried upstairs to the family rooms, and one for the mysterious guest who had arrived in the middle of the night, her head cracked open by some ruffian – so went below-stairs gossip.

Alick Wolfe had been lying awake since seven in the morning, reluctant to rouse his sleeping wife curled beside him, a hand casually flung over his arm. He gazed down on her face, amazed still by her beauty and his good fortune in being loved by her. Her long russet hair lay in a loose plait behind her, her skin slightly flushed from the warmth of their bed. Her fingers were stained in places by the pigments she used for painting the portraits that were beginning to bring her fame. He felt an irresistible urge to kiss her.

As he bent his head, her eyes opened and met his. 'Good morning, Mr Wolfe, I hope you slept well?'

He pulled her close and tucked his arm round her back. 'I slept very well until dear Rav came calling at three in the morning.'

'Good heavens! Why on earth? He has his own home to go to. Was he too foxed to notice he'd come to the wrong door?' She laughed.

'No, my darling Cory, by the time I saw him he'd sobered up. But I'm afraid we have a house guest.' Alick looked rueful.

Corinna struggled to sit up and said, a note of urgency in her voice, 'You mean your American cousin has arrived early?'

'No, this is a stranger to us both. A young woman run over by his lordship last night, travelling too fast and in his cups. As you can imagine, Taz was most put out.'

'Poor girl! Is she injured? Who is she?'

'Well, that's the mystery. Her name is Eliza but she cannot remember anything else. Rav, of course, has called her Miss Mysterious, which amuses him greatly.'

'I suppose he couldn't take her home without a chaperone, to protect them both,' Corinna mused. 'Is she hurt, Alick?'

'She had a crack on the head but it had stopped bleeding by the time she arrived at our door.'

'Goodness! Perhaps that accounts for the lost memory. I'd better get up and see to her.'

Alick Wolfe's arm around Corinna's shoulders tightened as he folded her close to his chest. 'Not yet, my darling Mrs Wolfe.' He smiled down at her, his eyes intense with desire. 'You're so warm and soft, and smell as sweet as hay, and I cannot resist you. Thank ye gods I no longer have to!' They both laughed and slipped lower under the embroidered quilt.

'So I smell as sweet as hay, sir! You make me sound like one of your favourite hunters.' Corinna's giggle ended in a sigh. 'Oh, Alick! I can't be long. I want to welcome this young woman to breakfast. And our little Emma will soon be scampering in, having escaped from Nurse.' She lifted her arms from the warmth of their bed to slip around his neck, murmuring, 'But it's very nice to be woken up like this...'

* * *

Eliza too was awoken early, but by the solitary tolling of a church bell, and a tide of powerfully mixed emotions washed over her. Most insistent was a sense of dismay; this passing stranger had imposed her upon his friends in such a high-handed manner that she felt ashamed. She was also in awe of her surroundings. Since she was seven, she had only had a dream of home. Found by Mrs Prebble, wandering, lost and crying, on the streets of Bath, she had been taken to live at Prebbles Flying Circus. There was no settled home for her even then, for the troupe moved from town to town, staying in lodgings or sometimes making do as best they could in the woods and the fields. Gazing round this beautiful room, Eliza wondered if this was what having a home meant. But in the morning light it seemed more like a palace and she, an imposter princess.

She tried to take it all in, knowing it would only be hers for a day; she would have to go and find work and make her new life as best she could. She gazed at the two large windows and the prettiest hand-painted wallpaper that transported her into a garden. The bed was hung with what looked like silk, embroidered with green willows and small figures with colourful parasols. She wriggled into the depths of the warm, soft bed just as there was a knock at the door and Polly entered, carrying a steaming pitcher of water. 'Morning, miss, I hope you slept well.'

Eliza sat up and stretched. She gazed at her calico dress hanging in the morning light, her spirit suspended between the insecurity of her past and hopes for a future, as yet completely unknown. As she slipped into her plain gown, she felt how incongruous it was with this grandly elegant room. She attempted to examine her wound, probing gently with her fingers. It didn't seem to be oozing and so with care she combed out her long fair hair, so pale it was almost translucent in the light. When she was performing she wore it loose as an essential embellishment to her persona as the Winged Venus, but for the rest of the time she braided it into two long plaits and coiled them round her head. She peered into the looking glass, meeting with an anxious frown the reflected gaze of her unusual eyes, one lilac-grey, the other greeny-gold.

She left the room, her heart unsteady, readying herself to meet the strangers who had taken her in, under duress she feared. The staircase and hall looked much more friendly as early sunlight spilled in through the large east window. Ancestral portraits no longer appeared to be following her with suspicious eyes and she could hear a child's voice somewhere, and the clink of china. These domestic sounds of a great house come awake settled her nerves.

Eliza was drawn to an open door and peeped in. There sat a woman, her russet hair in a loose bun, her head bent over a book of accounts with a cup of coffee by her side, its steam curling lazily. Eliza knocked lightly on the door and the woman looked up, her beautiful hazel-green eyes meeting her own as she rose to her feet. 'My dear, come in. My name is Corinna Wolfe, I think you met my husband, Mr Wolfe, last night?'

Eliza walked towards her and was not certain if a curtsey was required in greeting. Instead, Corinna grasped her hand and squeezed it. 'How's your poor head? May I see?'

Eliza had to remind herself not to slip into the everyday talk used by the circus folk. 'Mrs Wolfe, I'm very grateful for your and your husband's care. I won't impose on your kindness any longer.' Her voice sounded careful and stilted to her ears.

'My dear! Of course you'll stay until you've recovered and your memory has returned. There is no way that we could coun- tenance letting you leave until you know who you are and have somewhere to go. Now let me see your wound.' Corinna led Eliza to a chair by the table and poured her a cup of coffee, then walked behind her to examine the back of her head. Gently parting the hair, she said, 'Well, you're lucky it is just your memory you have lost. You must have had quite a bang. It's still a trifle swollen but looking good. Do you have any headache?'

'No. And I slept very well in your lovely room, thank you.'

Corinna walked back to her chair. 'Well, I hope you will consider it your room until you are restored to health.'

Eliza felt a surge of joy. Such generosity meant she could be safe for a while. She met Corinna's eyes which were intent upon her face. 'Now, Miss Eliza, what do you remember? Lord Purfoy said it was clear you were used to horses and liked them.'

'I do love horses. That much I know. And my name is Eliza but I can't remember anything more than that.' Eliza's voice wavered as she was clutched with shame at lying to this kind, trusting woman, but she was so determined not to be taken back to the circus that she knew she had to continue with her charade until she had had time to work out what to do next.

'It must be a most alarming experience. You may have family worried sick about you.' Corinna's face was wreathed in concern.

Eliza was saved from answering by a giggle behind her. The door was pushed open as a blonde child toddled in carrying a cloth doll. Corinna put her arms out and said, laughing, 'Meet our little daughter, Emma.' In one deft movement she lifted the small wriggling body onto her lap. As she gazed down at her, her face was suffused with love.

The child's nurse stood at the door. 'Mrs Wolfe, Miss Emma's so determined and insisted on seeing Mama. Her talk is coming on wondrously well. She manages sentences!'

Corinna laughed. 'I know, Meg, she's a most forward child. I'll bring her through to you after breakfast.' She smiled at the small bright face and gestured towards their guest saying, 'Emmy, this is Miss Eliza.'

Eliza put out a finger for her to grasp. 'How do you do, Miss Emma.'

'How do, Miss Eliza.'

Eliza felt her heart skip a beat; did the lively child remind her of her own lost childhood, or was it that she ignited the old longing in her for family?

Corinna was watching the face of this stranger who had arrived like a creature from another world. She was so simply dressed, and her remarkable hair was coiled in a way that made her look like a maiden from the Norse countries. The delicate beauty of her face and hands and her slender, athletic build reminded Corinna of a dancer, but she sensed that beneath this ethereal beauty was steely courage and strength. She was struck with how much she'd like to paint her portrait. 'Miss Eliza, I'm a painter and I wondered if you'd be happy to sit for me this afternoon?'

Eliza was taken aback that anyone would be interested enough to want to paint her, but nodded, her eyes bright with the realisation that this relaxed, comfortable household would be her home for a few more days. The occasional whinny from the mews beyond the garden made her long to discover what kind of horses they had stabled there, and perhaps see again the little wizened man who had helped his master recover her from the roadway. 'Do you think, Mrs Wolfe, I could see your stables?'

'Of course. Riding is one of your interests?' Corinna gave her an enquiring look.

When Eliza nodded again, an idea lightened Corinna's face. 'You seem to have brought very few garments with you. Until you remember where you live, would you like to borrow some of my clothes? I have so many that I can no longer fit into. But you are very slender, as I used to be before I started breeding.' She laughed ruefully, then looked up as Alick Wolfe came into the room, and once again her face glowed as she wordlessly lifted up their child for him to take in his arms.

Eliza was surprised at how tall and broad he looked in daylight, dressed in such good clothes that even she recognised their distinction. She had only seen him in his dressing gown, woken from sleep, and her embarrassment at being imposed on him and his family in the middle of the night meant she had barely met his gaze. This morning she noticed the crinkle at the corner of his brown eyes as he looked fondly at his wife and baby, then turned his smiling face to her.

'Miss Eliza, how good to see you restored to health. I hope you slept well?'

'Thank you, sir, it's a most comfortable room. I am more grateful than I can say for your and Mrs Wolfe's kindness.'

Corinna interjected, 'Alick, my dear, I've offered to lend Miss Eliza some of my clothes that no longer fit.'

'That's the best news!' He laughed. 'Perhaps once this new Wolfe cub is in the world you'll stop trying to return to a sylph again. I appreciate the armful you've become.' Eliza realised then that her hostess was with child.

Alick sat down next to Corinna and put Emma on the floor between them as Corinna continued, 'I've also asked Miss Eliza to sit for me. I'd love to paint her portrait.' When Alick looked surprised, she added hastily, 'Until she recovers her memory and knows again who she is and where she belongs.'

Eliza thought she should leave her hosts to their breakfast and stood up. 'I'll go to the mews to see the horses, if that's acceptable?'

'Of course.' Corinna looked up and gestured to the way. 'Go down the back stairs to the garden and you'll find there's a green door in the wall.'

Eliza's heart quickened as she stepped into the cobbled yard with the carriage house ahead and stables for the horses, lads busy cleaning out the night's straw, feeding and saddling up the hunters ready for their exercise. She loved the sounds of a busy stable and the animals and the sweet smell of hay. She found herself drawn to a striking black horse that reminded her of Percy.

The Wolfe groom came forward. 'Morning, miss. My name's Davey. Should I saddle a mount for you?'

Mild panic overcame her. She had never ridden a horse with a saddle and certainly had no idea how to handle a side-saddle which was the only way well-brought-up ladies were expected to ride. 'Thank you, Davey, but not today. It's just good to see your beautiful horses.'

'If you like the best horses money can buy, you should see Lord Purfoy's in the next mews.' He indicated the serried ranks of stables behind the house next door where there was even more activity with horses coming and going. Eliza walked into the yard, feeling shy. A huge black hunter loomed above her, led on a harness by a stable boy. The horse was even more beautiful than her Percy. She reached up to stroke its arching throat.

'Eh, miss! Ye've chosen our best. That's m'lord's stallion, Horatio.' She whirled round to face the small man who stood beside her. His eyes seemed black in his weather-beaten face and they gave the impression that he'd seen the whole of life. It was Taz, the tiger who had helped rescue her last night. 'This is my domain,' he said, flinging out his arm to encompass the neat rows of stables and carriage houses that a nobleman, known for the finest horseflesh in London, needed to maintain.

'Oh, good morning, Taz. What a grand horse he is.' It was a relief to be able to relax with him.

He was watching her closely but with an amused eye. 'Ye a horsewoman are ye?'

'I suppose I must be. I feel at home with them.'

'Well, ye can ride out wi'me, if ye like.'

'I would like. But I'm afraid I don't know how to ride side-saddle.' Eliza felt oddly ashamed but Taz just nodded, with little trace of surprise on his face.

'I think a young miss with yer skills will master it quick enough.'

'But mostly I long to ride bareback.' Eliza was suddenly concerned by what she may have given away with this thought-less remark, but Taz seemed unmoved.

'If ye ride astride, without a saddle, it'll be at dawn before any of the gentry are up to see ye.' He laughed. 'But tomorrow, wear a riding dress and ride wi'me. If it pleases ye, come at seven.'

'What will Lord Purfoy say?' Eliza was anxious to impose as little as possible on her hosts.

A wicked grin flashed across Taz's face. 'Ah, 'is lordship's not risen from 'is bed until eleven o'clock. 'E won't know what we do. The prancers are my concern.'

When she returned to the breakfast room, Eliza was taken aback at the sight of a man she had not met. He was sitting in the sun reading the newspaper, a cup of coffee steaming at his elbow. When he looked up, she met sky blue eyes in the face of a Renais-sance angel, his golden hair tousled in a halo round his head. He stood up and smiled, surprised to see her too. 'Good morning.' He took her hand. 'I'm a friend of the Wolfes, Ferdinand Shilton. I live just down the road.'

Eliza stopped herself sweeping him a curtsey and instead bowed her head in acknowledgement. 'Good morning, sir. I'm Miss Eliza. I'm afraid I can't remember the rest of my name.' She blushed.

'Mrs Wolfe told me you had been run over by Raven Purfoy's

curricle last night. I'm sorry. He's such a bang-up driver, he must have been deep in his cups.'

He motioned to a chair for her to sit and then walked to the door to find a chaperone. He returned with Polly who settled in the window seat carrying a lace tablecloth she was mending. Ferdy Shilton took his seat and sipped his coffee, his candid blue eyes on Eliza's face. 'Before Alick married Mrs Wolfe, Lord Purfoy, Mr Wolfe and I would meet for breakfast under my roof, but now the Wolfe house has become the meeting place for us all.'

'Mr and Mrs Wolfe have been very kind to take me in.' Eliza felt comfortable in his presence, even though she had never before seen such a finely dressed man in her life; she gazed on his sky blue coat tailored to perfection, widening his shoulders and emphasising his slender waist. Suddenly she was aware how hungry she was and helped herself to some toast.

'You've lost your memory, I've heard. Dashed rum do, that. Don't know what I'd do if I couldn't remember where my home was, who my friends were.' Ferdinand Shilton's eyes clouded with the thought of how much he had to lose. 'Worst of all, what my name was! Dammit!' He glanced at her, a look of horror on his face at having sworn in front of a woman. 'Apologies, Miss Eliza, but losing your family name, that's devilish bad.'

At that point the door opened and another man, more panther than peacock, slipped into the room. Eliza saw clearly for the first time the man who had run her down in the night and was struck by just how tall and elegant he appeared. His face had all the equine nobility she had recognised on the shadowy street, his dark eyes gleaming with some secret amusement under distinguished flyaway brows; her initial impression of his astonishing good looks was borne out in the light of day.

In an amused voice Lord Purfoy said, 'Good morning, all. I

see, Ferdy, you've already made the acquaintance of Miss Mysterious.' He approached Eliza, his eyes narrowed. 'Now let me see how that wound is healing.' Feeling shy in his presence, she uncoiled her plaits and without touching her, he peered at her crown. 'Mmm. Not too bad.' Then looking back to Ferdinand Shilton, Lord Purfoy continued, 'This young miss sprang in front of the horses. Could have broken one of 'em's legs!' He sounded mildly peeved.

Mr Shilton's chivalric nature was outraged. 'Rav! You cracked this young lady's crown so badly she now can't remember who she is!'

'Mmm, so she says,' he murmured, pouring himself some coffee. His dark eyes fell on Eliza's face and person and their languid gaze flickered with interest for a moment. It was the first time he had seen her cleaned of grime, and in the clear light of morning he was unsettled by the sight. Lord Purfoy had first thought he'd run over some foolish wench but had quickly realised she was not what she seemed. Now, before him, this young woman's elegance of face and manner gave him pause. 'How are you, Miss Mysterious?' He watched her as he drank his coffee.

Eliza took a deep breath. 'Much better, sir, thank you.' She felt her cheeks flush and her breath come a little faster. He unnerved her. His lordship was like a high-bred stallion whose energy was barely contained under his glossy dark coat, and yet he appeared so cool and restrained, as if nothing much ruffled his composure. She had ridden stallions like him, quivering with tightly wound energy and she sensed that, under that carefully cultivated demeanour, Lord Purfoy's passions were only just controlled.

Corinna swept into the room and her eyes alighted on her old friends. 'Ferdy, Rav! What a treat. You have made the acquaintance of our guest, Miss Eliza?' Both men had stood up to greet her and she grasped their hands and kissed them on the cheek. 'I'm just going to lend some of my clothes to Miss Eliza, so excuse us, gentlemen.' She smiled.

'Don't forget to include Ferdy's school breeches. You've never looked more fetching than when you wore them, Cory.' Raven Purfoy's eyes glittered with mischief and humour.

2

AN AMERICAN ALIGHTS IN LONDON

Corinna led Eliza up the stairs. 'I apologise for Lord Purfoy's remarks. He's teasing about the time I came to London looking for my father and could only travel alone disguised as a young man.'

'Did you find him?'

Corinna paused on the landing and turned to her young guest, her face soft with the memory. 'I found him just in time, in this very house. Having a father was all I had dreamed of.' She led the way into the master bedroom. 'This used to be his room when he was in Town.'

Eliza looked at the grand canopied bed, surmounted by a coronet, facing two full-length windows spilling light. The silk-hung walls spread their sea-green calm over the space. 'It's beautiful,' she said in wonder.

'It is. It's a continual delight to me that it is now my family home when for so long I feared I'd have neither family nor home.' Corinna gestured to the bed. 'That is where my father died and it's where his granddaughter Emma was born. It's where this baby will be born.' She put her hand protectively on her stomach.

Eliza felt emotion rise in her throat and clasped her hands together as she said, 'Oh, how I'd love to have a family too.' Her voice faltered. This was the first time she had ever said this out loud.

Corinna looked at her, her face puzzled. 'But you'll recover your memory and will be able to find them, won't you?'

'I fear I've never known my family.' Eliza's voice was a whisper.

Corinna stifled her curiosity and instead of more questions, put her arm around the girl. 'Let's manage what we can control and let the rest fall as it may. Come into my dressing room.'

Having lived in the most makeshift places for as long as she could remember, Eliza's short time in the Wolfes' house was providing undreamed of surprises and delights. Corinna's dressing room was a treasure trove of every kind of sartorial luxury; there were shelves of folded snowy white linen chemises, racks of hanging gowns for all occasions, matching silk stockings and gloves in every hue, and a special rail for her ball gowns, shimmering and gauzy in the morning light.

Corinna led her to the end of the rail. 'Here are the clothes I no longer wear.' She smiled as she pulled out a selection of day and afternoon dresses, holding them up to Eliza's cheek. 'I think these will suit you very well.' She looked at her guest's high plain gown and said gently, 'You'll need stays, so I will give you some of my smaller ones. They are very comfortable. I'll ask Polly to help you lace them.'

Eliza coloured. No woman had ever helped her with feminine dress and she felt singularly incompetent about how to wear it. 'That's very kind, Mrs Wolfe.'

'You seem to have led a sheltered life,' Corinna murmured as she laid out a wardrobe of chemises, stays, stockings and muslin and cotton gowns. She added a couple of spencers and pelisses, one in pearl grey and so elegantly trimmed in ermine it would enhance every outfit. 'You love horses too? So you'll need my old riding habit.' She reached out for a very smart riding coat and a matching full skirt in a fine woollen broadcloth of deep burgundy red. Eliza's heart quickened. All these lovely clothes for her to wear, and a riding habit too; she would be able to ride with Taz tomorrow after all.

Corinna reached up to the shelf where a series of bonnets were arrayed, wrapped in tissue paper. 'Of course as a young lady in Society you will need a bonnet for every occasion. I have so many I'm sure I can spare you a few.' She laughed as she placed three neat straw hats on the bed, each trimmed in different coloured ribbons and embellished with fabric flowers. 'And here's one to wear with your riding habit.' Eliza took in her hands the prettiest headwear she had ever seen, a small curly-brimmed top hat with a short black veil and a jaunty cockade of dark red feathers.

'Mrs Wolfe. I haven't the words to convey what your kindness means to me. I've never had such beautiful clothes to wear. I'm sure I've never even seen such lovely apparel. Thank you.' Eliza put her hand to her heart.

Both women carried the clothes up the next flight of stairs to Eliza's bedroom. They could hear the sound of men's talk and laughter from the library where the old friends were discussing the latest political gossip, horse racing results and gaming news. It warmed Eliza's heart to hear such conviviality. Although the bond between the performers was strong, circus life was stressful and tempers volatile, with much swearing and shouting. But this ease and bonhomie she supposed came from privilege and wealth which saved men and women from the daily struggle to survive.

Corinna left, saying over her shoulder, 'I must attend to my friends but will ask Polly to come and help you put these away. Come down when you're ready.'

Eliza sat on the bed feeling dizzy; her heart and mind had not yet caught up with the extraordinary change in her circumstances. Having always been a good mimic, she had found it less of a strain to talk in a ladylike manner but was still getting used to the luxury of this life into which she had stumbled.

Polly knocked, entered and started folding and hanging Eliza's borrowed clothes. With a pretty blue muslin in her hands, she turned and asked, 'Miss Eliza, would you like to put this on? I think it will suit you and I can help you with the stays.'

Eliza stood up and, feeling self-conscious at being dressed by another, took off her calico gown and the maid quickly slipped a freshly laundered chemise over her head. Eliza stroked the lawn that felt like silk against her skin. Then Polly held out the stays for Eliza to put her hands through the arm holes, the cotton cups fitting round her small breasts, making them more pronounced than she had ever seen them before. As Polly laced the stays up the back, Eliza looked down at her newly revealed shoulders and bosom and was suddenly shy.

The dress fitted her well and the maid secured the waist with a blue silk sash. Eliza caught sight of herself and blushed. Having grown up in the circus knowing she was only valued for her acrobatic riding skill, Eliza had never paid much attention to her looks and now, for the first time, thought herself attractive. Polly picked up a brush. 'Would you like me to dress your hair, miss?'

Eliza put her hands up to unpin her plaits and sat down on the chair in front of the looking glass. Under Polly's deft fingers and with care not to disturb the healing wound, Eliza's fine pale blonde hair was brushed out, reaching in waves to her waist. Then it was quickly coiled into a soft chignon with loose tendrils round her face. 'Now that's better, isn't it, miss?'

Eliza peered at herself and was not sure what she thought. In just fifteen minutes she had been made into a fashionable lady, but she knew herself to be far from the demure young woman who gazed back at her from the mirror. She did not want to seem ungracious so smiled and said, 'Thank you, Polly. You are very clever.' Tucking her ringlets behind her ears, she descended the stairs with some trepidation and, drawn by Corinna's voice and male laughter, she entered a different part of the house.

Eliza stood tentatively on the threshold. The room was large and lined with more books than she had ever imagined existed in the world. The sight of such a library excited her greatly; to be able to read anything, openly, was an unimaginable pleasure she hoped she would stay long enough to enjoy.

Her gaze turned to the occupants of the room who troubled her more. Everyone's eyes were on her and Alick Wolfe came forward, smiling. She felt more at ease when he said, 'You're back, Miss Eliza, and looking well in your new clothes.'

'They're lovelier than anything I could imagine. I'm honoured indeed to borrow them.'

Lord Purfoy's eyes had not left her face and he drawled, 'Our little Miss Mysterious gives us all kinds of clues that we have to piece together until the miraculous day when she recovers her memory.'

Eliza wished her skin weren't so fair that every emotion was writ large on her face for she felt her cheeks colour, but Corinna was quickly by her side. 'Come in, my dear. We were just discussing Lady Bassett's ball.' She led Eliza to a seat by the fire and offered her a cup of tea. 'I shall look forward very much to starting your portrait this afternoon, if you're still agreeable?'

Ferdinand Shilton looked up from *The Sporting Magazine*. 'I was the first person to have my portrait painted by Corinna and it's so high-flying that I've hung it over my drawing room fireplace. In fact, she's so famous now, I boast about being her first and greatest patron.'

Corinna smiled across at him. 'You know I owe you more than I can say.'

Raven Purfoy was swilling a glass of whisky, his dark eyes watching Eliza over the rim. He caught Corinna's eye. 'Immortalise her as the hoyden girl who nearly lamed my best horses. I prefer her in her natural state.'

Ferdy Shilton objected to his friend's lack of courtesy and leapt up. 'Rav! You forget you're a gentleman. Have some care with your talk!'

'Oh Ferdy, calm down.' Lord Purfoy patronised him as if he were a younger brother. 'Methinks our little Miss Mysterious has had to deal with many ungentlemanly gentlemen before now.' He flashed a knowing smile.

Before Eliza could speak, Alick also sprang to her defence. 'Rav! I won't have you talking thus about any young woman under my roof!'

Lord Purfoy was unfazed by the umbrage of his friends and continued, 'You should have heard the way she talked to me before she realised who I was and that I had not come to rob her. She told me to get my hands off her using the salty language of the street. Mind you, I was attempting to check her pulse. But I'm right, am I not, my little Miss Spitfire?'

Eliza knew he was right. She had inadvertently revealed just what disreputable company she had kept since she was a child and it was already clear to her that Lord Purfoy's narrow eyes and penetrating mind never missed a thing. The dangerous thought made him more appealing.

Ferdinand Shilton changed the subject. 'Al, this American cousin of yours. When do you expect him?'

'Any day now. He's doing the Grand Tour before he settles down with a wife and family back home.'

Lord Purfoy asked in a sly voice, 'Which part of the big, bad, Wolfe family is this? The criminal branch, deported to the New World this last century for mayhem and murder?'

Alick Wolfe was the most genial of them all and rarely took offence. 'Actually, you aren't far wrong, Rav. His father was a soldier who went to the Americas to fight in the Revolutionary War under General Cornwallis and decided to stay.'

Ferdinand Shilton said, 'There's probably a woman at the heart of it. Why else live in that benighted country?'

'No doubt there's a woman to blame. Isn't it always our fault?' Corinna said with a laugh.

Alick took her hand. 'Be that as it may, I think Mr Flynn made a fortune trading fur and opium and it's his son Zadoc who will be coming to stay.'

'That's quite a name to conjure with,' Ferdinand Shilton said. 'I thought our own "Raven" was exotic enough.'

Alick laughed. 'He probably had a fanciful mama.'

Lord Purfoy put down his glass and uncrossed his legs to walk to the window and gaze out on the mews. 'Well, Mr Handel certainly liked it – named his finest anthem "Zadok the Priest".'

'When should we expect him?' Corinna looked at her husband, thinking of which of the bedrooms she should ask the housekeeper to prepare.

'Depends on the Atlantic winds, but I would think very soon. His packet boat has probably already come to port at Falmouth. He intends to travel from Devon to London in stages.'

Corinna laughed in exasperation. 'I wish you men were better at communicating practical details. I hope he thinks to send a message once he lands.' She was ready to begin work and asked Eliza if she'd like to see her studio at the back of the house. As the two women left the library she spontaneously grasped her husband by the arm and kissed him fleetingly on the lips.

Once the door was closed, Lord Purfoy expostulated. 'You two! There's something improper about such uxorious love. By now, I'd hoped you'd be indifferent to each other, if not actually ruing the ball and chain.'

Alick chuckled. 'Rav, it's time you discovered for yourself the settled pleasures of married life.'

Lord Purfoy's handsome face was spoiled by a sneer. 'Save me from the thin gruel of *settled pleasures*! What can marriage offer me? I have hazard and Burgundy, hunting, racing and riot. And when cupidity raises its siren head, I have the comforts of the beauteous Mrs Cornford. What more do I need?' His eyes were cast down as he stretched his legs towards the fire. 'Certainly not bawling brats and a cold, complaining wife!' He looked up, a roguish expression lightening his face. 'Not that you could ever call Corinna that, the only woman I came close to wishing to marry, but you nabbed her first!'

Alick sprang to the offense. 'Don't blame your lack of agency on me, Rav. It took me an age to realise the woman I loved was right under our noses. You could have sued for Cory's hand any time.'

'Ah, but you captured her the moment we met when you played Sir Galahad.' Ferdy Shilton smiled. 'After that we didn't have a chance.' They all recalled with nostalgia and amusement how the friends had first come across Corinna on her way to London, a penniless orphan, dressed as a boy so she could travel alone. And how it was Alick who, with one blow, felled the brawling carter to protect her from his belligerent fists.

Alick was gazing into the fire. 'Sometimes we need the threat of loss to make us realise what has always been in our hearts.'

Purfoy's mood also turned ruminative. 'How I miss those days when she was just one of us! What fun we all had before she revealed she was really a gal, and we men had to be more careful with a female in our midst.'

Alick took Raven Purfoy's arm. 'As Corinna often says, we know you as the most loyal and warm-hearted of friends, the best of men. Why not drop your cynic pose? Don't you think there comes a time to marry and create your own family?'

Their eyes met as Raven said, 'My only family are my friends and my horses. As long as I have you all, and Taz caring for my prancers, I have all I need.' He sank back into his chair and toasted his friends with his glass.

* * *

The women walked down the hallway and Corinna opened the door into a small sitting room that to Eliza's eyes was an almost magical space. The light was diffuse and cool, illuminating with a silvery sheen the canvases stacked against the walls and a large easel standing before the window. Through the glass could be seen the garden and the mews beyond. The floor was bare with just a canvas covering to protect the wooden boards from paint. Most distinctive to Eliza was the smell of turpentine and oil that reminded her of the circus and everything she had left behind.

Corinna pulled a chair forward and gestured for Eliza to sit. She smiled as she said, 'I hope you don't mind my looking at you closely. I need to see the distinctive planes of your face and the set of your features.'

Eliza sat in the pool of light and the women met each other's gazes. Corinna slipped into a sleeved pinafore to protect her clothes, placed a medium canvas on her easel and picked up a stick of charcoal, talking as she worked. 'You have an unusual beauty, my dear.'

'I've never really considered myself much. There were few looking glasses where I lived.' Corinna glanced at her quizzically. Eliza regretted that she had let this slip and so wished she could confide in this competent, affectionate woman about who she was and where she'd come from, but was afraid of being cast back into the life she had escaped, or into a life she could not know.

'Have any memories returned of your life before the accident?' Corinna asked gently as she started sketching out the shape of her sitter's head, so delicately poised on her slender neck and shoulders.

Eliza thought it was perhaps safe to talk of the distant past which she could barely remember or understand herself. 'I lived in a big house when I was very young but all I recall clearly was the large orangery. Unripe oranges and lemons sometimes fell to the ground and I'd collect them to throw like bowls along the marble floor towards the doorway to the garden.'

'That's a nice memory. Did you have siblings?'

Eliza had often wondered this, but no memory had ever surfaced of another child; however, she smiled as she recalled her loyal companion, Lucy. 'Only a little black and white dog,' she said.

Corinna was sketching Eliza's large almond-shaped eyes. 'Did you know you have different coloured irises?'

'Yes, but I've never thought much about it,' Eliza replied truthfully.

Corinna stood up and led Eliza to the window. 'Well, I think it's quite remarkable. I knew there was something very striking about your gaze when I first saw you. But let me see in the full light.' She peered close. 'Your right eye is violet-grey and your left eye an amber-green. They are beautiful and only really obvious when you properly look.'

Eliza shuddered. She suddenly recalled being mocked as a changeling child when first taken to the circus by Mrs Prebble. Only now did she realise that it was probably the sight of her unmatched eyes combined with her unusually pale hair which reinforced in the Prebble entourage the uncomfortable feeling she was not at all like them.

Corinna put a hand on her arm. 'Miss Eliza, it is a rare characteristic but not something to be ashamed of. You are a beautiful young woman and your eyes give your looks even greater distinction. I see a face filled with dreams but allied with unwavering will and courage.'

In a rush of emotion, Eliza felt the rare pleasure of having someone interested in her spirit, and the sense of being understood, something she had never known before. Corinna returned to her easel and cast a cloth over the beginnings of her drawing. 'Let's do this again tomorrow, if you're happy?'

As they walked back to the library the men were about to leave. Ferdinand Shilton was the first to take both women's hands and bow. 'Farewell, Corinna, Miss Eliza, I do hope you are going to grace the Bassett ball. In that throng of Society absurdities, it is consoling to find a few lovely faces one knows.'

Corinna turned to her companion. 'Would you consider accompanying us, Miss Eliza?'

Lord Purfoy was slipping on his coat as he drawled, 'Miss Mysterious has probably forgotten how to dance.'

Eliza found this unexpectedly funny and laughed, 'I probably have!' She had never been taught the formal ballroom dances but incorporated much of the improvised steps into her routines in the ring.

Corinna was pleased and said, 'Well, you've got a dancer's way of moving. I should think you'll quickly pick it up again. I have a very good teacher, a Mrs Wilson, I'll ask her to attend you here.'

Lord Purfoy took Eliza's hand and bowed, his voice still languid but less sardonic than before. 'I am sorry, Miss Eliza, to have caused you such injury. I hope you are truly on the mend. If you and Mrs Wolfe are attending the Bassett crush, then I shall break my usual habit and hope you may keep one dance for me. Much as I prefer the card tables, I owe you that at least.' With a rueful smile he brought her fingers briefly to his lips, then was quickly down the front steps and away.

'Off to his club, no doubt. Thank goodness he's rich and skilled enough at cards and dice not to be beggared long ago by his habits,' Alick Wolfe said, his arm around his wife's waist as he watched his friends depart. Eliza looked at him and thought his good humour and generosity of spirit drew everyone to him, his humanity as large as his frame.

* * *

That night Eliza did not sleep well. Her conscience troubled her; the kinder everyone was, the more she felt at home and the more urgent it became to end her imposture and face the consequences. She determined she would tell Corinna in the morning after she returned from her ride with Taz. As the dawn light seeped through her curtains, she climbed out of bed. It was too early for Polly with her pitcher of hot water so Eliza decided she would scramble into her clothes and wash on her return. She had never worn the appropriate apparel for riding before and was amazed by how voluminous her skirts were to prevent her legs being glimpsed as she rode in a decorous side-saddle. She shuddered to think how inappropriate her clothes had been in the circus; what would Mrs Wolfe and her friends think of her once she told them the truth?

Eliza picked up her hat and tiptoed down the stairs, out into the garden and on to the mews. The Wolfe stables were intercommunicating with Lord Purfoy's next door and Eliza weaved her way through the morning activity of mucking out and saddling the horses for their morning exercise. She found Taz with Lord Purfoy's elegant black stallion. He looked up at Eliza's approach. 'Morning, miss. Keep away from Horatio's back legs. 'E's an ugly customer until exercised.'

Eliza was struck again by the noble grandeur of this horse; she moved close to his head and offered her hand. 'I've never seen a finer stallion.'

Taz's beady eyes peered at the girl who then put her cheek on Horatio's neck. 'M'lord's pride and joy. Loves 'im better than anyone.'

'Can I ride him?' she asked shyly, her heart beginning to speed at the thought.

Taz rarely showed astonishment but his wizened face looked shocked. 'Lawks! Miss Eliza, don't even consider it! No one rides that prancer but m'lord! I'm only allowed on 'is back in the mornin' 'cause the boss's abed 'til noon.'

He then gestured to a handsome bay with dark eyes: ''is lordship doesn't own any ladies' palfreys but 'is most amenable mount is Clio. She'll not mind the saddle.' A stable boy emerged carrying a side-saddle and proceeded to buckle it round the horse's belly. Eliza laughed as the horse nuzzled her ear, and said to Taz, 'How do I manage that preposterous thing?'

He turned his all-knowing eyes towards her and winked. 'I know ye're a fine 'orsewoman just by yer demeanour. Ye'll soon learn.' Then without ceremony he offered his hand and in one deft movement Eliza was in the saddle. 'Crook that right knee over the pommel.' He grabbed her lower foot and slipped it into the stirrup. Now she understood how necessary it was for a lady to have the voluminous skirts of a riding habit fall in ample folds over the legs, revealing only the most modest portion of booted ankle. 'There, miss! What ya think?' he asked.

It was the first time Eliza had sat in any kind of proper saddle and it felt odd to have her movement so restricted. But she was blessed with natural balance and athletic strength and easily settled into this new constraint. 'It's very good to be on a horse again.' Her face was shining.

Taz led her up and down the yard, watched with some interest by the stable boys who recognised a natural horsewoman in the way she sat and moved with the gait of the horse. 'I'm getting used to it.' Eliza smiled down at him.

'Just remember to sit up straight.' Taz, as small and wiry as a jockey, sprang up onto Horatio's back, a horse standing at a good eighteen hands and restive as he sidled and pranced. Within moments the horse was relaxed and leading Eliza and Clio out onto Davies Street, heading for Grosvenor Square and the Park. It was early and the morning was crisp, the horses' breaths wreathing in the cold air as they trotted in through Grosvenor Gate.

There were a number of young bloods exercising their steeds and grooms mounted on their masters' hunters but all eyes were drawn to Horatio and Taz, both well known. Lord Purfoy was proud of his reputation for having the best horses in London. When a friend had ribbed him about the expense of maintaining such a high-bred stable, he had dismissed him with an airy hand. 'I have no children; my prime bloodstock are a much more rewarding way of laying waste to the cash.'

Eliza was aware of the stir her presence caused, mounted on a fine Purfoy horse and in the company of Taz, famed as the best tiger in London. She felt entirely at home on Clio and even though using the side-saddle was a novelty and she would rather hitch her skirts up and ride astride, she felt at one with her horse. She longed to let the reins drop and give the mare her head. As if Taz could read her mind, he said sternly, 'No gallopin' in the royal parks, Miss Eliza. Just canter and that's it. Anyhow, I don't want yer fallin' off.'

Eliza swung round to face him with indignation. 'I'd never fall off, Taz!' She met his eyes which were dancing with amusement.

'Keep yer 'at on, miss! I reckoned that.' He chuckled to himself. 'Just like windin' ye up.'

Eliza laughed. She liked his manner; his lack of deference reminded her of the people she had grown up amongst. She admired him for not altering his demeanour at all when in the company of Lord Purfoy and his noble friends. Taz was immutably himself.

'Can I canter to that copse of trees?' Eliza asked and when Taz nodded, she dropped her reins and Clio sped up the grassy incline with Taz on Horatio beside them. It was thrilling to share her delight in her speed and grace with her horse, so powerful beneath her, both of them feeling the fresh morning air fill their lungs. They came to a halt by a stand of oaks and Eliza turned to Taz and said in an impulsive way, 'Could I ever work as a groom, do you think?'

'No, you could not!' Taz was emphatic.

'But why not? I really know about horses and love being with them.'

'Well, ye're a lady and come from the Quality.'

'I'm no lady. And I'm not elevated in any way.'

Taz looked at her quizzically. "Ow d'ye know? Ye lost yer

memory, haven' yer?' He was watching her and Eliza suspected, as she had from the beginning, that he knew far more than he let on. She was so tempted to tell him the truth but he changed the subject.

'Ye look like ye've always ridden side-saddle. Very elegant, Miss Eliza.'

Eliza titled her head in acknowledgement, her cheeks flushing. This was praise indeed from such an equine master. 'But as you know, I long to ride without a saddle.'

Taz lost his twinkle. 'Everything ye say, miss, is shocking in polite society. Ye had a 'oyden upbringin', ain't ya?'

They were just cantering back towards the entrance to the Park when a man rode towards them, a gleam in his eye. It was his horse that Eliza first noticed, a flashy grey with a very long tail, luminous in the light. The rider was dark and lean-faced. He gave her a piercing look as he passed, then stopped and wheeled his horse to come alongside. 'Do I know you, madam?'

Eliza was startled. She gazed into his face, striking in a furtive, ferrety way, and said emphatically, 'No, sir. We have never met.' In a protective gesture, Taz rode Horatio alongside Clio's flank.

The man peered closer. 'I didn't say we'd exactly met, my dear. But that charming profile is unmistakeable. Once seen never forgotten, eh, Miss Clorinda? Although looking slightly more ladylike than when I last saw you.' He leered.

Eliza flinched. She had not expected to be recognised and his impertinent innuendo alarmed her. She had to brazen it out and pulled herself up to her full height in the saddle. 'I don't know who you have mistaken me for, sir,' she said in her most haughty voice, 'but I tell you again, I do not know you.'

Taz reached for his whip, tucked into his saddle, and said with fierce authority, 'Move away, sir. Ye're discomfortin' the lady.'

The stranger's vulpine eyes flickered towards him. 'Such insolence from a mere groom. You deserve to be horsewhipped. Your master is Purfoy, is it not?'

'No man's me master, sir. But m'job is to care for Lord Purfoy's horses.'

'Well then, I'll take my complaints to him. You can tell him you've crossed swords with Davenport.' He tipped his hat to Eliza before spurring his horse into a fast trot and disappearing into the crowd of horsemen congregating around the Serpentine.

Eliza was shocked by this chance meeting; he had brutally reminded her of her duplicity and the vulnerability of her situation. She turned to Taz with a worried expression. 'I should tell you something, Taz.' Her voice dropped.

'No, Miss Eliza. Ye don't need to tell me anythin'. I already know. But ye do need to tell Mr and Mrs Wolfe.'

Eliza was astounded. 'How do you know?'

'When I first saw ye I suspected then ye was a circus chit.'

This answer unsettled her. 'Oh no! Was it so obvious?'

'Only to me.'

'Had you seen me performing?'

They had arrived back in the mews when he answered, 'Like to keep up to snuff on all good prancers. Circus folk 'ave an eye for a flashy steed.' He dismounted and walked round to offer a hand to her. Lithe as a dancer, Eliza extricated her foot from the stirrup, stepped lightly onto Clio's back, picked up her heavy skirts, sprang to the ground in a balletic move and bowed, a mischievous smile on her face. Taz chuckled. 'Yer a knacky one! Ye can manage far greater feats than that, I ken.'

Eliza felt her exhilaration rise. Taz understood and accepted her. 'Thank you, Taz. I really enjoyed our ride.' She stroked Clio's neck and went on tiptoe to kiss her. Then she realised with a jolt that this friendship would be short-lived. This morning she would tell Corinna the truth of her life.

'Ye like to ride again tomorrow, Miss Eliza?'

She hung her head. 'Once I tell Mrs Wolfe where I come from I don't expect to still be living here. But it has been a pleasure to meet you, Taz.' Eliza put out her hand to him. 'If the man who accosted me causes you any trouble with your employer I'll vouch for your behaviour.'

Taz swore and spat on the cobbles. 'Davenport, that scurvy nob! World would be a better place without such 'ell-begotten brawlers. I'm not worried, lass. But for 'is 'orses, Lord Purfoy's as unmoved as Lucifer. Cares not a whit about Lord Dastard.'

Despite her worries, Eliza laughed and said over her shoulder, 'That's not his name, as you know!' She walked out of the mews and, turning into Brook Street, was startled to see a giant travelling coach pulled up outside the Wolfes' house, disgorging brass-bound trunks and portmanteaus. She picked her way through the luggage where the kindly old butler was directing everything to be carried upstairs. 'Good morning, Gibbons, where's Mrs Wolfe?' Eliza's anxieties about her coming revelation to Corinna were amplified by this unexpected arrival.

'The lady's in her studio,' Gibbons said in a distracted way as yet another trunk entered his domain. Eliza knocked on the door and found Corinna in front of her easel, deep in thought.

'Excuse me, Mrs Wolfe.' She stood uncertainly on the threshold.

Corinna turned. 'Oh, Miss Eliza, come in.' She looked her up and down, noting she was dressed in her own riding habit, her hat in her hands. 'That looks even better on you than on me! Did you enjoy your ride?' Eliza nodded, her mind on how best to raise the subject of her provenance as Corinna motioned her to the chair opposite. 'Alick's relation, Mr Flynn, has turned up sooner than expected.' Corinna continued in a rush, 'I've just been thinking that with this new young man under our roof I must arrange for a proper chaperone for you. Perhaps Polly will be best? I can use one of the housemaids as my own maid for a while.'

Eliza coloured. 'It may not be necessary, Mrs Wolfe. I have to tell you something that will change everything.' She was just steeling herself to admit that she had never in fact lost her memory when there was a knock at the door and the tall figure of Alick Wolfe entered, followed by an even larger man.

'Ah, Miss Eliza, you're back.' He turned to the visitor who stood beside him. 'This is Mr Flynn, from New York.'

Eliza had stood up and the man walked towards her with his hand outstretched. Before Alick could introduce them formally, the newcomer said in an Irish brogue, 'Good day, Miss Eliza. I'm pleased to make your acquaintance.' His handshake was so firm it was almost painful and she gazed up into the bluest eyes she had ever seen. He still had hold of her hand as he addressed Corinna. 'Mrs Wolfe, I commend you on your handsome house. So much grander than it appears from the outside.'

Alick laughed at the surprised look on his wife's face. 'Zadoc has been telling me how cramped and dingy the houses looked in Falmouth, where he came ashore. How attractive the people, but smoky and mean their cottages.'

Zadoc Flynn released Eliza's hand to clap Alick on the back. 'But as I say, the interiors are beautiful and grand.' Eliza had been examining this surprising stranger while he spoke. He was wearing a large coat with a lustrous sable collar. Underneath she could see his shirt was of pale blue silk, not snowy white linen. His clothes looked expensive but of a more elaborate style than the austere perfection favoured by Lord Purfoy. Most surprising of all to Eliza was the sight of a large emerald on his little finger, and another as a stud in his right ear. This fascinated her. Not even the circus men, who could be flamboyant in their costume, wore gemstones in their ears. He had reddish-brown hair and his face was weather-beaten, whether from his life in America or the sea crossing she could not be sure, but he looked outlandish, and she liked it. She remembered she was still dressed in her riding habit. 'Excuse me. I must change.' She walked towards Mr Flynn whose bulk blocked her exit.

'Do you have to go, Miss Eliza? I like a woman who's dressed for action.' His blue eyes were laughing, oblivious of the surprise in the room at his forwardness. Eliza sensed this visitor had unsettled the easy, well-run household. As she dashed up the stairs she looked back and thought she saw the kind, elderly Gibbons give her a wink. She smiled.

Quickly washing in the water that was now cold, Eliza then slipped into a simple aqua-blue muslin dress and re-pinned her hair in a passable bun. She glanced at herself in the looking glass and was secretly rather thrilled by the image. Could this unfamiliar beauty really be her?

As she descended to the hall she almost bumped into a tall, elegant man who was about to pass his hat to Gibbons. He turned and Eliza's heart missed a beat. Lord Purfoy stood in his immaculate coat, his dark eyes amused at the sight of her. In his languid voice he enquired, 'How's that cracked head, Miss Mysterious?'

She involuntarily put a hand to her crown and said, 'I can barely feel where the wound once was.'

Lord Purfoy's eyes narrowed. 'Heads heal well. But may I examine it? I've had some dealings with such injuries in the boxing ring and when riders are thrown from their mounts.' Without waiting for a reply, he walked behind her and slipped his fingertips through her coiled fair hair. In a business-like voice he enquired, 'Is this still sore?' His fingers gently probed the line of the wound.

'No.' Eliza could barely speak the word, so overwhelmed was

she with the reminder of when he last touched her with such sensitivity. She put up her hand to cover his and keep it there, for that delicate gesture conjured up a fragment of memory of herself as a small child; the remembrance of such long-lost tenderness was too precious to relinquish. Eliza turned to face him with tears welling in her eyes. But there was something more than just the painful nostalgia; an unexpected curl of excitement at being touched by a man with such attentive care made her catch her breath.

Raven Purfoy was startled. Why was she so overwhelmed with feeling; why the tears? Was she still in pain, despite her protestations to the contrary? But then he too had been disconcerted. The feel of her fine skull had unexpectedly moved him. Being reminded of the fragility of life was not comfortable and he shuddered. How close he had come to snuffing out this young life too. But to his shame he also found a thrill in the intimacy of that touch. His susceptibility alarmed him. He withdrew his fingers delicately from her hair and struggled to regain his unruffled poise.

Eliza noticed his stricken face. 'I'm quite recovered, my lord,' she said quietly.

Lord Purfoy shook his head imperceptibly and his cool, cynical manner was again ascendant. 'So, tell me, has some miracle yet occurred and your memory returned?' He offered his arm as they walked towards the breakfast room from where snatches of chatter and laughter could be heard.

Eliza hesitated. She had been about to reveal all but had been sidetracked by the unexpected arrival of Alick's relation. As they entered the room she felt the muscles in the arm beneath her hand contract. Everyone had looked up and there in Lord Purfoy's favourite chair sat Mr Flynn, appearing as a hulking interloper in this familiar domestic scene. Alick and his cousin stood up to greet them and Zadoc Flynn became even more of a looming presence, with his unconventional clothes, tanned face and smiling blue eyes.

Alick strode forward to take his old friend by the shoulder. 'Rav! You're in time for breakfast. And I see you've met up with Miss Eliza on the way. Come in. This is my relation from the Americas, Mr Flynn.' Both men walked forward to shake each other's hand as Alick continued with the introduction. 'And this, Zadoc, is one of Corinna's and my oldest and best friends, Raven Purfoy, lord of the rolling acres of Hertfordshire.'

'How many acres, Mr Purfoy?' Zadoc Flynn asked with interest.

Alick intervened with a laugh, 'It's actually Lord Purfoy, but he'll answer to Purfoy.'

Raven Purfoy was at his iciest. It was infra dig to enquire about a gentleman's assets at any time, let alone on first meeting. 'My ancestral estate runs to about five thousand acres.'

'Oh, I've just bought about the same in Kentucky. Farming some cattle and breeding horses there.'

Alick said with a sly gleam, 'Oh no, Rav doesn't *farm* his acres. He leaves that to his tenants.'

Corinna and Eliza watched the meeting of these two opposing masculinities; both were fully aware of their own good fortune and elevated position in the world, beneficiaries of inherited wealth, one from the New World and one from the old. They were both tall, one dark and elegantly dressed with a sardonic cast to his handsome features, the other more brawny, his reddish hair dishevelled, his face beaming.

Everyone turned as Ferdinand Shilton walked into the room, benign and exquisite in his azure coat and pale yellow pantaloons, his blond good looks bright and eager as the day. 'Did I hear the immortal words "breeding horses"?' he asked.

Alick came towards him and took his arm to introduce him too to Mr Flynn. Ferdy Shilton enquired in his cheerful way, 'So you too have an eye for a good prancer? Pity you have none of your bloodstock here. The Owners' Race at Epsom is the one event in the calendar no one misses.' He turned to his friend. 'Rav, here, usually wins it. Has the best horses in the country and is a mighty fine rider too.'

Zadoc Flynn laughed. 'I'm afraid I'm rather too big for the fleetest animal to carry.' With a cheerful grin he glanced at Eliza and said, 'I suppose lady riders are not allowed? I must say I approve of the fine habits worn by Englishwomen. What we'd call fine and dandy.' Lord Purfoy winced at these words then, catching sight of Flynn's appraising glance lingering on Eliza's form, he frowned.

Eliza's response surprised them all. With sparkling eyes she declared, 'I would very much like to ride in a horse race.'

Raven cast her a dark glance and asked in his droll way, 'I wonder what this might reveal of your mysterious past, Miss Eliza? I presume you are an accomplished horsewoman? Why would that be, do you think?'

Eliza felt a tremor of anxiety. If Taz and Lord Davenport had recognised her, she felt increasingly sure Lord Purfoy had not been fooled by her ruse. She turned from his all-seeing gaze. Corinna broke into the conversation. 'Gentlemen, help yourself to breakfast, you can continue your equine conversations then. I have to concern myself with the event of the Season, Lady Bassett's ball. I presume I must request two more invitations? You will join our party, Mr Flynn?'

Her new guest looked delighted. 'I'm here for the experience and am grateful to join you in any enterprise, Mrs Wolfe.'

As Corinna turned to go, Eliza followed her and said, 'I have something I must tell you.'

Corinna had a distracted expression on her face. 'You have yet to have something to eat, my dear. I must drop a note to Lady Bassett and then see little Emma. You'll find me in the studio in an hour.'

Eliza realised how famished she was after her early morning ride. In the circus she had become used to being hungry and had learned not to notice but now, with the smell of warm bread and coffee wafting through the house, she was overwhelmed with a desire to eat.

The men were laughing as Mr Flynn regaled them with his first impressions of English womanhood. 'Your Falmouth lassies are such comfortable armfuls.' He had a mouthful of toast when he continued, 'And the fashions here! So much more daring than at home. These ladies are barely dressed, with just a bit of muslin between the world's gaze and what God gave them!'

Alick laughed but when Ferdy noticed Eliza had returned he remonstrated, 'Mind your language, sir!'

The men got to their feet and offered Eliza a chair while Lord Purfoy poured her a cup of coffee, glancing with some disdain at the newcomer in their midst who was still talking with little care for Ferdy's social niceties. 'These rosy-cheeked goddesses had useful footwear in that seaside town of steep, muddy lanes. They all clatter over the cobbles in their wooden pattens, as agile as mountain goats, turning a pretty ankle too.'

Eliza had helped herself to a cinnamon bun and noticed Polly enter the room and sit in the window seat with some sewing; it was obvious she had been asked by Corinna to act as chaperone. Eliza found herself taking the chair next to Raven Purfoy. He had been watching her and said quietly, 'I recognise that when we met you were fleeing from somewhere, from something. If there is anything I can do to help, don't hesitate to ask.' His intense eyes slid from her face as he turned his gaze to the window. 'I too know what it is to be alone. To be without kin.'

There was a guffaw of laughter from the other side of the room where Zadoc Flynn was holding forth on the wonders of English posting inns and their accommodating staff. Eliza was not sure she had heard Lord Purfoy's words right. He was so satirical and coolly constrained that she knew it was a rare emotional revelation she could not ask him to repeat. Instead, she said, 'You could not have brought me to a kinder place.'

He looked at her again and his face softened. 'The Wolfes are my dearest friends.' He finished his ale in one draught then added, 'I know you are a horsewoman of some skill. You should ask my tiger, Taz, to select a mount for you while you're here.'

'I went riding with him early this morning. He saddled up Clio for me.'

A look of irritation crossed his face as he said in clipped tones, 'Taz treats my horses as his own, to do with as he will.'

Eliza was sorry to have been so frank and attempted to smooth the waters. 'Not so, my lord, Taz is very particular. He would not let me ride Horatio, who is the most magnificent horse I have ever seen.'

This elicited a volcanic response. Lord Purfoy's eyes flashed and although he'd lowered his voice, it was full of suppressed anger. 'You are never to even think of riding my horse. If he bolted or threw you, it could kill you. Only I ride him. And occasionally Taz when the steed needs exercising.'

Eliza's eyes were also fiery, but with indignation. 'No horse has ever thrown me, sir! But I promise I will not speak of riding Horatio again; I will not even look at him if you'd prefer!'

Suddenly the atmosphere between them lightened into amusement and Lord Purfoy, his colour heightened, turned to her. 'Apologies for my excessive reaction. I've seen too much death from a rider mismatched to the horse.'

'You don't have to worry about me, my lord.'

'Well, it's obvious that I do, since you threw yourself under my horses' hooves.' He spoke with some exasperation then regained his usual composure. 'Anyway, in this case it's not you I'm concerned for,' he drawled, once more cool and detached. 'It's Horatio.' He stood up, offered his hand and in a low voice said, 'I think I've heard enough enthusiastic travellers' tales for my taste. I'm off to my club.'

Eliza knew Corinna would be in her studio. She took her leave of the men and Polly folded up her sewing and followed her out of the room. Eliza knocked and entered. The mistress of the house was working on a drawing she had done of her daughter Emma, her small bright face full of sweetness and mischief.

For a moment Eliza watched Corinna, thinking her the most attractive of women with her thick russet hair coiled loosely on her head and her body swelling like a goddess with her coming baby. Corinna turned and smiled. 'Now, at last I have some time for you. I apologise for the early arrival of Mr Flynn, but he seems charming enough.'

Eliza sat down and took a deep breath. So long pent-up, the words tumbled out without preamble. 'I am ashamed to have to tell you that I have deceived you and all your friends. I did not lose my memory when Lord Purfoy's horses ran me down.' Corinna's eyes were on her face as she continued, 'I was so afraid that if I admitted who I was and from where I'd come, that Lord Purfoy would return me to the life I'd left.'

'So who are you and where did you come from?' Corinna's voice was quiet.

'I'm not certain about who exactly I am but the night I was brought here I had been running away from Prebbles Flying

Circus. I was one of their performers, Clorinda the Winged Venus.'

Corinna's initial expression of astonishment changed to one of suppressed amusement. 'That's quite a name to live up to.'

Eliza smiled with relief. 'I know. Perhaps you can understand why I've grown tired of it and wish for a normal life?'

'So how did you come to this extreme?'

'I was lost in Bath when I was seven years old and Mrs Prebble found me and took me back to the circus who were performing in Henrietta Gardens. They trained me as a dancer on horseback.'

'What a shock that must have been for you. To lose your family like that. What do you recall of them?'

'We did not live in Bath but were visiting, I think. I have a vague memory of my mother and as I've said, I don't think I had any siblings. But the one thing that kept me hopeful through all the loneliness and toil of my childhood was the certainty that my mother was looking for me, and that she is somewhere still. And I must find her.' Tears had sprung to both women's eyes.

Then with a stronger voice, Eliza continued, 'My most vivid memory was walking with my nurse over a pretty bridge of shops in the centre of Bath. The rush of water below was thrilling and alarming.' She shivered at the memory. 'Then suddenly a troupe of acrobats and jugglers emerged and I was swept along with them. When they had gone I was alone. That was when Mrs Prebble found me crying on the street. I could not remember the address where we were staying so she took me back with her.'

Corinna knew that newspapers published advertisements begging for news or sightings of lost children; if they were very young the chances of being reunited with their original families were slight. Her maternal heart was touched to the core and she put out her hand to take Eliza's in hers. 'Do you know your full name?'

'I've always been called Eliza; perhaps I was once an Elizabeth? My surname is Gray, but I had a favourite pony who was a grey and have wondered if I just assumed she and I were siblings.'

'As a lonely child myself, I can appreciate how that could happen. But do you have any memories of where you lived?'

'Just that it seemed a huge rather empty space; I was a small child and so many places seemed vast. It was in the country because I remember a garden with woods and a stream beyond. I enjoyed mimicking the speech of the chimney sweep and our servants which amused them and made them treat me as one of them. I realised very young that there were different ways of speaking for different occasions.'

Corinna nodded. 'It's a useful knack. Hence your ability to speak in ways befitting both Society and the circus people with whom you grew up.'

Eliza felt such relief at having told Corinna the truth as far as she knew it, but was anxious about what came next. She looked up and met Corinna's concerned gaze. 'I so regret my dishonesty, when you and your friends have been more than kind to me. But I wonder if you could help me one more time, to find work as a maid, perhaps in the house of one of your friends? I don't want to have to go back to Prebbles Circus.'

Corinna was reminded poignantly of her own search for belonging and the deceits that this involved. She stood up to embrace Eliza. 'My dear, the most important task is to find your family and your true home. I too was like you. Finding my father and understanding my past meant everything to me.'

Eliza was taken by surprise, her heart touched by Corinna's

reaction. With a break in her voice she said, 'But I am a stranger to you. Why be so kind to someone who has deceived you?'

Corinna continued with her explanation. 'I was helped by these three friends, Alick, Ferdy and Raven, who took me in when I had nothing, thinking me just a lad from the country, in need of help. They made all the difference to my life, and it makes me happy to repay some of their generosity by helping you.'

The burden of lies, the relief after days of anxiety and guilt overcame Eliza; in the face of such kindness, she put her hands to her face and cried. Corinna placed an arm round her shoulder and through gulping sobs, Eliza managed to say, 'Thank you, thank you. But I feel I must do something to repay you in return.'

'You are going to sit for your portrait. That is a treat for me. And I very much look forward to your accompanying us to the Bassett ball. Everyone who is anyone will be there, and who knows what strange things may come our way?'

* * *

That evening Eliza sat down to write to Rose Bowman, her only friend, and tell her she was safe. She ended with a greeting for Percy. 'Hug his neck for me and whisper in his ear that I will never forget him.'

3

LEARNING TO BE A LADY

The Wolfe household was a hive of activity when Eliza returned from her morning ride. Zadoc Flynn was already in the breakfast room laughing with Alick about a report in *The Sporting Magazine* of a duel fought by two 'Gentlemen from New York' who continued to shoot at each other and miss until a Mr Bartout, known to Mr Flynn, was finally wounded in the calf and limped away. Still chuckling at the idiocies of life, both looked up as Eliza entered. They sprang to their feet. 'Good morning, Miss Eliza,' Alick said, pulling out a chair for her.

Zadoc looked at her quizzically. 'I'd like to join you on a ride tomorrow. Would you be agreeable to showing me the Park?'

Eliza answered with a smile, 'Of course. I meet Taz, Lord Purfoy's groom, at seven in the morning, if it's not too early for you?'

Alick said, 'I think I can find you a sturdy hunter. Purfoy's horses are high-bred beasts, perhaps too light for you.'

Eliza realised she had to change out of her riding habit before she could join them for breakfast, so bobbed a quick curtsey and dashed up the stairs to slip into a morning dress of spotted grey muslin. She attempted to make her mass of fair hair look a little neater. How much easier it was when she could just plait it as she did at the circus when not performing. Confecting even a simple coiffure demanded three hands to deal with the quantity of unruly hair that wanted to spring out into waves and tendrils.

Returned to the breakfast room, she sat down with a cup of coffee just as Corinna entered with Emma on her hip. 'Now don't forget, Miss Eliza and Mr Flynn will be needed for dancing lessons later this morning when I've booked Mrs Wilson's services.' Eliza cast a doubtful glance at Mr Flynn. She had forgotten that Corinna was set on taking her and their new American visitor to the Bassett ball, and had determined that both her unexpected guests would be able to acquit themselves well in the best society.

Gibbons then announced the arrival of Lord Purfoy. Their neighbour strode into the room, as immaculately accoutred as ever. Alick hailed him with a chuckle. 'Rav! This is far too early for you. Are you well, old friend?'

It was true that his lordship's day rarely began before noon but the comfortable patterns of his life had been unexpectedly disturbed by the dramatic arrival of Eliza, then disconcerted further by this uncouth intruder from America who unaccountably irritated him. He could not remain luxuriating in bed, taking a few hours over his toilette, catching up on the news from *The Times* and his domestic correspondence while he knew that next door, this hog-jowled American was holding court with his coloured-up tales of travel and derring-do.

Overhearing Corinna's plan for the dancing classes made him bridle; this man was over-familiar and the idea of him dancing with Corinna, or Eliza, made an unwelcome curl of unease rise in his breast. Raven Purfoy did not care for this feeling and could not fathom the reason; neither of these women were his responsibility except that he'd almost killed one and once had his heart touched by the other.

'I'm no company for anyone until I've had some coffee,' he murmured, catching Corinna's eye.

She laughed. 'I was about to hand Emma to you while I poured you a cup but then I remembered that when it comes to infants, you're more of a Herod than a St Nicholas.'

Purfoy gave her a sly smile as he subsided into a chair. 'It's a mercy I didn't ask you to marry me, Cory. You've proved far too keen on maternity for my taste.' Alick had taken his daughter from his wife and went in search of the child's nurse, while Corinna poured out second cups of coffee for her guests. Raven looked round the room and greeted everyone with an incline of his head. 'All we need now is Ferdy to walk through that door and the old band of bucks will be together again. Those were the days, before Alick was domesticated.'

Corinna passed him an almond biscuit. 'Hush, Rav. You and Ferdy one day will also marry and become better men because of it!'

Eliza had been listening to this banter and, try as she might, she could not prevent her own heart from beating a little faster. From the moment she had first seen Lord Purfoy, as she lay bleeding on the roadside, she had thought him beautiful in the same way her horse Percy was beautiful, with his haughty, aristocratic head. She loved their habit of command, their natural arrogance and nobility and grace, although Percy never narrowed his lustrous eyes in the sly way Lord Purfoy did. But Eliza was not entirely certain Percy wouldn't get cranky and give her a warning bite, and she sensed a similar unpredictability in this high-bred human. She knew she would have to tell him the truth of her life as far as she knew it. And she was certain he would then disdain her for her dishonour in deceiving him – in deceiving them all.

Just at that moment, Mr Shilton was announced by Gibbons and the room was immediately sunnier with his arrival in an expensively tailored sea-green coat and buttercup-yellow pantaloons, appearing as cheerful as a daffodil. Zadoc Flynn looked up from *The Sporting Magazine* and rose to his feet to greet both the men who had joined the party. 'I find I could easily become accustomed to this leisured way of life.'

Ferdy Shilton's face was merry. 'We know no other. No English gentleman worth his name would dream of being industrious. Against our code, don't you know? Just consider Lord Byron; he refuses all pecuniary gain for those books of poetry sold in their thousands, much to his publisher's delight.'

'Well, I'm no English gentleman then.'

Raven Purfoy gave a slow smile. 'You do things differently in the colonies.'

'A colony no longer.' Mr Flynn's riposte was uncharacteristically sharp.

Alick interrupted the conversation by hailing the new arrival. 'Ferdy! Where were you last night? You were missed at the club, you know.'

'I went to Astley's.'

'Again?' Alick raised an eyebrow.

'Why not? I wished to see the horses. A particularly fine black one I have my eye on.'

'With a particularly fine lady riding on his back, no doubt.' All the men laughed.

Ferdinand Shilton was offended by their levity. 'Actually no. The Winged Venus has flown away. She was no longer in the show.'

Lord Purfoy's eyes were on Eliza's face and she felt her colour rise. 'I wonder why, and where to. It's quite a conundrum... is it not?' he drawled.

Zadoc Flynn responded in his friendly way, 'But there was another fine equestrian there. A good-looking filly she was too.'

'You were at Astley's with Ferdy?' Purfoy gave him a piercing look.

'He knew I had some fine bloodstock at home and thought I'd like to see the circus horses. Pretty they are too. But I'm sorry to have missed the Winged Venus. Mr Shilton sang her praises to the skies.'

Eliza could bear the deceit no longer and knew that it was now that she would have to tell them the truth. Corinna had just re-entered the room and her presence gave her courage. She stood up, her cheeks pink, and said, 'I have something shaming to admit to you all. I can only apologise from the bottom of my heart for not telling the truth at the time.' The men's eyes were rapt on her face and Eliza took a deep breath and clenched her fists to maintain her resolve. 'When Lord Purfoy knocked me down in the street, I was running away from Prebbles Flying Circus.'

Ferdy Shilton looked thunderstruck. 'No! You're not Clorinda?'

Zadoc Flynn did not fully understand the social gulf between an itinerant circus performer's life and the high society his relation and family and friends inhabited. 'So, you're this famous trick rider? I'm pleased to make your acquaintance. We have such skilled horsemen in America but they're men, the best being the Sioux Indians.'

Lord Purfoy's eyes narrowed as he responded, 'Sioux Indians being rather thin on the ground in this country, such horsemen come mainly from Irish stock, and women are a rarity. For good reason.' His voice was stern and uncompromising. He turned his intense gaze on Eliza. 'You seem rather out of place in such reckless company. How did you become a circus performer, may I ask?'

The room was silent and attentive as she answered, 'When I was seven I became separated from my nurse while we were visiting Bath. Mrs Prebble found me and took me back to the circus. She trained me as a tumbler and dancer on horseback.'

This news upset Ferdinand Shilton greatly. He did not like his settled view of the world disturbed. Here was someone who had been deprived of her natural place in society, possibly even a member of the nobility, and it made him uneasy. 'So who are your family? Where are they?'

'I don't know. I ran away from the circus in the hopes of finding them and to have a more settled life.'

Corinna interrupted, her voice filled with emotion. 'I understand this well. I longed to find out where I fitted in the world, and you friends...' She hesitated as her voice broke and she looked from Mr Shilton and Lord Purfoy to her husband, then continued, 'You three helped me do just that. I've extended the hospitality you showed me to Miss Gray until she discovers what happened to her all those years ago.'

'Aha, no longer Miss Mysterious, but Miss Gray now. We must all be grateful your memory has returned,' his lordship murmured while crossing his legs and leaning back in his chair.

Eliza sat down. It was done. The truth was out and no one yet had turned away. In fact, Mr Flynn said casually, 'Where I come from, most people have lost touch with their families. There's a freedom to it, you know.'

Raven Purfoy had not taken his eyes from Eliza's face. Flushed and animated, her eyes gleaming with unshed tears, she reminded him poignantly of someone he had tried not to think of in years. He shut out this unwelcome thought and turned instead to the near present, saying in a quiet voice, 'We found Corinna's father through a gift she had, with a coronet engraved in the silver. Do you have anything that could provide a clue to your origins?'

Eliza shook her head. 'Only a blue glass ring I gave to Rose, my friend at the circus, as a keepsake when I left.'

'Well, you do have unusual looks.' Purfoy's eyes were amused. 'Not many people have such flaxen hair and piebald eyes.'

Eliza was taken aback. 'My lord, my eyes are just different colours, that's all.'

He laughed. 'Whatever they are, they're a warning of trouble. I had a horse once with one gold and one brown eye. She was the most beautiful mare but the friskiest minx who only did what she chose.'

Zadoc Flynn said, 'In my experience, obstinate animals need to know who's master.'

Lord Purfoy's glance slid over Mr Flynn's genial face and the icy blast of his disapproval froze the smile on the American's lips. 'I do not treat my horses thus,' he said with the utmost disdain.

Gibbons knocked on the door and entered in search of his mistress. 'The dancing teacher is here, madam,' he said. Corinna smiled her thanks then indicated that Eliza should follow her.

'Mr Flynn,' Corinna called to her visitor, 'if you would like to learn the English dances, Mistress Wilson has arrived.'

Eliza was relieved to have endured her truth-telling unscathed, at least for now. She bobbed a quick curtsey to the men and followed Corinna up the stairs to the drawing room where the piano-forte stood waiting.

Mrs Wilson was an excellent dance teacher, somewhat better than her much more famous husband. She greeted Corinna like an old acquaintance and Eliza had a chance to size her up. She was of medium height and middle years, slender and quick in her movements; her bright eyes, in a thin wrinkled face, seemed to miss nothing and find amusement in much of what she found. She was introduced to Eliza just as Zadoc Flynn came into the room in his stockinged feet, having left his boots at the door.

Corinna sat at the piano-forte while Mrs Wilson marked out the basic steps of a quadrille. Following her directions, Eliza started to practise the steps in the square formations that characterised the dance. Mrs Wilson clapped her hands together with delight. 'You're obviously a natural dancer, Miss Gray. It will not be a difficult task to teach you, I can see.'

Zadoc Flynn was apologetic. 'I'm afraid I, on the other hand, am not a natural dancer. All I'm used to is country reels,' he said as he attempted to follow the moves.

Mrs Wilson smiled in encouragement. 'Your experience with American reels, sir, will make the country dances and Scottish reels seem straightforward enough. To make things easier, there's usually someone calling the changes at a ball.'

Corinna was playing a cheerful melody as Mrs Wilson, Eliza and Mr Flynn skipped and swirled through the steps of a reel, Zadoc only trampling the women's feet a few times, accompanied by apologies and laughter. Mrs Wilson turned to Corinna and asked her to play a waltz and partnered Eliza with a loose hold to show her the steps. She called across to Zadoc Flynn who was watching closely, 'Sir, can you attempt a simple waltz? Take Miss Gray as your partner and follow my lead.'

Eliza was suddenly shy as she took Mr Flynn's hand and placed her other on his arm. Propriety demanded they dance with space between their bodies but, as Mrs Wilson explained, on a turn it was natural to be held closer to enable a smooth motion round the room. Eliza may have been a performer at Prebbles Flying Circus but she had never danced with anyone else. Here she was in the arms of a stranger who seemed to share none of her reservations. His big hand grasped hers and he did not smell of horses, a familiar scent she loved, but indubitably something human and male. It was novel and disconcerting, even exhilarating.

They managed the steps of this new and daring dance competently and Eliza enjoyed creating graceful patterns across the drawing room floor. As she and Mr Flynn managed to perfect the steps, she began to appreciate the pleasure of being in the arms of a tall strong man who at times seemed to know how to dance.

She was laughing up into his face after a mistake that had made her almost trip and did not notice the striking dark figure of Lord Purfoy watching from the door. Then Mr Flynn attempted an overambitious turn and his stockinged feet slipped on the polished oak boards. He tumbled to the floor, pulling Eliza over with him. She gasped in surprise and shock and quickly sprang to her feet, offering him a hand up. The foolishness of their fall struck them both and they gasped with laughter, still holding hands while Mrs Wilson admonished Mr Flynn for his over-wide stride and clumsy feet.

Wishing to make his farewell, Raven Purfoy had sought out Corinna and had followed the sound of voices and music to the drawing room. He stood for a moment on the threshold, his eyes narrowed as he watched Eliza being steered round the room by her beefy, be-stockinged partner. Her elegant form and pretty dancing feet made him feel protective and possessive and he hated the vulnerability these emotions evoked. Seeing the dancers suddenly tumbled on the ground and Eliza's muslin gown flounced to her knees, revealing the unexpected but surprisingly affecting sight of her slender calves and fine ankles, gave him a jolt of long-forgotten feeling. In a fluid athletic movement she was quickly upright again, and she and Flynn were laughing together as if old friends as Raven Purfoy's fists clenched with long-suppressed emotion.

He couldn't bear seeing this interloper making such a pig's ear of the dance: he could not bear seeing Eliza in his clumsy embrace. Lord Purfoy's much-vaunted control cracked and he strode into the room in his top boots. Corinna had stopped playing and looked up to see her old friend almost shoulder Mr Flynn aside and offer his hand to Eliza. 'I think you should see how the waltz is properly done, Miss Gray. Would you play, Corinna?'

Eliza was suddenly encircled in his lordship's commanding embrace and felt the call of some unruly emotion she had not experienced before. How strange the effect, she thought, and how could dancing with each man elicit such different emotions? Both were tall and strong, both filled with virile energy, but while in Zadoc Flynn's arms she felt safe and light-hearted, Lord Purfoy's embrace perturbed her body and soul to an almost unbearable degree. Her knees went wobbly as Raven Purfoy swept her across the floor. She could not think what steps to make next, her breath was fast and she was unable to meet his eyes. She had never been so close to him before and the feel of him, the scent of him, filled her senses.

'Don't look at your feet, Miss Gray. Just trust in your partner and dance.'

Eliza looked up into his face and immediately lost her steps, trod on his foot, apologised, then laughed nervously. On an impulse she placed her small feet in their dancing slippers on the toes of his immaculately polished boots and said, 'Perhaps this is the best way to dance with someone so much better than me.' She glanced up mischievously and was met by the most inscrutable countenance.

Raven Purfoy danced on a few more steps with his balletic

passenger standing on his boots, but he was taken aback. He was already regretting his impetuous intervention and was confused by how disconcerting it was to have this young woman in his arms, her breath rapid as a captive bird's, her shapely waist under his hand, her breasts perilously close to his chest. Such behaviour was so out of character for him and had thrown his feelings into turmoil; assailed by the desire to hold her even closer, he was alarmed by the sense of his loss of dignity, his loss of control.

Lord Purfoy stopped in the middle of the room and regained his habitual sangfroid. The music stopped too and Corinna stood up, delight on her face.

Her friend continued as if nothing untoward had happened, bowing in acknowledgement of Eliza and Mr Flynn and, taking Corinna's outstretched hand, said, 'I must be gone. I'm riding Horatio in the Park with Taz. He's slightly concerned with his gait. He has to be fit for the Owners' Race, ye know!' He flashed her one of his rare smiles.

Zadoc Flynn came forward. 'The Owners' Race, eh? It sounds amusing.'

'It's the most anticipated race of the Epsom season. Horses can only be ridden by their owners, and it's highly competitive – and deadly serious, I assure you.'

Corinna attempted to ease the situation and said with a laugh, 'And Rav and Horatio are the unassailable champions.'

Eliza's heart was thumping but she was not certain what had just occurred. It was as if a tempest had suddenly entered the domestic scene, scattered all conventions and settled feelings to the winds, and then left as rapidly as it had come, leaving unimaginable changes in its wake.

As they returned to Mrs Wilson and the dancing lesson, Mr

Flynn said almost to himself, 'Perhaps I need to get myself a mighty fine racehorse after all.'

* * *

Eliza was about to go through to Corinna's studio to sit for the next stage of her portrait when Gibbons delivered a note to her in a hand she recognised. He bowed and said, 'This was delivered by a ragamuffin who dashed off before I could question him.'

Thanking him, she settled herself into the chair opposite the easel to wait for Corinna, and began to read. She was suddenly alert to a sentence:

An American Gentleman comes to see me after the Show. He is friendly and tells me he has Horses at his Farm.

With a shock Eliza realised that Mr Flynn was probably Rose's 'American Gentleman'. She knew he had been to Astley's with Mr Shilton but had not suspected his acquaintance with Rose had progressed to something more than fleeting. What was in his mind? Was he offering a lure of some kind, she wondered? The possibility added to her concern for Rose.

Just as Eliza was folding up the note to put in her pocket, Corinna entered. She whisked off the cloth that had covered the canvas and sat down. 'Mrs Wilson will come back tomorrow for one more lesson but it's clear to me you'll manage very well with the dances at the ball. Mr Flynn is less naturally gifted, but his warmth of character and general bonhomie will carry him through any embarrassments.' She smiled. 'Now let me look at you again and get the proportions of your features right.'

Eliza settled back into the chair, her spirits less agitated now that she had confessed to her origins and had not been met with dismay. As if she could see these thoughts written on her sitter's face, Corinna said in a soft voice, 'There is no shame in being an orphan or a lost child, you know. There are so many. I thought I was all alone in the world until I found my father.'

'You were very lucky.'

Corinna was peering at Eliza's face as she mixed her pigments with oil and started to paint in the flesh colours. Before her was a sitter with the fine-boned beauty of a Holbein drawing. She marvelled at the delicacy of the eye socket and the curve of the cheekbone, the sculpted elegance of the nose and jawline, with the added surprise of the full mouth that seemed to belong to a more sensual, less refined face. She answered Eliza in an abstracted voice, her mind on her painting. 'I was lucky. My father was still alive and had been seeking me. But you cannot know what you will find once you start to look.'

'But where do we start? You had a crest on a silver cup. I have nothing to distinguish me.'

Corinna wiped her brush on a piece of linen. 'Aha! But you have your unusual looks.' Corinna continued to scrutinise the face in front of her and murmured almost to herself, 'Such a shapely head with a charmingly noble nose.'

Eliza laughed out loud. 'I sound like a racehorse! In fact, after being knocked down in the road, when I first opened my eyes and saw Lord Purfoy's face, I thought him as beautiful as Percy, my horse, left behind at Prebbles.'

Corinna chuckled. 'He surely is the handsomest of men, or indeed even of horses! But beware, his heart is bound in armour. Something happened in his youth he will not speak of. He is not a man to give your love to, my dear, unless you don't mind it returned in pieces.'

Eliza immediately coloured. 'Oh no! I didn't mean I *loved* him as I love my horse, just that I thought him as fine-looking as Percy.'

'Well, *you* are very fine-looking. I think even if we don't find your family, you will attract a good man to love you.'

Eliza bridled. 'But I ran away to find work and freedom, I'm not looking for a husband!' she said with indignation.

Corinna was matter-of-fact. 'I came to London with the dream of becoming a portrait painter, but I needed a home and some means of survival before I could establish myself. Finding my heart captured by Mr Wolfe provided me with all the pleasures of love, but also the necessities of life.' She put down her brush and reached across for Eliza's hand, aware this young woman had nobody to instruct her about life. 'A married woman has greater freedom than if she remains unmarried, unless she's very rich and distinguished, or exiles herself from Society by becoming a pirate or lawless brigand!'

They both laughed and Eliza felt a rush of gratitude towards Corinna for her motherly care – something, she realised, which had been entirely absent and much missed for as long as she could remember. Emotion welled up in her chest; she had never allowed herself to think of the love that had been denied her when she was severed from her family so young.

Corinna noticed the flush of feeling in Eliza's face and her own heart was touched. She said impulsively, 'I would very much like to buy you a special dress for Lady Bassett's ball. I think my cast-off gowns work very well for the every day, but I want you to shine. I think you need something made especially for you.' She stood up, once more assuming her practical manner, and said, 'With the ball next week, we have no time to lose. Could you accompany me to my modiste this afternoon, perhaps?'

Eliza wanted to kiss her, so grateful was she for everything, but knew such a gesture was far too forward. Instead, she grasped her hand and brought it to her lips. 'Thank you, Mrs Wolfe. I shall be honoured.'

* * *

Raven Purfoy, as immaculate as ever in his riding clothes and polished top boots, strolled round to the mews to talk to Taz. 'Show me what's concerning you.' The men eyed the great hunter, glossy and black as ebony.

'It's mendin', guv. Ridin' this morn' with Miss Eliza, 'e were a sweet goer.'

Lord Purfoy's eyes flashed as he met his tiger's mischievous gaze. 'That girl's not to be let near him, you hear. No gal can ride a stallion as mettlesome as Horatio.'

'Well, if anyone can, it'll be Miss Eliza. Y'know she dismounted by standin' on Clio's rump, then leapt to the ground! 'alf expected 'er to somersault on the way.' He chuckled.

For a fleeting moment his master looked astonished then amused, but his voice was stern in response. 'Taz, I can tell you're susceptible to that young woman's charms. Heed what I say on the matter!'

'Never fear, m'lord. Nothin' with fewer than four legs charms me.' And he flashed his gap-toothed grin.

Horatio was growing restive so Lord Purfoy settled himself in the saddle and trotted out of the cobbled mews, heading for Hyde Park. As they entered through Grosvenor Gate he felt his tension ease; the air was fresh and acquaintances greeted him as they passed. He released the reins and felt his favourite hunter's energy uncoil as he set off into a fluid canter. Raven Purfoy permitted Horatio far more freedom to act on the impulses of instinct and spirit than he allowed himself. He knew his own heart was walled up, neglected, left to sicken and die, and it was painful to have it stirred back to life.

Purfoy cantered up towards the copse of oak trees and leaned forward to run his hand over Horatio's shoulder muscles, feeling the animal's strength and exhilaration. He was surprised by a pang of sorrow that he could not live as simply in the present as this. He had learned how dangerous it was to abandon himself to feeling, how fraught it was with pain. As the Oxford Street Turnpike came into view, he wheeled his horse around and headed downhill towards the Serpentine.

The day was growing warmer and hazy with the arrival of spring. The wildfowl scattered with enthusiasm across the water, coots chirruping as they foraged in the muddy shallows, while ducks paddled with haughty disregard for the moorhens flashing in and out of the reeds. Purfoy watched their diverting busyness. Out of the corner of his eye he saw a horse he recognised and coveted. White as snow with a long floating tail, the stallion commanded attention. He had tried to buy him from his owner, despite his own hearty dislike of the man. Lord Purfoy's eyes moved from admiring the beautiful animal to the dark, lean-faced rider who approached and tipped his hat.

'Davenport,' Purfoy drawled, 'I haven't seen you at the club for some weeks. I hope you've been well?'

Lord Davenport gave him a knowing glance. 'A touch of the old malady, ye know. 'Tis rife in Covent Garden. Strumpets up from Wapping Docks for a better trade than the scurvy Jack Tars.'

Lord Purfoy's lip curled in disdain and he was about to turn and ride away when this most notorious of gamblers said something that made him pause. 'Life is a game of chance. My mother's cousin is further ailing. Soon I'll be saved the bore of having to marry an heiress.'

'You're his heir?'

'I am, and in the nick of time.' Davenport's pale face looked triumphant. Then he cast a sour glance at Lord Purfoy. 'We're not all fortunate enough to sup with a golden spoon from the moment we enter the world.'

'I've been lucky indeed. But I've been careful to husband my fortune.'

Lord Davenport snorted with derision. 'If gambling deep and buying the best bloodstock is "husbanding your fortune", then that's news to me.'

Lord Purfoy was reminded again of just why he disliked this man so much and turned his horse to go, but Davenport put out a hand. 'Talking of which, that insufferably rude tiger of yours needs some masterly discipline.'

Purfoy's manner turned even more icy. 'I do not need your advice on how to handle my staff. Taz is the finest groom in London. I trust him with my life. More importantly, with the lives of my horses.'

Lord Davenport knew he had needled this most self-possessed of men and he enjoyed his unaccustomed power. In an insinuating voice he added, 'Your unruly tiger was accompanying that little chit from the circus, Miss Clorinda.' He spat out the name. 'I'm surprised, Purfoy, you advertise your low taste in female company. She's enchanting enough, 'tis true, but why flaunt her in public, and on one of your horses too? Any such betrayal of our class is better kept behind closed doors, don't you think?'

A white rage rose in Raven Purfoy's breast. His voice was quiet and menacing as he said, 'I should call you out for that slur against my name, and Miss Gray! But I won't stoop to deal so with you.' He wheeled Horatio around and cantered towards Grosvenor Gate, irate, unsettled, spoiling for a fight. He hated being in thrall to passion. Loss of control alarmed him; if his iron grip on his life began to give way, what chaos would ensue? As he trotted through Grosvenor Square, Purfoy rued the night he had refused to listen to Taz and had run into that confounded girl.

* * *

Eliza had never been to a dressmaker of any kind, let alone a fashionable modiste in Bond Street. She dressed in the smartest walking gown that Corinna had given her, a confection of green twilled sarsenet with a plaited collar of cream ribbon, and over that a matching pelisse with a ruffled hem. On her head she wore a fetching Leghorn bonnet trimmed with pink and green Italian silk, quickly tied under her chin as she descended the stairs. Corinna met her in the hall. She smiled. 'We just have to walk to the end of the street. Madame Delaunay's shop is not far.'

The afternoon was bright as they set out, walking briskly east. The moment they reached Bond Street, Eliza's eyes widened at the sight of so many finely dressed men and women. She had been gratified by her own appearance but here were such elaborate bonnets, coats and pelisses embellished with contrasting ribbons, flounces and fur, they quite eclipsed her own modest attire. She took Corinna's arm. 'These women are so brightly clothed I feel like a sparrow amid the parakeets.'

Corinna tutted. 'Many of these gowns are more truly theatrical dress. I wouldn't want to see you so tricked out.' But Eliza found the sight of so much colour thrilling. She had been brought up with outfits made from tawdry cloth but bursting with decorative extravagances. This was the first time, however, she was exposed to the power of fine clothes, the effect on the wearer and the messages they gave to the world. Eliza noticed a hatchet-faced woman with sallow cheeks dressed in exquisite rose silk and an operatic bonnet trimmed with a fan of golden ostrich feathers, and thought she looked queenly and magnificent. It seemed even the most plain and disconsolate of women was made distinguished by the quality of the garments she wore.

As they weaved their way through the crowd of shoppers and promenaders the sky grew ominously dark as storm clouds obscured the sun. Eliza could smell the rain on the air. A sudden clap of thunder brought a deluge that caught everyone unawares and there were cries of dismay as people ran for cover. Corinna steered her young charge into the nearest coffee shop. 'We'll wait here for the worst of the rain to pass. I'll be back in minutes with an umbrella from a shop I know.'

Eliza settled on an upholstered bench next to another young woman sheltering from the weather. She pulled her skirts close. 'I'm sorry to splash your pelisse.' Eliza looked down at the damp stains spreading on her neighbour's blue silk. 'My name's Eliza Gray.'

The young woman looked up with a merry expression. Her serene oval face and wide clear brow attracted Eliza greatly. 'I'm Marina Fairley,' she said. They managed an awkward handshake, so closely were they packed with other shoppers and their chaperones. The young woman peered into Eliza's face as she said, 'I don't recognise you. Is this your first Season?'

Surprised this frank young woman should have suspected she might be a debutante, Eliza replied, 'I'm not doing the Season as such, just attending Lady Bassett's ball.'

This elicited a vivid smile from her new acquaintance who then said, 'You are lucky on two counts. To have escaped the torture of the Season and to have an invitation to the Bassett ball.' Her golden brown eyes were alive with humour and intelligence.

Eliza laughed. 'Is that a contradiction of desires?'

Marina Fairley shook her head and said emphatically, 'The ball is fun but the Season most decidedly is not. This is my third.' She pulled a face, her eyes full of mischief. 'I'm not beautiful like you and have no dowry – and indeed no desire to marry. So you can see why I'm such a failure.' Eliza was struck by how the wry expression on the young woman's face belied the meaning of her words. What she said next revealed the reason for her levity. 'My mama has promised if I haven't found a husband by the summer, then she'll give me up as a *lost cause*' – she gave the words melodramatic emphasis – 'and let me pursue the life I choose.'

Just as Eliza was about to ask her the nature of the life she chose, Corinna returned with a very large umbrella. 'Look what I found. The competition for them was fierce!' Eliza introduced her new acquaintance to Corinna and stood up to go.

Miss Fairley put out a hand with a visiting card between her fingers. 'I'd so like to see you again, Miss Gray. I'm at my grandmother's house at Albermarle tomorrow. Shall you come to tea at three?'

Eliza looked questioningly at Corinna. 'Would that be acceptable? Do you need me to sit for my portrait tomorrow afternoon?'

'It's a very good idea to meet more young people. Polly can accompany you. We have Mrs Wilson's dancing lesson in the morning and I can paint you when you get back.' They made their farewells and stepped into Bond Street where the tempest had passed but had left the street running with malodorous sludge. Picking up their skirts, they scurried past two more parades of shops: the mantua-makers, milliners, glove-makers, jewellers and modistes, their windows gay with elaborate displays.

Corinna pointed to a shop sign swinging in the wind with the name *Delaunay* inscribed in a swirling cursive hand. 'There it is.

With that lovely pelisse in the display.' She indicated a pretty bow window with a pale primrose velvet coat with ermine collar and cuffs adding a sense of drama and luxury. Corinna led the way up the steps and in through the door.

Parting the curtain at the back of the shop, a woman of indeterminate years stepped forward, her eyes lively under black eyebrows and with greying hair swept off her face into a small bun at the nape. On sight of Corinna her face softened with a sweet smile. 'Mrs Wolfe! What a pleasure to see you again.' She came forward with her hands outstretched.

When Corinna introduced Eliza and suggested Madame Delaunay might be able to make her a ball gown in a matter of days, the modiste rolled her eyes. '*Mais oui*! I'm a fairy godmother who can work miracles!' She laughed. Then she appraised Eliza's figure and colouring. 'You are very *petite* and elegant. But those eyes! *Oh la la*! We must emphasise their remarkable colour.' Madame thought for a moment, her gaze intent on Eliza's face. 'The paleness of your hair too is very dramatic. I think lilac lace over blue tiffany will show your beauty to its advantage.'

She clapped her hands and a willowy young woman appeared from the workroom at the back and gave an uncertain smile. 'Tea for Mrs Wolfe and her friend, please, Harriet.' Madame Delaunay then disappeared into the stockroom to emerge some minutes later carrying a bolt of filmy tiffany in a shimmering sky blue. 'This will be for the underdress,' she said as she put it on the sofa beside Eliza. Within a few seconds she was back with a beautiful Flanders lace in lilac.

Eliza put out a hand to touch the airy folds. 'It's exquisite,' she said, barely believing it could be made into a dress for her to wear.

'Well, Miss Gray, I'll show you how beautiful it will be. Now stand in front of that mirror.' Madame Delaunay approached with both bolts of fabric and draped the blue tiffany round her body then overlaid it with the lace, gathering it under Eliza's breasts to imitate the narrow bodice and skirt. 'There!' The modiste looked with satisfaction at Eliza. 'What do you think, Mrs Wolfe?' she said over her shoulder.

All three women gazed at the reflection in the mirror. Eliza stifled a gasp. The fabrics' colour combination made her eyes strangely vivid and gave depth to her coils of fair hair. Madame Delaunay's austere face softened at the sight. Corinna was the first to speak. 'It's perfect. Now, what style do you think?'

The modiste stood back and scrutinised the young woman standing before her, swathed in fabric. She was once more business-like in her manner. 'Miss Gray has an elegant neck and her shoulders are fine. I think the dress should enhance these features. In Paris now they reveal more of a woman's back. An exposed décolletage is passé. The back and nape of neck are the new focus of desire.'

Eliza looked at Corinna with some alarm. In the circus she had not thought of her physical charms at all; she was costumed and masked, playing a part, and only her physical prowess in acrobatics and her skill with horses were of note. She was afraid of drawing too much attention to herself as Eliza Gray, of unknown parentage and doubtful prospects, no longer the Winged Venus with supernatural powers. However, Corinna met her panicked look with a reassuring smile and said, 'What do you have in mind?'

Madame Delaunay became animated, excited by the prospect of creating a striking new gown for a beautiful young woman who would wear it well. For one of her garments to be seen at the Bassett ball could only do her business good. She arranged the lace over Eliza's shoulder as she explained, 'I think the blue tiffany should not fully line the bodice. Miss Gray's shoulders and back to below her shoulder blades will be covered only in the lace. I'll have specially designed stays sewn into the bodice so as not to spoil the elegance of the transparency of the lace at the back.'

Eliza glanced at her reflection and felt excitement rise at the unfamiliar idea that others might find her attractive, that her parents might approve of the woman she had become, that Lord Purfoy might think her no longer a disreputable girl but an elegant beauty fit for his arm. That last thought transfixed her. How clothes might make her acceptable to someone as elegant and high-born as he. Until she had ruined it by standing on his boots, he had danced with her in Corinna's drawing room as if she were to be taken seriously as a worthy partner. If such a transformation could be wrought, it was all due to Mrs Wolfe's generosity.

Eliza grasped Corinna's hand. 'Thank you for the chance of having such a lovely gown to wear to the ball.' Then she turned to Madame Delaunay. 'And thank you, Madame, for your craft which makes this possible. The first dress ever made especially for me!' Both older women could tell by the slight catch in Eliza's voice how affected she was by her change in fortune.

Madame Delaunay clapped her hands again and Harriet emerged through the curtain at the back, a tape measure around her neck. 'Please take Miss Gray's measurements.' She then glanced back to Corinna and smiled. 'Mrs Wolfe, my seamstresses will finish this in two days as a special favour to you, but you do realise I'll have to charge you more.'

'Of course. I think your plans for the dress are perfect. This is Miss Gray's first entry to Society and such a gown will give her courage.' After the measuring was done, Corinna then took

Eliza's hand and they were soon on the street again, trying to keep their fine calfskin boots free of the worst of the dirty puddles. Corinna laughed when she looked at Eliza's anxious face. 'Having had no siblings, I'm enjoying treating you as a younger sister. You will look so rare and distinguished, I'm quite excited myself.'

After the deluge, Bond Street was filling up again with strolling dandies and men driving their flashy phaetons and curricles, showing off their horses and driving skills and ogling the young women hurrying past with their chaperones. Corinna and Eliza drew many an admiring glance. Corinna was used to it and took no notice, but Eliza found herself colouring at some of the leering faces and fragments of lewd comments that made the young men's companions guffaw. Only by becoming diverted by the shop windows did she prevent her eyes from meeting theirs.

In the reflection of a milliner's window, Eliza saw a gleam of light and glanced back into the road. There in the distance were a team of two beautiful grey horses she knew well from her last encounter with them. Her heart began to beat faster and she recognised the familiar, smart, navy blue curricle with the crest on the door. It was Taz who caught sight of her first. He saluted and prodded the driver in the back and pointed.

Lord Purfoy held the reins in one hand as with the other he tipped his curl-brimmed beaver to his acquaintances. Eliza thought with some amusement that it was like a royal progress, but then she knew he was considered quite the Corinthian, the best in London. A shiver of excitement caught her unawares. Standing on the pavement, seeing him almost as a stranger, made him particularly compelling. He was so commanding in his good looks, wealth, his skill and competence. Watching him drive his mettlesome steeds with such ease and authority made her heart leap. Eliza hugged herself. Whatever lay in the future, just now it was enough for her romantic heart to know he lived and walked the same earth as her.

Corinna noticed their approach too. 'Look, there's Rav!' she cried and waved. 'He's incorrigible. He's driving too fast but he and Taz are laws unto themselves and make a stir wherever they go.'

The greys were suddenly alongside and were pulled up, stamping and whinnying. In an instant Taz was at their heads and muttering endearments to quieten them. In one athletic movement Lord Purfoy had leapt to the ground. He swept off his hat to greet Corinna and Eliza on the pavement. 'What a pleasure. My two favourite women,' he drawled with an inexplicable gleam in his eyes.

Corinna slapped his proffered hand with a laugh. 'Don't try to gammon us, Rav. I know there are few women you rate and to be your favourite is less flattering than it might sound.'

He smiled in response. 'You know me too well, my dear. I should be more careful of what I reveal to an inquisitive being like you.' His eyes, more lively than usual, appraised Eliza's face and outfit. 'You're looking most charming, Miss Gray. That bonnet becomes you. But I must say, I do prefer my name for you: Miss Mysterious. I'm a little sorry your memory has miraculously been restored to you.' His dark eyes sparkled with amusement.

There was cursing and consternation in the road as carriages were attempting to manoeuvre round the Purfoy curricle carelessly parked at an angle. Taz was giving as good as he got with some salty words only he could summon up from his years living on the street. Lord Purfoy turned to watch the show then addressed himself again to the women. 'My apologies, ladies, for Taz's language. I fear I should not try the patience of the Bond Street dawdlers any longer. May I offer you both a lift home? It'll be a squeeze but we'll manage.'

Eliza was keen to see more of Lord Purfoy and Taz but Corinna said, 'Thank you, Rav, but no. In my condition I'll need the whole seat to myself. If Miss Gray is happy to walk? It isn't far.'

Lord Purfoy bowed and replaced his hat on his head. 'Perhaps I'll see you both at the ball, dazzling all with your distinctive beauty?'

Corinna put out a hand. 'So, you are going?'

He brushed her fingers with his lips. 'I may. Indeed, I may even dance. It'll be interesting to see what Mrs Wilson has managed in two short teaching sessions. I hope we may do better than last time.' He raised his eyebrow. 'But then there are all kinds of miracles attached to the intriguing, mysterious Miss Gray.' With that he sprang back into his curricle. Taz saluted both women as he let the horses' heads go and took his place on the platform behind the driver. They headed off into the melee with Taz tossing a rude gesture at the irate horsemen and grooms who had been inconvenienced by the bottleneck the Purfoy vehicle had created.

'Taz, you bring my name into disrepute.' Lord Purfoy was mildly reproving.

'They know not to mess with me, guv'nor,' he said with some satisfaction as they bowled down the street towards Piccadilly.

* * *

The two women headed back up Bond Street. Eliza was unsettled by Lord Purfoy's teasing. She had never experienced family life and although living amongst circus folk gave her an understanding of men like Taz, whose downright frankness and wit was familiar, she was quite unprepared when faced with a sophisticated and cynical member of the aristocracy. Eliza took

Corinna's arm to ask, 'Does Lord Purfoy choose always to converse in badinage?'

'He does a lot of the time, 'tis true, but perhaps as a mask. For some reason he has to protect his deepest feelings.'

'But you touched his heart, did you not?'

Corinna squeezed Eliza's hand. 'He likes to claim that he would have married me if Alick hadn't stepped in first, but isn't that easy to say? It saves him from unlocking his heart and risking pain.' She looked into Eliza's face. 'He's a tricky man to love. There are many other men this Season you'll find more reliable and rewarding, you know.' Then she chuckled. 'What do you think of Mr Flynn? He's a good man and a wealthy one, he'd be a far more sensible choice of a husband.'

Eliza was taken aback. She had not thought of Zadoc Flynn in a romantic way. She laughed. 'He's more like a dray horse than a thoroughbred.'

'That may be, but such beasts are useful, hard-working and trustworthy, even though they may not quicken your heart with their grace and speed.'

Eliza met Corinna's amused eyes. 'You obviously understand me well. The closest I've had to family have been the circus horses. I compare every man to them.'

'I suspect the attraction of Lord Purfoy is his likeness to your beloved horse, Percy, but we can't be fanciful when it comes to something as important as marriage. Zadoc Flynn is a steady character and very rich indeed.'

They were almost home and hurrying as the sky was growing dark again with another gathering storm. Eliza asked Corinna, 'Why should Mr Flynn's money interest me?'

Exasperated, Corinna stopped in the middle of the pavement to remonstrate with this young unworldly guest for whom she felt such responsibility. 'Eliza! You can't go on being all sensibility, you know. Good sense has to come into it too; money is the road to freedom. When you have none, it is not a luxury but a necessity. Until my father bequeathed me his house in Brook Street, where we now live during the Season, I was lonely and afraid. I had no home and no way of surviving, except if I was very lucky and obtained a position as a junior governess in a household somewhere. But it would still have been a mean and precarious life.'

Eliza was struck with the stark reality of her situation. 'I'm not qualified to become a governess, I'm only book-learned from my own random reading. But I thought I could work in a shop?'

Corinna's voice softened. 'You could, or in the theatre, given your experience with performance, and your beauty. But I want first to see if you can find your family and be reconciled. Until then I am more than happy to offer you a home, as Ferdy did so kindly to me.'

Eliza met Corinna's anxious face with eyes dancing with mischief. 'If money's so important in this world, Lord Purfoy is rich, isn't he?'

This sly comment lightened Corinna's mood. She laughed. 'He is. Very rich indeed. Though at the rate he spends on his horses and gambling I don't know how much longer he will be. Too many once-wealthy men are reduced to debtors' prison or exile abroad through profligacy.'

'But Lord Purfoy is not profligate!' Eliza felt indignant on his behalf.

''Tis true. He's a lucky gambler and astute with his horse trading.'

Eliza could not stop herself from wondering: if money mattered so much in the wider world and love and desire mattered so much to her, surely Lord Purfoy combined both handsomely? But she was wise enough not to labour the point to Corinna who seemed to have other concerns.

The rain had held off and they arrived home tired but pleased with their expedition. The dress would be lovely and Eliza knew that wearing it would bestow on her something of its magical power to transform.

4

THE CONSOLATIONS OF SISTERHOOD

After a stormy night the morning was as crisp as if laundered, the air fresh and bright as the sun rose on a new day. Eliza had slept through the rumbles of thunder and the drumming rain and was only awoken by Polly carrying a pitcher of water through to the dressing room. 'Are you riding again this morning, miss?' the maid asked as she opened the curtains to gaze out on the mews.

'I am. It's the best start to any day.'

'Well, Mr Flynn seems to have risen early too and his man has laid out his riding clothes.'

Eliza yawned and padded across the floor to the dressing room. 'Thank you for reminding me, Polly. He did mention he'd like to join Taz and me.' After a quick wash, she was helped to dress in her riding habit by Polly who buttoned the tight short coat that nipped in her waist, contrasting with the voluminous skirts. A part of Eliza longed to be divested of all this cloth to instead ride freely in her close-fitting circus costume, but she was also attracted to the ladylike elegance of her borrowed outfit that showed off her figure and colouring to such effect. Polly twined her mass of blonde hair into a loose low bun so that Corinna's smart top hat would fit, the short net veil making her eyes mysterious and its ostrich feather curling round the brim.

Colouring slightly, Polly said, 'I've been to Astley's, miss, with Davey on me night out. I've seen ye perform.'

Eliza turned to face her with a look of surprise. 'Did you, Polly? What did you think?'

'I thought ye was a marvel. Davey agreed.'

'That news pleases me greatly. It's a show for the people.'

'Well, the people loves ye. The best thing in it. I'm honoured to help ye in any way,' Polly mumbled in some embarrassment as she turned to tidy the room.

Touched by this, Eliza walked into the mews with a lightened step. Taz had already saddled Clio for her. 'Miss Gray, we 'ave company.' He jerked his head towards the neighbouring Wolfe mews where Eliza could see a big bay hunter with Mr Flynn sitting easily on his back. As Taz gave Eliza a lift into the saddle she said, 'Yes, he's from the Americas and really knows his horses.'

Taz looked sceptical and sucked his teeth. To his mind, only his employer and himself were gifted with an almost mystical eye for the best bloodstock: no one else came close to understanding horses as they did. 'We'll see,' was all he said as he sprang into the saddle as agile as a cat. They trotted together over the cobbles and met with Mr Flynn who raised his hat and said in a cheery voice, 'Good morning, Miss Gray.'

Eliza appraised him with a more interested eye. He looked well on a horse, despite his height and breadth. His good humour was also attractive and, most importantly, he did not consider her circus background as demeaning but rather something curious, even admirable. This democratic approach was refreshing, for Eliza knew most of her fellow countrymen and women looked down their noses at such a provenance.

They rode together through Grosvenor Square, avoiding the carts loaded with flowers and vegetables destined for the basement kitchens of the grand houses. Children with their nursemaids were already running round the central gardens chasing their hoops. As they approached the gate into the Park, it was thronged with riders on horseback and a few promenaders taking advantage of the fine weather after a day and night of storms. Acquaintances greeted one another and some rode off in twos and threes. The grass was saturated and already churned up into muddy ruts by horses' hooves. Mr Flynn sat back in his saddle and surveyed Hyde Park, seemingly unimpressed. 'It's rather a small area of green for such a large city.' He turned and gazed directly at Eliza. 'I wish you could see my acres in Kentucky. Wide expanses, big skies, and we could ride all day and not reach my neighbour's land.'

Eliza smiled, meeting his eyes which were sparkling in the morning light. She knew he was thinking of home with some nostalgia and the emotion this roused in her caught her off-guard. Then she glanced at Taz trotting behind her, his face distinctly unimpressed as he muttered, 'Humph! Ride all day to traverse yer land – m'lord prefers a faster 'orse.' She almost laughed out loud at how transparent his scorn was for this rich stranger, boasting about his acreage. Mr Flynn was oblivious; to anyone who did not know Taz and his canny skills, he was a mere servant and not worth consideration.

Zadoc Flynn pointed to a distant stand of plane trees. 'Let's give our horses their heads and canter up to that thicket.'

When Eliza nodded, they let loose their reins. Eliza's mount, Clio, was in the wake of Mr Flynn's large hunter and Eliza was aware of the mud flying up from the speeding hooves in front. When they reached the clump of trees, both were exhilarated and breathless. Taz moved in close, aware he was chaperoning

Eliza, just as Mr Flynn noticed the mud splatters on his companion's face and bodice. He laughed. 'You look like a spotted lynx,' he said as he brought his horse alongside hers and took out his linen handkerchief. 'Let me clean you up.'

Eliza lifted her face as he dabbed at the gobbets of mud. The dry linen was not proving very effective, instead smearing the dirt across her skin. Mr Flynn was not someone to give up and continued to scrub at the sticky marks, turning her cheeks red and streaky in the process. They were laughing at the mess he was making just as they heard the thunder of approaching hooves. Turning in unison they saw Horatio cantering towards them in long flowing strides with an elegant figure in the saddle, his face like thunder.

Raven Purfoy reined in his steed, his dark eyes blazing as they fell on Mr Flynn and Eliza, she looking surprised and inexplicably shamefaced. But he directed his ire at his groom. 'Taz, I didn't expect you to skulk off to accompany Miss Gray when I needed you.'

Taz brushed off any rebuke. 'I never skulk, as ye know, guv. Offered to ride wi' Miss Gray only for I knew ye to be still abed.'

'Well, as you can see, I'm no longer abed. In fact, I think I'll be up most mornings to exercise Horatio myself.' He was shocked to hear himself saying something so uncharacteristic – and inconvenient. Since he was a student at Oxford and could please himself, he was never up before noon. Leisure and languid pleasure were the order of the day. What had the arrival of Miss Gray done to him? He looked across at her and saw the mud smears on her reddened cheeks and the splatters of mud on her bodice and in an instant knew the American fool had botched it.

'Here, let me clean you up. You're not fit to be seen in public, certainly not on one of my best prancers.'

'I don't mind how I appear, my lord,' Eliza said.

'Well, I do. My horses are well known, ye know.' He took out a handkerchief from his inner pocket. 'Now to do the job properly this linen has to be wet; shall it be my spittle or yours?' His voice was matter-of-fact but the thought of his saliva on her skin seemed somehow shockingly intimate. Eliza took the handkerchief, spat on it and passed it back. Lord Purfoy had moved Horatio alongside Clio and the stable mates nuzzled each other as he reached over to place a forefinger under Eliza's chin and tilted her face upwards. 'Now I can see better what I'm doing.'

Raven Purfoy's unexpected touch made her hold her breath. She always found his proximity disturbing and was never certain what might happen next. She glanced up at his face but his expression was intent on his task as he deftly whisked away the mud from her cheeks. When Lord Purfoy had finished, he sat back in the saddle to survey his handiwork. 'You're respectable again, if looking a trifle scrubbed.' He smiled and handed over his handkerchief. 'I'll leave you to clean your riding habit.'

As Eliza rubbed away at the cloth, she glanced up and met his eyes. 'It's my fault Taz has been taking me riding. I miss my horse, Percy, so much. I had to leave him at the circus, you see.'

'It's typical high-handedness on Taz's part that he offers you one of *my* best horses, as if they belonged to him.' His lordship's words were severe but his eyes were sparkling, and Taz and Eliza shared a wry smile. Then, unexpectedly, he added, 'But I have to agree with him: you match Clio well – not many riders could.'

Gratified by this compliment, Eliza returned to cleaning the mud from her bodice, unaware of much beyond her concern for Corinna's habit. Taz, however, had noticed on the tree line a flashy grey, its white tail streaming like smoke as its rider cantered down the incline towards them. He muttered, 'Somethin' wicked this way comes.'

Everyone turned. 'It's not like you to be so melodramatic,'

Purfoy said to his tiger – then he too recognised the horse. 'But you're right, if not exactly wicked, then very disobliging indeed.'

Lord Davenport reined his horse in alongside Eliza. Looking sly and furtive, he said, 'Good day, gentlemen.' He tipped his hat. 'And good morning to you, Miss Clorinda. I wondered who the wasps might be around the honey pot, and now I see.' His pale lean face surveyed the men. 'I thought it might be Purfoy, of course, with his unruly groom, but a stranger too?' He gave a questioning look.

Barely hiding his contempt, Raven Purfoy said, 'Our companion's name is Miss Gray.'

Lord Davenport smirked. 'Pray, accept my apologies, Miss Gray.'

Mr Flynn extended his hand in his genial way. 'Zadoc Flynn, visiting from the Americas, taking advantage of the hospitality of my kin, the Wolfes of Brook Street.'

'I'm pleased to make your acquaintance, Mr Flynn. I hope you'll be accompanying your hosts to the Bassett ball tomorrow night. Our enervated nobility could do with some new blood.' Davenport's laugh expressed neither warmth nor delight. He lifted his hat in farewell but as Eliza turned to meet his gaze for the first time, her face was lit up in a shaft of sunlight that made vivid her unusual eye colour. Lord Davenport paused, looking at her intently. His face visibly drained of its remaining colour before he wheeled his horse around and spurred it into a canter.

'Do you know that scoundrel?' Lord Purfoy's voice was harsh as he addressed Eliza, indicating Lord Davenport's receding back.

'No, but he recognised me from seeing me ride at Prebbles.'

Raven Purfoy's voice was sarcastic. 'Oh, I forgot. That's when my tiger brought my name into disrepute by indicating he was prepared to horsewhip him.'

Eliza lifted her chin, feeling protective of Taz – not that he needed anyone to fight his corner. 'He was just defending me, my lord.'

His lordship's glittering dark eyes held her gaze as he drawled, 'Miss Gray, you seem to have an unerring capacity to unsettle any custom and every equilibrium.' Eliza could not read whether it was amusement or exasperation in his voice. 'I'm ready for breakfast,' he said as he turned Horatio and headed for the Grosvenor Gate. Eliza, Zadoc Flynn and Taz followed in his wake. It was the first time Eliza had had an opportunity to see Horatio's movement as he cantered with his master elegantly poised on his back. Man and horse moved as one and it excited her to see such fluid symmetry and consummate skill. As they entered the mews, Taz leapt down to take the horses' reins and Lord Purfoy dismounted and walked round to offer a hand to Eliza. With a mischievous chuckle, Taz said, 'Miss Gray don't need yer help, m'lord. She can somersault to the ground!'

Eliza coloured. 'You are mistaken, Taz,' she remonstrated as she noticed Lord Purfoy's eyes register surprise. 'I wouldn't attempt a somersault in these clothes! I'm practising being a lady,' she said, unhooking her leg from the pommel and slipping down Clio's side to take Raven Purfoy's proffered hand.

'I'm gratified to hear that,' he murmured. 'On past performance, it seems you have a deal of practising still to do.' He continued to hold her hand as he looked deep into her eyes. 'Who are you, Miss Gray? Where do you come from? A changeling left by the fairies? Your distinctive appearance might suggest as much.'

'I too would like to know.' Eliza's response was subdued.

Before their conversation could continue, Zadoc Flynn strode through the arch dividing the mews. He walked up to his lordship. 'Purfoy, I've decided to buy a fine stallion of the best racing stock to ship home. For my breeding mares back in

Kentucky. May I have your permission to ask Taz to accompany me to the sales at Tattersalls? I would appreciate his experienced eye.'

A fleeting look of irritation crossed Purfoy's face before he regained his composure and the courtesy befitting his rank. 'Of course, Mr Flynn. Check with Taz when he may have some time to spare. Early morning is best, is it not?' He turned to catch the eye of his groom, busy unsaddling Horatio.

Despite Taz being unimpressed with this visitor, the chance to handle some top-class bloodstock never failed to thrill. ''Tis true, guv'nor,' Taz said, not wishing to give away his delight at the prospect.

His lordship continued, as if musing to himself. 'Of course, you couldn't do better than buy Davenport's beautiful grey. As fine as any I know. But you'd have to wait for that blackguard to beggar himself at the gaming tables before you could acquire it, the only living creature he loves.' He had released Eliza's hand and she turned and crossed the garden to enter the Wolfes' house. He watched her small, graceful figure until she was out of sight. The fibres of an unseen chord dragged at his heart. How dangerous, how foolish, the senseless, pitiable folly of allowing himself to stray into such perilous waters again!

* * *

After Mrs Wilson's dancing lesson, Eliza was feeling confident that she would manage to acquit herself perfectly well. Mr Flynn was less proficient but of a more devil-may-care character, unconcerned at how he might be judged. Eliza thought that growing up with the comfort of great wealth had made him attractively immune to self-doubt and the anxieties of less fortunate citizens. She also admired his utter lack of interest in trying to be an

English gentleman; he was happy in his own skin, and that appealed to the rebel in her.

In a thoughtful mood, she dressed carefully for her first visit to Marina Fairley at her grandmother's house. It struck Eliza as novel and intriguing to have a grandmother, to have family to whom one bore a likeness and belonged, and she was excited at the thought of this expedition.

The afternoon was bright and warm as she and Polly set off on foot, turning left into Bond Street. This shopping area was always busy with people coming and going, chatter, horses, carriages and every kind of spectacle. Tantalised by the passing show, the young women paused to gaze in shop windows until the ogling and comments by saunterers and dandies hurried them on. Soon they'd reached Grafton Street and then, there it was, the grand edifice of Miss Fairley's grandmother's house at the corner of Albermarle Street.

The door swung open to reveal a hallway painted canary yellow, an imposing but grimy chandelier hanging from the ceiling and the walls lined with portraits in gilded frames. The summery colour lifted Eliza's spirit. The old retainer, also dressed in yellow but the fabric faded and slightly frayed, seemed to be expecting them and led the way towards the back of the house where a large panelled mahogany door opened to the library.

Marina Fairley met her at the threshold, her glossy brown hair piled on her head in an untidy bun. 'Good afternoon, Miss Gray. I'm glad to see you again. Come in and meet my grandmother.' In a spontaneous gesture she grasped Eliza's hand and walked with her arm in arm towards the fireplace while Polly disappeared down the back stairs to the kitchen quarters. Eliza stood before an elderly woman sitting by the fire with a book in her hand and a pair of wire-rimmed spectacles on the bridge of her thin nose. 'Grandmama, this is my new friend, Miss Gray.'

Then, as Eliza extended her hand and dropped a small curtsey she added, 'Miss Gray, this is my dear grandmama, Mrs Penrose.'

Eliza was reminded of a bird, but not of the garden variety. Mrs Penrose had the striking presence of a raptor with the far-seeing eyes and calculating stillness of a hawk.

These steely eyes were sizing her up, then in an instant they softened and the hawk became a twinkly grandmother. Eliza sat in the chair opposite while Marina Fairley headed for the door, saying over her shoulder, 'I'll just ask Cook for tea and biscuits.' Eliza was intrigued by the surprisingly dark room. The only light came from a single large window, veiled with the soot of ages, falling dimly on walls lined with handsome mahogany shelves filled to overflowing. Books were everywhere; they lay open on all available surfaces, bright fabric ribands marking the page, and were stacked in small piles on tables and chairs, green and red leather spines glowing in the crepuscular light. For a young woman who had had to snatch what reading matter she could and indulge in secret, such an abundance quickened her imagination.

Lettice Penrose noticed her wide-eyed interest in the room and held up the book in her lap. 'Do you know this? An acquaintance of mine, Mrs Carter, some years ago translated and published the works of the philosopher Epictetus, and this is the result.'

Eliza had neither heard of Mrs Carter nor of Epictetus and was relieved when her friend returned. Marina had caught the last of her grandmother's words and laughed, 'Miss Gray, my grandmother is one of the old *bas bleu*. She belonged to the Society of Blue Stockings when she was my age.' She sat down beside the elderly lady and took her hand. 'She is a great supporter of me against my mama whose prosaic views of life and women's place in it need to be resisted.'

Eliza had heard of the *bas bleu*, admittedly as a derogative description of a woman writer in *The Sporting Magazine*, and also recalled one of her favourite novels. She asked, her eyes shining, 'Mrs Penrose, did you ever meet Mrs Thrale? I loved *Evelina*. I found a copy and managed to read it when everyone else was asleep.'

'But why so clandestine, child?'

'I wasn't encouraged to read books.'

'Why heavens not?' Mrs Penrose looked disbelieving, as if a life without books were unimaginable.

Eliza coloured. It was always nerve-wracking revealing her irregular past but she sensed, and hoped, Marina Fairley and her grandmother would be sympathetic and accepting. She took a deep breath. 'I was lost as a child and taken in by a circus family and trained as a dancer with horses.'

Both women sitting opposite her looked aghast. Mrs Penrose was the first to speak in a shocked voice. 'Brought up in the circus?' She recovered her natural courtesy and continued with a practised emollience of tone, 'Apart from the lack of books, that sounds like an adventurous childhood, my dear.'

Eliza agreed her life until this point did indeed sound like an adventure, however, she quietly explained it was one she could have done without, adding, 'But I really longed to live a more normal life, and most of all to find my mother from whom I was severed so young.'

Marina came to sit beside Eliza and took her hand in sympathy. 'My troubles shrink in comparison.' Her eyes were bright with tears. 'I complain about my mother but at least I have one, and my grandmother is a continual delight to me.'

Eliza thought she should elaborate a little more. 'I ran away thinking I could find some work in a shop, perhaps, or as a lady's maid, until I could discover who I was and where I came from.

But all the while I was unsure how I could ever trace my family. Then I was offered hospitality and help from Mr and Mrs Wolfe.' She turned to meet Marina Fairley's sympathetic gaze. 'You met her when we were sheltering from the rain.' She continued, 'And for the first time I feel hopeful there is a way ahead for me.'

Mrs Penrose had been watching Eliza's expressive face and said softly, 'You have a most distinctive look. You remind me of someone but I can't recall who. It was too long ago. Is Eliza your full first name? Or are you an Elizabeth, perhaps?'

'It is the only name I know, ma'am. Perhaps it's not even my given name. I was so young when I was separated from the life I knew.'

Marina squeezed her hand. 'Well, I too feel I know you and have known you for ever! Perhaps we can be like sisters to each other?'

Eliza felt a rush of gratitude for such openness of heart. Suddenly shy, she said, 'May I ask, as you reject your mother's plans, what is the kind of life for which you hope?'

'My hopes are more easily realisable. I wish to be free from the imperative of marriage. I want to live the life of the mind,' Marina said dramatically, with a flourish of her hand.

Her grandmother chuckled and indicated the book in her lap. 'I'm just reading here, *First say to yourself what you would be, and then do what you have to do.* This is one of Epictetus's prescriptions for happiness.'

'Well, that is true indeed. And *you*, dear Grandmama, have made it possible with your offer of an annuity so I can live as I choose.' She smiled at her grandmother, then turned to Eliza. 'You see, I wish to do what Grandmama's friend Mrs Carter did, translate and publish some ancient text my father sent to me.'

Eliza's face was eager. 'Is your father a scholar too?'

Marina snorted with laughter. 'No! So far from a scholar. He was a gamester and libertine and died in exile from his excesses.' Eliza was taken aback at such frankness. Miss Fairley noticed her expression and patted her arm. 'I don't mean to sound so *uncivil* and flippant. You see I never really knew him. He was a nobleman who ruined my mother. Hence her obsessive desire to see me respectably settled!'

Eliza was doubly surprised at such openness about personal matters, but thought perhaps the intellectual influence of her grandmother must have made Miss Fairley unguarded.

Mrs Penrose interceded with a stern voice and once more became hawk-like and uncompromising. 'My daughter, Lydia, was a foolish ninny and he was a disreputable rake whose behaviour with a young woman of her class was disgraceful. He wasn't fooling with one of the maids, ye know! Lydia was a vain numbskull, and he had no excuse and fully deserved his fate.'

Both young women looked at each other, startled by the emotion in Mrs Penrose's voice. Suddenly, Eliza was gripped by a need to know and asked Marina in a quiet voice, 'Was your father's name Fairley?'

'No. My mother quickly married the local squire, a Mr Fairley, who gave me the cloak of his name. But she never forgot her noble seducer and was proud of the grandeur of his bloodline. Her vanity meant she could not keep it from me, as discretion and good manners demanded. Instead, she confided my parentage, hoping I would aim higher in marriage myself.'

'Lydia always lacked imagination,' Lettice Penrose added. 'Takes after her father, I'm afraid. Very dreary and lugubrious he was. Having coddled himself all his life, he was carried off by a chill caught one rainy afternoon as he tried to stop jackdaws nesting in our chimneys. Why he didn't leave it to one of the gardeners, I'll never know. But I always wondered if it was really his tedious doggedness that was fatal in the end.'

'Oh, Grandmama! You don't need to be so disobliging.' Miss Fairley's amused voice belied her disapproving words. 'He knew his limitations. I remember him saying that the most beautiful women should be left for unimaginative men like him. He was looking at you at the time.'

Her grandmother laughed. 'That's one of his wittier sayings. I was beautiful once, 'tis true, but not as beautiful as your friend.' Mrs Penrose smiled across at Eliza. 'Miss Gray, mark my words, your looks will lead you to your family, or at least to marriage so you can make your own family. The fairness of your hair and skin, the cast of your features, and those oddly coloured eyes are most individual.'

Eliza blushed with pleasure at a compliment from such an exacting woman. She had grown up admonished rather than praised, and approval of any kind surprised her with joy. 'Thank you, Mrs Penrose,' she said, the colour still suffusing her cheeks.

'I feel for your plight my dear, although not all families are loving and sometimes are best lost to us! But the wise philosopher has a message for you too, Miss Gray: *Mourn not for that which you lack; rejoice in what is yours,* great beauty, goodness of nature... and the skill of a fine horsewoman.'

Now it was Eliza's turn to be amused. 'You're teasing me, Mrs Penrose. No classical philosopher would mention my horsemanship!'

The once young Blue Stocking threw back her head and laughed as gaily as if she were a girl again. 'You're right, I added that! But the first exhortations belong to Epictetus as certain as night follows day. Look, it's here.' She tapped the open page of her book. 'You must celebrate what you have. You are a lucky young woman to be so richly endowed with gifts.'

'Thank you. I will endeavour to do just that. I've been

learning to dance properly and hope this will prove to be another of my skills.'

Both Marina and her grandmother looked at her with a question in their eyes. 'Is this in preparation for the Bassett ball tomorrow?'

'It is. Are you both attending?'

Lettice Penrose answered, 'I'm too old to find much of the Season diverting, but Lady Bassett's ball is always worthwhile, purely because everyone will be there. I enjoy seeing how much old acquaintances have aged over the past year, and how many are still alive!' She got to her feet and the young women stood up too. 'Now I must say farewell, Miss Gray, until we meet again. Perhaps at the ball tomorrow?'

Eliza felt this was a sign that she should leave, but Marina held onto her arm. 'Do sit down, Miss Gray. We have so much more to talk of.'

It was true, she longed to know more about her new friend. Eliza studied her face and noticed her expression of meditative calm, but Marina Fairley had a look too intelligent, too steady and full of purpose to be considered just a dreamy girl. Intrigued by her talk of translating classical texts from their original source, Eliza asked, 'Where did your father find this manuscript that you intend to work on?'

'When he was a young man on his Grand Tour, before Napoleon and his wars ended all that, he was in Venice and was invited to the library of San Marco. He copied some poetic fragments in Latin.' Marina paused and looked thoughtful. 'It made me feel closer to him to know that through all his profligate ways he never lost these pages. When he heard I was a bookish child and good at languages, he sent me this precious copy just before he died. I wish I'd had the chance to share my interest with him.'

Eliza was touched by this story of estranged father and

daughter coming together over Latin. 'I'm impressed that you'd been taught the classical languages,' she said, painfully aware of her own educational inadequacies.

'I grew up with my mother and Mr Fairley in the Manor Farm and had lessons with Lord Ashley's young sons and their tutor at neighbouring Ashley Court. That's the only reason I learned Latin and Greek. I can teach you should you wish?'

'If that would allow me to become a governess then I might ask you to do just that.' Eliza laughed but could not ignore her anxiety about how best to earn her living, should she fail to discover her family.

'You should not need to work at some menial task. A governess's life is but a half-life. With Grandmama's stipend there will be enough for two. You could always come and live with me, then we would please ourselves, paying no heed to Society and the aspersions so readily cast on old maids!'

Eliza felt a wave of astonishment and gratitude for her new friend's blitheness of spirit. Whatever happened, she was no longer entirely alone. She squeezed Miss Fairley's hand. 'You have given me the greatest gift of friendship. With you in my life, my future looks more hopeful.'

Eliza stood up, ready to take her leave and Marina stood beside her. 'Do you think, as sisters under the skin, you might be happy to call me Marina?' She looked suddenly shy. 'And may I call you Eliza?'

Overcome with feeling, Eliza hugged her. 'Of course. I would be honoured.' Was this what having family was like, she wondered, as she felt arms encircle her?

* * *

When Eliza returned with Polly to Brook Street, there was a letter waiting for her in the hall. She recognised the hand of Rose Bowman and carried it up the stairs to her room.

As she read, her unease grew. It was full of Mr Flynn's plans, not least to escort her to the Bassett ball. What was Mr Flynn offering Rose? Eliza knew she was a worldly young woman and not easily gulled, but what was their relationship already? And most immediately concerning was the news that Mr Flynn intended to bring her uninvited to the grandest ball of the Season. Eliza could not bear Rose to be publicly scorned as Lord Davenport had privately scorned her. She also, more shamefully, felt uneasy about her old life intruding on her new.

Not wishing to misread the situation, Eliza did not express such misgivings to her friend and only sent in reply an encouraging but non-committal note. She was just asking Gibbons to have it delivered when Mr Flynn entered through the front door, his eyes lighting up at the sight of her. Eliza took his arm. 'Mr Flynn, can you spare me a moment?' She steered him into the small sitting room at the front of the house. 'It won't take long, so I hope it's not indelicate if I don't call for Polly.' She smiled at him over her shoulder.

When he could, Flynn ignored the niceties of English customs and shrugged. 'I've just been to see the Palace of Westminster. What a building! I'm very much enjoying being the tourist about town.' They sat down in chairs on either side of the fireplace as he continued his enthusiastic talk. 'Before I return home I'd like to see Bristol, from where my father set off as a young man. Bath, of course. Who can come to England and not see that town? Then Ireland beckons, the country of my ancestors.'

Eliza's face was serious. 'Mr Flynn, my concerns are more

immediate, I'm afraid. Rose Bowman sent me a note about accompanying you to the ball tomorrow.'

He looked surprised. 'Yes indeed. She said she'd never been to a soirée let alone a ball, and I thought I could give her that pleasure.'

'That is a generous thought. But I'm worried you have no invitation for Miss Bowman and it is a very grand ball to which only those invited can go. I'm protective of her. I don't wish her feelings to be injured by the prejudices of some.'

'What prejudices could there be?' He looked genuinely puzzled.

'There are some in English society who are sticklers for the rules and conventions. I was abused by a nobleman in the Park who recognised me from the circus. Miss Bowman is much more distinctive as she does not wear a mask when performing.'

Mr Flynn looked triumphant. 'Well, she will be unrecognisable. I have bought her a special dress as a present. I was on the strut with Mr Shilton and he pointed out the best mantua-maker in London for glossing with satin and style any discrepancies in a woman's breeding.'

Eliza laughed. 'That sounds just like what Mr Shilton would say. He is an advocate both for the power of beautiful clothing and that of conformity to the rules. Things must be seen to be done in the correct manner.'

'Well, what can be your concern? I will bring Miss Bowman late to the ball, after her performance is finished, as she is not meant to leave the premises, as you know.'

Eliza's feelings were so stirred by what she was about to say that she involuntarily leaned across to touch his arm, to make sure she had his attention. 'You are an American, you are very rich and this makes it possible for you to break rules and conventions with little censure. We women, especially if we lack financial means or breeding, have to guard our honour as carefully as our lives.'

He snorted with derision and Eliza snatched her hand back in exasperation. 'It's perfectly true, what I say! It is only your insulation through wealth and the privileges of your sex, and your lack of imagination' – she paused, surprised by her rudeness, then continued – 'means you can ignore the true limitations on women who lack family, property or status!' Her voice had risen and her cheeks were flushed with feeling.

Mr Flynn took her hand in a conciliatory gesture. 'I'm sorry, Miss Gray. I'm just a country bumpkin – is that what you call here what I would call an ass at home? – I am grateful that I have not been schooled in an English gentleman's subtle refinements.'

Eliza felt her indignation subside. She smiled. 'Men are asses here too.' However, still wishing to make her point, she continued, 'I fear the disadvantages of women without status are as true in your country. This is why I hope you will be careful what you offer Miss Bowman. She is not a fool, but dreams can make fools of us all.'

Zadoc Flynn was himself unsmiling when he answered, 'I'm conscious of the lure of the new and ignorance of the unknown. I take my responsibilities seriously, you can rest assured.' Eliza was aware how long they had been talking and stood up ready to go. He forestalled her. 'Miss Gray, just one more thing. Taz is escorting me to Tattersalls, first light tomorrow. He has a very high opinion of your horsemanship. Would you come with us? I'd be grateful for your skill in riding when I buy what will be the most important horse to establish my racing bloodline. I'm too heavy to truly test these beasts bred for speed.'

Eliza paused, her heart beating fast. She would love to see the best horses in the land, she was gratified to hear how highly Taz rated her, and she longed to be able to ride a potential racing star.

But would it be too bold, she thought, to dress so she could ride as she did at the circus, free and astride? The clothes she had been lent included Ferdy Shilton's old school breeches and jacket. Would it be indelicate for her to wear them in public just for a couple of hours? Her rebel spirit thought it was worth the risk for the thrill of the ride. She met Mr Flynn's questioning face. 'Yes. I should be glad to ride the horses for you.'

* * *

Eliza was strangely agitated by the day's events. She ran up the stairs to her room to dress for dinner and to have a few moments to think. Her friendship with Marina Fairley was an unexpected pleasure. There was an instant understanding and affection between them which pierced her loneliness. Perhaps her strike for freedom was not so foolhardy after all? Perhaps in running away from the only home she had known, in pushing open the most alarming door of all, she had found all kinds of other possibilities, of other doors ready to spring back, revealing unimagined worlds.

The chance of riding a horse astride again delighted her, feeling at one with the animal, instead of perched on its back in the proprietary side-saddle, looking elegant no doubt, but disconnected from the animal's power and spirit. And to top this pleasure was the fact that the two most highly regarded horsemen in London, Lord Purfoy and his tiger, Taz, commended her riding skill. She knew this showed an unbecoming vanity, but her riding prowess was the only skill she had and it was exciting to have it recognised by the people who mattered most.

Eliza put her concerns about Rose to one side. She could address them with her tomorrow, when she saw her at the ball. After a cursory wash she clambered into a dress of Corinna's that she had yet to wear. She loved the shell pink of the silk gathered into a pink and dove grey striped bodice with ruffled bands of grey ribbon sewn at the hem and sleeves. Her appearance no longer surprised her; Eliza was getting used to the new elegance of both her looks and her life. Her elocution too felt as natural as if she had been speaking this way all her life.

Polly popped her head round the door and asked if she needed help with her lacing or her hair. Eliza said with a rueful smile, 'I've made a passable attempt at a Grecian style, I think.'

'No, miss, you haven't.' Polly was firm. 'Let me help you.' She brushed out Eliza's hair. 'It's so long and there's so much of it, like spun silk, I'm not surprised you find it difficult to manage.'

'I used to wear it plaited which was easier but less elegant.' Eliza smiled at Polly in the looking glass.

'Well, miss, you could plait some of these side waves and then pin them into the main mass coiled into a bun on the top of your head.'

The maid's deft fingers did just this and Eliza stared at her reflection. 'That's wonderful. Thank you, Polly, for making me look more than passable.' She laughed. 'I shall try that myself but I don't know if I can replicate your confection.'

'You can always ask me, miss.' Polly was gratified at the praise.

'That's very kind, but I can't live here for ever under the benign care of Mr and Mrs Wolfe. I shall have to learn to manage myself.' She made an effort to keep her voice light-hearted, aware that Polly's life was far more conscribed than hers, even at its lowest ebb. Eliza then remembered the adventure that awaited her. A tremor of excitement ran through her and she turned her head towards the girl to say, 'Oh Polly, I'm leaving early tomorrow for a ride, so don't worry about bringing me water until I'm back.'

* * *

The usual band of friends was due for dinner before peeling off to their clubs or other forms of entertainment. The Wolfe household, with Corinna at its heart, provided the warm embrace of family without any answering responsibility. This was particularly appealing to Ferdy Shilton and Lord Purfoy who had obstinately eschewed matrimony for the carefree pleasures of bachelorhood, but enjoyed the comforts of home, run by a competent woman who created for them all such a seductive sense of kinship.

Eliza walked into the drawing room where Mr Shilton lounged like an elegant faun, one slender pantalooned leg crossed over the other. His manners were impeccable and on sight of her, he sprang with grace to his feet, took her hand and bowed. 'What a pleasure to see you again, Miss Gray.'

Zadoc Flynn was reading *The Sporting Magazine* and he too got to his feet. 'Miss Gray, it's not an hour since we last parted but it's always a pleasure to see you.' He bowed low in an amused parody of the expected mores. Eliza laughed.

Corinna joined them wearing a fine corded silk dress but her fingertips were still stained with paint. She handed a small leather-bound volume to Eliza. 'I thought you might enjoy this. Lord Byron's *The Corsair*. Alick ordered it from Hatchards to make sure he got a copy.' In delight, Eliza stroked the gleaming green calfskin as Corinna continued, 'It's wonderfully adventurous and romantic, I think you'd enjoy it.'

Just as they were settling round the table, Gibbons announced Lord Purfoy.

'Apologies, my dears,' he drawled. He was as panther-like in his grace as ever but paler than usual and seeming low in spirit. He subsided into his chair opposite Eliza and Mr Flynn and said to the room at large, 'The life of a nobleman is not a happy one!

Oh the utter tedium of having nothing worthwhile to do, and to spend so much time doing it.'

Alick had begun to carve the beef and looked up to meet the disconsolate eyes of his friend. 'Why not take on the management of your estates, Rav? You have such wealth in those fertile acres and the castle could do with some updating and care. Mine gives me great pleasure, second only to my family.' He waved his carving knife in the direction of his wife.

His friend scoffed. 'Life in the country is even more irksome than life in Town. What to do for diversion? I even find hunting and shooting a bore, certainly find the people who indulge in them so. The contemptible in pursuit of the inedible. Nothing to do in that benighted land but bet on the one-legged goose winning the race or shadow-boxing with the trees.'

Corinna was concerned. 'Why so melancholic, Rav? What has happened to disturb your mood?'

Ferdy intervened with a laugh, 'His lordship rose from his bed unconscionably early. I know how dangerous that can be for a man's equilibrium.'

Mr Flynn offered his own remedy. 'Why not breed racehorses as I intend to do? You have your own unerring eye and Taz's experience.'

Eliza felt her heart leap at the thought and blurted out, 'I'd really like to do that.' Everyone looked at her in surprise and she coloured. 'Of course, if I ever have my own family and home.'

Lord Purfoy's eyes were on her when he asked, 'What is family? Like you, Miss Gray, I have no family but my friends, my horses and Taz. Those alone I care for, they're all I need.'

Eliza had been held by his intense gaze as he spoke with more feeling than she had heard in his voice before. She leaned forward and said in earnest, 'You do have a home and security, a place in Society. Above all, you know where you've come from, my lord. That's what I long for.'

'But my home and my history merely bring further grief. You have a bare slate on which to write a new story, free of the pain of the past.' Eliza was so caught in his gaze it felt they were speaking only to each other, both in a storm of different thoughts and desires. He had everything she longed for but was discontented, and she had nothing but was full of hope. Somehow they were connected each to the other through a force neither understood, and a recognition of the loneliness of their souls.

The moment was broken by Ferdy's voice. 'Miss Gray, you're clinging to that volume as if your life depended on it?'

Eliza looked down at the book in her lap, amazed to see how white her knuckles had grown with the force of her grip. As if returning from a dream she said, 'Ah! Lord Byron's *The Corsair*, kindly lent to me by Mrs Wolfe.' She handed it to him with a reverence that he remarked upon and she replied, 'It is the greatest privilege for me to have a book to read when and where I choose. I was not brought up with books. In fact, they were frowned upon and I had to read in secret.'

Lord Purfoy laughed. 'There are some who think Lord Byron should not be read by the young or virtuous. I presume you fit both of those categories?'

'He came with some of his friends to see the performance of the Prebbles Flying Circus. There was such commotion. It was the night I almost fell off Percy while I was dancing on his back.'

'My only regret is that I never went to see you perform myself. Clorinda the Winged Venus conjures the most delicious image.' Lord Purfoy had returned to his teasing, sardonic manner and Eliza did not know what to make of him at all.

Alick was tucking into the food when he looked up and said, 'Well, Ferdy's seen Miss Gray's performance.'

'I have. And most affecting it was too.'

Corinna interrupted their masculine banter. 'Gentlemen, spare Miss Gray's blushes. I hope you will all be gracing Lady Bassett's ball tomorrow night?'

Men about Town liked to complain about the dullness of the Season's balls and musical soirées, largely because most hostesses refused to provide gaming tables. Experienced hostesses did not care to see the male guests drift away from dance floor or musical entertainment, seduced by the more diverting charms of cards and dice. But Lady Bassett was a gamester herself and very happy to combine as many pleasures as she legally could at her famous ball.

Ferdy Shilton was keen. 'I surely will. I can't ignore a chance to display my latest sartorial triumph. I've had Meyer craft me an evening coat in silver grey to wear with my oyster silk pantaloons.'

Lord Purfoy was less enthusiastic. 'As you know I'd rather be at my club but I promised Miss Gray a dance in penance for my reckless driving. I won't stay long. Such glittering gallimaufry adds to the deadly tedium of Town life.'

'Oh come on, Raven, you know you find it diverting seeing all the new debutantes and their mamas, the old roués and young sprigs jostling for preferment. You enjoy nothing more than casting a cynical eye over the passing show.' Alick knew his friend well.

Zadoc Flynn was emphatic in his delight. 'I'm pleased to be able to attend. It will be interesting to contrast a big ball during the London Season with the dances back home.' He returned to his meal but then mentioned his controversial plan. 'I intend to bring a guest. I know I haven't obtained an invitation for her, but she has never been to such an event and I thought it would be a treat for her to have a taste of a different life.' He looked rather shamefaced.

Lord Purfoy noticed his demeanour and asked, 'Different, how different?'

'Well, she's a performer at Prebbles Flying Circus, a friend of Miss Gray's.'

'And her name?'

'Miss Bowman, Rose Bowman.'

Ferdy Shilton looked doubtful. 'Beware, without an invitation, your guest may be turned away. Regardless of her own dubious past and unconventional present, Lady Bassett is an enforcer of the proprieties at her social events. I think she's afraid of a brawl breaking out, or any hint of scandal. Making a point of her virtuousness erases her scandalous record.' Eliza felt her unease grow. She did not wish either Rose or herself to be exposed and disgraced.

5

LOVE AND LOSS AT THE BASSETT BALL

Corinna woke early, her mind full of vague anxiety. Alick's hand lay on her stomach and in stirring she woke him too. He pulled her into his arms and buried his face in her hair. 'I hope you slept well.'

'I did until just now when worries assailed me.' She yawned and shaded her eyes against the shaft of early sun that streamed across the bed.

Alick propped himself on an elbow so he could see her face better. 'Why? What concerns you, my love?'

'Our guests. The reins are slipping from my fingers.' She laughed. 'You know how I don't care to be out of control of events. We have so much to think of: your work on the estate, my painting, time with Emma and now our coming baby.'

Alick had flopped down on the pillow again, his right arm slipping around her shoulders. 'Tell me what Miss Gray and Mr Flynn are up to that concerns you.'

'Eliza really needs to find her family and I'm not sure where we can begin in that quest. We have no clues, as I had with my father's gifts. But she has such a distinctive look, I can only hope someone recognises her.'

'That seems unlikely but it's all beyond our control anyway.'

It calmed Corinna's mind to feel her husband's physical warmth and strength of character. She looked up into his face. 'I know. But without meaning to be, Eliza's quite a disruptive presence. I've never known Raven so out of sorts; he's even breaking his lifelong insistence on sleeping until noon. These last days, he's been up early to exercise Horatio himself!'

Alick laughed. 'Don't you worry. Purfoy's proof against the most irresistible siren. He's made sure his heart has turned to stone. I'm not sure it's Miss Gray's fault he's out of his cot before noon.'

Corinna stirred, disconsolate. 'Then there's your wild relation from across the seas. He goes missing late at night. Ferdy says he leaves the club to go off to some show or pursue some lady love. Is he over here to find a wife or just to kick over the traces?'

Alick's left hand had begun to trace the blue veins beneath his wife's luminous skin. He murmured in her ear, 'I know he intends to buy a fine horse, which is probably a cheaper option.'

Corinna sat up abruptly, her eyes flashing and her hair in disarray. 'Alick, take this seriously!'

He chuckled. 'I'm finding it very hard to do so when you're so close to me and in such dishabille.' He pulled her to him again and enfolded her in his arms. 'I love your body swelling with our child. You are impossible to resist, darling Corinna!'

Corinna's face was under his chin and she remonstrated weakly as his lips moved slowly down her neck. 'I'm trying to talk to you about our troublesome guests and need your advice.'

'Well, wait until you've put on something to wear. I can't think of anything but you when you're in my arms, smelling so sweet and warm, rosy as the dawn.' His voice was muffled against her skin. In a deft movement Corinna extricated herself and skipped to the chair where his silk banyan had been tossed the previous night. Tying it firmly high above her swelling belly she returned to sit beside him on the bed. He looked at her, his hair unruly and his brown eyes full of amusement and desire.

Corinna was thoughtful. 'I feel a strange protectiveness towards Eliza. Is it just because she has not known a mother's love and care?'

Alick stretched his arms behind his head and with his eyes on his wife's face said, 'It may be you recognise your own plight in her. Your lack of family and need to belong somewhere. But you cannot be responsible for the whole world, my darling.'

'I fear the irresponsible are easier to love,' she said with a rueful smile.

He grasped her hand. 'Your care for me, for our children, for everyone in your orbit just makes you more desirable. I love you more than life, Corinna. My idea of paradise is to have you in my arms, pregnant with new life, with baby Emma beside us.'

She threw back her head and purred with pleasure. 'Well, I love you, darling Alick.' Then she added with a laugh, 'But I have no intention of being permanently with child, I assure you.'

She was still laughing as he pulled her back into bed. He buried his hands in her hair while gazing at her lovely face. 'That may well be so, Mrs Wolfe, but we both know you positively enjoy the hurly-burly of the marriage bed.'

'Oh Alick, shame on you!' She gave him a playful push and made as if to get up.

Undeterred, he put out his hand. 'Come, we have a few more moments left to us to be irresponsible.' Her protestations petered out as their lips met in their familiar embrace.

Maybe Corinna would have been less carefree had she known that Eliza Gray had early that morning tiptoed out of the house

wearing breeches and Ferdy Shilton's schoolboy jacket and
Eton hat.

* * *

Eliza had woken as dawn was breaking. Her pulse immediately
quickened as she remembered the adventure that lay ahead.
There would be so many fine horses to see and perhaps even to
ride. She dressed hurriedly in the borrowed breeches and shirt.
She could only really judge a horse's movement if she rode
astride but was aware she had to maintain her boyish
masquerade as there was always room for scandal if a young
woman was detected in such a disguise. She was slightly built
and the clothes fitted well enough, but her long hair was a problem. She quickly wove two thick plaits and coiled and pinned
them on her head before clamping them under Ferdy's old
top hat.

Eliza glanced at herself in the glass and thought she looked
quite passable as a young man. She felt liberated to be free of the
encumbrance of skirts and ran round to the mews feeling as light
as a gazelle. She found Taz had saddled up his own hunter and
was just about to put the side saddle on Clio. When he saw Eliza,
his knowing eyes widened and he chuckled. He had last seen
these clothes on Corinna when she was a slip of a girl and could
carry off the disguise. He ducked back into the saddlery to bring
out a regular saddle which he secured on Clio's back.

They heard the clop of hooves on the cobbles and Zadoc
Flynn appeared from the neighbouring Wolfe mews, sitting high
on his big hunter. His expression registered surprise at the sight
of Eliza in masculine clothes and his blue eyes gleamed. She said
brusquely, 'If you want me to give my opinion, I have to ride the

beast astride.' She then sprang up into the saddle as lightly as Taz himself.

Taz led the way. 'We'd best go across the Park. Head for the turnpike.' It was so early that only tradesmen's carts were on the streets, the boys scampering up and down the basement steps of the big houses, delivering meat, vegetables and flowers brought in daily from the market gardens surrounding the city.

Once they entered the Park they rode through the trees where mist still lay in drifts like sea-foam across the wet grass. Mr Flynn could not contain the excitement in his voice. 'Tattersalls must have quite an area to stable the horses and provide an exercising ring.'

Taz grunted in reply, 'Mr Tattersall has as much space as the Horse Guard Barracks just down the road.'

Eliza rode Clio up to Zadoc who seemed disconcerted by the sudden sight of her slender thigh beside his, clearly outlined in breeches. She asked in a low voice, 'Does Lord Purfoy know you've borrowed Taz for the morning?'

'He does, but didn't appear too enthusiastic about it. I don't think he approves of me.'

Eliza said in an amused voice, 'He doesn't approve of anyone apart from Taz. Oh, and he has a sneaking regard for Mrs Wolfe.'

Mr Flynn gave her a sidelong look. 'I don't think the noble gentleman is aware I've asked you to give your opinion too. No doubt I've flouted some central rule of English etiquette.'

'Well, Mr Flynn, I know you care little for that! But really, I'm as much an outsider as you. Just as uncouth.'

'That's not true at all. It's clear you're an English lady, despite everything.'

Taz heard this last exchange and never one to stand on ceremony, or show due deference, added his pithy opinion. 'Yon Miss

Gray's more than a lady, sir. None I know can ride like 'er or dismount a steed with an acrobat's tumble.'

'Thank you, Taz, for revealing my shame.' She was laughing and then caught sight of Mr Flynn's surprised expression. 'You see how uncouth I truly am!' They had just turned down Grosvenor Place and there facing them was *Tattersalls Horse Repository,* painted in large black letters over the entrance. Inside was a spacious half-covered yard with a stone rotunda and the stables all facing inwards, some with the heads of their curious occupants surveying the activities around them. Stable boys were busy cleaning out the straw and preparing the mounts to ride out for exercise.

A smartly dressed man in a dark coat and tall top hat greeted them, introducing himself as Mr Tattersall. Mr Flynn dismounted and shook his hand. He passed over a letter of credit from Drummonds Bank and the man visibly paled at the sight of the guarantee of such a significant sum of money. He gazed on the party of Mr Flynn, Eliza and Taz with renewed respect. Their mounts were taken to be stabled while Mr Tattersall summoned his best horses to be made ready for the parade.

Eliza was filled with excited wonder at the sight of so many stables and as many fine horses under one roof. Her heart ached for Percy. She did not expect him to miss her as acutely as she missed him, but could not believe she would never see him again.

Mr Flynn approached Taz and Eliza. 'I'd be grateful if you could look out for the physical conformation of the beast that would suggest his athleticism and speed. Good temperament matters too. Don't know how Lord Purfoy manages his prize hunter. So strong-willed and contrary.'

Taz sprang to the horse's defence. 'Horatio is more intelligent than most coves. Just mirrors my lordship's temperament. He's perfectly docile when handled with respect. I've never known him cantankerous.'

'Well, I admit he's the handsomest beast I've seen, and beauty matters too, but is not more important than physical prowess. I want a horse that can win the Epsom Derby.'

Mr Tattersall returned with a stable boy leading a high-spirited bay on a long rein and they watched as he put the horse through his paces in the manège. Mr Flynn shook his head. The next, a dashing black stallion, arrived in the arena, bucking and cavorting, refusing to do what he was asked even when the whip was flourished. Eliza felt her spirit flow out to the beast, but Mr Flynn shook his head again emphatically.

They inspected another five, all stallions, but none caught Mr Flynn's eye, or indeed made either Taz or Eliza feel a frisson of excitement. Mr Tattersall seemed increasingly desperate as he saw the chance of a rich profit recede. He went to prepare his last offering, then led into the courtyard an elegant but lightly boned animal, not big but coiled with energy, dun in colour. And a mare.

Zadoc Flynn was tetchy. 'I said I wanted a stallion,' he grumbled.

'You said you wanted a horse that was fleet of foot,' Mr Tattersall said mildly. 'This is a mare I was keeping back for the Duke of Beaufort.' This nugget of information silenced any further doubts.

Eliza was immediately drawn to the animal's side. Her golden eyes were full of liveliness and humour, her tail held high. She quivered under Eliza's touch which sensed the energy radiating through her warm skin. 'What do you think, Taz?' she asked over her shoulder.

He placed his hand on the horse's rump where the powerhouse of muscle and propulsion resided. 'She's small but I like her. She could be swift as the wind.'

'But how would she compare with the bigger stallions in a flat race?' Zadoc Flynn asked in a sceptical voice.

Taz was running his fingers down her fetlocks and with his head to her ribcage, listened to the beat of her heart. 'That's a big heart. She could fly. But she needs a light jockey.' He turned to Eliza and, wishing to maintain her disguise, did not use her name when he said, 'Why not ride her now and tell us what you think.'

Eliza was startled to be offered the first ride. Mr Tattersall, relieved to have a possible sale, turned to get her saddled up. 'Sir, tarry a while,' Eliza said. 'I'll ride her without a saddle. Her spirit and character will be clearer through the movement of her muscle and blood.' She looked across at Mr Flynn who nodded, his blue eyes beginning to sparkle with some of the anticipation Eliza felt. The horse was brought to the mounting block and Eliza sprung lightly astride her back. She asked that the stable boy detach the long rein and let her move freely; horse and rider set off fluidly round the ring, trotting until Eliza eased her into a smooth canter. The men watched the animal's movement and balance and Eliza felt a quiver of energy run through the mare beneath her. This lovely animal had so much more to give.

Eliza sprang to the ground without need of the block or a helping hand and she nodded her approval to a watching Zadoc Flynn. Taz then rode the mare and he too seemed impressed. Mr Flynn had seen enough. He drew Mr Tattersall to one side and with much waving of arms and hard-nosed negotiation they agreed the price with a handshake.

The small party rode back to Brook Street in a happy mood. Mr Flynn once more was his cheerful self. 'Thank you for your opinions. I'm disappointed she's a mare but if she wins races as she seems disposed so to do, then she will become the mother of my new stud in Kentucky. I will call her Ohio, after the mighty river that feeds our pastures on my farm.'

When they arrived in the mews, Mr Flynn turned his horse into the Wolfe stables and Taz and Eliza trotted through the intercommunicating arch to dismount. 'A good morning's work, Taz,' Eliza said.

Taz sprang off his horse and nodded. 'That young mare is summat special.' He looked up at Eliza and, with a mischievous grin, said, 'Now ye're in breeches, what 'bout yer circus dismount?'

She admonished him. 'You shouldn't encourage me. I'm trying to be a lady.'

Taz snorted. 'Well, ye're dressed in the wrong duds for that.' Realising how ridiculous it was protesting she was a lady while wearing Ferdy's schoolboy breeches, Eliza laughed.

Eliza had not noticed Lord Purfoy reading *The Sporting Magazine* while he leaned against the door jamb of a stable, awaiting Taz's return. His face was partly in shadow and she did not see his astonishment at seeing Taz was not alone, as he had expected, but in the company of a young man. Except when he saw the young rider's profile, he recognised with a visceral jolt that the fine-boned face was not masculine at all. Holding his breath, he watched Eliza fling Ferdy's top hat to Taz then stand lightly on Clio's rump before springing up and in one balletic move, somersaulting to land on her feet on the ground.

Taz chuckled in appreciation. 'Ye're a rum one, Miss Gray!' But Raven Purfoy was assailed with a complex mix of emotions: alarm at the danger – what if she had slipped and cracked her head again on the cobblestones? She might not have survived, this second time. But most disturbing to his peace of mind was coming upon her dressed thus. Before he knew she was female, Corinna had dressed in breeches in order to travel safely alone, and this had not troubled him in any way. But *knowing* Eliza Gray was a woman, it was disconcerting to see her long slim legs so clearly delineated in her borrowed breeches. Her narrow waist and the obvious curve of her hips as she worked alongside Taz, unsaddling Clio, troubled him with the clandestine intimacy of the sight. He had seen countless women before in various stages of undress, but to catch Eliza unawares and scandalously clothed tantalised him in a quite different way. He was caught off-guard, a situation he did not relish.

As he walked out of the shadows, folding the paper and putting it under his arm, Eliza noticed for the first time his dark presence. She gasped and her expressive face registered surprise, delight and then embarrassment in quick succession as she realised that once again she had taken advantage of his generosity without permission or acknowledgement. Yet again, she had revealed her uncouth ways in being dressed so scandalously in public. 'Oh, Lord Purfoy.' She crossed her arms in front of her. 'My apologies. I was meant to have changed into suitable clothes and be having breakfast by now.'

'Where have you been, dressed like that?' he asked in his cool way. 'No, let me guess! You thought it might be a lark to join my tiger in some wild scheme. Could it be to do with buying horses, by any chance?'

Faced with his sardonic amusement, Eliza realised the incongruity of standing before him in ill-fitting dandy-schoolboy clothes while he exhibited the understated elegance of his dark attire. She could not suppress a giggle and suddenly they were both laughing together. 'Is there nothing that escapes your notice?' she managed to ask.

'Not much, I admit. I'm over-responsible and ever vigilant. It is my curse.'

'Then you'll know just what we were up to, my lord. I don't

need to tell you, as I'm sure Mr Tattersall is one of your spies and has already sent a note.' With that she turned to go.

Lord Purfoy put out a hand. 'I realise, Miss Gray, I have never had the pleasure of seeing you perform your equestrian feats. Perhaps you will show me one day?'

Eliza could not tell whether he was serious or joking; his eyes seemed to combine both amusement and his usual languid superiority. 'I'm afraid my dear horse, Percy, is still at the circus. He's my best partner in all things.'

'Well, I suppose I should be grateful it wasn't you and Percy who fell into my path that fateful night, else I'd be responsible for him too.' He really *was* amused now.

Eliza was taken aback. 'Sir! I'd hate you to feel responsible for me. I intend to find my family and then set up my life again. If I ever have a home, I may even be lucky enough to take Percy with me.'

Lord Purfoy bowed as Eliza walked quickly back to the Wolfe house, surprisingly excited at the thought his eyes were upon her receding form.

Taz had saddled Horatio and as Purfoy was about to ride out, he looked down at his tiger. 'Well, what did Mr Flynn buy?'

'A dun mare, nice little mover.'

'Could she beat Horatio in a race?'

'Depends who's on board. Not with that great lummox in the saddle, that's certain.'

Purfoy nodded and set off for Hyde Park.

* * *

In the Wolfe household, breakfast was long over and Corinna was preparing to continue her portrait of Eliza when Lord Purfoy walked through the front door and followed his friend into her studio. He was still in his riding clothes and looked disconsolate, silently gazing at the face that was beginning to emerge on the canvas. Corinna put a hand on his arm. 'Raven, are you well? You seem less yourself recently.'

He turned stricken eyes to meet hers. 'If I'm not myself it's because I'm disturbed by memories of my sister Elizabeth. It's painful to revisit these thoughts, that dark time.' Corinna had long been puzzled by the nature of the tragedy in his past but something about his manner had always discouraged any questions. Still subdued he said, 'I have sought to keep my innermost self fearless and aloof, free of the least tremor of love or hate.'

'That's quite a task.' Corinna was unpacking her brushes and had her back to him which made it easier to talk about the deepest things. She continued in a quiet voice, 'Do you wish to tell me what happened to Elizabeth?'

Lord Purfoy slumped into the chair and as if the dam of his emotions was breached, at last the words began to cascade out unchecked. 'It was brutal but so shockingly simple. We were at home, at Hartfield Castle. She was sixteen and I was in my early twenties and responsible for her since our parents' death. She was a headstrong girl, an enthusiastic rider. My favourite stallion, Cromwell, was over-lively and she had the supreme confidence of youth. She was determined to ride him. Perhaps in too overbearing a manner, I had forbidden her to do so.'

He sighed as if his breath came from the depths of his being, then continued. 'One afternoon she decided she would ride him and prove a point to me. He took fright at a dog and bolted through our park with her clinging to his back. With such speed, when a low branch knocked her to the ground, her neck was snapped as quickly and easily as if it had been a spillikin.' His face was ashen as his head fell to his hand. Very quietly he continued, 'In that moment, all life, all happiness fled. On a perfect summer morning full of sunshine and birdsong, I found her lying in the grass under the oak tree whose branch had done the deed – so beautiful, so pale, so irredeemably dead.'

Corinna put down her brushes and stood beside him, her hand on his shoulder as he turned away, his face stricken, unable to meet the sympathy in her eyes. He continued, 'I blame myself for not selling Cromwell when I knew he was so fiery, but I loved him too much. If I'd been less selfish, less wilfully blind, Elizabeth would still be alive.' He then looked at Corinna. 'Do you understand now why I had to batten everything down in order to survive?'

Corinna met his eyes and murmured, 'The heart can only be suppressed for a time. Winter passes and with the warmth of spring it has to beat again.'

'If it hasn't died of neglect in the cold and dark.' He gave a bitter laugh. 'I know you will appreciate how shocking it was to see Miss Gray lying, apparently lifeless, on the road, through my own selfish doing. I was crushed with the sense that I had to relive this tragedy that had destroyed Elizabeth's life and ruined mine. My guilt could never be expiated.'

'But Miss Gray survived and is very much alive,' Corinna said gently. 'Nothing ever ends, just transforms into a new beginning.' Her concerned eyes rested on his face.

'But that rebirth, how agonising it is.' And with that he left the room to head back to his own house.

When Eliza entered the studio ready to sit for her portrait, she was unaware of the visitor who had just left as abruptly as he had come. Settling into the same chair, she met Corinna's painterly gaze. This woman who had offered her friendship and hospitality was only a few years older, but the nearest to a motherly presence that Eliza could remember. As she met Corinna's scrutiny, Eliza knew that she too understood her sense of being alone in the world. Corinna had come to London in search of family and had found it triumphantly: Eliza hoped with all her heart that this would be her story too, to tell her children.

As Corinna concentrated on painting the pale hair that waved in silvery spirals round her sitter's face, she recalled her own youth. 'When we long for the affection we lost as a child, it can make us unsure of it when it arrives. I remember myself feeling so bereft of meaning, not knowing where I came from and who I truly was.'

Eliza had been thinking of the morning and wondered if her longing for affection confused the realities of love. She was puzzled: why was it so easy to be in the company of Taz and even Zadoc Flynn, for whom she felt a brotherly affection? They shared an interest in horses and Mr Flynn's bluff good humour and tales of his travels entertained and comforted her. Yet Lord Purfoy never failed to unsettle and excite her. His presence made her blood pulse in her veins, her breath grow shallow, her skin prickle with the energetic life force that radiated from him. Why long to be with him, yet feel so uneasy when he was near? Eliza met Corinna's concerned gaze as she asked, 'Is this why stirring up deep emotions is so uncomfortable?'

'May I ask, is it Lord Purfoy of whom you talk?'

Eliza could barely acknowledge such a thought to someone who knew and loved him. 'No! I mean, how presumptuous of me. There is such a gulf between us.' Her pallor was suffused with pink.

Corinna picked up a pot of rose pigment and started mixing it. 'I want to capture that colour in your cheeks; it so enhances your eyes.' As she started delicately dabbing on the newly mixed paint she said, 'You'll find love is no respecter of boundaries.' She looked up, narrowing her eyes, and extended a paint brush as she measured the proportions of the face before her. She then put down her palette and folded her hands in her lap as her voice turned pensive. 'When I first saw Mr Wolfe, I was a young vagabond woman masquerading as a youth, without a home, family or prospects. He was a well-established young man with the world at his feet and no thoughts of love.'

'But you were brought up to be a lady while I lived amongst the circus folk: I know Lord Purfoy finds me shamefully unladylike.'

'That isn't the case, I assure you. I think his spirit is burdened with a weight of self-blame.'

Eliza leaned forward. 'Blame for what?'

'It's not my place to tell you any more, other than I think his sister's death may somehow be on his conscience.'

'He had a sister?' Eliza was pleased for any information about this unknowable man.

'Yes, she was called Elizabeth.' Corinna looked at her and the words were heavy with significance. Eliza felt a pang of connection but then checked herself; what a foolish fancy that she could share anything with an unknown beloved sister, mourned by her brother. Corinna watched Eliza's emotions pass quickly over her face. She said gently, 'Once you have discovered something about your family, you will feel more secure in the world.'

'But even if I were a lost heiress, it wouldn't make him love me.' Eliza's voice was defiant and she was shocked by the force of emotion, shocked that she had named it as love.

'My dear, nothing can make anyone love us. All we can do is live our own lives well and turn our faces to the sun.' They both laughed at the image as Eliza gazed towards the window where a suffused light cascaded over her face like water. Corinna then added, 'And don't forget, whatever you may currently believe, Raven Purfoy is not the only person worthy of your love.'

Corinna's words seemed to hit a raw nerve. Her eyes brilliant with feeling, Eliza said, 'I fear he is. There is no other. From that first sight of him kneeling by my side on the road, my spirit unfurled and seemed to meet his there in the cold and dark. I will never forget that night, that moment's recognition of another's soul, whatever the pattern of my life might turn out to be.' Eliza was shocked that her thoughts, so long suppressed, had burst from her like molten lava through a fissure in the rock.

Corinna seemed just as taken aback at the rush of emotion. 'My dear Miss Gray, you don't have to be so averse to compromise, so neck or nothing, you know. You are young and behind that flower-sweet face, there's a brave and reckless spirit. Recall the will for adventure that brought you here. Few young women would launch themselves on a dangerous world with nothing but intelligence and beauty to commend them.'

Eliza attempted a more conversational tone of voice, and smiled. 'I have never thought myself beautiful, and have no reason to consider myself intelligent. Until I came here and you pointed out my unusual eyes and lent me your lovely clothes, I barely thought of my physical appearance at all.'

'Well, tonight we will go to the Bassett ball where everyone who is anyone will attend and you will have your beauty affirmed by them all.' Corinna was closing the pots of pigment and looked up at Eliza and then at her portrait. 'Remember, you don't need anyone to tell you who you are, you already know.'

Eliza stood up to walk over to the painting. It was her first sight of it and it startled her so profoundly that for a moment she stopped breathing. She was silent for so long that Corinna glanced at her in concern. Eliza had grown up without mirrors; here before her on the canvas was her face as regarded by others. It was certainly recognisably her, but revealing something she had barely acknowledged in herself: love, courage, vigilance, but also with an eagerness for life. Moved by the revelation, she turned to Corinna. 'I have longed to be seen, to be known; you have seen me and shown me myself.'

Corinna put her arms around her. 'I'm glad you think so. But it is you who have shown me yourself. Unschooled and natural as you are, you have a transparency that is rare. There is only a light veiling of the soul within.' Corinna placed a linen cloth over the painting and they left the studio. Gibbons had just opened the door to a young messenger boy with a large dress box, tied with a bow.

Eliza ran forward. 'My dress from Madame Delaunay! All thanks to you, Mrs Wolfe!'

Corinna smiled. 'I'm very much looking forward to seeing you wearing it tonight. Ever since I had my first fine ball dress made for me, I've realised beautiful clothes are the wings that give us flight.' Eliza took the box from Gibbons and dropping Corinna a slight curtsey, ran up the stairs to her bedchamber.

* * *

She stood at the window watching a grey bank of cloud blow in across the rooftops. The sky grew dark and she shivered. This was the stormiest of springs and another squall was on its way. Sudden gusts of wind began to beat the branches of the beech tree in the mews and the air grew electric. Just as a streak of lightning and thunder rattled the windows, the rain arrived in rods slanting out of the sky. Eliza always found storms exciting but was pleased to be safe and warm inside when they struck, not camping with the circus in a field somewhere.

Polly's rap on the door went unheard, so great was the elemental power unleashed on the city. Corinna's maid had appeared early to help Eliza with dressing and styling her hair. The lace and tiffany ball gown was hanging in the dusky light, appearing shimmering and enchanted. Polly's eyes widened. 'Lawks, miss, that's a dress fit for a fairy princess!'

Eliza laughed with delight. 'You're right, Polly. It's more beautiful than I could have imagined.' She had just finished washing and stood in a loose gown, her hair slightly damp and curling at her neck. 'It has special stays sewn in as the back of the bodice is cut low. Only the lace covers my back and shoulders. It's a style from Paris, apparently.'

This also meant Eliza could not wear the usual lawn chemise but stood naked as a water nymph as Polly slipped the dress over her head. The pared-down stays laced at the side so the wearer could manage to dress herself. Polly offered to fasten them, then smoothed down the blue tiffany lining. She let the lilac lace fall over the skirt and Eliza moved to check it in the looking glass by the window. She could barely believe that the wild circus girl she had been could look like this. The small bodice was lined at the front with the silk and her décolletage was exposed, as was the fashion, but her puff sleeves and the rest of the bodice back was only covered by the airy delicacy of the lace. She was entirely clothed with the silk and filigree of the lace, yet from her breastbone to her shoulders, spine and shoulder blades, she appeared practically naked, surprising the eye and making her skin luminous.

Eliza let out an involuntary sigh. 'Oh!'

'You look beautiful, miss,' Polly could not help herself exclaiming, then turned practical and extracted from the shelves in the dressing room a long pair of silk satin gloves in dove grey. 'That finishes off the look. Now I must do your hair.'

* * *

The thunder had not rumbled away but continued to rattle above the louring clouds that extinguished the last of the light. Eliza descended the stairs and picking up an extra candlestick, entered the drawing room, the precious copy of *The Corsair* in her hands. She settled down to read while she waited for Mr Flynn, Corinna and Alick. She was engrossed in Byron's great bravura epic and wondered why it affected her so much, like a message from another world. As she read on she realised the lonely, mysterious hero was her Lord Purfoy.

Zadoc Flynn entered the room, dressed for the ball in his dark superfine coat, satin pantaloons, silk stockings and almond-toed shiny black dancing shoes that somehow managed to make his large feet look quite elegant. 'I've just had these clothes made for me by Mr Shilton's tailor,' he said with pride, showing off the quality of the cut.

Eliza thought he looked most attractive, his cheerful expression and weather-beaten face and the emerald in his ear contrasting with the fine tailoring of his newly acquired clothes in a most pleasing way. 'You look fine and dandy, Mr Flynn,' she said, smiling.

He let out a great gust of laughter, realising she was repeating back to him one of his sayings. 'Well, you look far too beautiful to be just fine and dandy, Miss Gray; I'd say more of a goddess escaped from Mount Olympus, which after your earthy outfit and performance this morning is close to a miracle!' He put out his hand, brought her to her feet and twirled her round. 'My, my, is such display allowed?' he asked mischievously as he saw her back for the first time.

Corinna and Alick had just entered the room and caught the end of his playful question. 'It is the height of Parisian fashion, Mr Flynn; beware your ignorance in such matters.' Corinna was protective and turned to Eliza, her eyes sparkling. 'That dress suits you just as well as I hoped. And so effective in its simplicity.'

Corinna herself was wearing a dress of silver tissue that shone in the candlelight and Alick, even in his most formal clothes, looked informal, as if he had dressed in a hurry and had better things to do. He smiled at the two women. 'Well, with the storm still raging and given that my companions are so beautifully dressed, I'm glad I've called for the best chaise.' Although Lady Bassett's mansion was just round the corner in Grosvenor Square, it was not acceptable to simply stroll round from Brook Street. The weather made this even less acceptable. They all put on their cloaks and Gibbons and the men wielded large black umbrellas to protect the women from the rain. The carriage traversed the few hundred yards towards the Bassett house but was stalled in a queue of other carriages filled with guests.

So great was the crush that wheels were barely moving, the horses growing restive in the driving rain. They could see the house ablaze with light a mere fifty yards away and when eventually they reached the portico to disembark, they were met by liveried servants who held aloft their own umbrellas to help the guests brave the weather and navigate the puddles underfoot.

Eliza had never been to a Society soirée, let alone a ball, and the extravaganza that confronted her quickened her pulse and filled her with trepidation. The hall and drawing room were thronged with brightly plumaged women and dark-suited men. The ballroom was built across the back of the house and led into an orangery and then into the garden beyond. Chandeliers and candelabra filled with burning candles were reflected in the rococo mirrors that lined the room, fracturing and multiplying the colour of the dresses and scintillas of light from myriad flames until it was a phantasy of feathered headdresses, spangled silk, jewels, laughing faces and twirling figures. She turned to Corinna, her face glowing. 'This is such a *spectacle*!'

'You are lucky to have the best as your first experience.'

The small orchestra was playing a reel. Eliza was stopped in her tracks as she listened to the rich complexity of sound that flowed from the violins, viola, violoncello and horn; to someone who had only heard Corinna's piano-forte or the percussive cornet and drum of the circus band, this sound was thrilling. The spirit of the music had infected the dancers with a *joie de vivre* which made Eliza long to join in. At her elbow, Zadoc Flynn said with a smile, 'We've practised this; I suppose we ought to risk our first public display.' He put out his hand in invitation.

Eliza followed him into a set and they began coordinating their steps with the other dancers, at first tentatively, then with the gay abandon that characterised everyone else in their group. Eliza could not help laughing as Zadoc Flynn grasped her hands to twirl her round and pass her on to the next dancer in line. As the music drew to an end, both leaned in together, at ease in their familiarity as they walked through to the refreshments room, exhilarated by the dance. Eliza scanned the crowd for her new friend, Marina Fairley, and, although she could barely admit it to herself, she longed to see Lord Purfoy.

The orchestra was starting to play again as Ferdinand Shilton strolled up to Corinna and Eliza standing with Alick and Flynn who were both drinking champagne. 'What a grand rout this is!' their dandy friend said, his blue eyes full of fun. 'And what a picture the two most beautiful women of my acquaintance make.' Most other men were dressed in coats of dark-coloured superfine but Ferdy Shilton, never one to hide his jack-a-dandy light under a bushel, was wearing his new silver coat and oyster satin pantaloons. He offered his arm to Eliza. 'Will you allow me to escort you to the dance?'

'I shall be delighted, Mr Shilton.' Eliza joined him in a set of four to dance a quadrille. 'Please forgive me my mistakes; this is the first time I've danced this with anyone other than Mr Flynn or our dancing teacher.'

'You're a natural dancer, Miss Gray. You forget I've seen Clorinda the Winged Venus perform.' He was murmuring his mischievous comment as the quadrille brought them close together before separating them again.

Eliza flashed him a reproving look and when the dance brought them close again she whispered fiercely, 'It is ungentlemanly of you, Mr Shilton, to speak of this in such company!'

He brought her hand fleetingly to his lips. 'You're entirely right, even though only the most discerning would ever recognise you dressed like this. My apologies as a gentleman.' As they came together again he said more seriously, 'Old Purfoy's a trifle troubled by what that American is up to in the equine stakes, you know.'

As the dance came to an end, Eliza answered truthfully enough, 'He's just bought a mare to take home for his racing stable.'

With a sceptical expression that sat incongruously on his angelic face, Mr Shilton led her to a sofa at the edge of the dance floor. 'Do you know if he intends to race her here?'

'Ah! Is that what most exercises my lord?'

Ferdy Shilton hated any kind of controversy and changed the subject. 'You acquitted yourself very well, Miss Gray; no one would ever take you for a debutante.' He bowed. 'May I collect some refreshment for you?'

Through the press of dancers, Eliza suddenly glimpsed Marina Fairley sitting on a sofa by one of the windows. She caught her eye and waved. 'Thank you, Mr Shilton, but I'll be joining my friend, Miss Fairley.' She indicated the young woman surreptitiously reading a small book she had half hidden under her reticule.

Eliza slipped into the seat alongside her friend. 'Marina, you're reading, not dancing!'

Marina's open face lit up with pleasure and relief. 'I am pleased to see you! As you know, I am fatigued to death with it all. But I have to at least turn up at a few grand occasions like this to please Mama until I've proved I'm unmarriageable.'

Eliza was struck by how cheerful Marina was in her defiance. She looked incongruous in this extravagantly dressed company in a simple dark blue muslin dress, unembellished by tucks or flowers, her hair in a simple bun. 'What are you reading with such attention?'

Marina removed the small volume from beneath her reticule and putting her wire spectacles back on her nose, turned it over to show the cover to Eliza. 'It's volume two of Mrs Edgeworth's *Belinda*. Illuminating about all these people and their desires.' She swept the ballroom with her hand.

'Is your mother here with you?' Looking around, Eliza was suddenly filled with unbearable longing that her own mother might be one of this throng. Her eyes strained to catch something familiar in the swirl of faces, her ears trying to differentiate a fond voice from the surrounding clamour. But her mother seemed as far away from her as ever.

Unaware of the consternation in Eliza's heart, Marina Fairley continued with a laugh. 'No, Mama thinks I should endure the unendurable without doing so herself.'

Struggling for composure, Eliza said in as equable a voice as she could manage, 'Well, I think it's really exciting to be here. Who knows what may transpire.'

'I was once wide-eyed like you too.' Marina laughed. 'Grand-mama is here.' She pointed to a knot of elderly women by one of the fires. 'Holding court with her friends.' Then she craned her neck and pointed to a striking woman talking to another at the entrance to the orangery, dressed even more plainly than herself. 'And there's my gorgon aunt, Lady Dauntsey. She loathes Society and disapproves of 'Our Profligate Age', as she calls it. She's always threatening to cloister herself in a nunnery, but still cannot resist Lady Bassett's ball.'

Eliza was struck by the lady's imperious profile. When she turned, she seemed to have the kind of censorious face that would be found carved on a church lintel to repel bad spirits. Searching Marina Fairley's looks in vain for some likeness she asked, 'Is she your mother's sister?'

'No, she's actually my father's family and enjoys disapproving of her brother.' She smirked. 'Like many of the pious, I think she's excited by wickedness.'

Eliza was intrigued by the mention of this most important but mysterious figure in her friend's life. 'Did you ever see your father?'

'No, by the time I was told of my connection to his noble family he had already fled into exile in Paris.'

'But he obviously knew about your existence?' Eliza hoped for her friend's sake she had mattered to her father, even a little.

'Yes, but he only showed the slightest curiosity when he heard about my interest in languages. It was then he sent me his copy of the manuscript I've mentioned.' Marina saw the sympathy in Eliza's face and said brusquely, 'Don't worry, I'm not as full of sensibility as you. I don't care for him and don't really mind how little he cared for me.'

The orchestra was tuning up for the next series of dances and Eliza could not stop herself scanning yet again the melee of colourful guests for someone she knew would come. She caught sight of the back of a tall, soberly dressed figure and held her breath, only to feel the plunge of disappointment and recoil as he turned and she recognised the profile of the predatory Lord Davenport.

Marina heard her intake of breath and put a hand on her arm. 'What's troubling you?'

'That man.' Eliza pointed Davenport out, laughing with a group of rakish bloods. 'He's so malign.'

Marina snorted. 'He's Lucifer's cockerel, as vain and malicious as they come. He happens to be Lady Dauntsey's son and the only thing of which she approves.'

'But if she's as strait-laced as a nun, how can she approve of him?'

'Maternal blindness and delusion!' Eliza laughed as her friend continued, 'I wish my mama suffered from the same disease.'

'But if Lord Davenport is Lady Dauntsey's son, is he not your cousin?'

Marina wrinkled her nose. 'I'd rather not own that relation. Neither does he choose to acknowledge me as a member of his family. I suppose my lack of legitimacy is his excuse.'

Alick Wolfe appeared at Eliza's elbow and requested a dance. Before Eliza left her side, Marina put a hand on her arm and whispered, 'Take care never to be alone with the cockerel.' Surprised by the urgency in Miss Fairley's voice, Eliza turned with a questioning frown as Alick led her into the fray.

* * *

Lord Purfoy had left his club in St James's and in a break in the storm, drove his curricle home with Taz on his perch behind him. He was reluctant to go to the ball but had promised Miss Gray one dance. He said over his shoulder, 'Taz, you must never again let me drive so in my cups. All kinds of trouble from that misjudgement flows.'

Taz let out a profanity and spat. 'Short of knockin' ye cold, guv, I couldn't stop ye. Wild and obstinate as a mule!'

'I don't care for your impertinence, Taz, nor for the animal analogy; a mule I am not! Mr Shilton's right, you need to show more deference to your superiors,' his master said with a sardonic smirk. 'Nevertheless, I hold you responsible for the accident with Miss Gray. Without that I would be warm by a fireside tonight, not expected to prance and cavort with the best of 'em.'

As they bowled home, the sky darkened further and the storm broke again with increased ferocity. Open to the elements in his curricle, Lord Purfoy was drenched through as he walked up the front steps of his house and divested himself of his dripping coat in the hall.

He stood in his dressing room wearing only his silk brocade gown, gazing out gloomily at the rain-swept scene beyond his window. His hair was still damp and curling and he felt strangely melancholy. Why had he allowed this unknown slip of a girl to so dominate his thoughts and disturb his settled world? Had it become a kind of madness? All the old certainties of his life were unmoored, his discipline loosened, and now he felt compelled to forsake his library and the decanter of finest French brandy for a tedious social event, designed to please mothers touting their daughters as marriage goods.

Lord Purfoy had refined the miscellaneous harlotry of his youth to a regular liaison with a beautiful widow, Amelia Cornford, who lived in an attractive house off Cavendish Square and appeared to enjoy his uncomplicated company as much as he did hers. He did not insult her by offering money, but was lavish with his gifts which he knew were probably fast transmuted into currency. His feelings for Mrs Cornford had never stirred his shackled heart; now, for the first time, he had grown dissatisfied with the thin gruel of unsentimental attraction. What was happening to him? The wild weather seemed to express the breakdown of order in his own internal world.

His valet, John, interrupted Lord Purfoy's unhappy train of thought by entering with a newly laundered linen shirt. His lordship dropped his dressing gown to the floor just as a streak of lightning illuminated the sky, sending a phosphorescent flash across the tall athletic figure who stood naked and gleaming as a young Zeus mustering his thunderbolts. John whisked the fresh shirt over his lordship's head and left to collect his satin breeches and silk stockings while his master sat in the chair, crossed one long bare leg over the other and picked up *The Sporting Magazine* to flick through the racing pages.

Lord Purfoy may be grateful that the almost supernaturally gifted Taz had deigned to stay on as his tiger, despite the blandishments to stray to even grander equine establishments, but he never feared his valet would be inveigled to serve a different master: John's admiration was for Lord Purfoy alone. To practise his craft to the highest levels he needed a fine figure of a man to dress; he felt honoured to have such a distinguished example of manhood as his lordship, with his broad shoulders, lean physique and elegant long limbs. Lord Purfoy was the Olympian ideal whose refined muscularity showed off superbly crafted coats, pantaloons and breeches to greatest advantage. His long shapely calves needed no padding and looked elegant in either top boots or silk stockings. His lordship's servants took pride in the fact that their master so thoroughly put his peers in the sartorial shade.

Shrugging into his greatcoat, he placed his curly-brimmed hat on his head, grabbed an umbrella and walked into the stormy night to climb into his chaise, brought round from the mews by Taz.

Lord Purfoy arrived late at the Bassett mansion and as he entered the wide hallway, he paused. Candlelight, usually so diffuse and soft, here, through force of numbers, multiplied a hundredfold in the reflections of windows, and mirrors dazzled the eye. The orchestra resonated through the vast room and a young woman was singing Handel's aria, 'Ombra mai fu'. All his senses were heightened.

Lady Bassett claimed him, delight suffusing her haughty features. 'My dear Lord Purfoy, how glad I am that you could come.'

He kissed her hand, meeting her calculating eyes with a half-smile. 'How could I consider missing such a celebrated gala?'

The grand hostess, who could subdue armies with one cold glance, was almost skittish in his presence. He bowed and proceeded into the room. His eye had alighted on Alick Wolfe, taller than most, leaning against a pillar talking to Ferdy Shilton, distinctive in silver. As he approached his old friends his eyes were searching the crowd – for people he knew, he told himself – but really only for Miss Gray.

Corinna caught him by the arm. 'Rav! How good to see you. I thought you'd think better of it once you saw the weather.'

He bent and kissed her on the cheek. 'You are as beautiful as ever, my dear.'

'Well then you'll have to break your habit and dance with me.'

Lord Purfoy smiled. 'All my habits are broken,' he smiled ruefully.

Corinna suspected the main culprit in this destruction and said, 'Miss Gray seems to be very much restored to health,' pointing her out dancing a waltz in Zadoc Flynn's arms.

Purfoy caught sight of Eliza's flaxen head in the swirl of dancers. She was turned away and her back appeared to be almost naked, covered only by the tracery of lace. Once again he felt jolted by the sight of her in such unexpected dress. He turned to Corinna. 'That's quite a surprising gown, Cory; I know it's your gift and I hold you responsible for inflaming the young gentlemen in her vicinity.'

Corinna bridled. 'It's the new fashion from Paris. To the cognoscenti it's not alluring at all, just the height of elegance.'

'Well, my dear, I commend you for its style and refinement but to a gentleman of lively imagination, it is a good deal more.' His tone was full of raillery but as he watched Eliza being steered rather inexpertly around the floor by Mr Flynn's meaty arm, he wanted it to be his hand on her slender back, and was shocked by such an unwelcome thought.

* * *

Eliza had been grateful that Mr Flynn was her partner for her first waltz in public. They had learned the dance together in their lessons with Mrs Wilson and understood each other's roles. She felt entirely comfortable in his broad embrace; there was something unexpectedly exciting about being in the arms of a large strong man who felt utterly dependable and safe. They were managing quite well, she thought, and congratulated him; he only trampled her once, their turns were thrilling and they managed not to crash into any other dancers.

Mr Flynn was in a fine mood. 'This is grander than any soirée I've been to in New York.'

Eliza asked him, 'Do you still intend to bring Miss Bowman to the ball?'

'Why? Are you still concerned I shouldn't?'

'It's just that I too am an outsider to Society and am ignorant of the complexity of its conventions. I fear all kinds of haughtiness and false pride rule.'

'Well, it doesn't bother me. I'm just a beef-witted colonial, after all.' He smiled his big grin. 'But I'll tell you one secret, Miss Gray. I'm entering Ohio in the Owner's Race at Epsom. But you're not to say a word.'

This news made Eliza uneasy. She knew this race was held in such high esteem by the Corinthians who fancied themselves the best horsemen in England with the most magnificent horses money could buy. At this point she scanned the room, looking for the most famous Corinthian of them all, and yet was taken aback to see him there at last. Lord Purfoy had arrived and was talking to Mrs Wolfe. Eliza could no longer concentrate on her steps and apologised to Mr Flynn. 'I'm sorry, sir, may we stop now and collect some refreshment?'

He bowed and escorted her to the room where burgundy, brandy, lemonade and ale were on offer, alongside small sweet and savoury pastries. Mr Flynn was congratulating her and himself for a fine first waltz when Eliza sensed the atmosphere in the room change. Her back was to the door and she feared she was deluded by her own longing and dared not look round. Then a tall figure appeared at her elbow. A cloud crossed Mr Flynn's face as Lord Purfoy nodded to him in greeting and put out his hand to Eliza.

'You've come!' she blurted out.

He smiled. 'I've kept my word. I have a long-held prejudice against prancing round a ballroom floor, but I promised you a dance and am not in the habit of breaking my promises.'

Taking her leave of Mr Flynn, Eliza placed her hand on Raven Purfoy's arm and allowed him to escort her back into the ballroom. Such had been the clamour from the younger dancers for another waltz that the orchestra began with a piano-forte introduction. Everyone took their positions in a circle and as the orchestra joined the melody, Lord Purfoy placed his arm with great decorum lightly on her waist and she rested her hand on his shoulder. Being in such close proximity to him was a completely different experience from dancing with Mr Flynn. Eliza wondered if this perturbation she felt in his arms was just her imagination. It was as if the atmosphere in the room was charged with the volatile turbulence of a coming storm.

They began the steps, formal at first, with physical distance between them. They did not speak but their eyes met and she found it difficult to look away. The music sped up and the couples were necessarily in a closer embrace as they twirled across the floor. Eliza was dizzy and smiled into his face. 'Lord Purfoy, you assert you don't dance but you do it so well!' He did not respond in his usual sarcastic way and his expression remained set, his eyes narrowed. He pulled her firmly to his hip as he took her into a fast turn, and then an extra twirl. She felt the muscles in his waist and thigh and his shoulders tense under her hand. She was reminded of his power and strength and her eyes widened with the almost unbearable pulsation of energy between them. He had danced them into the shadowy embrasure of a window and they stopped, both breathless.

Eliza was struck how candlelight revealed so much because its flickering light illuminated so little. In its luminous halo, all things shone with significance and around it waved the encroaching dark. All she was aware of was Lord Purfoy's face gleaming above her, a strange daredevilry in his eyes. His arm was still firmly round her waist and her dizziness made her cling to him. To Eliza's astonishment, he suddenly buried his face in her hair and said with such quiet intensity she could barely hear, '*Tu m'enivres.*'

She was shocked by the emotion in his words and had to know what he meant, asking, 'I'm not educated like you, my lord. Tell me again.'

'You intoxicate me.' His voice was almost a moan. So heightened was the moment and so unexpected his utterance that she found herself lifting her face to him as if for a kiss. His whole being seemed anguished and struggling for control. He gazed unseeingly out at the tempestuous dark as he said, 'It may be the stormy air, or that dress, or a fever upon me, but I'm so close to breaking every code I have lived by and running off with you into the night.' His brilliant eyes then met her startled gaze as he cried, 'What have you done to me, Miss Gray? Art thou some enchantress? To so fill my dreams with you...'

A small explosion in her heart made her stand very still, trying to take in the true meaning of words she never thought she would hear from his lips. Lord Purfoy released her. His eyes were as shocked as hers and he abruptly led her back to Corinna who was sitting on a sofa between the windows in desultory talk with an acquaintance. By then his lordship had recovered his composure and said with his usual drawl, 'Thank you, Miss Gray, for your charming company. Now it's off to the card room for a game or two.' She watched his elegant back weave through the crowd, and felt bereft.

Eliza did not wish to interrupt Corinna's conversation; she needed time to think about whether this was a revelation of Lord Purfoy's feelings or merely a misinterpretation by her own spirit, hungry for love. So unexpected was his outburst, so uncharacteristic of the noble sardonic lord, she wondered if indeed he was feverish, or in his cups. How tired she was of the ache of loss and longing, how she dreamed of putting the burden down at last.

Eliza slipped into the orangery where a few people sat in small groups while the rain continued to hammer on the glass roof. Distracted by her own thoughts, Eliza skidded on a squashed orange that had fallen to the floor. She put out a hand to steady herself and grasped the arm of a woman standing gazing at the sodden garden beyond the doors. 'My apologies, madam.'

The woman turned her head and Eliza knew immediately this was Lady Dauntsey, Marina Fairley's fearsome aunt. But as their eyes met she was unprepared for the thunderbolt of recognition she felt. For the first time in her life Eliza saw another with something of her distinctive looks. There, staring back at her, were eyes exactly like her own, one amber-green, the other violet-grey. So great was the shock of surprise, hope, fear, and a burning curiosity and need to know that Eliza gasped, 'Are we familiar to one another?'

The lady looked discomfited. 'What is your name?'

'Eliza Gray.'

Lady Dauntsey visibly paled. 'But she's long dead.' Her hand had gone to her throat.

Eliza's heart began to contract with fear. 'What do you mean, madam?'

The older woman had regained her composure and with great coolness said, 'She looked like you; perhaps you're related. I once knew an Eliza Gray who sickened and died soon after a family tragedy.'

This was the most painful truth that Eliza could hardly bear to hear but had been dreading all her life. It was so shattering of her hopes, but she had to have Lady Dauntsey confirm it. Meeting the eyes that seemed so like her own but painfully veiled with hostility and suspicion, she asked in a tremulous voice, 'Was the family tragedy the loss of her daughter?'

'I seem to remember it was,' Lady Dauntsey said with feigned nonchalance as she turned aside, offering only her forbidding profile.

The blow fell, crushing her spirit. Eliza had spent her life believing her mother was looking for her, desperate to reunite with her daughter, but in this casual remark her worst fear was made true. There was no mother to find. She was alone. With a sob, Eliza knew she had to escape. *Her mother was dead.* This terrible fact vibrated in every cell of her body. She had only endured the loneliness and harshness of her life because she had been certain her mother was waiting for her and that one day they would be restored to each other. Her longing for that primal love had ended brutally like this.

Eliza wrenched open the door to the garden and dashed out, oblivious to the rain. She did not know what she intended to do – escape through to the mews and lie down with the horses? The cold drilling of the raindrops seemed to give her an external distraction from the inner turmoil of her heart as it fell in pieces at her feet. She lifted her face to the skies. Was her mother some-where in that turbulent dark? Was she that distant star in the lowering clouds, almost lost to view but looking down on her daughter in her hour of need?

Suddenly she felt a hand grip her upper arm. 'Come out of the storm, Miss Gray.' She turned to meet the concerned eyes of Lord Purfoy. Forced back into the present, Eliza was aware of the rain mixing with her tears. The torches that lit up the terraces had largely been extinguished by the downpour but in the ghostly light that still emanated from the candle-filled mansion behind them she saw his face, wet and gleaming, his eyes dark and inscrutable. He led her back to the orangery where they were alone and stripped off his jacket. 'Wear this,' he said in a peremp-tory way as he extracted a linen handkerchief from his pocket and proceeded to dry her face and dab at her hair. 'Tell me, what ruinous event has compelled you to attempt a drowning, or at least to invite a fever?'

Eliza's eyes, intent on his face, were filled with the feeling she could barely articulate. 'My mother is dead.' Her words were so bleak, her voice so forlorn, that Lord Purfoy cast decorum aside, opened his arms and gathered her to his chest. Her wet mass of hair seeped moisture through his shirt as she breathed in the smell of him, warm and male, overlaid with a whiff of some green spice like bay. Her halting words continued, muffled by the folded linen of his cravat. 'I've spent my life longing for her, hoping she never stopped looking for me. But tonight, I'm told these hopes are as ashes. She died long ago, soon after we were torn apart. There was no one thinking of me, searching for me, for she had gone.'

'Who told you this?'

Eliza felt his voice vibrating through his chest. She wanted this extraordinary moment of intimacy to continue for ever but stirred, aware of other dancers approaching the orangery. 'My lord, I fear you and I should not be out here together without a chaperone.'

He released her. 'Well, my reputation in such matters was lost long ago, but to protect yours we'll go in search of Corinna. But tell me how you came to know this about your mother?'

'Lady Dauntsey.'

His face darkened as he muttered, 'Mother to that graceless blackguard, Lord Davenport!'

'I fear we may be related in some way. She has my eyes.'

'No! No one can have eyes quite as affecting as yours.' And he smiled a rare, sweet smile. 'Surely you wish to find out more about your family? Have you siblings, a father perhaps?'

About to enter the ballroom again, Eliza turned to him, her face anxious. 'Do I look a fright?'

'Yes, but I've always had a soft spot for the occasional fright. Let me pin that lock of hair back in position, make you a trifle more respectable.' He picked up a damp wing of her fair hair, twisted it and expertly reattached it to the bedraggled Greek goddess style Polly had so carefully constructed.

'You seem to be a skilled lady's maid, Lord Purfoy,' she said with a spark of her old spirit.

'I have all kinds of hidden talents, Miss Gray,' he said, retrieving his coat from her shoulders and holding it for a fleeting second to his face. Then, as if waking from a dream, he grimaced as he slipped his arms back into the damp sleeves. 'This seems not to have survived as well as your gown.'

He turned a serious face to her. 'I have an apology to make for my ungentlemanly conduct earlier. I do not wish to take advantage of you in that way.' His smile was wintry. 'I seem to be making a habit of apologising for unconscionable behaviour, Miss Gray. I hope you will forgive me for this further breach of my code.'

Eliza's heart and mind were once more in disarray. Did he regret everything he had said, or merely the manner in which he had said it? As they stepped through the glass doors and re-entered the ballroom awash in light, Marina Fairley accosted her, her face etched with concern. 'Thank goodness you're still here. My termagant aunt has upset you, I know.' She took her arm. 'You're drenched! Come and warm up.'

Eliza looked back over her shoulder at Lord Purfoy, a question in her eyes. He nodded. 'I hope you find out more,' he said, before turning on his heel to rejoin his friends.

Miss Fairley was animated and drew Eliza quickly to the fireside. 'My aunt returned from the orangery with a face as thunderous as the sky. I overheard her telling her son she knows who you are and I think she has information on your family. Are you happy to come with me and ask her what she knows?'

'Lady Dauntsey has already told me my mother is dead.'

As Eliza said these bleak words, Marina put her arm around her in sympathy. 'I am so sorry, Eliza. I know what heartbreak this must be, but let's find out what we can.'

Lady Dauntsey was sitting on a chair by one of the grand windows. As the two young women approached, she looked up. 'Miss Gray, Marina, good evening.' The noble lady was magisterial in her manner. 'I realise I owe you further explanation, Miss Gray. I believe I know who your father is, but it is not a straightforward matter.'

Eliza was astounded at the news so casually imparted that her father was still alive. Her hands flew to her face, unable to quite know how to cope with two such momentous pieces of news about her longed-for parents. 'But who? Who is he?'

'He's my cousin and he lives in Bathwick Court in Bath, permanently now as he is seriously afflicted with the gout and the waters bring him some relief. His name is the Marquess of Bathwick and he is an old, ill man with not many months left to live.'

Eliza curtseyed. 'Thank you, Lady Dauntsey. I cannot tell you how important it is to me to be told the truth. I am grateful for that.' She looked up once more into the haughty face with eyes so like her own, saddened that the first person she had met to whom she was related did not extend to her any warmth of family feeling.

Just as Eliza and Marina turned to go, Eliza saw the unmistakeable figure of Zadoc Flynn enter the ballroom with her friend, Rose Bowman, on his arm.

How good to see her old friend when she was in such need of familiar support. All her fears about Rose coming to the ball fell away as she ran towards her. 'Rose! I'm so glad you're here.' They hugged, laughing with pleasure at being reunited.

'Eliza, you're wet! Where have you been?'

'Oh, it's nothing. How did you manage to slip away?'

'After the performance, when everyone was asleep, Mr Flynn parked his chaise just outside my window and I climbed out and onto the vehicle's roof.' She giggled and clung to her rescuer's arm. Mr Flynn beamed, then went in search of some wine. Eliza looked at the transformation in her friend with some wonder. Rose had always been striking in her looks, dark-haired and dark-eyed, and here she was wearing a beautiful gown of pale pink organza that set off her olive skin to perfection. She seemed to have lost her diffidence and stood with her head held high.

Rose's dark eyes were full of delight at the sight before her. 'You look bloomy, Eliza. That gown's prime stuff. Not what we're used to!' She put out a hand to feel the quality then peered more closely at her friend. 'But you're a little pasty and more than a trifle topsy-turvy. Wet as a drowned rat. What's the trouble?'

Eliza's smile was wan. She was suddenly very tired. 'I've had a whirlwind of a night. I've lost a mother and found a place in the world, all in two hours. My heart is battered. I don't know who I am any more or where I'm going.' She did not mention she had also had a declaration of what seemed to be love, only to have it quickly withdrawn.

The music had temporarily stopped so the musicians could eat and drink. It was well past midnight and many young men were spilling out of the card room, well lubricated and boisterous, in search of more liquor. The sight of Eliza and Rose Bowman drew many curious eyes. The contrast in their colouring was dramatic, one so fair, one so dark. A couple of the bloods recognised Miss Bowman from Astley's Amphitheatre, and there was sniggering and muttered lascivious comments. Circus folk and other itinerant entertainers were unwelcome as equals in any part of polite society and their presence here, at the pinnacle of the haut ton, was considered by some social arbiters to be an insult to their carefully stratified way of life.

One gentleman had emerged with the other gamesters and was deeply in his cups and enraged by his losses at the gaming tables. Lord Davenport's bleary eyes alighted on these two women in animated conversation. He made his uncertain way through the crowd of guests and in an over-loud voice accosted them. 'I know who you are. This is no place for women such as you.'

Eliza and Miss Bowman looked at him with shock. The room quietened and all eyes turned towards them. Lord Davenport's colour was high and his speech blurred, suggesting the extent of his inebriation, but his slur on their characters and class brought a curious crowd closer, some hostile, some sympathetic. Into the centre pushed the unmistakeable figure of Zadoc Flynn. 'Sir! You are drunk. Apologise to the ladies and withdraw!'

'I will do no such thing!' He was riled at being humiliated in public by a nobody. 'These harlots have no right to be here, polluting the air for the rest of us.'

Eliza and Rose were used to insults and prejudice on occasions when they travelled with the circus, but to be so characterised and demeaned in such elevated company – and for Eliza in front of her new friends – was mortifying. Colour rose to their cheeks as every eye seemed to be turned their way.

Zadoc Flynn was outraged. He too was slightly the worse for drink. He ripped off his coat and cast it to the floor. Putting up his fists, he addressed Lord Davenport. 'Withdraw your slurs and apologise or I shall knock you down.'

The drunken lord sneered. 'I'll be damned if I will. You're just a clodpole from the colonies and you'll not make me do anything.'

As if from nowhere, Mr Flynn's right jab took everyone by surprise, not least the smirking man on whose face it landed. The room was silenced and aghast as Lord Davenport was floored. Helped by a couple of cronies who dashed forward, he struggled to his feet, bleeding from his nose. 'What the devil!' he hissed. 'I'll call you out for this. Name your seconds.'

The crowd parted as Lord Purfoy strode into the middle of the melee. 'Davenport, you're drunk!' His cold eyes flickered over the man's bloodied face. 'You're in no condition to call anyone out and Mr Flynn was entirely correct to defend these young ladies' honour and reputations.' His disapproving gaze swept over the other befuddled young blades who had gathered, hoping for a proper mill. 'This is Lady Bassett's ball and we owe it to her not to turn it into a common brawl. Get back to the tables.'

He shepherded Eliza, Miss Bowman and Mr Flynn towards the Wolfes who had been cooling off in the orangery. Corinna came forward, concerned at the exhaustion clear in Eliza's face. 'It's certainly time to go home. And you're wet too. I've called for the carriage.'

Zadoc Flynn was still fuming. He turned to Lord Purfoy. 'I want to kill that devil-begotten cur.'

Lord Purfoy took him aside and said with a curl of his lip, 'I'm afraid in England we don't aim to kill our antagonists in a duel. It is a matter of honour, not death.'

'Well, I brought Miss Bowman here to experience a dance and I intend to give her that pleasure at least.' Zadoc Flynn looked defiant. Then his face lost its mulish look and he smiled. 'And I'll apologise to Lady Bassett for my behaviour.' The orchestra had struck up again and he took Rose by the hand and said, 'Come on, Miss Bowman. I hear the strains of a waltz. I can't take you home without having the pleasure of one dance.'

6

TO BATH

In the intimate safety of the chaise with Corinna and her husband sitting opposite her, Eliza burst into tears and all the emotional turmoil of the evening's revelations tumbled out. All except for Lord Purfoy's oblique words; those she could not fully fathom and kept close to her heart. In a bleak voice she said, 'I have hung my life on a dream.' Corinna leaned across and took her hand as she continued, 'The dream that my mother was waiting for me; it sustained me through all these years.'

Corinna's voice was sympathetic. 'I'll accompany you to Bath. To find your father will answer so many questions.'

Eliza knew how momentous it had been for Corinna to find her father before he died, but could not believe that her own reunion could match her hopes.

In her room at last, Eliza was almost too tired to undress. It was past two o'clock in the morning. Polly had waited up for her mistress and was ready to unbutton Eliza's dress for her but, unwilling to keep a hard-working servant from her bed, Eliza dismissed her and managed the rest herself. After the most perfunctory wash, she climbed under the quilt and was immediately lost in dreamless sleep.

Eliza awoke to the tolling of a solitary bell from a distant spire and for a moment, lay in warm oblivion in that borderland between sleep and waking, unaware that her world had changed most profoundly. As she came to full consciousness, sorrow engulfed her. The north star by which she navigated her life had been obliterated with the knowledge that her mother no longer shared the earth with her. She walked to the window and gazed out over the roofs at the sky lightening to the east. The stars had melted into the dawn and only the slither of a crescent moon remained, a solitary silver brush-stroke in the milky sky. Eliza felt her sympathies flow out to that lonely moon and wondered if the promise of an unknown father could make her feel less abandoned in the world.

So central was the question of who she was and where she belonged that she could barely consider the other earthquake that had struck the night before: Lord Purfoy's unexpected declaration of passionate regard, so quickly withdrawn, had added further tumult to her stricken heart. She knew not what he meant. She had been warned by Corinna, who understood him as well as anyone, that he carried a burden of remorse that even she could not quite fathom. There was no mistaking the emotion between them, but so shattered by the revelations about her family, Eliza could barely find the energy to think of love.

She dressed carelessly and made a passable attempt at taming her hair into a bun, shocked at how pale she looked. She went down to breakfast but did not feel ready to eat anything more than a piece of dry toast. Corinna was there, also pale. 'Goodness, I can no longer thrive on late nights.' She sighed as she eased herself into a chair. 'Either I'm getting old or it's having a young child and another on the way that has altered my capacity for balls.'

'Well, I have no children as my excuse but I too feel as weak as watered milk.' Eliza nibbled at her toast.

'You've had a number of shocks to absorb. No wonder you're exhausted.' Corinna's face brightened. 'But I have some good news. Alick has an aunt with a house in Bath, in Great Pulteney Street. She's in Town for the Season and is happy to lend it to us.'

Eliza's spirits in part revived. This was a quest she had to follow to the end although she quailed at the thought of any more brutal confounding of her hopes. In a quiet voice she said, 'That's very kind. When do you think we should go?'

'Alick is staying in Town. But Mr Flynn is set on joining us. I saw him before he left to settle his new mare in the mews. He seems keen to see Bath; it's one of the central attractions on the English tour.' She poured out another cup of coffee for them both and added, 'I think we should set off in two days' time. Does that suit you?'

Eliza was taken aback. To go so soon alarmed her. She didn't feel ready for more shocks, but was also longing to find her father and hungry for information. To get to know Zadoc Flynn better was also appealing, if only to find out how serious he was about taking Rose to America with him.

Alick came into the room and threw himself into a chair, reaching out for a glass of ale. He looked more dishevelled than usual and ran his hand through his hair, adding to his general mien of distraction. 'Just bumped into Purfoy. He's off to his estate in Hertfordshire. Not like him to leave Town in the Season. But he's been out of sorts for a while.'

Corinna looked up at her husband with a questioning eye. 'Did Rav tell you why he's going?'

'No. You know how close to his chest he plays his cards. Could be that ladybird of his is on the move and he wants to keep her within touching distance.'

Corinna cast a quelling look at her husband who was unaware of Eliza's conflicted feelings for their friend. Certainly, Corinna was pretty sure Lord Purfoy was so discreet that there was no way her young guest could suspect such an arrangement with anyone like Mrs Cornford. She said hastily, 'I'm thinking we should set off in two days for Bath, if you're happy to do without us for a short while? I thought we'd take the large coach to accommodate Eliza and Mr Flynn, along with me and baby Emma, Nurse Meg and Polly.'

Alick looked at his wife with consternation. 'I don't want you tiring yourself in your condition. You'll have to travel over three days.'

Corinna was brusque in her response. 'I'm not an invalid, you know. I would enjoy a few days in Bath; it's a while since we were there, Alick, when we had such an enjoyable time.' Her eye caught his. They had spent a week in the city after their marriage and although it was rainy and unseasonably cold, she would always remember it with pleasure.

He smiled indulgently and said, 'Very well, I'll book rooms for you at The Bird in Hand at Knowl Hill and then for the second night, The Marlborough Arms. They'll be long days travelling. I hope you'll be comfortable enough.'

Corinna finished her coffee and turning to Eliza, said, 'I'm so close to finishing your portrait. Are you happy to sit for me one last time this afternoon?'

'I'd be pleased to. I'm excited to see it completed at last.' Eliza stood up. There were letters she had to write and she had been told to help herself to the writing paper in the library. She sat in the window seat and the peace of the room washed over her. The rows of leather-bound books glowed in the morning light, giving the sense of being in a golden cave, with all those words, all those ideas and lives, waiting for her to explore. Corinna's copy of *The Corsair* was tucked under her arm, a companion she could turn to in any empty moments and a connection with Lord Purfoy's soul. The suffering hero, both poetic and in life, found deep resonance in her heart.

She wrote first to Rose in her quick hand, deprecating the incident at the ball with Davenport and assuring her of her affection.

The second letter she wrote to her new friend Marina Fairley in a more formal manner.

> *Dear Miss Fairley,*
>
> *Would it be possible to meet you for a ride in Hyde Park? I suggest tomorrow, at two after Noon. Lord Purfoy and Taz are out of Town so I will be riding a different Horse.*
>
> *Yours ever,*
>
> *Eliza*

The words *Lord Purfoy and Taz are out of Town* took some of the lustre from the day. Why, she wondered, had she given her heart without condition to a man whom she had been warned was proof against love? Why was she so certain that there could be no one else for her? Was it that his face was the first she saw when she regained consciousness and, in that primitive impulse for survival in a moment of peril, she allied herself with the first living being who offered safety, deciding against all odds that her destiny lay with him?

Raven Purfoy was so mysterious and unknown that the unexpected anguish of his words to her meant they could not be forgotten. *You intoxicate me... Art thou some enchantress? To so fill my dreams with you...* For better or for worse, her dream had settled on his elegant, aloof person, never expecting he would love her and make the fantasy real. In her young life Eliza had learned to keep her deepest longings in the realm of fantasy as protection from an unforgiving world. It was hard to relinquish her self-protective habits and learn to trust again that sometimes a prayer could be answered, a dream, fulfilled.

Eliza heard the distant church clock strike twice and hurried through to Corinna's studio where the artist already stood at her easel while baby Emma practised her walking by staggering from chair to table before subsiding at her mother's feet.

Eliza sat and watched this plump, fair-haired child collect a box that had held her mother's pigments and with a torn piece of old cloth, make a bed for her wooden cat. The care and ingenuity shown by her intrigued Eliza. She wondered what kind of child she herself had been. She had no one to tell her, no one to remember. Emma started singing 'Rock-a-Bye Baby' surprisingly in tune and a distant memory was awoken that made Eliza catch her breath. For a moment she was back in her own nursery and the ghost of a face hovered over her crib and, as if drawn in air, faded quickly away.

Corinna had been concentrating hard on capturing the emotion behind her sitter's extraordinary eyes. And with one final speck of Naples yellow dabbed onto the canvas, she stood back and narrowed her gaze. 'Yes, I think that is done.' Her voice was quiet, almost as if she were speaking to herself. Her eyes remained on her painting as she said, 'Miss Gray, come and see what you think.'

Eliza moved to stand beside Corinna and looked on this finished representation of her self. Emotion rushed up into her chest and colour suffused her cheeks. Here was a woman she recognised, yet the expression in her eyes was so unlike any she had ever seen: caught off guard, pensive, ready for adventure but with a veil of melancholy. 'It's beautiful,' she said, 'but I seem so lonely.'

'I know. But that is what I see when I look closely at your face. In company you are full of vivacity and laughter but I see something solitary at your centre. It's very much part of you.' Corinna looked across at her young guest and noticed tears were coursing down her face. Dashing them away, Eliza seemed as surprised as Corinna who said gently, 'Sometimes to see a finished portrait of oneself can be a deeply affecting thing.'

Eliza could not stop herself from giving Corinna a brief, intense hug. She was shaken by how touching it was to be truly understood, and she felt an unexpected intimacy with the artist who had revealed to her this hidden self. Corinna said, 'When you have found your family and have a home of your own, it will be my gift to you.' She picked up Emma and slung her on her hip.

'This is the most precious present I could ever hope for. Thank you.' They both walked towards the door, Eliza stealing a look over her shoulder at the portrait drying on the easel, seeming to be alive yet left all alone in the room.

* * *

The next afternoon, Davey, the Wolfes' groom, had saddled up Sally, Corinna's pretty grey palfrey with a dark mane and socks. Eliza, accompanied by Davey, rode to Hyde Park to meet Marina Fairley and caught sight of her just inside Grosvenor Gate, the purple plume on her hat a bright flag in the sunlight.

They grasped each other's hands in greeting. Miss Fairley smiled broadly. 'I'm very glad to see you again, Eliza. How are you after that scoundrel drunk abused you and your friend at the ball? I'm ashamed to even think of him as related to me, so despicably rude was he!'

Eliza was serious in her response. 'It shocked us both. So unexpected and humiliating at such a grand event.' She frowned. 'But in some ways he's right. Polite society doesn't recognise irregulars like Rose and me.'

'Well, for that matter, polite society does not think highly of me either for being so happy to turn my back on the conventions of my sex and class. But if you don't feel the lack of your own household and family, why should it bother others?'

Eliza met Miss Fairley's eyes with the query: 'You don't feel the need for a family, do you?'

They trotted down to the Serpentine, scattering the waterfowl who were foraging amongst the reeds, their grooms in attendance a few paces behind. Marina Fairley gazed thoughtfully into the middle distance. 'No. The idea of childbirth fills me with dread. Pregnancy seems a death sentence. As dangerous as if we were to go to war!' She laughed bitterly. 'Then even if you survive, there's no guarantee the child for whom you suffered will have warm feelings for you, or you for the child. My mother can barely countenance me, and I find her a bore. I know I'm a disappointment to her, you see.' A look of sadness suffused her face but only for a second or two before she was once more composed and smiling.

Eliza was aware of the pulse in her veins that reminded her of her longing for love, knowing she could not endure a life without it. She asked her friend, 'But what of your heart?'

Marina Fairley laughed. 'You'll find I'm no sentimentalist. I aim to live without the distractions of love, a Stoic like the philosopher Epictetus, whom Grandmama so commends.'

Eliza, who was carried away by the red-blooded verse of Lord Byron, could barely contemplate such a rational view of life. 'So what sustains the spirit?' she asked as their horses cropped the grass at the water's edge in the shade of a copse of birches.

Miss Fairley said without hesitation, 'Virtue, knowledge, serenity; the storm of emotion is only destructive of such equanimity.'

Eliza looked at her friend and wondered if it was her self-belief, in the face of her mother's ambition and her aunt's disdain, that made her so admirable. 'Perhaps this is why I feel we are matched, although not even related? You are the calm centre of my storm-tossed sea.'

They had moved their horses into the open sward and trotted up the slight incline towards the Tyburn Toll. Miss Fairley was amused. 'Well, you can entertain me with tales of your trouble-some heart while I concentrate on living the virtuous life and pursuing my studies of classical philosophy!'

'Talking about troubles, how do you manage Lady Dauntsey's disobliging nature? I'm grateful that she told me my father's name, but the way she conveyed that my mother is dead was cruel in its starkness.'

'You just have to armour yourself and not let her arrows pierce your flesh.'

In the distance they saw a group of four gentlemen on their flashy steeds racing one another through the avenue of trees that ran parallel with the road. Galloping in the royal parks was forbidden, but these young blades were rich enough not to bother with the fines and willing to take their chances. Marina Fairley scoffed in derision. 'That one on the grey is the dastardly one of whom we speak. Devil Davenport is leading the charge.'

They watched from the protection of a copse of trees but as the men wheeled their horses around and slowed to a canter, they were suddenly upon the two women. Recognising them, Lord Davenport reined in his mount which sidled and reared, still coiled with unruly energy. Both Davey and the Fairley groom moved their horses closer to the women. Eliza watched in some admiration how his lordship handled the frisky stallion, entirely at ease in the saddle. 'Why, ladies...' His voice was insinuating. 'How do, Marina? And your little friend I've seen in all kinds of places from the highest to the low, good day.'

'Good day, Lord Davenport.' Marina was frosty. 'This, as you know, is Miss Gray.'

'Good day to you, Miss Gray.' He bowed his head but Eliza could not miss the sly flicker of insult in his drink-befuddled eyes.

Her dislike of him, however, was overborne by her admiration for his horse. She could not help but ask Lord Davenport about his handsome mount. 'Sir, is that goodly beast yours?'

He seemed surprised. 'He is. He's called Eros for obvious reasons.' He looked round at his fellow riders who had hung back, and they all laughed in a bawdy manner, casting impertinent glances at Eliza and Marina. The women realised all the young men were in their cups, despite the fact it was early in the afternoon. Still laughing at his coarse insinuations, he added, 'Eros is such a powerful stallion. I intend to ride him in the Owners' Race at Epsom and show the arrogant Purfoy that he and Horatio no longer rule the turf.' His men friends cheered. Lord Davenport tipped his hat to the women and joined his group as they cantered back towards Cumberland Gate.

'They are despicably drunk!' Eliza said with some indignation, adding, 'He doesn't deserve such a beautiful horse. I hope he cares for him properly.'

Marina Fairley tutted. 'Miss Eliza, beware the emotions. It seems yours are involved in everything; you are indifferent to nothing. Such commitment only courts grief. Davenport isn't worth your concern, and neither is his horse. Try for serenity.'

Eliza laughed. 'I could never be as you suggest. My emotions are as turbulent as the sea, not least because I go to Bath tomorrow and hope to find my father and discover something of my family at last.'

They had arrived at the gate out of the Park and, in the crush of horses, riders and promenaders arriving to take advantage of the spring sun, Miss Fairley grasped Eliza's hand. 'I wish you every luck with your quest. But take care of your heart; don't hope for too much. Hope is the graveyard of happiness.' Her words were bleak but her face was lively with amusement. They blew a kiss to each other as both women and their grooms turned their horses and headed for home. Eliza trotted into the mews, her spirits more settled by her new friend's calm wisdom about life. In the hall was a note waiting for her in Rose Bowman's hand. Eagerly she took it upstairs to her room where she sat by the window to read.

My dear Friend, do not concern yourself. I am less Romantic than you.
We endured insults both small and Large but I have a Plan for my life.
We have only our Selves – I intend to use the Advantages I have to
obtain what I need.

Your Rose

Eliza felt uneasy. What danger was her friend courting? How far did her responsibilities go towards someone she had grown up with and held in great affection? She hoped her own reckless behaviour had not encouraged her friend into even wilder schemes.

***

The large Wolfe travelling coach was pulled up outside the house at seven in the morning. They had a long three days' travelling ahead of them and needed to start early to take advantage of the daylight. Eliza had packed a couple of evening gowns for the soirées Corinna had warned her they would attend together, with a selection of day dresses, pelisses and bonnets, and a warm redingote borrowed from her hostess. Eliza climbed in and sat with Polly and Emma's nurse, Meg, on one seat while Zadoc Flynn settled in opposite. Corinna handed Emma to Meg then turned to her husband. He took her into his arms in a fierce embrace. 'Take greatest care of yourself and our children, my darling.'

Corinna slipped her hands under his coat and feeling the muscles in his back tense, she pulled him to her as she lifted her face for a fleeting kiss on the lips. Even as a married couple they had to maintain decorum in public. 'Alick, keep safe for me. My heart belongs to you who knows it best,' she murmured into his neck, then quickly extricated herself from his arms and climbed into the coach to sit next to Mr Flynn. Eliza noticed Corinna's eyes were bright with unshed tears and realised with a jolt how much she longed to feel that same intense connection with another, and could never practise Miss Fairley's reasonable stoicism. If even in the end her soul had to travel alone through the world, Eliza hoped, just once in her life, to experience this intense fire.

The coach moved off and Eliza was filled with excitement at travelling out of London in some comfort. Prebbles Flying Circus occasionally moved its entourage of performers and animals to another city but the travelling was painfully slow and uncomfortable; Eliza and Rose were usually despatched via the public stagecoach with the cheapest tickets which meant sitting on the roof, precarious and frozen to the bone. Here she was in a comfortable coach with fur blankets on the floor and heated bricks under their feet and in the most congenial company. It was astonishing to consider how fundamentally life had changed for her, but unsettling too that this could only be a transition to something she had yet to know.

She glanced across at Zadoc Flynn who was keen with anticipation, his guidebook open in his hand. 'I shall buy a bottle of medicinal water from Bath to take home as a souvenir. My father suffers from the gout,' he said, reading about the distinctive pleasures of the city they were about to explore.

Once they had left Hyde Park Gate behind, London receded as the Wolfe coach headed for the pretty villages of Knightsbridge and Kensington with their cottages and occasional big manor houses, built of brick and surrounded by gardens. The road was crowded with large wagons filled with produce, alongside racing curricles and flashy phaetons of the young bloods about Town on their way to an illegal boxing match or some other dubious entertainment. The fast mail coaches sped on their way, overtaking the overladen stagecoaches, creaking while their passengers clung onto the top rails, in peril for their lives and blue with cold.

As they passed the barracks, Eliza peered out of the window, hoping to catch a glimpse of Kensington Palace, aware that the Court retired here amongst the fields and trees for a change of air. The swaying vehicle had rocked Emma to sleep in her mother's arms and Meg and Polly were gently snoring too. Even Corinna's eyes were fluttering, but Eliza and Mr Flynn were too stimulated by the novelty of travel to even grow drowsy.

They were crossing the flat lands now, filled with orchards and market gardens feeding the expanding population in the great city to the east. As the coach approached Hammersmith, Zadoc Flynn consulted his book and pointed out a quaint roadside tavern with a distinctively high, red-tiled roof. 'Look, The Red Cow,' he said then quoted, '"Notorious haunt of the lowest of footpads and pickpockets. They passed on information on any rich travellers to the fine-dressed 'knights of the road' on their fleet black steeds with horse pistols ready. The coaches were sitting ducks in the bleak heathland to the west." Hide your jewellery, Miss Gray.'

'Luckily I have nothing worth stealing but my virtue!' she retorted with a self-deprecating laugh.

'That's priceless indeed. I'm going to have to lay my life down to protect you!' He reached up to where a holster swung above his head, checking to see if it contained a pistol and shot. His fingers closed around cold steel. 'This is more a lady's pistol. Back home we'd have a shotgun.' He noticed the surprise on Eliza's face. 'Our justice is more rough and ready than yours. We shoot first and ask questions later.'

'In that case I'm relieved you have no shotgun with you, Mr Flynn.'

Casting her a roguish look, he settled down to read his guidebook further.

Eliza thought this was a good time to raise with him what had been exercising her since reading Rose Bowman's letter. She hesitated and then in a rush of words, addressed him. 'Sir, I feel some responsibility for Miss Bowman. Forgive the presumption of asking what your intentions may be towards her.'

He looked up startled and seemed reluctant to answer. Eventually, he took a breath and said, 'Your concern is to your credit, Miss Gray. I hope I can reassure you when I say...' He paused, trying to find the right words. 'Forgive me for any indelicacy, but Miss Bowman is a young woman who knows her own mind. I assure you it is not me taking advantage of her but rather she determined on her own destiny. She has told me she wants to come to America with me to try her fortune.'

Eliza's eyes opened wide with astonishment. 'This is what she has told you?'

'She has.'

'And have you agreed?'

'I suggested she could come with me to my father's business in New York and work in the offices there, or she could help with managing my stud in Kentucky. But she's not as keen on horses or as skilled with them as you are.'

Eliza was taken aback by Rose's boldness but also admiring of her reckless courage and sense of adventure. Her anxiety about Rose's vulnerability as a woman without family, status or money, however, was not assuaged. 'I presume this arrangement does not involve marriage?' Her voice was quiet and her cheeks flamed with embarrassment at her temerity in asking such a thing, but she was concerned that her friend should know exactly the kind of arrangement she was entering.

Zadoc Flynn gazed out at the fertile green fields and answered, 'No, it does not. But then I don't think Miss Bowman would wish for that. Nor is it as important there as it is here. We are a new country and have not assumed all the constraints of the old. Irregular arrangements between men and women are not as disadvantageous for the women as you may fear.'

'You would, nevertheless, be responsible for her until she has found work and determined how she wishes to live.'

It was Mr Flynn's turn to colour with embarrassment. 'Of course! What kind of brute do you think me? I have the benefit of my father's successful business and my own efforts and I assure you money is no problem. Miss Bowman will want for nothing while she establishes her new life.' He was watching her closely as she processed this astonishing change about to happen in her friend's life.

Everyone in the carriage was still asleep as Mr Flynn leaned forward and took Eliza's hand, his face serious. 'Miss Gray, my country offers infinite possibilities for men and women alike, regardless of breeding or wealth. I may not be about to offer for Miss Bowman's hand but you are a different matter. I share your love of horses, I find your personal attractions unsettling. I would be honoured if you would consider accompanying me home to America as my wife.'

Eliza was astounded. She snatched back her hand and in a fierce whisper said, 'Mr Flynn! I could not object more to your mentioning in the same breath that you're happy to take my friend as your mistress but would consider marrying me! If this is an example of the manners and sensibilities of your countrymen, I want nothing to do with them.'

Mr Flynn's usually genial manner turned mulish. Aware of their sleeping companions, his voice was quiet and emphatic. 'I'm not a practised flatterer like the trifling dandies and men of the Town in your country, but a plain speaker and an honest one. My father is the richest man in New York and I'm wealthy in my own right, healthy, hard-working and of good temper.'

'Marriage is not like horse-trading, sir! Am I now meant to inspect your teeth? And anyway, this is hardly the place for such a conversation.'

'I'd like to point out, Miss Gray, it was you who raised it. I was contentedly reading my book when you decided to poke your nose into your friend's business.' He settled back, looking pleased to have claimed the last word. Eliza turned away. He was right, she had been patronising towards Rose whose letter had told her she knew her own mind and made her own decisions about her life. Eliza's thoughts whirled with so many new and shocking ideas. Rose would be gone from her for ever and she herself had just received a backhanded marriage proposal from someone she considered no more than a brotherly presence at best. Were Rose Bowman and Mr Flynn, with their pragmatic attitude to relationships between men and women, the wise ones – and she, the romantic fool? Lacking family connections or prospects, she had declined out of hand a new life and marriage to a good, decent, attractive man who was as rich as Croesus, just because she had given her heart to another who she had been warned could not return her regard. What folly was this?

Such disquieting thoughts were interrupted as the coach drew into Hounslow for a change of horses, the wheels of the Wolfe coach clanking over the cobbles as they turned into the yard of The Crowing Cockerel.

After a hurried stop, everyone scrambled back into the coach; before nightfall they had to reach Knowl Hill where Mr Wolfe had booked them rooms. As the vehicle rolled towards notorious Hounslow Heath there was a frisson of expectation, even though the tract of rough grassland and scrub was nothing like as dangerous as it was in the previous century, when hundreds of highway robbers on horseback or foot had lurked in wait for travellers. But its reputation remained, and Eliza saw the coachman place his blunderbuss across his knees. Although she felt sure she saw a horseman waiting half-obscured in a scrubby copse of stunted trees, the journey through this windy wasteland was without incident.

Soon dusk was falling and the coach arrived at The Bird in Hand. Eliza spent a restless night in a lumpy bed and could hear Emma wailing next door and Corinna and Meg's soothing voices. The child had seemed out of sorts on the journey, sleepy and grizzling, and Eliza hoped she was not ailing. She felt a sympathy for Corinna, on whose pale face anxiety was writ large. This onerous journey was all in aid of her search for family and she was aware of it being yet another imposition on her generous hosts.

At last, at the end of the third day, the coach and its weary passengers were finally on the outskirts of Bath, its pale lime-stone buildings gleaming pink in the sunset. The river Avon ran through its centre and wooded hills to north and south seemed like a great amphitheatre for the spectacle that was the city itself. 'It is beautiful,' Eliza said, craning forward so she could see better in the vanishing light.

Mr Flynn looked up from his book. 'I won't read out the disobliging comments in this guidebook about how Bath has declined since its grand days last century when it really set the rules of fashionable life.'

'I know, people complain it's now filled with the elderly, ailing and lame. And far too many sad, unmarried women who eke out their diminishing allowances as companions or guides.' Corinna was once again light-hearted, relieved that her daughter seemed to be better.

The coach lumbered over Pulteney Bridge, with its bright souvenir shops overlooking the tumbling weir below. It pulled up outside a tall, imposing house on the south side of Great Pulteney Street. The travellers climbed out, tired, hungry and stiff-limbed, and were relieved to find that Alick's Aunt Jane had left instruc-tions for the skeleton staff, who remained in residence, to welcome them in her absence. Her under-butler, Toby, opened the door. Still informally dressed, he ushered them in, taking bonnets and pelisses, then showed them the dining room where a cold buffet of roast beef, bread, ale, burgundy and pastries awaited.

Meg and Corinna had taken Emma upstairs to settle her for the night. Zadoc Flynn and Eliza were left alone and after he had piled his plate with meat and bread, he sat down with a tankard of ale. Suddenly aware of her own hunger, Eliza joined him at the table and he carved her some beef. 'I intend to race Ohio, as you know, and am very keen to try her out at this famous Owners' Race at Epsom.'

Eliza nodded. 'Lord Davenport has a beautiful stallion he intends to ride in that same race. I think he has an animus against Lord Purfoy whom he determines to best.'

'Well, Purfoy on Horatio is the champion. 'Tis a pity he's so haughty; everyone wants to beat him.'

Eliza sprang to his defence. 'He's not haughty! He is just the most skilled horseman with the best mount.'

Mr Flynn was eyeing her shrewdly. 'As you know, Miss Gray, I'm too heavy to ride Ohio in a race. But you could.'

It was the second time since they had set out that he had completely astounded her with a plan. 'Of course I can't ride. I am not Ohio's owner and I'm not a man.'

'Both of those obstacles can be overcome.' He was chuckling at his own ingenuity.

Eliza was even more emphatic when she said, 'And most importantly, there is no way I'd be part of a ruse to deprive Lord Purfoy of his rightful crown.'

'Oh don't be so prosy and honourable, Miss Gray. You're the best rider I know, and you're lightweight. There's little doubt in my mind you and Ohio would win.'

Eliza put down her ale glass and said, 'Well, Mr Flynn, you'll have to look to someone else.' She stood up just as Corinna entered and sank, exhausted, into a chair. Eliza picked up a plate and said, 'Can I collect you something to eat? It's been such a long day.'

'I'm so tired I think I'll retire soon.' Corinna sighed. 'At least Emma seems to have recovered. I'm so relieved.'

Both women bade goodnight to Mr Flynn then walked up the stairs to their bedrooms on the second floor. Eliza turned to Corinna. 'I can't believe I'm in the same city as my father. I'm so grateful to you for making this possible. I'm sorry it's been such a tiresome journey for you.'

Corinna laughed. 'Wait until you've met him, my dear. You may not be thanking me then.'

* * *

Eliza woke early and contemplated the day ahead. The sounds of the city in the street outside were unlike the sounds of London. The wide thoroughfare of Great Pulteney Street meant carriages were driven faster, so the horses' hooves sounded rhythmic and the jingling harnesses strangely soothing. The calls of the delivery boys were in a soft West Country brogue. There seemed to be more birdsong. Excitement rippled through her. She felt she was on the brink of a new stage of her life. She was about to meet her father and that thought alone made her heart beat faster. Perhaps once she discovered where she belonged in the world it would help her understand her restlessness and hunger for affection: perhaps it would put her feelings for Lord Purfoy and Mr Flynn's practical proposal of marriage into better perspective too?

Eliza dressed carefully in a day gown she knew flattered her colouring with its saffron silk twill and smart Cossack spencer in lilac wool to complete the outfit. She examined her appearance in the looking glass and felt such an outfit would protect her from any but the worst buffetings of life. As she was struggling to tame her mane of hair into a tidy bun, Polly tapped on the door and entered to immediately work her magic with plaits and tease her curls. 'You're very lucky, Miss Gray, to have such hair. Like an angel, miss.'

'Thank you, Polly,' Eliza said demurely but did not add what was in her heart: *I wonder whether anyone in my family shares the same hair.* She then ran down the stairs in search of some paper and a quill. The desk in the library was the obvious place to start and in the middle drawer she found a pile of creamy paper, some newly cut quills and a small bottle of already mixed black ink. It was difficult to know how to address a man she could not remember ever knowing. Her hand was shaking as she introduced herself, mentioning his cousin Lady Dauntsey, and asking for an audience.

Her signature was more constrained than usual; anxious as she was not to give the Marquess any reason to refuse her, she tried to make herself as unremarkable as possible. Quickly folding the paper, she addressed and sealed it, then handed it to Toby. 'Would you see that this is delivered to the Marquess of Bathwick at Bathwick Court?'

The young man was keen and talkative. 'I know the place. Gloomy pile at the end of the road and yon Marquess as tumble-down as his lair. I shall deliver it me'self. Do you need a reply, miss?'

'Yes please, Toby.' This longed-for reunion suddenly felt real. To steady her nerves she walked through to the dining room in search of some coffee.

Corinna appeared, her face pale and tired. 'Oh, coffee. Good,' she said as Eliza poured her a cup. 'Emma's not very well again. I don't know what might be ailing her.'

Eliza knew that childhood illnesses were dreaded by parents who understood too well how quickly a small body could succumb to infection. 'I'm so sorry. Is there anything I can do to help you with her?'

Corinna reached for some toast. 'I've left Meg with her and will return after I've eaten. But, Eliza, I want you to see something of Bath. Would you take Polly as your chaperone? Perhaps go to The Pump Room?' She was soon away, anxious to get back to her daughter, just as Mr Flynn walked in. 'Good morning, Miss Gray. After yesterday's rain, it's perfect weather for exploration, don't you think?' He poured himself some ale and sat down.

'I'm probably going with Polly this morning to see what's so special about The Pump Room,' she said, glancing out of the window, her nerves on the sharpest of tenterhooks, waiting for the sound of the front door and Toby's return.

Mr Flynn snorted. 'I'll have much more fun; I'm off to the races on Lansdown Hill.' He looked at Eliza's tense face and said with a smirk, 'Well, I fear you'll find the city but a refuge for the sick in mind and body. If you care for impecunious dowagers and ramshackle profligates who pander to a handful of rich old duchesses, that's your pleasure.'

Eliza was irritated by his levity and said severely, 'I don't believe any guide's editor would be so disobliging; you've made that all up, haven't you?'

Zadoc Flynn's spirits were irrepressible. 'Of course not! It's true—'

He was interrupted by Eliza jumping to her feet. She had heard the front door close and, excusing herself, dashed to the hall. 'Oh Toby, you're back!'

'Yes, miss. It took a while, the Marquess ain't the cheeriest of coves. Somethin' in yer note caused trouble. But here's the answer.' He held out a letter with a very grand crest impressed into the red wax.

Eliza returned to the dining room and sat to read the curt response.

Come at four after noon.

It was signed with a shaky B. She felt as shaky as that signature. It had been foolish to hope for more of a welcome to a long-lost daughter; after all, he was old and perhaps had every reason to doubt her claim. She looked up at Mr Flynn whose merry expression had faded.

'Bad news?' he asked solicitously.

'No, it's just I have a bad habit of expecting more of life than perhaps I should.' Eliza's smile was brave rather than cheerful.

'There's nothing wrong with expecting more, but perhaps the art lies in realising we may have to settle for less.' He gave her a peculiar look she could not fathom. 'Remember, if the more of life lets you down, then my offer of the less is still on the table.'

Eliza could not but be amused and somehow touched by his dogged business-like approach to life, his lack of pride. Perhaps he was a natural happy Stoic like Marina? And in the end both would suffer less than she. 'I thank you, Mr Flynn.' Her eyes met his and then looked away.

He leaned forward with a boyish and rather embarrassed expression on his face. 'Miss Eliza, you are the radiance in the dark,' he said, his voice quiet and full of feeling.

Eliza was startled by how out of character such an utterance seemed. 'That's a very kind thought, Mr Flynn, but what makes you say that?'

He smiled sheepishly. 'I know I'm not very romantic but found it in a book of poems and thought it a good line to say to a girl to persuade her I was otherwise.'

Eliza found herself admiring his honesty and an attractive humility. 'Really, Mr Flynn, you're fine as you are. Don't change in any particular. Certainly not to try and turn yourself into any kind of romantic.'

His handsome blue eyes looked relieved. 'Well, that is good of you to say so. But how am I to persuade you of my warmest feelings towards you?'

Eliza laughed softly. 'Ah, I'm afraid I'm a lost cause, Mr Flynn.' She stood up and said more brusquely, 'Now I must go and experience for myself the impecunious spinsters, rich old duchesses and fortune-hunting rakes to be found at The Pump Room.'

Accompanied by Polly, Eliza walked the hundred yards to Pulteney Bridge with its pretty shops and the torrent of the river Avon below; how disturbingly familiar this stretch of bridge and water seemed to her, stirring the deepest of memories. She was relieved to turn left towards the Abbey. Whatever Mr Flynn and his guidebook might say, Bath was a pleasingly compact city with everything within walking distance, and the backdrop of green hills with grazing sheep imparting an air of rustic charm.

The classic portico of The Pump Room faced both women as they stood on the paved courtyard outside the great Abbey church. There was a bustle round the entrance with people of every age and kind coming and going, some in wheeled chairs, some leaning heavily on walking sticks, many looking very fashionable indeed to Eliza's inexperienced eye. She was pleased she was wearing such a becoming gown and pelisse and had chosen the best of her bonnets for the occasion.

They pressed through the crowd to find themselves in a vast lofty room lined with pillars with two great fireplaces emitting heat and flame. Between these edifices and surrounded by a throng was a marble urn spouting a cloudy liquid. This, Eliza surmised, was where the legendary healing waters were dispensed, their sulphurous smell filling the air. The musicians in the small orchestra in the raised gallery at the farthest wall were playing as if their lives depended on it, while those visitors who could walk promenaded the room, chatting while keeping beady eyes on who might be of note in the wider company.

Eliza turned to point the waters out to Polly when a tall figure of a man caught her eye. His back was to her, and he was on his way out, but she thought he looked remarkably like Lord Purfoy. Her heart lurched. He was meant to be at his estate in Hertfordshire. Then she noticed that on his arm was a woman, tall and willowy, with an elaborate plumed bonnet that shielded her face from Eliza's gaze.

There had never been any talk of a serious woman in his lordship's life; surely she was mistaken in thinking this man him? She admonished herself for seeing him in any distinctive silhouette in her vicinity, but the uneasiness persisted. She turned to Polly and they both queued up for their small glass of murky waters, wrinkled their noses at the smell and mineral taste and sipped the hot liquid gingerly. 'I wonder if we're drinking this before or after it's been bathed in at the Baths?' Eliza asked with a grimace.

So noisy was the orchestra, so hot and stuffy the crush and malodorous the air, that Eliza took Polly's hand and they retreated to the street. They decided to walk into the Abbey itself and look at the tombstones, statues and inscriptions, but Eliza's mind was distracted by thoughts of her father and the unwelcome anxieties of whether Lord Purfoy had, for some reason, been drawn to Bath with a lady companion in tow. How painful it was to feel this confusion of operatic emotion. Perhaps Mr Flynn was right in treating marriage as a pragmatic transaction free of the agonies of love?

They walked home the long way, marvelling at the shops in Milsom Street, as colourful and enticing as those in London's Bond Street. The clouds were gathering and the wind had increased. Bath was notoriously wet and suddenly spots of rain were falling in big splashes on their faces. 'Come, Polly, it's not far, let's hurry home.' They picked up their skirts and ran as decorously as possible, weaving in and out of the umbrellas and soon were at their house, tumbling through the door, laughing and soaked to the skin. Not even their bonnets had kept out the deluge. 'I'll have to try and dry my hair before I have to go out. And you'll come with me, Polly? Just before four?'

'Of course, miss,' she said. 'I'll come now and help you with your wet clothes.' Once more dressed and warm, Eliza decided to visit Corinna and see how Emma was. She knocked on the door and when she entered, found Corinna sitting in the window reading while Emma slept in her mother's bed. 'Oh, Mrs Wolfe, how is she?'

Corinna's face was not as drawn and pale with fatigue as at breakfast but her words were serious. 'She has a mild fever which Meg and I are containing with cold towels. But I think after you've seen your father I may have to decide to return to London. I'd rather rely on our own physician than the Bath ones, more used to ailments of the elderly.'

'Of course. I'll be ready to leave whenever suits you. I'm granted an interview with the Marquess this afternoon. Then my work here is done.'

'Come and tell me what you find out. I hope it is all you hope for.'

Eliza had tidied her hair and dressed in one of her borrowed afternoon gowns in palest lilac ribboned muslin, with a small straw bonnet lined in cream silk that flattered her face. It was still drizzling with West Country rain and although they could have called for the chaise to be harnessed, they decided to walk the furlong or so to Bathwick Court, sheltered under two large black umbrellas.

The house was distinctive from afar as yew trees in the front garden, once tamed with topiary, were now so overgrown and unkempt their black branches stretched into the sky and over-bore the roadway. Eliza opened the gate and the women walked up the mossy path to an oak door, bleached by the years. She knocked and waited. Listening intently, they noticed that no bird-song penetrated the dark canopy of trees. Eliza knocked again just as the door opened a crack and two beady eyes peered out.

'I'm Miss Gray. Lord Bathwick is expecting me.'

The door opened wider to reveal an elfin figure. He was small and of indeterminate age with a lively expression on his yellowed wrinkly face. He nodded. 'Come.' They were led through the echoing space of the vast hall to the back of the house where he rapped on a double door.

A faint voice said, 'Enter.'

Eliza asked Polly if she would wait for her and then stepped into the room. The curtains were drawn and the light so low she could barely see from whence the voice had come. The air had the miasma of the sickroom: a pungent camphor combining with the sweet smell of opium.

By the fire was a makeshift bed and there, amongst the mound of bedding, lay the Marquess, his large head as bald and smooth as an egg. He had his back to her and she saw him put out a bony hand to grasp a perruque and place it haphazardly on his head. 'Come closer, girl, let me see you,' he said in a queru-lous voice.

Eliza held her breath. Here was her father at last. She stood before him and gazed tentatively into his face – so thin and dessi-cated it looked barely more than a skull, paler than parchment, the skin tight across the bone, his sunken eyes the only sign of life, restless with pain. 'Good afternoon, my lord.' Not certain what to do, she gave a small curtsey.

'None of that's necessary, my dear.' The old man's voice was kinder as he grasped her hand. 'Lean closer, I need to see you properly. Just keep away from my foot, I'm in the devilish agony.' She glanced down at his swollen foot, bandaged and placed on a cushion. 'The gout, you know. Such intensity of sensation makes a naturally irascible man a brute.'

'I'm sorry you endure it so, sir.' Eliza felt a rush of sympathy for his suffering. Indeed there were beads of perspiration glistening on his waxy pallor, his anguished eyes scanning her face.

'You're a beauty like your mother,' he said in a strangulated voice that cracked with such emotion that it took Eliza aback.

'I heard from Lady Dauntsey that she had died soon after I was lost. I'm sorry for us both in that.' He cast her hand away from him with some force, his face distorted.

'Can I fetch you anything for the pain?' she asked.

'No! My pain is unassuageable, beyond endurance!' His hands covered his face. Eliza felt powerless to help him and sat on the edge of the chair next to his bed. She searched intently for some familiarity in his face. He continued, his voice barely audible, and she leaned closer to hear. 'I have not the energy for politeness or dissembling. I'm not long for this world. Look into my eyes, Miss Gray.'

Eliza met his tormented gaze, puzzled and increasingly alarmed. He turned away. 'I can barely look on you. Your eyes are the evidence that damned your mother.'

Eliza's pulse began to race, so fearful was she of some terrible revelation to come. 'Sir. I do not understand,' she said, her own voice barely audible.

'I could not make your mother happy, but when at last you were born she was filled with joy. As was I. Until your baby blue eyes began to change and become this devilish mixture of green and grey Then I knew that you were not my daughter.'

This news hit Eliza like a body blow. She sat back as if

winded. 'How can that be, sir? What do you mean?' Her voice
trembled.

But Lord Bathwick was not listening. It was as if a dam had
burst and he had to unburden his spirit at last. He continued,
quiet and intense, his emaciated hands gripped together until the
knuckles shone white. 'She would not tell me who your father
was so I was unable to demand satisfaction with the sword.
Neither could I endure her pleasure in you. I could not bear to
look on you, the daily reminder of my wife's betrayal, my humiliating cuckoldom. I was driven almost mad with jealousy.'

Eliza feared what she was about to hear. Had he killed her
mother? She could barely allow such an unnatural thought into
her mind. It was unendurable hearing any more, but she was
rooted to the spot, unable to move. Her eyes fixed on his wig,
which was slightly askew, and this trivial detail helped her to still
her racing heart.

Lord Bathwick continued, speaking rapidly and with anguish.
'I have to tell you. I have to confess this guilt before I die. When
you were seven we came to Bath to take the waters for my gout.
The physical agony was a magnification of the pain in my heart
that tormented me so. I had to exorcise it the only way I could.'
His hands fluttered to his face as his voice sank even lower. 'I am
filled with the shame of bribing your nursemaid to lose you
during the Solstice revelries when the streets were thronged with
every kind of roisterer and merry-maker.'

Eliza's head dropped with the weight of this terrible fact. 'So it
was not an awful accident? I was lost on purpose?'

His nervous fingers touched her hand briefly and his voice
softened, but he still could not look at her. 'Almost immediately, I
understood the cruelty of my deed. Your mother was so grief-
stricken I was filled with remorse for her suffering. I tried to find
you, through every office of enquiry. I even contacted London's

Bow Street Runners and offered a large reward. But you had disappeared.'

'The circus folk found me and I remained with them until a month ago.'

'I am sorry I did such a wicked thing. And I have been in hell these long years for it. Your mother's grief turned into malaise and the doctors could do nothing for her.' He hesitated as if he could hardly bear to continue. Then with a sigh, he said, 'She faded away and was dead within the year.'

'So you did kill her!' The words burst out of Eliza in an agony of shock and horror. She had leapt to her feet, incapable any longer of stillness and self-effacement. 'You deprived me of my mother and her of me! You deprived me of my family, of knowing to whom I belonged. You destroyed my chance of love! I carry these wounds inflicted by you throughout my life. You have unburdened yourself but have plunged your confessional knife into me. And I still don't know who my father could be and whether he might love me.' Her voice rose with the heartbreak of it all and she strode towards the door, intent on leaving.

'Wait, Miss Gray.' His voice was still weak but carried a force that made her pause. 'I have her jewellery box for you.' She walked slowly back to his bed. 'There's nothing of value. All her jewellery was Bathwick jewellery and so goes to my heir, but this box contains some of her own beads and brooches. They are for you.' He pointed to a small rosewood box on the floor by his bed. Eliza's emotions were in so much turmoil; to be offered something of her mother's was almost too much to bear. She picked the box up and ran to the door. Before she left a thought struck her with the clarity of revelation. 'Pray, my lord, who is your heir?'

'My will has long been ratified. As I have no legal male heir, I have left what I have to a distant cousin. I would have preferred to leave something to you, now I know you have survived, but I have not the strength to change it. Instead it remains as it always has been.' His voice was fading with the effort of speech. In barely a whisper he added, 'My heir is Lord Davenport.'

Eliza's dispossession could not have been more complete; with neither family, nor home, and the inheritance that might have been hers placed instead in the avaricious grasp of the most despicable person she knew, her shock was too deep for tears. The old man sensed the terrible import of all he had told her and, in a last gesture of attempted conciliation, pulled from his finger his great ring glinting with its ancestral crest, and offered it to her. 'This is the Bathwick seal. The family crest is centuries old and it now belongs in your keeping.' It fell like a stone into her hand.

7

RISING FROM THE ASHES

Thrusting the ring into her pocket and holding tight to her mother's jewellery box, Eliza dashed from the room, collected a startled Polly, and left Bathwick Court as fast as her buckling legs would carry her. Outside, the light was gloomy and the rain had turned from Bath-drizzle to downpour. The door of 10 Great Pulteney Street looked very distant as the young women set off, pulling their umbrellas low over their heads. To keep the shock of these revelations from overwhelming her, Eliza concentrated on not stepping into the puddles that were rapidly forming on the uneven pavement. The hard wooden edge of the box dug into her chest as she held it close under her pelisse and this kept her focussed, her emotions locked away, protecting her from the full tragedy of what she had been told.

They had just begun walking down the long, wide street that led to their door when a carriage pulled up in a flurry of horses' hooves and splashy water. She heard Taz's voice. 'Huzza, Miss Gray! Two drowned rats on the highway!' Eliza looked up into his familiar smiling face, sitting atop the carriage seat dressed in his caped greatcoat, his hat low on his brow.

'Taz!' She was so pleased to see him. Then she realised where Taz went, Lord Purfoy was sure to be.

The door of the smart chaise opened and Raven Purfoy drawled, 'Get in; this weather's for frogs and ducks, and you are neither.' Eliza and Polly bundled themselves in along with their dripping umbrellas. He looked at the two young women opposite, so wet and bedraggled, an amused smile on his lips. '*Mon Dieu*, ladies, you've brought the flood with you.' He flicked some stray raindrops from his immaculate breeches and looked straight at Eliza. 'At least you didn't throw yourself under my horses' hooves like the last time we met on the highway.' But then he noticed her pallor and how close she looked to tears and realised his levity was ill-timed. 'Forgive me, Miss Gray. Is everything well?'

Eliza knew she could not speak of her momentous encounter with Lord Bathwick in front of Polly, so talked of other matters. 'Indeed sir, but Mrs Wolfe is concerned about baby Emma who has a fever and I think we return to London tomorrow.'

He looked immediately anxious and alert. 'I'm sorry to hear that. I'll offer her my fast chaise. I have my own teams of horses stabled at the posting inns along the way so the journey is more comfortable and can be done in two days.'

'That's very kind of you, sir.'

'I would do anything for Corinna and Alick. They are the closest I have to family.' His voice was unusually emotional. When the coach pulled up outside number ten, Polly climbed out before Taz had opened the door and dashed through the rain up the front steps. Lord Purfoy put out a hand. 'Wait a while, Miss Gray. I want to know what's really troubling you.'

His dark eyes were intent on her face and she knew she could not prevaricate with him. She took a deep breath and said, 'I came to Bath to see my long-lost father, the Marquess of Bathwick. However, it seems I am not his daughter but another man's natural child.'

He nodded sagely. ''Tis common enough, but not usually until the first child and heir has been legitimately born.'

Eliza's emotions were in such turmoil she found it hard not to let the floodgates give way. She said in exasperation, 'It may be common enough, my lord, but when you are that child it can be destructive of all happiness.'

Lord Purfoy pulled out his linen handkerchief and handed it to her. He leaned forward and murmured, 'Are these raindrops on your cheeks, or tears?'

His kindness was her undoing. She covered her face with her hands. 'You would cry too if the family you had longed all your life to find turned out to be a monstrous chimera!'

'That sounds most hideous indeed. Do you want to tell me more?'

Eliza took a gulp of air and continued. 'My legal father knew I was the daughter of another man and that my mother loved me, and so to punish her and relieve his own hatred, he paid my nursemaid to lose me in a crowd, here in Bath. I was just seven.'

Usually sardonic and controlled in everything, Lord Purfoy swore. 'Hell and damnation to him! I've never heard of anything more devilish.' He spontaneously reached for her hands. 'And you so young, abandoned to a merciless world!'

His sympathy for her plight was too much for her own control. It seemed a lifetime's tears were ready to fall and Eliza's breath came in hiccoughing sobs. 'My mother never recovered from her grief and died soon after. I'll never know her, or her love,' she said. 'I believed wishing hard enough would make it so. But I was wrong.'

Lord Purfoy's eyes all the time were on her face. 'The past can imprison us and petrify our hearts. I have known this too.' His voice and manner were gentle. 'These painful truths will free you from the tragedies of what has been.'

Eliza pulled the Bathwick ring out of her pocket and put it into Lord Purfoy's hand. 'At the last moment the Marquess gave me this.' He examined the ancient engraving and read out the latin motto. '*Omnia vincit*'.

'What does that mean?'

'It conquers all.'

Eliza looked at him expectantly. 'What does that "it" refer to?'

'It refers to love,' he said with quiet emphasis.

Eliza's voice was bleak. 'It's not a motto the current marquess appears to live by.'

Lord Purfoy took her hand and unfurled her fingers to place the ring in her palm. 'You will find love and live again. Believe me, for this has happened to me.'

In the maelstrom of grief, Eliza knew he was telling her of his salvation through love and with plunging spirits, she recalled her sight of him that morning. She knew now it must have been him, and blurted out, 'I saw you at The Pump Room. I thought you were at your estate and it couldn't be you. But here you are.' She looked up, hoping for a reassuring explanation she knew she had no right to expect.

Lord Purfoy withdrew his hands from hers and gazed out at the pouring rain. 'Yes, here I am. I came to Bath at the request of a friend.' His voice was matter-of-fact.

It was clear to Eliza now, this 'friend' was the new love that had saved him from his past. It should be no concern of hers and would only bring her pain, yet she had to know for sure. 'Is that friend the lady I saw on your arm this morning?'

His eyes met her gaze but all sympathy had fled. 'It's really no business of yours, Miss Gray,' he said coldly, but his irritation was with himself.

'Of course it isn't. But I can't help being disappointed.' Eliza was shocked she had said the words, and how revealing they were of her own presumptuous hopes.

The stricken expression on her face was just as eloquent of her feelings, and her words and forlorn mien wounded Lord Purfoy's heroic idea of himself. The fact that anyone he cared for considered him less than admirable punctured his pride. Anger flared and with it, a mortifying guilt that he had not lived up to some impossible vision she seemed to have of him. His words were stinging. 'You show an astonishing lack of understanding of the world, Miss Gray. I apologise if I do not conform to the ideals of a romantic miss as to how an unmarried man in his late twenties should conduct himself. Would you have me be a monk?'

Eliza's nerves were already frayed to breaking and she wished to get away from the tension between them. She gathered her skirts, held her mother's box tight against her chest, and grasping her umbrella said stiffly, 'Thank you for bringing us home.' In her haste she struggled to open the door but Taz was there and helped her out. His dark eyes missed nothing. 'Don't upset yerself, miss. There's always the 'orses. They don't let ye down.'

Lord Purfoy's voice was once more languid and drawling as he called after her retreating figure, 'Tell Mrs Wolfe that I'd be happy for her to have use of my coach and horses, and Taz too, should she wish to return more speedily to Town. She can send me a note at The White Hart.'

Eliza found Corinna in the small sitting room with Emma, bundled in a blanket, drowsy on her lap, her cheeks cherry-red. 'How is she?' She knelt by her side.

'She seems to be stable but I still think we should return to London as soon as we can. I'm sorry to draw your visit to such a precipitous close.'

'I'm keen to leave myself,' Eliza said.

Corinna looked at her sharply. 'I haven't asked you the most important question. How was the meeting with your father?'

Eliza knew she could not burden Corinna with her own woes when she was so taken up with the dangers to her daughter's health, so merely said, 'He was not what I had hoped. And in fact is not my father after all. But he gave me his ancestral ring and my mother's jewellery box, and for that I am grateful.' She indicated the box still clutched in her lap. Standing up abruptly, she said, 'I must go and change out of these wet, muddy clothes. Oh, and Lord Purfoy is in town and offered you his fast chaise with Taz driving. With his own horses at the posting inns, he says the journey should only last two days. Should you wish to take advantage of his offer, he can be contacted at The White Hart.'

She left and ran up the stairs. The box in her hands was weighted with significance and she could not wait to open it and have something at last that her mother had touched. She stripped off her damp clothes, slipped on a dressing gown and sank onto the bed. The box revealed a tangle of glass and bone necklaces. She carefully separated them and held each close to her cheek, hoping to catch a whisper of her mother's scent. There was a strand of fair hair caught in the clasp of a blue stone *rivière* and for a moment her heart stopped. This was as close as she could come to her.

Removing a cameo brooch of Persephone and a gold ring, Eliza found a small sheet of paper with a list in a neat fine hand.

2 yds Venetian Ribbon, same pink cording, 20 bugle beads, 1 yd silk tassels, celadon plume, 2 linen fichus.

Eliza smoothed the paper with her trembling fingers. This was her mother's handwriting, a meaningless list for the haberdasher but so full of meaning for the daughter who would never know her, except through these tiny personal scraps.

Eliza had piled the necklaces into her lap and was about to replace them when she noticed a small ribbon left in the empty box. She tried to pick it up but found it attached to a flap that opened a secret compartment at the base. Her heart was in her mouth as she slipped her fingers inside and pulled out a small, folded letter together with a miniature painting in a simple gold surround. She found herself confronted by a red-headed man in a tricorn hat with a roguish expression that seemed to challenge her own startled gaze. This face was thrillingly familiar. She could not know the colour of his eyes but something about their shape reminded her of her own. She knew immediately here was her father. Looking for a name, she found nothing inscribed on the back. The letter was yellowed at the edges and she unfolded it carefully. An untidy black cursive script had scrawled on the top right-hand corner, *On board the hellish 'Medusa' that carries me from you.*

Eliza's hands were shaking with the realisation this was a letter from her mother's lover, possibly the man in the portrait, and most probably her true father. She read on:

My most Beloved,

The miles of Shifting Sea that separate you from me rob my Hopes of seeing You and little E again.

How can I Bear this? I hear you in the Wind, I see you in the Bright unfurling Foam, you are the Air I breathe and your Beauty calls to me. I was as Free as an untethered Cloud until I saw You and in that moment Loved you. The Bliss! You Loved me in return and In our path we left a Trail of Light. And little E is the Reward of that Love we shared. When I have paid my Dues I will return to claim

You, the only Woman I have never wanted to Flee. You have Given
my Soul back to me.

It was signed with a flourish of an *R* and splashed with water
marks, presumably from sea spray.

Eliza flung herself back on the bed, pressing the two pieces of
paper and the portrait to her breast. After the anxieties and
uneasiness of the last few days, she felt a peace descend. It
seemed clear to her that her father and mother had loved each
other, that she had been created with love. This settled her
fevered mind and she knew with clarity that she could not agree
to a convenient marriage with Mr Flynn, however much comfort
and wealth he offered. She intended to live for something more
transcendent than friendship, more rousing to the blood than
good sense; even should the cost be that, like her mother, she
died alone.

Eliza also now knew with the same serene clarity that we
cannot control whom we love. She knew she was asking more
than life was disposed to offer by setting her deepest hopes on
Lord Purfoy, a man who had told her his stone-cold heart had
been miraculously revived through love, but for another. This
was her destiny. In this moment of recognition, Eliza felt
magnanimous towards her parents, towards Mr Flynn and the
decisions of his life, the opposing choices made by her friends
Rose Bowman and Marina. For loving, even into a void, was
better than not loving at all.

Eliza dressed hurriedly, put the Bathwick ring in the box and
fastened round her neck one of her mother's necklaces made of
beads of clear quartz. She then slipped into her pocket as a
talisman the note to the haberdasher and her father's love letter,
and descended the stairs for dinner.

Corinna was in a happier frame of mind, having made the decision to return to London in the Purfoy coach with Taz in charge. She excused herself for a minute to check again on Emma. Zadoc Flynn was elated after his rainy day at the races. 'The horses were padnags compared to Ohio, my fleet-footed Pegasus.' He greeted Eliza with ebullience, delighted with his judgement in choosing such an outstanding filly. 'She has every chance of winning the Owners' Race. We've got ten days to prepare.'

Eliza took her place at the table and asked, 'Have you decided on your jockey yet?'

'No. It would be ideal if I could get Taz to ride her. But he's too well-known already in the equine world and they would ken he wasn't Ohio's owner. He's also my arch-rival's prize asset. I could never persuade Taz to ride against Lord Purfoy and Horatio.'

Eliza's renewed lightness of spirit had made her reckless. She surprised herself by saying, with some defiance, 'Well, I don't owe Lord Purfoy my loyalty. If you still want me to ride Ohio, I will do it.'

Mr Flynn leapt to his feet, almost knocking over his chair in his enthusiasm. 'Do you mean it, Miss Gray?' He grasped her hands in his large paws. 'We'll have to embark on some early morning training with a light saddle. Are you happy with that?'

'You overlook an important point, Mr Flynn. What do you do about the fact that I'm not Ohio's owner, nor am I male?' Eliza extricated herself from his enthusiastic hold.

'That's easily overcome. I'll transfer ownership of the mare to you, and you'll ride her as a lad.'

'You ask so much of me!' She gasped as the full enormity of the deception hit her.

'No more than you are capable of, Miss Gray,' he said, his

broad face alight with enthusiasm. 'No more than you did when we went to Tattersalls.'

Corinna came into the room. 'So what's the news?'

Zadoc Flynn was aware of the loyalties between old friends and carefully said, 'I'm entering Ohio in the Owners' Race.'

Corinna frowned. 'That's rather rash; it's Raven Purfoy's race, or rather the race he always wins. He won't be pleased, you know.'

Eliza felt her resolve falter; she was naturally loyal and would be so to Lord Purfoy until the end of time, but she had to remind herself of today's revelation that she was no more to him than an inconvenient responsibility since their collision those few weeks ago. She met Corinna's gaze with pain in her own eyes. 'Lord Purfoy seems to be happy with his new love. He is with her in Bath. I don't see that a horse race will be quite such a priority now.'

Corinna was puzzled. 'Are you sure?'

Eliza wondered if she was being too impetuous in her decision, but the chance of riding Ohio in her first race was an exhilarating thought. 'He implied this was the case. And I had earlier seen him with a woman with whom he seemed familiar.'

Corinna murmured, 'I don't claim to know Rav's heart but that seems highly unlikely to me.'

Eliza did not wish to pursue it; she could barely contemplate any further loss. Everyone she had longed for seemed to have been stripped from her grasp. But what wild impetuosity had sprung her into Mr Flynn's camp, to ride against Lord Purfoy, to deceive her generous, loving hosts? She was close to reneging on her promise to ride Ohio when Zadoc Flynn stood up to go.

'On my last night here I'm off to join the gaming tables at the casino. I'll see you for breakfast.'

* * *

As Eliza rushed from his coach, Lord Purfoy remained deep in thought. He feared his heart had finally broken its bonds and was out of control. But his damnable pride! What damage had he done in not explaining Mrs Cornford to Eliza? She had caught him unawares with her question and had imbued the incident with such unwarranted significance. Now more than ever he knew this was a strand of his emotional life that he must clarify.

Taz's face, streaked with rain, appeared at the door. 'Where to, guv?'

'Back to The White Hart.'

Purfoy entered the front door of the hotel and ran up the stairs, two at a time, to the first floor where he had his rooms. He divested himself of his redingote and hat and without pause, crossed the corridor to knock on the opposite door.

'Come in,' a woman's voice answered, and he walked in to find Mrs Cornford reclined on the sofa in a charming gown made of blue silk and lace and tied at the front. Her eyes met his and her seductive glance became more guarded. His lordship did not look like he was bent on pleasure. 'You seem discontented, my lord?'

He dropped a fleeting kiss on her cheek. 'My apologies, Amelia. How ill-mannered of me.'

'Come sit beside me.' She patted the satin. 'It's seldom I have the diversion of your company for more than an hour or two.'

He sat slightly apart from the voluptuous curve of hip and breast and took her hand in a more formal gesture. 'Amelia, we have been good friends to each other, I hope you can agree?'

She nodded, her expression placid but her eyes betraying anxiety as to what was to come. ''Tis true, my lord. We never aspired to more.'

'I hope you understand that circumstances have changed for me.' He met her eyes with a soft expression.

She smiled, slipping her feet to the ground. 'I always knew this time would come. Perhaps it is you have fallen in love?'

'Indeed, I am shocked at this alteration in myself. So unexpected, in some ways so unwelcome. How much more comfortable to continue as before. But love changes everything, and I am changed.'

He took both her hands and brought them to his lips. 'Thank you, dear Amelia, for your generosity and understanding, for the pleasure we have shared.'

'Well, my lord, we never pretended it could be anything more. I can only wish you but fair weather for the future. She is a lucky young woman.' They both stood up and held each other in one last long embrace.

As they broke away, Purfoy said, 'I know you are staying in Bath to see your sister, but I will be leaving tomorrow. When I'm back in Town, I will ask my bank to set up an annuity. But you are to come to me if ever you are in trouble.' With that he kissed her hand and was gone.

* * *

The following morning dawned clear and bright, perfect weather for a long journey home. Everyone was up early and breakfasted and once again two maids and Zadoc Flynn climbed into the coach and made extra space for Corinna carrying baby Emma, wrapped against the dawn cold but already looking less flushed. The Purfoy coach was the most luxurious Eliza had ever seen, with its navy satin interior and tasselled blinds. She traced her finger over the gilded coat of arms on the door. *Audaci Venus ut*

Fortuna favet. She was intrigued and turned to Taz. 'What does this mean?'

He chuckled. 'Oh that's the Purfoy family motto; 'is lordship is very keen on quotin' it. Summat like, *Venus, like Fortune, favours the bold.*' She looked at him, trying to fathom what amused him so much about his master and his conduct. She wrote it hastily into the small notebook she carried in her reticule. Then she climbed in and they set off.

The large wheels and well-oiled springs meant it was a much more comfortable ride and the horses were swift and so well-matched they seemed to fly over the miles. It was clear to everyone why Taz was considered the best man to drive any vehicle. Under his skilled hands, the whole equipage worked with optimum speed and efficiency. They spent an uncomfortable night at The Rising Sun in Reading and after another long day's travel, rolled wearily into Brook Street.

Everyone fell ravenously on the cold supper Cook had to offer and then hurried to bed. Eliza was delighted at the chance to ride again and looked forward to the morning. Before allowing herself to succumb to sleep, she wrote a quick note requesting a meeting and addressed it to Marina Fairley. She hoped this new friend would help her discover who her real father was and she placed his letter, the miniature portrait and her mother's haberdashery list on the table beside her bed, alongside Mr Fox, and fell asleep with her hand resting on the precious pile of relics.

* * *

Alick Wolfe carried his daughter up to bed. Corinna put a hand on his arm. 'I've been sleeping with her and think I should tonight. The fever seems to have passed but just to make sure she is all right.'

Alick looked down at his wife and said quietly, so as not to wake his sleeping child, 'There's no way you and I are not sharing a bed after these days apart. Emma can sleep in with us.'

'Well then you'll have to help Meg bring the cot in to be beside me.'

After she and Meg had settled Emma, she looked up at Alick. 'We'll get the doctor tomorrow just to check she is truly getting better.' Polly had unlaced her and she was sitting in her dressing gown, brushing out her thick russet hair while Alick, propped on an elbow against the pillows of their bed, watched her. 'Poor Eliza had a terrific shock. Her longed-for father has turned out to be not her father but a monster who, wishing to punish his wife, manipulated a maid to wilfully lose her young daughter in a crowd.'

Alick's smile froze on his face as he sat up abruptly. 'There are some iniquitous people in this world.' Then he met her sympathetic eyes and his face softened as he added, 'How lucky you were with your father – and your husband.'

'I know.' She was ruminative. 'Then this wicked man informed her in the coldest manner that her mother was dead of grief, it seems! But Eliza thinks she has a miniature portrait of her natural father. So we will see if that helps her find out a little more of her family.' As she put down her brush and started to plait her hair for the night she continued, 'And your relation, Mr Flynn, has a wild scheme to race his new horse against Horatio. I fear the ructions.'

Alick sighed. His relation was proving to be rather a trial and he was hopeful that he would move onto the next stage of his Grand Tour and head for Ireland. 'Sometimes excessive wealth can lead to scattered brains and untrammelled appetites.'

'And our dearest Rav seems so out of sorts. I don't want him further upset.'

'Well don't tattle to him. It's not our business and anyway, it may not happen.'

'Eliza said something else that troubles me. She said Rav had indicated to her he was transformed by love – for a woman she saw on his arm in Bath. Who could this be? Has he confided in you, Alick?'

'No. But then it's not something Rav would talk about. *Transformed by love* doesn't sound much like his lordship either.' He snorted with laughter. 'Anyway, I wouldn't have thought that he'd characterise what he feels for Mrs Cornford as anything close to love.'

'You're mistaken, my darling. Something has loosened the bounds round his heart, but I thought it was our beautiful guest who was responsible for that.'

Alick sat up in bed and opened his arms to her. 'I'm tired of talking about Rav's romantic escapades. The bounds on my heart sprang free the moment I saw you felled by a beefy carter's fist. It was suddenly simple. I adore you and am lucky indeed that you love me in return.'

'Shh, don't wake Emma.' Corinna put her finger against his lips.

'I've missed you so much. Come to bed, mistress mine!'

* * *

There was a week to go before the race and Eliza and Zadoc Flynn were up with the dawn to ride in Hyde Park, accompanied by Taz, when almost nobody else was about. Here they could gallop Ohio without being seen and Mr Flynn experimented with the saddle and length of stirrup to see what best suited Eliza. He had seen a few of the jockeys in America shorten their stirrups and ride out of the saddle instead of sitting upright, as they did in England. Taz was impressed. 'Good to lift the bumfiddle off a racer's engine.'

Zadoc Flynn was taken aback at Taz's language and sounded surprisingly disapproving. 'Taz! Don't forget Miss Gray is a lady.'

Taz was unabashed and laughed. 'Lady or not, Miss Gray 'as a bumfiddle along with the rest of us!' He adjusted the stirrups. 'Or would ye prefer summat more fancy like *derrière*?' And he rolled his Rs in mockery.

Eliza interrupted. 'I agree with Lord Purfoy. Taz has such a talent with the horses he can speak how he likes. I'm quite aware that dressed like this and riding off the saddle, my "bumfiddle", as Taz calls it, is more prominently on show certainly than the average lady's.' Eliza turned to Mr Flynn. 'What do you think of Ohio after that?'

'For a trial ride, she looks fine and dandy.' He was happy again and Taz nodded in agreement.

Eliza added her verdict. 'I've never ridden so fast before. She's a wonderful ride, smooth and flowing; it was as if I were winged like a bird carried on the wind.'

Everyone felt exhilarated as they made their way back to the mews. As Eliza dismounted she asked Taz, 'When are you expecting Davey and the Wolfe coach to return?'

He gave a wink. 'Ye mean when's 'is lordship back?'

Eliza coloured and said brusquely, 'No, I don't. I was wondering when Davey was back so he could accompany me on my rides.' But of course it was Lord Purfoy for whom Eliza longed, admonishing herself for such foolishness; it would take time to extract him from her heart.

'Well, methinks two days. 'Tis a slower journey than it would be with me drivin' the guv'nor's best prancers.'

Eliza returned from the stables before her hosts were up and dashed up the stairs to change out of her borrowed schoolboy clothes. She feared most of all deceiving Mr and Mrs Wolfe and wondered what a nest of intrigue she was creating once again. After washing, she slipped into her blue muslin morning dress, rearranged her hair and went down the stairs to breakfast. She was just eating her toast and reading yesterday's *The Times* when Corinna and Alick came into the room together. Eliza sprang up and took Corinna's hand. 'How is Emma?'

The tension had lifted from Corinna's face and she smiled with relief. 'The fever has passed and she had a peaceful night for the first time in three days. I think she was exhausted. I certainly was.'

Alick poured them all some coffee. 'This morning I'll fetch our doctor. You can never be too careful with sickness in the very young.'

Zadoc Flynn came into the room bringing a gust of the outdoors with him. 'Good morning, everyone,' he said in his bluff manner. 'I'm hungry!' He piled his plate with bread, pickle and ham and sat down with a jug of ale and *The Sporting Magazine*.

Alick looked across at him with a smile. 'At this rate you're going to be far too heavy to ride that pretty little filly you've bought.'

'I know. It's hard relying on others but we have some fine jockeys back in Kentucky so I shall just have to enjoy being a spectator of her flying hooves.'

Gibbons knocked on the door and entered. His benign old face seemed to be smiling even when he was not, and Eliza understood just why he was so loved in the Wolfe family. This morning he proffered a silver salver with a letter upon it and, smiling at Eliza, said, 'This is for you, Miss Gray.'

Eliza was delighted to find that it was an answer from Miss Fairley.

Dear Miss Gray,

　　What a pleasure to hear from you. There is much News to share.
Would two hours after noon suit you? I've just read this and wonder if
you agree, 'Alter ipse amicus' – a friend is another self. That is what
you are to me.

　　M F

Eliza held the paper to her breast. How that sentiment
warmed her heart and made her spirit soar! She looked up and
asked Corinna if she could borrow Polly as a chaperone for an
hour or so. She then made her way into the library to finish re-
reading *The Corsair,* feeling all the while consoled by having her
father's letter and mother's list close, slipped between the last
pages for safekeeping.

Miss Fairley lived only a short walk away and Eliza had been
listening out for the chimes of the clock in the hall, counting the
hours. Slipping the miniature into her reticule, her fingers closed
protectively around the portrait, newly found and so precious to
her. Polly was pleased to be coming too on this most perfect of
spring afternoons, fresh, not quite warm, with a stillness that
seemed to suspend the day, birdsong floating in the air. 'No better
afternoon for an outing, don't you think, Polly?'

As they walked through Grosvenor Square, the circular
gardens at the centre seemed to sparkle with new life and for
once there were no carriages or horsemen clattering over the
cobbles. Time stood still. Eliza glanced towards Lady Bassett's
mansion and shivered; how much had happened since that night
of the ball some two weeks before. As the women turned into
Mount Street, Eliza was jolted from her reverie by the bustling
activity of the street and they came at last to a row of modest
houses on the west side where the Fairleys lived.

A maid answered the door and led Eliza through the narrow hallway to the drawing room at the back of the house. Miss Fairley sprang to her feet and dashed forward to take Eliza's hands. 'How good to see you again.' She drew her towards the fire. 'I've asked for tea and some just-baked cakes, if that's to your liking?' The maid closed the door and headed for the kitchen with Polly.

'Well? Tell me what happened in Bath?' Miss Fairley's voice was urgent and excited.

They sat together on the small sofa, the fire warming their faces, and Eliza told her the events that led to the shock of hearing how her mother died and how her father was not her father after all. 'I think the person who holds the clue to my natural father is your dragon aunt, Lady Dauntsey. She knows more than she's telling.'

'She always knows something and withholds more. This way she divides and rules and wields the most power.'

Eliza put her hand into her reticule and said, 'The Marquess gave me my mother's jewellery box and in a hidden compartment, I found a letter from a lover and this miniature portrait.' Full of suppressed excitement, she passed the oval gold frame to her friend.

As Miss Fairley turned it over, she gave a small gasp. 'He looks such a rogue!' she said.

Watching her friend's face, Eliza thought in a flash of unexpected clarity that he looked like Miss Fairley. Something in the brows and the set of the eyes and nose. Could it be he was Marina's reprobate father too? That would make her and Miss Fairley half-sisters. The thought that such a coincidence would unite them was thrilling. But Eliza quickly dismissed it as she had learned that wishing so much for something only led to bitter disappointment.

'Do you think he's your father?' Marina Fairley's eyes were dancing at the thought of this mystery to unravel.

'I do, especially when I read this letter.' She held out the love letter that appeared to mention her.

'Oh, this is so romantic. He really loved your mother, and you?' Marina's voice faltered with emotion and Eliza realised how important it was to feel loved by your parents.

She put out a hand and took her friend's in both of hers. 'Dear Marina, you know something of your father. Do you think this could be a portrait of him? That this is your father too?'

Eliza watched Marina's face lose its merriment, her cheeks, their colour. Gazing again into the eyes of the man in the portrait for what seemed an age, her friend eventually replied, 'I think you're right. He seems so familiar to me.' She held the portrait to her breast. 'What a wonderful thing this would be. To know what he looked like: that I looked like him. But most of all, that we are sisters after all!' She reached across for Eliza to embrace her, the thought of their sisterhood thrilling.

They separated and Eliza said, her voice trembling with excitement, 'I fear we'll have to talk to Lady Dauntsey to be sure, to get to the truth. Will you come with me?'

'Of course! I'd be most disobliged if I didn't.' Marina looked suddenly mischievous. 'In fact, we must beard her in her den and walk round now, uninvited. She lives in Davies Street, just a footfall away.'

Eliza realised there was someone closer to hand who could possibly identify the portrait. 'Would your mother help?'

Marina's face fell. In a low voice she said, 'My mother is so haunted by her heinous sin, I fear for her sanity if I were to confront her with the source of all her shame.'

They were distracted by the creaking door and looked up to see the maid with a tray of tea and cakes. Behind her was a thin, colourless wisp of a woman with darting pale eyes and a disconsolate mouth. Marina Fairley went towards her and took her hand. 'Mother, come and meet my friend, Miss Gray.'

Mrs Fairley hesitated then gave a vague smile as she was led towards the fire. Eliza took her hand and bobbed a quick curtsey. 'How do you do, Mrs Fairley.' The lady said nothing but perched on the sofa where Eliza had sat and accepted a cup of tea from Marina. Eliza found little resemblance between mother and daughter and wondered if all her friend's good humour, intelligence and courage had been inherited from her father.

Mrs Fairley's eyes were on Eliza's face in a pale, unnerving stare. She looked from one young woman to the other and said in a querulous voice, 'Marina, why could you not be as beautiful and charming as Miss Gray?'

Eliza winced, but Marina seemed quite untroubled, answering cheerfully, 'Mother, no one could be as beautiful and charming as Miss Gray!'

'But if you at least tried you might make yourself more amenable to a husband.' Mrs Fairley's voice became an exasperated wail.

'As you know, Mama, I do not wish to marry. I'm more than content as I am.'

'Well, you are a foolish girl to be so obstinate and proud. Marriage saved me from the ignominy of your birth. Every woman must marry, this is an accepted fact of life.'

Realising this was an old sore between mother and daughter, Eliza changed the subject and turned to her friend to ask, 'Miss Marina, how goes your translation work?'

With a wide smile, she answered, 'I'm enjoying it more than I can express. I'm enchanted with Sulpicia. Just six short poems of hers in Latin; they're a love story for her and me.'

Mrs Fairley's pale cheeks flushed with annoyance. 'What

possible use can a facility with Latin or Greek be for any woman's prospects?' She had finished her tea and stood up to leave, putting out a hand to Eliza. 'I'm pleased to meet you, Miss Gray. I trust you'll have a good effect on Marina.' Eliza recognised her as a malign mother, disappointed in life and frustrated by how little sway she had over her daughter's resilient spirit. It was suddenly clear to her that only in the dreams of those who longed for them were families always happy and benign.

Marina led the way to the door. 'Let's collect your maid and see what we can find out from Lady Dauntsey, if she'll see us.' With Polly in tow, they hurried out of the front door into Mount Street, their bonnets on their heads and pelisses flouncing behind them. Marina slipped her arm through Eliza's and drew her close to say in a quiet voice, 'My mother is bitter against my father. Meeting him ruined her life, she says, as if she had nothing to do with it. I know she became obsessed and pursued him.' Turning left into Davies Street and holding onto her bonnet in the breeze, she continued, 'My father was a rakehell, 'tis true, attractive and rich and irresistible to some foolish women, who then wrung their hands when he would not marry them.'

Eliza was struck by this rationale. Did Marina categorise her as one of those foolish women, obsessed with a man who would not love her?

'Is love always a weakness?' she asked as they hurried up the street.

'If you're a Stoic, then yes. The highest virtue is reason.' They had arrived outside a grander house than the Fairleys, with pillars, a portico and a black shiny door. 'Deep breath, Eliza. We're entering the dragon's lair.' They both reached for each other's hands.

The butler asked them to wait in the hall while he climbed the stairs to the drawing room. Eliza had mixed emotions as they were ushered into Lady Dauntsey's presence. She was surprised by how pretty the room was, painted in rose pink with a large butter yellow carpet. In the middle sat Lady Dauntsey, like a black and white magpie in a white lace cap, the prettiness at odds with her severe, forbidding face.

The two young women hesitated at the door and were motioned over by a peremptory hand. 'Good afternoon, Marina, and Miss Gray.' She inclined her head and Eliza once again noticed her compelling eyes, like her own but steely in their cold regard. 'To what do I owe this unexpected visit?'

Miss Fairley walked forward. 'We hoped you could clarify a mystery about who Miss Gray's father may be.'

Eliza added, 'Your cousin, the Marquess of Bathwick, told me that I am not his daughter. As you and I share our eye colours, I wondered if we are in some way related. Could this be so?'

Lady Dauntsey motioned them to the chairs facing her. She was sitting ramrod straight and fixed the young women with a hard gaze. 'Marina knows I strongly disapprove of her father. He happened to be my brother, but all his actions scorned my religion and affronted my God.' She turned to a locked drawer in the table beside her and took out a small package and held it on her lap. 'As for you, Miss Gray, I cannot tell you who your father may be but I know that my brother, Lord Rotherhyde, may well have had many unacknowledged children. I live in dread of who will crawl out of the slime.'

Marina Fairley leaned forward, her voice fierce. 'Lady Dauntsey, your language is very intemperate. For better or worse, he was my father and he may also be Miss Gray's.'

'Well, it is nothing to celebrate, my dear. There's no glossing over the truth. You were both born in sin and your father died of his wickedness.'

Eliza had in her hand the portrait of the man she believed

was her father and felt protective of him. 'I thought our religion required us to practice Christian charity towards others,' she said, trying to control the outrage in her voice. She held out her hand with the miniature and asked, 'Could this be your brother?'

Lady Dauntsey's face blenched as she examined the man in the painting. In a softer voice she said, 'He was once young like this and the world was yet to corrupt him.' She handed the portrait back to Eliza. 'That is Lord Rotherhyde. I nightly pray for his soul.' She then looked speculatively at Eliza, as if uncertain how to proceed. With a sigh, she appeared to have made her decision and handed over the package in her lap. 'When my brother died, his few belongings were sent back to me from Paris. This was found in an inside pocket in his coat.'

Eliza's fingers trembled as she unwrapped the sheet of paper that was folded over something hard. There was a small silver-framed watercolour drawing of a woman with a baby on her lap. Was this fair-haired young woman her mother? Was she the baby in the picture? She could barely hope that she had a representation at last of how her mother looked. Overwhelmed, she could not speak.

Lady Dauntsey said with some impatience, 'Yes, that is Eliza, your mother. It's how I remember her too. I presume the child is you.'

Eliza looked up and met the eyes so like her own, but hers were brimming with tears. 'Thank you. You cannot know what this means to me. To be no longer buffetted on an ocean with neither mast nor sail. You have given me a compass and a map and now I know better who I am. Thank you.' She handed the portrait to Miss Fairley for her to see and only then noticed that the paper that wrapped it had a line in her mother's fine cursive hand. She smoothed it out and read:

*Since your Leaving dimmed the Flame, our Child born of Love stirs
these Embers once again.*

Eliza's heart stopped. She was loved. Her mother had loved
her. Her father too; he had kept the portrait in his inner pocket,
close to his heart. This momentous thought swept away the years
of uncertainty, the loneliness and longing; her empty dreams of
family had been filled and given meaning.

'Well, Eliza, she certainly looks like you.' Marina's words
flooded warmth into every cell of her being. *I'm part of a line of
ancestors. I belong as a branch on this great tree.* Then her friend
continued, holding the miniature of Lord Rotherhyde in her
hand, 'And this red-haired rogue is *our* father. We are sisters!' It
was confirmed. They reached across to each other and embraced,
a fountain of joy bubbling between them.

'I've always longed for a sister!' Eliza said laughing.

'So have I! We've now a blood bond against the world!'

Lady Dauntsey's face turned stony, her disapproval was
implacable. 'I think your behaviour shows a lack of moral education. Rather than unbridled delight in your parents' licentious-
ness, you should exhibit modesty and shame. Neither of you are
born of Christian union.'

Miss Fairley was uncowed by her aunt's thunderous disapproval. 'Surely the Bible teaches us: "First cast out the beam from
thine own eye and then shalt thou see clearly to cast out the mote
in thy brother's",' she said calmly with a smile.

Her aunt was momentarily disconcerted. Then standing to
her full height, she said, 'I wield the righteous sword!'

'More the self-righteous sword!' Marina muttered to her
sister.

Eliza took Lady Dauntsey's hand and gazing into those
remarkable eyes, said with warmth, 'What you have told me

today has changed my life. What you have given me I shall treasure all my days. Thank you.'

The noble lady momentarily relaxed her stance. 'I am pleased I have brought some light to your life. And it is indeed true that the sins of the father should not be visited on the child. I wish you both well, and perhaps we will see each other again. After all, our blood unites us, however shamefully.'

The young women bobbed quick curtseys and fled from the room, Eliza clutching to her breast the priceless portraits and the crumpled piece of paper in her mother's hand. They collected Polly from the hall and walked back to Mount Street first so Marina Fairley would not travel unchaperoned. Marina was once more whispering in an urgent voice so Polly could not hear. 'Sister, I meant to tell you that my despicable cousin, *our* despicable cousin, *he who should not be named*, set off yesterday in a hurry. Can you surmise where he was headed?'

'I have no idea.' Eliza felt the warmth of the conspiracy between them.

'Well, he was speedily to Bath. He had heard that the Marquess was not long for this world and intended to make sure he was there at the end so nothing could come between him and his Bathwick inheritance.'

For all the new-found warmth of sisterly feeling, Eliza felt a peculiar shock that her legal father was nearing death; it was saddening to feel she had never known him and now never would. Sad too that his estate and title would go to a distant cousin who cared not a single jot for him or the property. She turned to Marina. 'What will he do with the house and land? With the Bathwick jewels my mother used to wear?'

'He's an inveterate gambler with prodigious debts. No doubt he'll raise money against the property. Then he can continue at the tables night after night, as is his wont.'

They embraced on the doorstep in Mount Street. 'I am most glad to have found you,' Eliza said into her friend's shoulder.

Marina hugged her closer and replied, 'You're all and more than I could have hoped for in a sister. If you too decide not to marry, perhaps we can live together as two old maids?' She laughed as they pulled apart and their eyes met.

Eliza said in a rueful voice, 'The only man I have ever wished to marry does not want me, and someone I do not care to marry has made me a business-like proposition. I think your suggestion is most attractive.' She squeezed Marina's hand then waved and with Polly, turned for home. As she walked, Eliza considered what lay ahead. As the illegitimate daughter of one earl and the legal but unrelated daughter of a marquess, with neither property nor wealth, she had a circumscribed future, possibly as a lady's genteel companion. Living congenially with her sister was a much more appealing proposition; perhaps she could teach small children to ride?

As they entered the Wolfe house in Brook Street, a rumble of carriage wheels made Eliza pause and watch as a familiar carriage was brought to a halt outside the Purfoy mansion next door. Her heart immediately began its hammering. How much she hated feeling like this, her body's reaction beyond her control. She saw a dark figure climb out, with a certain weariness in his manner. Not wishing to be seen, Eliza moved quickly inside as Gibbons closed the front door. She ran up the stairs to her room, carrying her family trophies she would show Corinna later.

She flung herself on her bed and placed the two portraits together on the coverlet and gazed at them. 'My parents. My family. With me between them.' She then opened the paper that had wrapped the portrait found in Lord Rotherhyde's coat, and read the lines again, written in her mother's elegant hand.

Since your Leaving dimmed the Flame, our Child born of Love stirs
these Embers once again.

She placed this and her father's letter on her heart and folded her hands over her breast, closing her eyes and breathing slowly in and out, savouring the sense of being part of something bigger than just herself.

Eliza was so exhausted by the day's events she fell fast asleep, only to be woken by Polly asking her if she would like to join the family for dinner. She was still deadly tired but dressed and descended the stairs where Corinna and Alick, Ferdy Shilton and Zadoc Flynn awaited.

The meal was lively but Eliza was subdued throughout and became more so when the talk between the men moved to the coming Owners' Race. Nobody but Corinna noticed Eliza's silence and she drew her outside after the first course and asked her if she was well. Eliza confided, 'I learned the name of my true father, Lord Rotherhyde. Perhaps most upsetting is that he died when I was a baby, in exile in Paris due to his debts.'

Corinna took her hand between both of hers and squeezed it in sympathy. 'I'm so sorry, my dear. Fate seems to have robbed you of all your closest family.'

Then Eliza's face lightened and she smiled. 'But I also learned today that I have a half-sister and I could not be happier to be no longer such an orphan in the world.'

Corinna hugged her. 'You seem exhausted. Why not go to bed early; I find the greatest clarity and calm tends to arrive with the morning light.'

Eliza nodded. The idea of her comfortable bed and the oblivion of sleep seemed especially seductive. She bade everyone goodnight and climbed the stairs.

* * *

The morning did in fact bring a certain calm. Eliza lay in her warm bed gazing at the ceiling high above her, thinking she now knew better where she belonged. To have been loved made her orphanhood more bearable.

When she descended the stairs to breakfast, there was a letter gleaming white on the Jacobean chest in the hall with her name in a hand she did not recognise. Opening it, she was struck by the Purfoy crest printed and embossed, with the motto *Audaci Venus ut Fortuna favet* in small gold letters. In black ink his lordship had scrawled, with fine splatterings of ink that gave the impression of having been written at great speed. Dated the previous night, it read:

> *Miss Gray would you honour me with your company tomorrow at eleven ante-meridian Perhaps we could ride to the Park*

Lord Purfoy had used no punctuation and then signed off with a flourishing *P* that seemed to have a life of its own.

Eliza carried the note through to breakfast. Once again she was up early and sat alone with her coffee and a piece of toast. She could not fathom what he could want from her and continued to try and control her leaping spirit at the sight of his person, or even his name. She dressed in her borrowed dark red riding habit that fitted her well, if a little snugly over the bosom, and placed the matching smart hat on her head. She then asked Davey to saddle up Sally and returned to the house to wait impatiently for the clock to chime eleven.

As the first chime died away there was a knock at the door and Gibbons opened it to the impressive sight of Lord Purfoy in his riding clothes; buckskin breeches, high boots and coat, cut more generously than his close-fitting evening apparel. His hat was in his hand and Eliza noticed for the first time his hair was not black but dark brown, caught by the sun as he stood on the doorstep, his distinctive dark brows looking less forbidding than usual. He held out his gloved hand. 'Good morning, Miss Gray. Shall we go and collect our horses?'

They were soon mounted and with Davey behind them, set off for the Park. Lord Purfoy glanced across at her. 'You look very well this morning.' He looked closer. 'I think I recognise that riding habit. It does you justice.'

'Thank you, my lord,' Eliza said demurely, uncertain as to the purpose of this expedition.

It was a fine morning and he seemed to be in a tense frame of mind as he made an attempt at light conversation. 'I've been hearing quite a lot from Taz about your equestrian prowess. It's not easy to impress that tiger, I can assure you.'

She started. Had Taz told him she had been riding Ohio? She calmed her nerves with the thought that Taz was no fool, and not one to gossip. In the coolest manner she could conjure, she said, 'I rate his opinion highly.'

Lord Purfoy smiled ruefully. 'I can assure you, Miss Gray, we all do. He's a stickler when it comes to horse management.' He turned to her, a curious expression on his face. 'He tells me you ride without a saddle and can balance on a cantering horse's back and dance.'

The thought of her outrageous circus act juxtaposed with this austere, patrician nobleman both amused and embarrassed her. 'Only in the right circumstances,' she said in a prim voice.

'Well, perhaps one day there will be the right circumstances for you to show me.' He was not looking at her but a certain excitement suffused her cheeks and she turned away. They entered Hyde Park and there met a throng of horsemen and women, and curricles with teams of glossy horses showing off their paces, the riders and drivers hailing one another. Lord Purfoy was afforded a deal of attention for his celebrated riding and driving skills, and the unmatched beauty of his bloodstock. Men approached on horseback and saluted him, engaging in some desultory chat. Horatio appeared to like the attention and held his head and tail proud while his master was polite, yet distant. His presence in the company of a very striking young woman just added to the frisson of their interest. Lord Purfoy was aware of their prurience and tipping his hat, shepherded Eliza away. They cantered up the slight incline towards Tyburn, Davey following at a discreet distance.

Eliza had only once before seen Lord Purfoy riding freely on Horatio and as she and her horse followed him, she marvelled at the bond between man and beast. Both were dark, big and proud and they moved with such fluid grace in easy unison; she recognised just how difficult they would be for her and Ohio to beat in the coming race. But her eyes were more than professionally interested. Raven Purfoy was surprisingly graceful yet muscular and imperious in the saddle and the sight turned her heart over in a potent mix of recognition and forbidden desire, for who was she to harbour such hopes of his regard?

They pulled their horses up in the shade under a stand of beech trees near the perimeter of the Oxford Road. Lord Purfoy dismounted quickly and was by her horse's side before Davey. He offered Eliza a hand. 'I've seen your trick dismount but I presume in that heavy skirt and riding side-saddle you're not about to entertain us with another gymnastic feat?'

Was he laughing at her? Eliza's voice carried a hint of reproof. 'That was not meant for your sight, my lord.'

His severe manner turned roguish and he surprised her with a chuckle. 'I realised that. It made it all the more enjoyable.'

She unhooked her leg from the pommel and slid into his hands. The intimacy of his touch never failed to quicken her blood from the first night when she recovered her wits after the accident to find him searching for her pulse. This time he was not frantic but measured as he held her waist firmly for a moment, her feet still off the ground. How easy it was for him to hold her thus, how light he made her seem and the thought of his unshowy strength thrilled her again.

'Sir, please put me down. There may be others watching.'

'Do you really think I give a damn, Miss Gray?'

'No, but I do. When a woman has not the protection of wealth or family connection, her virtue is the only thing of value left to her.'

He swung her to the ground, chastened. 'You're right. I can be cavalier with my own name in a way you cannot be with yours. I apologise.' He gave her his arm while Davey took the horses' reins and followed at a distance. 'It seems I have much to apologise for, Miss Gray.' Eliza looked at him with a question in her eyes and he continued quietly, 'Mrs Wolfe tells me my conversation with you in Bath was ambiguous and did not convey my meaning clearly enough. The lady you saw with me is Mrs Cornford, a widow whom I have known a long time. We offered each other a kind of friendship and esteem.' He took a deep breath. It was obvious he found this difficult. 'She has not expected marriage from me and I have not been able to offer it.' He looked into her eyes. 'But it is you, Miss Gray, I was speaking of. And I am sorry for confusing the matter. I am myself confused, unused as I am to this tumult beating in my brain.'

Eliza was wary. She had reconciled herself to mattering little in his life and could not bear any further plunging disappointment. He continued quietly, as if he barely understood his feelings himself, 'For so long I've prided myself on my impervious heart, unmoved by either love or hate. But now that resolve has cracked, the gates of my soul have opened and fear like an assaulting army has stormed in. Fears of loss once more are hammering on my door.' His face had grown anguished with memory. 'When I thought I had killed you with my horses, my heart stopped; you lay on the ground as lifeless as my poor sister had lain all those years ago. It once more felt like a repeat of that nightmare. But this time, I thank God *you* opened your eyes, filled with life, not dimmed by death. I knew then you would live, and that I had met my fate.'

Eliza's chest was constricted as she faced the full import of his words. She reached for his hand to try and steady herself; could she be hearing this right? That in that moment when their eyes first met, he had recognised her as she had him? In a voice full of wonder she asked, 'Can it be you pierced through the careful mask I showed to the world and saw me for who I am?'

In answer he held her hand against his chest. 'Feel that heart-beat, Miss Gray. No longer as slow as a hibernating bear's, now racing like my hunting greyhound in the chase. You have so unsettled me. My thoughts are filled with you by day and haunt my dreams by night. How can I maintain sanity? What am I to do?' Eliza's hand seemed to be vibrating in rhythm with his thrumming heart and the intimacy of that moment was all she had ever longed for; a connection soul to soul was hers at last, and she felt light-headed with joy.

His dark eyes were searching hers. 'Desire and reason assail me. I see the right way and approve it, but then am mesmerised by your eyes and cannot but follow the wrong.'

Eliza's hand was still held by his and she said quietly, 'My lord, what is wrong with following your desires?'

'No man is free without being master of himself. Detachment

and reason were the gods keeping me from chaos. I fear untrammelled emotion; I cannot become a gibbering ghost of myself.'

Eliza remembered his family's crest; wrinkling her brow with concentration, she recalled Taz's translation and quoted it. '"*Venus, like Fortune, favours the bold*" – what of your family motto now?'

Raven Purfoy looked startled, then amused. 'So you're an advocate as well as an equestrian artist and outrageous beauty!' He was once more serious and said with intensity, 'Miss Gray, can I hope that you might grace me with your affection, and teach my poor heart to love?'

Overwhelmed with feeling herself, she wished to answer, 'Yes, yes, yes!' but before she could utter a word, a man on a striking grey horse cantered up to them. Eliza snatched her hand away and turned her face so her heightened colour was obscured by the flaring brim of her bonnet.

'Why, if it isn't the Winged Venus and my haughty Lord Purfoy. I hope I'm not interrupting anything.' Ignoring Raven Purfoy's thunderous look, Lord Davenport continued in his suave way, 'I have had some good fortune. Through a stroke of unruly fate, I have become the Marquess of Bathwick and lord of the Bathwick estates in Somerset. My pecuniary embarrassment is over, thanks to the vagaries of family inheritance.'

'So you are no longer under water with the clubs?' Lord Purfoy enquired with a sneer.

'No indeed. I shall return to the game, my pockets filled with gold.'

'No doubt there will be many gamesters glad to hear that.'

Then as Lord Davenport wheeled his horse round to return the way he had come he said, 'I'll see you at the races, Purfoy. I think it'll be a battle between the black and the white, and this year my ambition is that my ghostly beauty will beat the invincible Horatio.' As he gathered his reins to leave he said, 'I hope you bring your pretty little filly with you.'

Eliza gasped at his wanton talk. She stole a glance at Raven Purfoy. His jaw was set hard and she could see a muscle twitching as if he were attempting to keep his emotions in check. Through gritted teeth he hissed, 'Davenport, that is no way to speak of a lady. Apologise to Miss Gray, now!'

Lord Davenport drawled with his furtive smile, 'I had no intention of disrespecting you or anyone. My apologies, Miss Gray.' He inclined his head and then in an instant he had spurred his horse and was gone.

This crass interruption had broken the mood between them. Eliza was shaken by the news of Lord Bathwick's death, so casually imparted, and said to Lord Purfoy, 'The Bathwick title and estates were my legal father's.'

His face had lost none of its grimness. 'I'm sorry you had to hear of his demise like this.'

'I did know it was close. A friend, my half-sister as it turns out' – she still could barely believe the words – 'told me Davenport had sped down to Bath to ensure no legal deflections in his inheritance.'

Lord Purfoy looked at Eliza with a brooding expression. 'My newly sensitised heart means I now hate as passionately as I love. And I am disconcerted to find how much contempt I have for that man. I intend to deprive him of as much of the Bathwick inheritance as I can. I shall set to work with that purpose tonight on the gaming tables at White's.'

Davey approached with the horses and they both set off in silence back to Brook Street. As they reached the mews, Lord Purfoy drew Eliza aside to say, 'I'm sorry about that rude interruption. I hope this time I've made my feelings clear. With you I have come to see what life is, what love can be. Is it too much of a burden to place in your hands?'

A wave of the emotion of the last few days broke over her. Family loss and gain had wracked her spirit, but most miraculous of all, the man she thought could never be hers was offering her his life.

Her voice shook as she answered, 'From the moment I first saw you my heart was yours. If you will have it.'

He took both her hands and pressed them to his lips. Taz had emerged to unsaddle Horatio and, seeing this last gesture, smiled.

As Eliza ran upstairs to change, a feeling of dread fell heavily on her spirit. She could no longer ride Ohio for Mr Flynn in the race. After Lord Purfoy had opened his heart to her, she could not humiliate or betray him by masquerading as a jockey to compete against Horatio. It was necessary to find Zadoc Flynn immediately and tell him.

Dressing quickly, she asked Polly, 'Have you seen Mr Flynn?'

'Don't think he's up yet. He was out late last night.'

Eliza grabbed her copy of *The Corsair* and went through to the dining room where breakfast was still laid out, ready for any late-comers. Agitated, she poured herself some coffee and started to read, trying to calm her spirit. The house seemed strangely silent. No voices from the Wolfes, no high fluting giggle from Emma, no sound of industry from the kitchens; it was as if she had been left alone on a desert island. She closed her book; the richness of Byron's poetry was drawing her into an imagined corsair's world.

Zadoc Flynn came through the door as silently as a cat. 'Oh, Mr Flynn!' She jumped. 'I didn't hear you.'

'I'm not feeling the best. Don't talk too loud, my head is pounding.' He slumped into a chair and Eliza looked closely at him. His skin was pale, with a yellowish tinge, and his eyes were bloodshot.

'You look sick as a dog.' She quickly poured him a cup of coffee and thrust a currant bun into his limp hand. 'Eat something, Mr Flynn, it might help.'

'I don't think I could let anything else pass my lips without casting up my accounts.' He looked rueful. 'If you'll forgive the vulgarity, Miss Gray.'

Eliza's heart sank. He was not in the best condition for her to deliver her blow, but deliver it she must. 'Mr Flynn, I have something important to tell you.' He cast her a bleary look and she continued, 'I'm sorry but I cannot ride Ohio in the race.' She clasped her hands together to strengthen her resolve.

This news had an instantly sobering effect on Mr Flynn who sat up erect and said, 'Why ever not? It's all agreed. A gentleman's agreement between us.'

'I'm sorry, I should never have said I would in the first place. I did it out of pique with Lord Purfoy and I'm ashamed of my pettiness.'

'Well, Miss Gray, this is no time for finer feelings. It's too late to get out of it. The race is in two days' time and I've already transferred ownership to you. Ohio is entered for the race and you are her owner and rider. You can't back out now!'

'I'm mortified at the trouble I've caused you, Mr Flynn, but I can't beat Lord Purfoy. It's his race to win.'

'Ah, so he or Taz have got to you, have they?'

'No, no! Lord Purfoy has no idea I'm riding in the race. That's the main trouble.'

'Well, there's not much likelihood you'll win. Horatio is a mighty brute of a stallion, strong and fleet of foot. Davenport's flashy grey, Eros, is a likely challenger, not our little filly.'

'But Horatio is being ridden by a big man; he's probably half as heavy again as I am. And Ohio is so light and fast.'

'Then hold her back. I just need her to have been placed in an English race before I take her back to Kentucky. Please, Miss Gray. You're my only chance.'

Eliza's head dropped. He was right. She had given her word and could not renege on their agreement so late. She would have to ride Ohio as if they were in a social race and make sure she did not win and that Lord Purfoy would never find out.

8

IS THE RACE EVER WON?

That evening's dinner was full of the usual bonhomie when the friends were together. Ferdinand Shilton entertained the company with talk of his country estate at Nonsuch, where they would stay for the Epsom races. 'My servants are all atwitter at having the old house inhabited again. It's only half an hour from the Downs.'

Corinna passed him the bowl of roasted potatoes and said to the assembled company, 'I'm staying here with Emma. I don't want to tire her after she's just recovered from the fever. Polly can chaperone Miss Gray.' She smiled across to where Eliza sat quietly, embarrassed by the secret she and Mr Flynn by necessity kept from their friends.

Lord Purfoy also seemed abstracted, gazing into the fire. He stirred and met Mr Shilton's blue eyes. 'Ferdy, it's very kind of you. If my memory serves me right, Nonsuch Place offers mighty fine quarters. We'll be most comfortable, thank you.'

Alick Wolfe handed out slices of beef on the point of his carving knife. 'Rav, I saw your under-groom setting off with Horatio this morning.'

Lord Purfoy accepted the beef and nodded in response. 'Yes, he'll take him down in easy stages and settle him. It's only some fifteen miles away.'

Ferdy had also despatched his hunter. 'I'm riding Avatar this year, my speedy bay. He's young so it's really just practice for him.' Unlike the other owners who tended to be accoutred in sober colours for the race, he insisted on wearing a jacket of canary yellow, a flash of sunshine on the sombre field.

Alick waved some beef at Zadoc Flynn. 'I suppose Ohio's already down at Epsom?' he asked and his cousin mumbled agreement, his mouth full of food.

The wine was flowing freely but Lord Purfoy demurred. 'I have work to do later and need a clear head,' he said as his friends turned their enquiring gazes his way.

Eliza only met Lord Purfoy's eyes once and she quickly looked away, ashamed at her duplicity. She was relieved when he abruptly stood up, ready to leave. 'I'm off to my club,' he said with a certain grimness. He bowed at the men then took Corinna's hand and kissed it. 'Thank you for a delicious meal. I'm sorry we won't have the pleasure of your company on the Downs. Since breeding, you're not as much fun as you used to be.' He smiled his rueful smile.

Corinna laughed. 'Oh Rav, I know you have little time for the squallers, as you so sympathetically call them. And as for my dull character, I have long said that the irresponsible have always been easier to love, as you know full well!' She gave him a knowing look.

Lord Purfoy still had her hand in his and said, 'Well, my dear Mrs Wolfe, never easy nor dull, but always entirely lovable.'

Alick intervened with a snort of amusement. 'Careful, Rav, that's my line. Don't forget she's my wife. You missed your chance!'

Lord Purfoy saluted his friend then he turned to Eliza, his austere features softened with humour and a strange tenderness. She wondered if it was thoughts of Corinna or herself that wrought this change in him. He took her hand lightly in his and she felt the thrill of his cool touch. As if there were nothing between them, he said, 'Miss Gray, I'm pleased you will be joining us at Epsom. I promise it'll be a day to remember.' And without further ado, he was gone, and the energy in the room settled back into predictable comfort.

Mr Flynn expostulated, 'Alick, how can you countenance him treating Mrs Wolfe with such familiarity?'

Alick chuckled. 'We are old friends and he knows Corinna well. He means no harm. It is his way of complimenting her and flattering me. I know where my wife's heart lies.' He looked across at Corinna with a warm gaze.

Zadoc Flynn was a different kind of man and could not see what Lord Purfoy's friends appreciated in this elegant, haughty aristocrat. He too was privileged with everything that great wealth bestowed, but the Flynn fortune had been ruthlessly wrested by his father from the emerging industries of a new republic, and now consolidated by his son. The Purfoy millions were deeply rooted in the mists of time: ancestral lands awarded by the great King Henry for extreme valour fighting the French, nearly three hundred years before. So it was that Zadoc Flynn looked at Lord Purfoy and saw a man with an unattainable sheen of sophisticated confidence and elegant sangfroid who did nothing but race his horses, gamble and drink with his cronies, while Lord Purfoy considered Zadoc Flynn an uncouth adventurer whose recent fortune could not gloss the fact he had barely strayed from his uncultured roots.

The Wolfe cook was famous for her plum pudding and it was brought to the table still tied tight in the linen cloth in which it had been boiled. Corinna unwrapped it with ceremony and started to carve the ball into segments which she placed on plates that were passed around, accompanied by the sauce boat filled with a mixture of butter and brandy. Zadoc Flynn looked down at the slice of bready mass mottled with raisins and said, 'English plum pudding has a reputation abroad. I'm delighted to be able to report back to my family that I've eaten of the pudding that made England great!'

Eliza took a spoonful and it lay heavy on her anxious stomach. Noticing her pallor, Ferdinand Shilton said in his cheering way, 'I think you'll like Nonsuch, Miss Gray. I've asked that the Queen's bedroom be made ready for you. It's called thus because it was my mother's. It's very pretty with a lovely view of the Nonsuch parkland and the distant Downs.'

Eliza smiled at him. Mr Shilton was the kindest of men, without a shadow on his soul. His wealth and angelic looks had awarded him a charmed life through which he moved on winged feet. 'Thank you. I've never been to the races before.' Her voice trailed off as she realised that when she was young, the Prebbles had taken their circus to Epsom Downs for the Derby fair, one of the most riotous days of the year. It all seemed so long ago and she was tired, and happy to withdraw with Corinna and leave the men to their brandy.

Corinna was on her way to check on Emma when she put out a hand to waylay Eliza. 'My dear, may I have a quick word?' She led her into her studio and closed the door. 'I do not wish to pry but I have affection for both you and Raven Purfoy.' She met Eliza's eyes with her own concerned gaze before continuing, 'He has endured some great tragedy in his life. His heart is neither as cold nor as armoured as he may like it to seem. I haven't known him this emotional and vulnerable to wounding before. Take care, dear Miss Gray, I fear you don't know your power.'

Eliza looked at her, startled. 'I would never seek to wound Lord Purfoy. He is the only man I have ever loved. I knew this from the first moment I saw him.'

Corinna nodded, an anxious frown still on her face. 'I understand your sentiment entirely. That first recognition of love is irresistible. But it's not always what's best for us, you know.' She took a deep breath. 'Mr Flynn has told me that he has asked you to marry him and accompany him to New York?'

Eliza's answer was emphatic. 'And I have told him I cannot agree.'

'Are you sure? He's a good man, and with little family to detain you here you would have a comfortable life, an adventurous life in America – and you are an adventurous spirit and full of courage. You should be proud of how you set out alone to make your way in a world too often harsh and hostile to a young woman such as you.'

'Why do you want me to consider him, Mrs Wolfe, when you surmise Lord Purfoy might return my affections?'

Corinna coloured at the direct question. 'You're right, it seems contradictory of me when I want Raven Purfoy to be happy. It's just he's a complicated man and perhaps not easy to love. Whereas Zadoc Flynn is plain-woven and as regular as they come, with a happy gift for optimism.'

Eliza felt a rush of affection for Corinna. She recognised she had a maternal concern for her happiness too. So rare was this in her life, it touched her heart. She put a hand out and grasped Corinna's. 'I know Lord Purfoy is difficult; perhaps with the sensitivities of a thoroughbred, he'll rear up, throw me off and bolt. But when someone has captured your soul, how can you give it to another? I am prepared for the challenges.' She coloured at the thought that she even had a chance. 'Anyway, I'm skilled at handling high-bred stallions.' She met Corinna's eyes and they both laughed.

'Well I'd rather it be you with that particular tricky beast than me,' Corinna said, still smiling. 'I'm very happy to have a steady prancer in my dearest Mr Wolfe.' She kissed Eliza on the cheek. 'Sleep well. I must check that Emma is still peaceful. You see, responsibilities rather militate against the kind of transcendent passion you would live by.' And with that, she turned and ran up the stairs to the nursery.

At last Eliza could climb into bed and sleep. Her candle illuminated with a flickering light the two portraits of her parents on the table beside her and she gazed at them in turn, wondering how strangers could be so imbued with emotion that they seemed completely familiar, as if she had known them for ever. Mr Fox, who had accompanied her through life, sat faded yet alert between them, his beady black eyes seeming to twinkle in the guttering flame. She lay down on the mound of pillows and placed her hand on all three symbols of her family and gave a silent prayer. *Help me, dear God, to do best what must be done.* She blew out the candle and within minutes was asleep.

* * *

The next morning the household was up early. Everyone but Corinna was travelling to Mr Shilton's house that day and there was a festive atmosphere. Lord Purfoy had elected to drive his racing curricle for the sheer pleasure of it, with Taz up behind him organising the tolls on the way. Ferdinand Shilton, Alick Wolfe, Zadoc Flynn and Eliza and Polly were sharing the legendary Shilton travelling coach. When it drew up in stately splendour outside the Wolfes' house, Eliza happened to be gazing out of the window. She gasped at the sight of the vast glossy carriage, shaped like a boat and still swaying, even once the wheels had stopped moving, so deep were its springs. It was drawn by a team of six beautiful, matched bay horses with a postilion riding on the lead horse. Despite her anxieties about her duplicitous role in what was to come, Eliza felt her own spirits rise. An adventure was about to begin!

Mr Flynn and Alick Wolfe climbed into the ship first, carrying a barley scone each and a flask of brandy. Their valets had travelled ahead in Lord Purfoy's chaise with their masters' luggage. Polly accompanied Eliza in a show of decorum as she was sharing the carriage with three men. The women climbed in and settled themselves in the extravagantly padded and buttoned interior. 'I've never seen such a grand conveyance!' Eliza said, stroking the emerald green satin. 'Mr Shilton truly knows how to travel in comfort and style. I almost expect him to have outriders blowing their horns.' She laughed with the ludicrous pleasure of such ostentatious luxury.

Zadoc Flynn looked at her quizzically and said, 'I wonder if I should order myself such a carriage. It would certainly create a stir back home.'

Ferdinand Shilton lived just a stroll away and had yet to arrive. His coachman was on the driving seat ready to go, with the Shilton valet beside him. All awaited their master.

Alick grumbled, 'It's not like Ferdy to be late. Rav, yes, but Ferdy's so punctual.'

Just at that moment a cheerful if rather pale face appeared at the window. 'Apologies, ladies.' Mr Shilton climbed in and settled himself between Alick and Mr Flynn. He lifted his silver-topped cane and rapped on the roof and the great equipage moved off, much to the excitement of two small boys who were passing with their hoops and stopped to watch, faces agog.

'Ferdy, you look a trifle haggard. Did you overdo it at the club last night?' Alick had placed a hand on his friend's knee. Eliza had never seen Mr Shilton look less than rosy with health and bonhomie and he did indeed appear pale and fragile, with shadows under his eyes.

Ferdinand Shilton yawned and answered his friend, 'Kind of you to be concerned, Al, but I was first of all at Lady Ogbourne's rout in Berkeley Square. Such a dull affair. But the night was much improved by bumping into your sister, Miss Gray.'

Eliza looked across at him, surprised and pleased that Miss Fairley should publicly claim their connection. 'I'm surprised she was there. She professes to disdain such society gatherings.'

'Well, she certainly looked pretty unimpressed. She was reading a book in the window embrasure. Miss Fairley was most amusing, relating stories on the dizzy-eyed matrons and their artless daughters, clustering round the few eligible men.'

Eliza laughed. 'She's suffered through three Seasons and no doubt recognises the type.'

Zadoc Flynn was slouched half asleep in the corner of the coach. He stirred to add with a snort of derision, 'What I've seen of the London Season is a damn sight more entertaining than the social scene in New York. Prettier women too.' His eyes met Eliza's before she looked away.

Ferdinand Shilton interrupted with a laugh. 'Don't go judging all English women by the example of Miss Gray. As her sister said to me, she's the *nec plus ultra* of feminine beauty. After she'd explained that she meant the peak of feminine beauty, I could only agree.'

Eliza was both embarrassed and surprised. 'Mr Shilton, you're exaggerating; she didn't say that!'

'Yes, she did, and she also said you were the bravest woman she knew. Has she seen you ride at the Prebbles Flying Circus?'

Eliza had coloured and mumbled, 'No, she hasn't. Only you and Taz have seen me perform.'

Alick was kind and perceptive and he intervened with a laugh, 'Ferdy, stop your yammering. You're boring us and embarrassing Miss Gray.' Changing the subject, he said, 'I'm surprised to see Purfoy up so early, racing his curricle down to Epsom at first light.'

Eliza withdrew *The Corsair* from her reticule, and began to read it again, determined this time to learn the epic off by heart so that it would be with her always. But as she listened to the men's conversation, her concentration slipped from the words in front of her to the thought of a dark lord as he drove down alone with his finest horses, headed for the wilderness of Epsom Downs and the annual gladiatorial combat. Lord Purfoy was almost as mysterious and fascinating to his male friends as he was to her. Ferdinand Shilton said, 'Rav is a law unto himself. I think he has a wager with a friend about who would arrive first. Al, did you see him at White's last night?'

Alick responded with a frown. 'He was deep in play with that hell-begotten dog, Davenport, although that blackguard now insists on being called Bathwick in recognition of his new inheritance. That's your family name, isn't it, Miss Gray?'

He looked across at Eliza who nodded. 'Not that the family wished to recognise me.'

'Well, you'd think Rav was out to avenge you!' Alick continued with some admiration in his voice. 'Ye gods! I've never seen him as concentrated, grim and stone-cold sober.' He glanced across at Eliza.

Zadoc Flynn muttered sleepily from his corner, 'Don't know why everyone's so impressed with him. To me he's just an arrogant nobleman who has earned neither his title nor fortune.'

Alick chuckled. 'Come now, Zadoc. It's your father who earned your millions, so that's a bit rich coming from you.'

The coach had passed through the villages surrounding London and was travelling down ancient drovers' roads sunk between grassy banks with green hills rolling away to the horizon. Ferdinand Shilton sat forward, pointing to the middle distance where sheep were grazing in the shade of a stand of trees. 'Do you see that large clump of mighty oak? That is Shilton land and it means we will be at Nonsuch Place in fifteen minutes.' All the occupants of the carriage leaned forward, alert and expectant.

After following a long driveway meandering through meadows filled with wildflowers and then over a stream, they caught a glimpse of the great house. Nonsuch Place shimmered in the afternoon light, its tall Elizabethan chimneys dominant against the pale blue sky. The lacy stonework framed a mosaic of glittering panes of glass that looked like jewels reflecting the sun. Eliza stuck her head out of the window to better see. 'Mr Shilton, this is the most beautiful building in the land.' Her eyes were round with amazement.

Ferdinand Shilton, born in Nonsuch's great ducal bedchamber, had never called anywhere else home so was always pleasantly surprised when friends were awestruck on seeing his ancestral house for the first time. He smiled as they all climbed from the carriage and stretched their legs, gazing up at the grand front looming above them. The lush parkland, dotted with ancient spreading oak trees, rolled away on all sides. The whole place was beautifully kept with an atmosphere of opulent calm.

Eliza walked into the soaring hallway. Everything sparkled, from the central chandelier with a hundred candles to the windows spilling late afternoon light. Most country houses were left with minimum staff when their owners and the rest of the servants headed for London and the Season. Ferdinand Shilton, however, was keen on upholding tradition and had the means to do so, keeping two complete sets of staff in his town house and his country mansion. Thus, walking into Nonsuch during the Season, his guests were greeted not by dust motes and the musty smell of damp, but by warmth, light, cleanliness and the fragrant scent of burning apple wood in the many fire grates.

'Ferdy, this house never fails with its warm welcome.' Alick clapped his friend on the back.

'My housekeeper, Mrs Plover, will show you your rooms. Tea, cake and burgundy in the library in half an hour?'

Mrs Plover was a handsome woman with a large upholstered bosom and an imperious air. She led Eliza up the wide oak staircase to the first floor and pointed to a bedroom as large as a ballroom. 'That's the master's room.' Then crossing the landing, she led Eliza into a beautiful room lined with blue silk and almost as large. 'This was Mr Shilton's mother's room.'

The room was almost as grand with three windows across, their many panes of glass fracturing the view of Nonsuch parkland into a kaleidoscope of fragmented gold and green. In the centre was the great four-poster bed, its silk curtains falling from a coronet suspended in the dusky heights of the ceiling. 'Thank you, Mrs Plover, it's a room fit for a queen.'

Polly had followed her and stood there awestruck. 'Bless me, Miss Gray!' She unpacked Eliza's clothes, looking askance at the boy's jacket and breeches she found folded at the bottom. 'This house is so grand I feel all atwitter.'

'Don't fear, Polly. It's just Mr Shilton's home, it's not a palace. He is the best of men and I'm sure his servants are equally friendly.'

'It's that housekeeper. Looks as unforgiving as the Gorgon.'

Eliza laughed. 'Really, Polly, you shouldn't let your imagination run away with you. We're only here for a few days then we go back to Town.'

'Will you need my help later to dress for dinner?'

'To save us time, I'll dress now.' Eliza too was rather intimidated by the grandeur of Nonsuch Place, but she would not admit it, even to herself.

Polly headed for the door. 'I'll get some hot water, Miss Gray.'

'Oh, Polly, I'm too tired. I think I'll just put on my dress, spend a little time at dinner, then early to bed.' She slipped on the pale rose gauze dress with the ivory rosebuds round the neck and sleeves. It was comfortable and yet she knew it suited her colouring well. She threw a Braganza shawl around her shoulders as it was chilly in the window seat where she settled with her book. Eliza loved this poem that reminded her of Lord Purfoy, and determined to learn it so well that, like a creeper, it would twine into her heart and become one with her. Carried away in her reading, she lost track of time and a soft knock on the door sprang her from the Aegean Sea and a mysterious and lonely hero.

Polly popped her head around the door. 'Mr Shilton asked me to tell you it is time for dinner.'

In a fluster, Eliza closed her book, dashed to the dressing table and attempted to tidy her coiffure. She had so much very fair hair she wondered how she was going to disguise it tomorrow, under a hat, riding as a male jockey. Anxiety and shame suffused her spirit. She hated the deception involved in keeping her promise to Mr Flynn. Sticking her hairpins back into the relaxed bun on the top of her head, she noticed it was already unravelling into fine ringleted strands round her face. Still wrapped in her shawl, she ran down the stairs, just as Lord Purfoy entered the hall.

His dark eyes imperceptibly changed from their usual narrow gaze. 'Why, Miss Gray, you seem in a hurry. Are we late?'

Eliza was unexpectedly breathless. 'I've been lost in my reading.'

'Still *The Corsair?*' he asked in an amused voice.

'Indeed. I intend to learn it.' Then without thinking she quoted:

> *His heart was formed for softness – warped to wrong,*
> *Betrayed too early, and beguiled too long.*

She stopped abruptly. What had induced her to say that? She had so clearly exposed her feelings for *The Corsair,* and for him.

But the subject of her effusion just smiled. 'Indeed.' He offered his arm to escort her into the dining room and, as she laid her hand on his, he murmured,

> *Yet tempests wear, and lightning cleaves the rock;*
> *If such his heart, so shattered it the shock.*
> *There grew one flower beneath its rugged brow,*
> *...The granite's firmness and the Lily's growth.*

Eliza coloured. 'You know it too?'

'I do. When you mentioned you were enjoying the poem I determined to read it, to keep step with you, to beat with your heart as it beats, follow the story where it leads.'

Eliza felt something inside her unfurl, all tension fled. They walked into the dining room together and she felt entirely at ease, at one with another, no longer an orphan, no longer alone.

Everyone looked up. 'Oh there you are, Rav! And you've

found Miss Gray, too. Come and sit down. It's haunch of venison.' Ferdinand Shilton waved them to their seats as his best burgundy was broached and its ruby liquor splashed into rummers engraved with the Shilton crest.

'As I'm in the position of your honorary chaperone for the night, come and sit beside me, Miss Gray.' Alick Wolfe's avuncular warmth was extended to her and Eliza slipped into the seat next to him while Lord Purfoy was shown to a chair on the opposite side of the table.

The talk between the men turned to last night's gambling. Alick was ladling buttered carrots onto his plate from a dish proffered by the under-butler and called across the table, 'Purfoy, I saw you at White's deep in play. What time did you get to your crib last night?'

''Twas more like this morning.'

'And did you win?' Alick was intrigued by his friend's virtuosity at the tables.

'I'm on a prolonged mission against a dastardly foe.'

His lordship's face was severe in the candlelight and Eliza, her imagination still full of her reading, said, *'There was a laughing Devil in his sneer.'* She thought she had barely spoken out loud but everyone turned to look at her, not certain to what she referred.

Raven Purfoy knew and answered, *'That raised emotion both of rage and fear.'*

Their eyes met as he raised his glass, watching her intently over the rim. Ferdinand Shilton expostulated, 'Don't know what you're both going on about, but luckily you seem to understand each other.'

Still looking at Eliza, his lordship said, 'Luckily, we do.' He put his hand on his dandy friend's arm. 'It's just one of Lord

Byron's poems both Miss Gray and I have been separately reading.'

'Well, that noble cove must know you well – *laughing Devil in his sneer* – he's certainly got your humour to a T!' His friends snorted in amusement and Eliza watched the brotherly comradeship between them. Ferdy continued, 'I hope you're going to beat Davenport in the race tomorrow, otherwise there'll be no end to it.'

Eliza's warm sense of belonging drained away as quickly as if a sinkhole had opened up in front of her, and every good thing in her life was fast disappearing into the void. She looked across at Zadoc Flynn who appeared oblivious to her moral crisis. She would have to speak to him again. She could not ride against Lord Purfoy; this was the man she loved, who seemed to return that feeling – there was no way she could be implicated in such a dastardly plan.

It was difficult to get Mr Flynn alone. The men were all intent on opening the port and discussing playing a few rounds of hazard. Eliza was tired and desperate to go to bed when to her relief, Zadoc Flynn called out to his friends, 'I must get some coin from my luggage.'

As he left the room, Eliza slipped out after him and waylaid him on the stairs. She determined not to weaken by telling herself it was better to betray Mr Flynn and go back on her word than to betray Lord Purfoy, who mattered to her more than anything in the world, even her good name. In a steady voice she said, 'Mr Flynn, I cannot ride Ohio for you.'

He stopped and whirled around. 'What do you mean? Are you ill?'

'No, I'm not ill, but I cannot in good conscience ride Ohio against Lord Purfoy.'

His colour was heightened and his look suddenly exasperated

and condescending. 'Why? Because you fancy yourself in love with the arrogant lord?'

Eliza felt similarly riled. 'No, I do not. But it is a poor way to repay him his kindness to me.'

Zadoc Flynn snorted. 'What kindness? In running you over and cracking your crown? You owe him nothing and you owe me the value of your word. I cannot take Ohio back to Kentucky as a brood mare of the highest quality without winning a place in a Blue Riband horse race in the old country.'

Eliza felt her chest tighten with a knot of panic. 'You didn't mention she had to be placed in the race. I thought she just had to compete and we could come in last.'

'No, fourth, or at a pinch fifth, is the minimum that will be registered.'

'But there is little chance I could ride Ohio to such a placing and not be noticed by Lord Purfoy. I can't risk it.'

Mr Flynn turned steely in a way Eliza had not seen before. 'So with a belated missish sensibility, you are prepared to go back on your word and rob Ohio of her chance of glory?'

This appeal to her respect for the mare and the horse's celebrated future in America did catch at Eliza's heart. She did not want to be the reason for Ohio's failure in her new role as the mother of the next generation of Kentucky racehorses. She was aware her ramrod spine was beginning to buckle. This was something she would have to follow to the end, with the minimum of fuss. 'All I ask then, when the race is over, is that you help horse and rider to disappear into the crowd. If you promise you'll whisk Ohio and me away so no one properly sees us, then I'll ride her. But, Mr Flynn, you have to protect my anonymity.'

Zadoc Flynn took her hand and with a gentle voice said, 'If you married me, Miss Gray, you wouldn't have to worry about your reputation, or Lord Purfoy, or anyone. You'd have a stable yard of beautiful horses to ride and everything you could possibly desire. The offer is still there, should you change your mind.'

Eliza squeezed his hand. 'Thank you, Mr Flynn. I don't disdain your offer at all.'

He turned serious. 'Leave your riding clothes by my door tonight and I'll take them to Epsom in the curricle.'

'Thank you. I'm travelling down with Mr Wolfe and Polly in one of Mr Shilton's fast chaises. He has so many carriages, and even more horses!'

'He's a rich man who loves his bloodstock. As do I.' He was about to resume his journey up the stairs when he paused. 'I'll see you at the racetrack tomorrow. Don't be alarmed. It will all work out fine.'

Eliza returned to wish goodnight to the friends. She put her head round the door to a scene of fraternal merriment. The men had pushed their chairs back from the table, loosened their neck cloths and were settling down for a night of friendly banter and scurrilous gossip, lubricated by countless glasses of Mr Shilton's finest alcohol.

They looked up, their expressions sparkling with delight in their own company. Ferdinand Shilton waved. 'What a charming flower is come amongst us!'

'Goodnight, gentlemen. I will see you in the morning.'

Lord Purfoy looked more relaxed than usual, his eyes glittering and cheekbones flushed. He met her eyes and murmured to the puzzlement of his friends:

> *She bowed her head, and turned her to depart,*
> *And noiseless as a lovely dream is gone.*
> *And was she here? And is he now alone?*

Eliza felt her heart leap in recognition of their private understanding, for this was Byron's corsair addressing his saviour, Gulnare, prepared to risk her life for his. Then Eliza did in fact bow her head, but it was in shameful acknowledgement that she was risking her life not for the man she loved, but to fulfil another man's ambitions, and in the process she was betraying *her* own hero's trust and belief in her. She too turned to depart, her eyelids stinging with tears.

As Eliza was climbing wearily to her room, Polly emerged through the door. 'Oh Miss Gray, I've just left you a pitcher of water. Do you need help with undressing?' She nodded and Polly returned to unbutton her dress and unlace her stays. 'Polly, please accompany me to the Epsom races tomorrow. We'll go with Mr Wolfe.'

Polly's face lit up. She had a liking for Davey, the Wolfes' groom, and an outing to the races was well known as a time of jollity and bacchanalian revelry; they would be able to grasp a short time together to visit the stalls selling gewgaws and various drinks and foodstuffs.

After a quick wash, Eliza slipped into her nightdress and climbed into bed, so tired she hoped to fall asleep without delay. But her mind was filled with contradictory emotions and fear. Not even Mr Fox could settle her unease. He sat on the table by her bed and in the moonlight, one of his beady eyes glinted as if he were watching over her, but admonishing her for what she had agreed to do; for once his guardianship did not soothe her qualms as it had through the years.

As sleep came at last, her waking fears became a series of fragmentary dreams; she was the girl who was prepared to kill to save a corsair from death but he seemed to have assumed the dark good looks of her own lord; she was falling under the hooves of galloping horses, one black like Horatio, one white like

Davenport's Eros. She was caught in a vortex of faces and voices with no way out.

Eliza was dragged from troubled sleep by Polly's knock on the door. Struggling to sit up, she looked towards the window where the early sun was slanting through the curtains, promising a fine day. As Polly walked to the dressing room to sort out her clothes, Eliza felt it was time to confide in her. 'Polly, can you keep a secret?'

'Oh yes, miss.' The young maid's blue eyes opened wide with excited anticipation.

'I've agreed to be the jockey on Mr Flynn's horse for the main race today.'

Polly's cheeks flushed at the mention of such scandalous derring-do. 'That's a brave lark, miss!'

Eliza told her firmly, 'No one knows but you and me and Mr Flynn. You have to keep it to yourself, Polly. I am not proud of deceiving others but I had promised to help Mr Flynn's new mare race to third or fourth place so he can take her to America to establish a new bloodstock line.' These treacherous words sounded to Eliza quite reasonable in her desperation to minimise the plan's potential for disaster.

As Polly picked up a day dress, Eliza said, 'I'm going to have to change discreetly in a stable so luckily that gown has buttons I can reach.' Eliza also determined she would abandon her stays and just wear a spencer over her dress to disguise her lack of support.

'How to hide your hair, Miss Gray?' Polly asked as she brushed out the fine waves.

'Perhaps plait it and then I can pile it under Mr Shilton's old Eton hat I've brought with me.' She picked up the hat and also her cloak, even though it was going to be a warm day.

When she arrived in the dining room for breakfast, the men

who were racing had already departed for the Downs. Only Alick Wolfe remained, relaxed, his legs crossed, reading yesterday's newspaper. He put down *The Times* when Eliza entered and poured her a cup of coffee. 'Good morning, Miss Gray. As you see, we're the last to leave for the races.' He smiled. 'Is Polly ready to join us? It's a festive place on race day and we should set off soon.'

They climbed into the spare Shilton chaise with a team of four glossy bays, with one of their host's grooms driving. Alick Wolfe sat with his back to the horses and seemed as relaxed as a cat in the sun. 'There'll be so many deep wagers today. I cannot bet on anyone other than Rav winning, he'd never forgive me otherwise.' He laughed and with his gaze turned on the lush green hills that marked the approach to the racecourse, he did not see Eliza wince. There was so much greater significance attached to this one race than she had ever considered possible. How naive and foolish she had been! She reproached herself for impulsiveness and misplaced loyalties; into what trouble had they led her? She sat on the edge of her seat, unable to relax.

The chaise turned a corner and there before them was laid out a panoramic scene of the Epsom Downs seething with the most motley crowd of people Eliza had ever seen. Every type of person, from the tinkers shouting out their wares to the working men and women for whom this was a yearly festival, to the grandest noblemen with their open barouches filled with guests quaffing champagne, their grooms handling their horses and house staff serving grand picnics on the greensward. Young men had drawn up their carriages and some sat on the roof for a better view of the course. The Shilton groom parked the chaise alongside another of the Shilton carriages and Alick Wolfe, Eliza and Polly climbed out.

Proud racing steeds were led around the paddock by their

grooms with gamblers eyeing them, weighing up the odds. There were pennant flags flying from wooden sheds where the horses were saddled and jockeys could help themselves to jugs of ale. Everywhere was gaiety and laughter as people milled about the Downs, intent on pleasure. Men and women were dressed in their festive finery; Mr Shilton's sunshine-yellow coat would be entirely unremarkable and Lord Purfoy's habitual immaculately tailored coat and trousers in black superfine would stand out as incongruously urban and austere. The air was filled with the aroma of food being cooked on braziers in small tents, boiling cockles and fried onions and roasting almonds and sweet chestnuts.

Alick Wolfe led the way towards a knot of his friends, huddled discussing what money they would bet on each rider. Eliza took Polly's hand. 'Mr Wolfe, I wish to find Mr Flynn. Don't be concerned, Polly will chaperone me. I'll seek you out later.' She didn't wait for any demur and walked speedily towards the sheds where the horses were being prepared for the important next event, the Owners' Race. The first shed was filled with restless horses and their owners with their grooms. Eliza was alarmed at the prospect of bumping into Lord Purfoy and Horatio and was relieved that he was nowhere to be seen. Neither was Mr Flynn, but the moment she walked into the second shed, he was unmistakeable by his bulk.

He met Eliza's eyes with a smile of relief. 'Miss Gray, come with me.' He led the way into a small room at the back. 'Your clothes are here. We've got half an hour to make it to the starting post.' Eliza quickly whisked off her gown and chemise while Polly guarded the door. Although Mr Shilton's schoolboy breeches and jacket were a little too large, his boots fitted well and were beautifully made and comfortable. Eliza coiled her thick plait into the crown of Ferdy's curly-brimmed hat and then crammed it on her head. She emerged to face Polly's scrutiny. 'How do I look?'

Polly could not hide her astonishment. 'You look very... fine, miss.'

'No, I mean do I look like a jockey? Will I pass as a man?'

'Well, Miss Gray, I suppose you might, but a rather pretty young man.' She looked unconvinced.

'Well, it's as good as I can make it, so we'd better go and find Mr Flynn.'

Together they left the shed and found Zadoc Flynn standing with Ohio's reins in his hands. His wide-eyed glance seemed to suggest he agreed with Polly, that she was not entirely plausible as a male jockey. However, she leapt into the saddle without his help and he began to shorten her stirrups. 'You're athletic enough to ride like our best American jockeys, with your weight out of the saddle.'

'Is this cheating, Mr Flynn?'

As he finished buckling the leather straps, he looked up at her. 'Of course not, Miss Gray. If English riders are fool enough to ride heavy in the saddle like squatting on a stone, that's their choice.' This response did nothing to quell Eliza's anxieties. But when she began to walk Ohio down to the starting post, she felt the horse's spirit and excitement flutter under her. Mr Flynn walked beside his horse, a hand on her neck. She was a small, graceful mare, her dun coat polished and gleaming.

Eliza leaned down to whisper to Mr Flynn, 'I do not wish to be seen by Lord Purfoy.'

'Don't worry yourself with him. He's probably already at the start. The race will begin before he bothers to look at the horses and riders bunched in behind him.' The afternoon was sunny and unseasonably warm, the air growing heavy and thundery. Eliza noticed Lord Davenport's beautiful grey, always a horse to stand out from the crowd. She knew this was Horatio's main rival and she hoped beyond hope that Lord Purfoy would beat him easily, then she and Ohio could melt away in the crowd. Catching sight of Mr Shilton's yellow coat ahead settled her nerves. She would tuck in behind him and then just make sure she could race Ohio into third or fourth place at the finish line, and fulfil her promise to Mr Flynn.

Then Eliza saw him, the only person she longed to see. She felt her soul caught in a gust of passion so unexpected it made her shudder. The power of this new emotion shocked her, but she knew she had to be calm. Strategy was needed in this race, especially as she had never ridden in one before. Horatio was the biggest horse there and Raven Purfoy sat tall in the saddle. They were both dark and striking and once Eliza had seen him, she could not take her eyes off him. How much she loved this man, but what a delicate path she was about to tread. He had no idea there was a traitor in his midst. And she shuddered again, but this time with real foreboding.

Zadoc Flynn patted Ohio and looked up into Eliza's face. 'You know it's a mile. Don't let her have her head until the last furlong. She's the fastest little filly I've ever seen. But hold back that speed 'til the last sprint.' He was about to leave her with the other milling horses and riders but turned back, a soft light in his eyes, and said, 'Take care, Miss Gray, it's a dangerous sport and your life's far more important than glory.' He grasped her hand and kissed it. 'I'll see you at the finish.' And he walked briskly away.

The race entrants were called to the starting line. Eliza's mouth was dry. She looked for Mr Shilton's yellow coat and headed towards his end of the field, well away from the Lords Purfoy and Davenport. The race starter climbed up the ladder to his little wooden platform and raised his arm holding a red flag.

Waiting for everyone to bunch up in an approximate line, he let his arm fall and they were off.

Eliza could feel Ohio's excitement. The mare seemed to have energy pulsing from every cell and Eliza had a struggle to hold her back, but she did try the new riding style of American jockeys and lifted her rear out of the saddle, shifting her weight forward. Ohio sprung down the course in pursuit of the herd ahead. Eliza watched Horatio and Eros take off like primed rockets, so quick they left the rest of the field far in their wake. Clods of damp earth and grass were gouged out of the course by the galloping hooves ahead and flicked into the faces of the pursuing riders and their mounts. Eliza was concerned. Would those two leading horses keep up their blistering pace or tire? She prayed that Lord Purfoy and Horatio could maintain this commanding lead while she husbanded Ohio's speed and remained in the middle of the field.

Riding out of the saddle was an unaccustomed stance for her and put a strain on her thighs and knees, so she sat down for a furlong or two but could feel Ohio's strength and frustration at being held back. The crowd's roar was deafening and where it confused Eliza, it excited her mount. Ohio just wanted to be given her head and run free. To Eliza's consternation, Horatio and Eros, although still well ahead, were themselves tiring; Lord Purfoy's and Lord Davenport's contempt for each other was such that they had both thrown caution to the wind, each intent on leaving the other in the dust, and now their mounts were tiring. It was passion, not strategy, that had dictated their race and their lead was eroding fast.

Just as the final furlong post loomed, Eliza raised herself out of the saddle and let the reins drop in her hands. The crowd and the mass of gamblers who had wagered on this unknown outsider roared with excitement. Ohio was propelled like a bullet just fired from a gun. She stretched out her legs and threw back her head, then with her neck and ears flexed forward, she galloped in pursuit of the front runners, as if her life depended on it.

Eliza felt the pure thrill of speed, being in partnership with a magnificent animal whose fluidity, strength and grace was as one with her rider. She noticed with some alarm that they had easily passed Mr Shilton on Avatar. Too late she wondered if she should attempt to rein in Ohio, but was aware that so much money was wagered on this race that she would be heavily censured if deemed to do anything to alter the outcome.

The dark figures of Horatio and Lord Purfoy were still ahead of her but the gap was narrowing and she felt a terrible sense of imminent doom. It was too late; she could do nothing now to change her fate. Suddenly, as the flags marking the finish were in view, Ohio surged ahead and crossed the line first. The sky was rapidly darkening and as Eliza wheeled Ohio off in a large loop, she could not bear to look at Lord Purfoy. Zadoc Flynn was there in an instant, as he said he would be, and put his hand out for Ohio's reins to lead them off into the crowd.

'Wait a moment, sir!' Lord Purfoy's voice rang out.

Eliza turned and met his scowl, more thunderous than the sky in a face pale with shock. She dismounted and waved for Zadoc Flynn to take Ohio back to the stable and rub her down. Lord Purfoy had also dismounted and Eliza noticed Taz riding up from the starting line, and even his face was grim.

The crowds and horses were thick around them when Raven Purfoy took her arm and steered her to the shade of a nearby tree. Eliza's heart was beating inordinately fast, all her senses heightened. She noticed the raindrop that had fallen on Lord Purfoy's shoulder, the smell of the damp air, the intense stormy light that seemed to gild everything with a greenish glow. There was a sudden gust and Taz looked up at the sky and sucked his teeth. 'A storm is runnin' on the wind,' he said to no one in particular.

Eliza was aware of the pressure of Lord Purfoy's fingers on her elbow, how close he was to her, and she met his eyes at last. He said in a quiet voice full of suppressed rage, 'Is this the way you show your contempt for me, Miss Gray? Disguise yourself, keep it a secret, then humiliate me?'

'No! I'd agreed to ride Ohio for Mr Flynn before you...' Her voice tailed off; she was about to say *before you told me you loved me*, but had he really declared his love? It was so complicated and upsetting that she hastened to add further explanation. 'I only ever meant to ride for fourth – at the most, third place. And I never intended for you to recognise me!' Her voice rose with emotion.

'How could I not recognise you? I'd know that pert profile anywhere, even swamped by a ludicrous hat. And don't forget I've already seen you riding astride in male clothing. Your figure and style are not unknown to me!'

The rain was beginning to fall in large drops that splashed Eliza's face. 'I never meant to win,' she said in an impassioned voice.

'So, it was just an accident you won!' He clapped his hand to his forehead in disbelief. 'That is even more demeaning. I'm riding Horatio flat out yet cannot beat you, a chit of a girl riding a small frisking mare, with no intention to win!' He was pacing, rage, humiliation and disappointment creating havoc in his breast.

Eliza made the mistake of trying to assure him of her best intentions, and added, 'Horatio should have, would have won. It's just you rode him out too fast at the beginning.' She heard Taz's sharp intake of breath. It was a reckless move to criticise his master's horsemanship.

This reasonable but injudicious statement hit such a sore nerve, Raven Purfoy whirled round to face her again, his hair whipped by the wind and rain, his dark eyes blazing. 'Miss Gray, I don't need any lessons from you! I'm a far better judge of horse-flesh and indeed racing than you could ever be. But you've shown me how very poor my judgement is of women and love.'

His words were so bleak and damning Eliza could think of nothing but getting away. She had no horse, Mr Flynn having taken Ohio back to the stables. In her distress, her eye fell on Horatio quietly cropping the grass. Driven by her determination to escape this dreadful debacle of her own making, she leapt onto the horse's back in one balletic move.

'Do not ride Horatio!' Lord Purfoy commanded. His voice was forceful and overlaid with panic. But just as Eliza thought better of her spontaneous action, a deafening crack of thunder over-head made everyone jump and Horatio reared up into the tempestuous air, whinnying in fright. He bolted off back down the racecourse with Eliza on his back clinging to his mane. She struggled to hold on. The reins were inaccessible, dangling down his chest, and the stirrups were too long for her feet to reach; she had never ridden a horse so large, so full of power and will, and Eliza was terrified. The rain was beating into her face, almost blinding her; her hat had blown off and her hair was unravelling and whipping across her eyes. She knew that being thrown at this speed could break her neck and all she could do was cling on, hoping this great beast beneath her would tire of his own accord.

Raven Purfoy lost not a second. He grabbed Taz's horse and threw himself into the saddle to take off in pursuit. He was in the grip of such historic fear, he could barely breathe. The nightmare from which he had been in flight these last seven years was repeating itself and he knew his spirit could not survive the same fatal ending. To protect himself, his heart so newly unfurled began to harden once more to stone. Horatio was ahead of him and the small, bedraggled figure of Miss Gray was still lodged on his back. 'Hold on! Hold on!' he muttered to himself. Desperate not to see her tumble off to lie under the flying hooves, motionless as a rag doll in the mud, he spurred his horse on. Luckily this mount had not been ridden in the race and was fresher than Horatio, but far from as powerful. His bolting steed's headlong gallop meant Eliza and Horatio were soon approaching the starting line, having covered almost a mile.

The rain was still pouring down in rods, lightning occasionally zigzagged across a tumultuous sky and thunder rumbled intermittently over the Surrey hills. The operatic heavens were reflected in Lord Purfoy's emotions as he drew his horse alongside a tiring Horatio. 'Hold on, Miss Gray!' His voice was peremptory. He leaned out of the saddle to grasp his runaway horse by the bridle and then slowed both animals to a canter then a trot, finally bringing them to a halt. He immediately dismounted and put his hand up for Eliza who fell into his arms. She felt safe at last. The fear was over. She had survived and now was held in the close embrace of the only person she ever wished to hold her so.

Lord Purfoy's emotions were more complicated and intense. Despite Eliza's mesmerising proximity and his overwhelming feelings of protectiveness and relief she was alive, a primitive fear had the upper hand. It burst out of him with force. 'How dare you take Horatio! I've warned you before no one rides him. He's too spirited for anyone but Taz and me. How dare you refuse to listen to me, to risk your life like that! So reckless! So selfish!' All the tightly constrained pain and distress of the past came tumbling out of him.

'I'm sorry, Lord Purfoy. I was so ashamed and angry I just

wanted to get away.' Eliza had extricated herself from his arms and stood before him like a drowned rat, her clothes drenched, her fair hair down her back tangled and dark with the rain, her face streaming with water.

Lord Purfoy looked at her, full of life, her spirit bright as the sun, and gratitude to the heavens overwhelmed him. With a catch in his voice, he said, 'I was so afraid you would die, like my little sister, Elizabeth. The person I loved best in the world, the person for whom I was responsible. She disobeyed my order not to ride my horse and was thrown, her neck snapped in an instant, like a twig.'

He put his hands over his face and Eliza realised with a shock what terrible memories she had re-awoken. The rain had begun to roll away down the valley but the sky was still storm-ridden. She put a tentative hand on his arm. 'I had no idea. Why didn't you tell me of this?'

He threw off her hand. 'Because I could not bear to relive those days. And you, in your outrageous wilfulness, have made me do just that. I cannot survive such loss and guilt again. You are as headstrong and as reckless as she, how can I trust my heart to you? How can I love again, give myself to you who are capable of taking me to the edge of reason?'

Eliza gasped at the damage she had wrought. He was right; her wilfulness and selfishness had brought them both close to the brink of ruin. Corinna had warned her of her power over him and she had abused it. Realising this too late, she was filled with remorse and overwhelmed with a sense of mortification. 'How can I atone?' she asked, her face taut with anguish.

His eyes met hers, distant and dead, as he answered in a flat voice, 'By letting me go. Don't fill my heart with longing, don't haunt my dreams. Just leave me to my own designs. It has taken me the years since Elizabeth's death to work out how to survive. I cannot return to that agony.'

Eliza could not bear the bleakness of such a vision. 'Surely love is worth the pain. I too have loved and lost, but isn't denial of love the bitterest of all?'

He had taken the reins of both horses and they began to walk to the makeshift stables. The storm had passed and in the silver light, everything was renewed; the trees were sparkling, their branches dripping diamonds, the sodden turf as green as emeralds and somewhere, birdsong floated on the air. But for Eliza and Lord Purfoy the storm had entered their souls. Staring straight ahead, he said, 'Loving you lifted the weight of grief from me, only for it to return today with crushing force. I realised I could lose you too and I prefer bitterness to demolition and insanity.'

Eliza had no answer and bowed her head, feeling her own weight of grief at what she had done and the gulf between them. He still did not look at her and asked, 'Where is Polly, to chaperone you? Your recklessness about your reputation, your carelessness of your life, makes you dangerous!'

'No one knows I'm a woman,' she said hastily, tucking her hair into the back of her jacket.

'I'm afraid, Miss Gray, you do not make a credible man. You're far too beautiful and your shape gives you away.' His voice was still matter-of-fact and cold but Eliza suddenly felt exposed and self-conscious, keen to dress again in her own clothes, which at least hid the form of her body from the eyes of the world.

Polly came running towards her. 'Miss, I was worried you were caught in the storm. Are you all right?'

'Yes, a horse bolted and Lord Purfoy rescued me.' Eliza was suddenly very cold and her teeth began to chatter.

He took her by the arm and walked her up to her maid. 'Polly, your mistress needs to be in the dry and warm as soon as possible. I'll get Taz to take you both back to Nonsuch Place in my curricle. Five minutes.'

'But you too are drenched to the bone, sir!' Eliza protested. She looked at him standing before her, his hair blackened and spiky with the rain, the shoulders of his beautiful coat oozing damp, water still clinging to his eyelashes and streaking his pale face, and she shivered.

'Don't worry about me. It's more important you get back and warmed up. Shock too can be delayed. You will need some brandy.' He paused, his face harrowed as he said, 'I have told you I love you, and honour you, and would hold you dearest in all the world. But you have flung this back in my face; now give me leave to go.' And with that he strode off, the horses following obediently behind him.

Polly hurried Eliza back to the room behind the stable which had stood in as a makeshift dressing room. She stripped her of the wet clothes and drying her with her own pelisse quickly dressed her in the chemise, day dress and spencer she had arrived in, and then wrapped Eliza close in her cloak, trying valiantly to pin her hair back into a passable bun. Shock had made Eliza's limbs as lifeless as a puppet's, incapable of their own agency. She could not bear to think that in one rash and thoughtless act she had destroyed this man, his love for her, her future with him. He had asked her to let him go; she owed him that respect at least.

Taz arrived outside the tack room, driving Lord Purfoy's flashy greys harnessed to his famous navy blue curricle. He sprang down to hand Eliza up, followed by Polly. They were snug on the seat beside him and Eliza once more felt the familiar warmth of Taz's presence, so like the no-nonsense men she had grown up amongst. He set the horses off for the short drive back to

Nonsuch and cast her a wry smile. 'Well, Miss Gray, ye know how to set the wolf among the fold. Never seen 'is lordship so devil-ridden.'

'I didn't mean to be so troublesome.' Tiredness engulfed Eliza and she found it hard to speak as she laid her head on Polly's shoulder.

'Ye may not mean to be, Miss Eliza, but ye surely are.' It was the first time Taz had offered any reproof of her and it made her already injured heart shrink under the flail. Not another word was uttered while Eliza's soul cried in the silence, *What he requires of me will break my heart but set him free.*

9

THE LONGING FOR HOME

Eliza was so cold she quickly undressed with Polly's help and slipped into bed. Their early return was unexpected and the housemaids had yet to prepare the bedrooms. She noticed the fireplace where last night's ashes lay on the dusty hearth, and shivered; how her heart, her hopes, were now as those ashes! 'Polly, could you ask that the fire be lit for me, please?'

'Of course, miss. I'll bring you some warm broth too. That'll restore you to yourself.'

I don't think anything will restore me to myself, was Eliza's silent riposte. She lay curled up as the bed slowly brought some warmth to her limbs. She had the sense that today marked an end to hope and youthful dreams and the start of her new reality. How more than kind everyone had been to her, a stranger collected off the street, more than generous with their hospitality, but she could no longer be protected by their wealth and charity. She had to stand on her own feet now and decide what to do with her life. The burning question that had fuelled her through her youth had been answered; she had discovered who she was, an orphan now but given a glimpse of parents, although she could never know or speak to them. Her hand reached out for Mr Fox who slumped lopsided by her bed, companion through every vicissitude of her life, and picked up the small box with the portrait miniatures and the two sheets of her parents' handwriting. She folded all to her breast and attempted to draw strength for the future.

Not everyone for whom she had longed was lost to her. Lord Purfoy may have turned away but at least he still existed alongside her in the world. Eliza told herself, *It's enough that at night I share with him the same canopy of stars.* Would he look up and think about her, as she did about him? This thought alone would be enough.

There was a light knock and Polly entered with the under-housemaid who bobbed a curtsey and began to sweep the hearth and stack the new wood. Polly brought a tray with a bowl of chicken broth and set it on the table beside her. 'That'll soon put you right,' she said with maternal solicitude.

As she helped her to sit up, Eliza felt dizzy and her chest and nose congested. 'Oh Polly, I hope I'm not sickening with anything.'

'Nothing that a good sleep won't fix.' Polly was brisk with her advice and Eliza gazed up into her face made attractive by her sweet expression, apple cheeks and the soft curls of brown hair that escaped her cap. She smiled. 'Thank you, Polly.'

'The gentlemen have just returned from the races, full of rois-ter-doister. It's probably best you rest here. They've been cele-brating their successes. All but Lord Purfoy who's black as thunder. He's off to London, before breakfast he says.'

Eliza thanked her and added, 'Would you apologise for my not joining them for dinner? Say I have a chill.' In fact, she felt strangely weak and tearful. Her childhood with the Prebbles had taught her not to cry as it only elicited greater ridicule or chastisement. But she felt like crying now. The last weeks had been filled with so much painful discovery, delight and despair, there had been little time to think about what it meant and how she truly felt. Eliza lay back on the pillows and listened to the crackling of the newly lit fire. As she felt the warmth seep into her body, her mind expanded into freewheeling thought.

These six weeks living with the Wolfes at the heart of London Society had shown her she was not trained for anything, especially not for being a lady. True, she could dance but she could not play the piano and her sewing was of the rough and ready kind. She neither managed light, meaningless chatter, nor was she educated enough to hold her own with discussions about the great classical authors that engrossed her new-found half-sister, Miss Fairley.

Eliza knew now how naive it had been to think she could become a lady's maid. All she excelled at was riding and doing tricks on the back of a horse. With a heavy heart she faced the confounding of her dreams of freedom, but there was the relief too in returning to the familiar, of going back to the life she had known, returning to the circus where she excelled at something.

Over all these thoughts of her future loomed the large figure of Zadoc Flynn who had offered adventure and a business-like marriage from which love might grow. He was an attractive prospect and a good man, but accepting him meant she would travel to America with him and never see Miss Fairley again. Even more impossible to accept was no longer inhabiting the world Lord Purfoy bestrode. Eliza turned restlessly in her bed. How wilfully blind she was, how deluded, to allow her love for this man to so overbear the sensible decision to marry another.

There was a knock and Polly's bright face appeared at the door. 'Miss Gray, Mr Flynn asks if he can see you fleetingly. In my presence of course.'

Eliza felt strangely flustered. Could thinking about someone conjure their presence? She sat upright in bed, feeling dizzy, and pulled the covers up under her chin. 'Yes, that would be possible. Let him come in.'

Zadoc Flynn had been waiting in the corridor and walked in looking shamefaced in a way Eliza had never seen before. He stood quietly at the foot of her bed and said, 'I have to thank you for your extraordinary skill this afternoon, Miss Gray. You have made certain Ohio's value as a champion dam and I could not be more grateful.'

'Well, as you know, I very much regret agreeing to your plan.'

He hung his head. 'I can see how wrong-headed it was of me to insist on your keeping your bargain. It was selfish and I'm sorry if I've caused problems with any of your friends.' He met her eyes as colour flamed into her cheeks, then continued. 'Purfoy's angry enough with me. He won't talk except to tell me you were on Horatio when he bolted in the storm. I'm sorry my taking Ohio so quickly off the course put you in danger and caused you such trouble.'

Eliza gave him a pale smile. 'It's done now.' She was struck by how weary she was. 'Mr Flynn, I must rest. I'm fatigued by the events of the day.'

'Of course. I hope you sleep well, Miss Gray.' He inclined his head. 'I just have to say, you know there was no financial prize for winning the race but it seems fair that I offer you 20 per cent of all Ohio's subsequent earnings in races or as a champion dam.' He did not wait for an answer and left with as little fanfare as he had come.

Eliza sighed; how typical that Mr Flynn's brain for business never ceased. She was too tired to even think what this meant but she knew that even the most generous offer was as ashes and could never compensate for the damage that ride had done.

Polly wiped her hands on her pinafore. 'Well, that man is easier to like when he's less cock-a-hoop.' She then coloured at speaking out of turn. 'Beg pardon, miss.'

'Don't worry, Polly, I know what you mean. But I'm just too tired to think any more.' Eliza slipped down the bed and pulled the quilt over her head. All her natural optimism was exhausted; all her courage and heart that had helped her survive deprivation and difficulty just drifted away, leaving her with a sense of emptiness and loss. Her mind groped for sleep but found only wraiths and shifting shadows.

The voices that haunted her were not a loving mother's; she had been too young to recall her and it was all so long ago. Instead she heard the exasperated echoes of Mrs Prebbles. *Who are you, that anyone could love you?* asked harshly when she came upon her dreaming of a larger world. Perhaps Mrs Prebbles was right; who was she, the discarded child, to hope for a love greater than life itself? She heard the muttering, *Your mother lost you on purpose, you must have been such a naughty girl!* These were the interwoven stories of her childhood, the foundation of her memory, that clamoured in her head when weak or ill. It was hard to stay brave in the face of such ghosts.

As Eliza slipped farther into sleep, a fragment of Mrs Prebbles's kindness floated to the surface of her mind. *Hope for little and ask for less, my dear, that way you avoid discontent.* Now lying in her warm bed in this oceanic room in Ferdinand Shilton's mansion, Eliza wondered if all her misfortune had come from her inability to follow this advice. To have hoped for so much and to have asked for even more; to be reunited with a loving family, but even more boldly to be loved by Raven Purfoy as she loved him, without limit, bound together by Fate for eternity. Was her own lively fantasy of love the source of her downfall?

Eliza smiled to herself; she knew what Corinna Wolfe would

think, what her new sister Marina would say: *Life is not like this, love is not as simple; you will learn to trim your sails to the wind and accept what is.* But Eliza knew this *was* her life, this was her love and how prepared she was to stand by it, even into a solitary old age, the price exacted by her romantic soul. Eliza's mind was as tired as her body and she sank into a fitful sleep, filled with dreams of doors slowly shutting before her while she ran down a dark corridor that had no end. She could not remain in this fearful place but knew not how to awake.

* * *

'Good morning, Miss Gray.' Polly's cheerful country brogue cut through Eliza's dreams while light streamed in from the drawn-back curtains. 'Are you feeling better?'

Eliza struggled to sit up, her eyes squinting against the bright morning. 'I think so. It's hard to tell until I stand.'

'Good. If you are well enough, the gentlemen thought they would set off back to Town once breakfast was finished.'

Eliza climbed out of bed and found the early sun almost too dazzling. Stretching, she rubbed her eyes and stood by the window. 'Storms are always followed by a new-swept day,' she said to Polly while looking out on the deer park luminous in the sparkling light, its ancient oaks spreading their branches low over the tussocky grass. A herd of deer sheltered in their wide embrace and she watched a leash of hares bounding across the sward back to their forms, to snooze away the day.

As Eliza gazed out on this pastoral scene she began to feel the seduction of rural life lift her mood. She would be happy living here, and could not prevent an idle curiosity entering her mind – what kind of estate was Lord Purfoy's?, she wondered. She knew it was in

Hertfordshire and had heard the men talk about its attractions but how its noble owner was so much a creature of the Town that he rarely visited. She suddenly wished to see it, but now never would.

She sat before the looking glass so Polly could help with her hair; even the tangle after the drenching of the previous day did not seem to daunt her busy fingers. She brushed and plaited and pinned and within a short time, Eliza was looking an elegant young lady once more. She had dressed rather hurriedly in the blue cambric in which she had travelled down and Polly fastened her ultramarine wool spencer over the top for warmth. Eliza pinched her cheeks to try and look a little less pale and then descended the stairs, drawn towards the conversation that floated from the breakfast room.

As she stood on the threshold she surveyed a comic tableau of young men paying the price for the night's excesses. All were pale and hollow-eyed, their host Ferdinand Shilton's skin so transparent it had a greenish hue as he stretched with a shaky hand for his cup of strong coffee. Zadoc Flynn had celebrated Ohio's triumph into the night and was looking tousled, his eyes bloodshot, as he slumped in a chair, chin on his hand.

Only Alick Wolfe, always more steady, appeared as usual, but pale and barely able to do justice to the table groaning with the Shilton cook's largesse: bread, a hock of ham, beef in aspic, sweet pastries and candied fruit were glistening in the morning sun. He got to his feet and met Eliza's eyes with a smile. 'Good morning, Miss Gray. You look better than most of us feel!'

Both Ferdy Shilton and Mr Flynn stood up to greet her and pull out a chair. Alick said, 'We have much to thank you for. We all made money yesterday betting on Ohio, such an outsider with long odds. We didn't know until the finish line and Raven flew into high dudgeon that it was you riding the mare.' His face registered his amusement. 'Corinna will reprimand me for not taking greater care of you in her absence.'

Ferdy Shilton was disapproving and said in a weak voice, 'I'm too nauseous to remonstrate, but really, Miss Gray, it's no way for a lady to behave. I only lent my clothes to Corinna when I thought she was a lad; I'd never knowingly approve of a young woman wearing them. I'm with Purfoy. No wonder he's left in a fit of the blue devils.'

Before Eliza could answer, Zadoc Flynn interrupted. 'It's entirely my fault. I put pressure on Miss Gray to ride Ohio for me as I was too heavy for the mare. When Miss Gray tried to back out of our agreement, I wouldn't allow it. I owe her a public apology.' He took her hand and bowed over it.

Eliza's voice was expressionless. 'I must apologise to you, Mr Shilton, for upsetting proprieties when I was taking advantage of your hospitality, and you too, Mr Wolfe, who with Mrs Wolfe have shown me the utmost care and generosity. My deceit may have been necessary but that does not make it any less reprehensible. My sincerest apologies to you all.' She had made up her mind about her next move and added, 'I will be making other arrangements when we get back to Town, and so will no longer be taking advantage of everyone's kindness.'

The men looked abashed. Alick Wolfe was quick to say, 'No, no, Miss Gray, you are no burden on any of us. It has been the greatest pleasure to be able to help you find your family and work out your plans.'

Cups of coffee were once more poured and handed around. Zadoc Flynn said, 'In two days, Alick, I'll no longer be in your hair. I'm off on the next stage of my tour of this island race. I'm off to Ireland in search of my people.'

Ferdinand Shilton snorted. 'When you see the poverty there,

you'll be grateful to your papa that he took the King's shilling to fight in America's Revolutionary War.'

Zadoc Flynn had been born after his father had begun to make his fortune as a fur trader in New York and had never known poverty. However, like the scion of many an immigrant family, he had been brought up on nostalgic tales of home. He had a proud look in his eyes as he said, 'I'm told 'tis the country of poesy and music, where faeries and leprechauns live by the hearth and in the woods. But the people are ferocious as wild beasts and no government can subdue them.'

'Well, sir, you'd better take your pistol then,' said Ferdy Shilton with a shudder. 'Nothing is more ruinous to civility than brutishness and violence.'

Eliza had retreated into her own thoughts while she nibbled on an almond cake. Alick broke into their reveries. 'If we wish to get back to Brook Street well before the light fails, let's be ready to leave in an hour.' Everyone prepared to return to their rooms where their valets and Polly were packing the valises.

There was a light knock at the door and the Shilton butler appeared, imperious in his formality. He wore a powdered wig and the frock coat of the previous century in the Shilton colours of blue and yellow. In his white gloved hand was a silver salver on which lay a letter sealed with scarlet wax. 'A missive for Miss Gray,' he said in a dulcet voice.

Eliza was startled. She immediately recognised the bold, black-inked letters and her hand trembled as she took the folded paper. The wax was impressed with his seal, the ancient Purfoy motto clear in the morning light. Not wishing to read the contents in public, she ran up the stairs to her room. Unfolding the paper, she thought of the meaning of that motto, translated by Taz for her and since graven on her heart: *Venus, like Fortune, favours the bold.* How sorry she was that Lord Purfoy's boldness and her own had been washed away in the storm.

She read his letter with trepidation.

> *My dear Miss Gray,*
>
> *My apologies for our rude parting but perhaps if you can forgive The Corsair you may forgive me too? Lord Byron says it more eloquently than I managed.*
>
> > *And She – the bright and solitary Star*
> > *Whose ray of Beauty reached him from afar,*
> > *On her he must not gaze, he must not think –*
> > *There he might rest – but on Destruction's brink.*
>
> *I just wished to assure you it is my deficiency of heart not yours.*

Then he signed it with a large single P. Eliza could barely control a sob. Lord Purfoy's nobility of spirit, even in the face of disappointment and betrayal, touched her to the core. His taking the blame for their parting filled her with even greater shame. Employing Lord Byron's poetry just amplified the message and speared it straight through her heart.

* * *

The large Shilton travelling coach was pulled up outside the portico, its team of horses snorting, ready for their return journey. Once again Eliza and Polly sat together and the three men were ranged opposite. Everyone was subdued, the men still queasy and tired, Eliza thoughtful and tense about what lay ahead.

The storm-swept brilliance of the light and the burgeoning

countryside was lost on them as they slumped in their seats, drowsy, distracted, inward-looking, while outside the coach windows the market gardens and villages were bright in the noonday sun. When the carriage wheels eventually rumbled over the cobbles of Brook Street, everyone was relieved to disembark and reacquaint themselves with the Wolfes' homely mansion again. Eliza stole a quick glance at the neighbouring house, hoping to catch a glimpse of its noble occupant, but the windows met her eager eye with a blank stare.

As they entered, Corinna appeared, carrying Emma, and ran into Alick Wolfe's open arms. 'I have missed you both so,' he said, lifting Emma into the air and slipping an arm around the child's mother. 'I hope you have been well,' he murmured into her hair.

'You have much to tell me,' she said smiling, and led him through to her studio where she quietly shut the door.

The men went through to the kitchen to scavenge some food from Cook and Eliza ran upstairs to read her letter once more. She knew the passage Lord Purfoy quoted and pondered how the words made their separation a matter of his survival. She could not argue with something so momentous but, on an impulse, took a piece of paper from the drawer and picking up the quill and ink pot that lay beside it, scratched her riposte, again from the poem they were both reading:

> *How strange that heart, to me so tender still,*
> *Should war with Nature and its better will!*

She signed it with her own initial E. Before Eliza could question the wisdom of her reply, she ran downstairs. Gibbons was nowhere to be found and in an impetuous moment, she decided to deliver it herself. Dashing down the front steps and up the neighbouring flight, she knocked on the door. It opened quickly and she was startled to find herself looking up into Lord Purfoy's dark face. His eyes, usually so languid, widened with shock. There was no opportunity to turn and disappear so she thrust her missive into his hand without a word, and hurried back to the Wolfes' house.

Mr Gibbons had returned to the hallway and Eliza was greeted by his cheerful voice. 'Miss Gray, it's good to see you back from the country. I have a note from a young lady whose maid dropped it in yesterday.' He removed a folded and sealed letter from behind the clock on the hall table and handed it to her. Eliza thanked him and walked into the morning room to sit by the fire. Marina Fairley had neat, precise handwriting and Eliza was surprised how pleased she was to see it again, requesting her presence at tea the following day at two.

Eliza was gazing into the fire, contemplating the unexpected arrival of friendship and love in her life, when the door opened and Corinna entered. She looked tired, her pregnancy more noticeable. 'Miss Gray, may I join you?'

'Of course. I'm glad to see you as I wanted to thank you properly for your kindness to me these last few weeks, and particularly to apologise for my deception over the race.'

'It's been our pleasure. Alick told me something of what transpired at Epsom yesterday.'

Eliza felt her spirits falter. 'Yes, I very much regret the subterfuge and dishonesty in riding Mr Flynn's horse. It was a shabby way to treat you all after you'd extended such hospitality to me.' Her voice was formal and subdued.

Corinna took her hand in reassurance. 'I'm not concerned with that. After all, necessity made me masquerade as a young man to seek my fortune. I could not accuse you of betrayal for doing as I had done.'

'I think it's the betrayal of Lord Purfoy that I am most ashamed of.'

'He's proud, and under that cool demeanour is a sensitive spirit, as I know you have already recognised. But I didn't want to talk about him, I want to talk about you.' Eliza looked at her, her expression wary and uncertain as Corinna continued. 'Alick tells me you feel you have no option but to leave us, to make your own way. I want you to know you'll always have a home here, should you need it.'

Eliza was struck with the power of that word *home*. Her longing for a home had been the sole impetus of all her recklessness. She shook her head, holding back the tears. 'That's the kindest offer I've ever had, Mrs Wolfe, but I cannot rely on other people's charity. I have to find a way of living that does not assume the generosity of others.'

'My dear. I was like you, an orphan without family or means, but then a stroke of great good fortune led me to a father who left me in his will this house and the resources to live. This is why it would honour him to share his largesse with you, another young woman disinherited through no fault of her own.'

Corinna then got to her feet. 'I can hear Emma calling for her mama. But remember, Miss Eliza, what I have said.'

Eliza returned to her room to write her acceptance to Miss Fairley and also a letter to Rose Bowman and Mrs Prebble telling them she would be back at the circus in two days' time. She had made up her mind and felt it was now the only honest thing to be done. Having made her decision, Elizer was sadder but calmer. After all, the circus was the closest thing she had ever known to home. Leaving the ease and warmth of the Wolfe house, the friendships of them and their friends, would tear at her heart but it had only ever been a temporary resting place.

* * *

Raven Purfoy was on his way to his club when there was a knock on the front door. He opened it and there was Miss Gray, her face raised to him like a flower, her eyes as startled as he felt. He had determined not to see her while he attempted to regain his equilibrium and return to the settled way of life that suited him best. But here she was, not even bothering to wear a bonnet, looking soft and ruffled as a rose. She thrust a letter into his hand and wordlessly dashed away. He returned to his library and read Eliza's note, an unexpected fluttering in his heart. Her hand was unschooled. It lacked the copperplate flourish of the women of his acquaintance, but the words carefully printed in a pleasing symmetry cut him deep and found their mark. He read them twice, running his fingertips over the paper, feeling the indentation where her quill had pressed:

> *How strange that heart, to me so tender still,*
> *Should war with Nature and its better will!*

He recognised the lines and frowned; Lord Byron had much to answer for. But a slight smile tilted the corner of his mouth and he did not crumple the paper into a ball and toss it on the fire as he had so many missives from women before. Instead, he refolded it carefully and slipped it into his breast pocket. Standing before the fire in his library, he stared into the flames. What was he to do? If he could not love her in the way she desired and deserved, could he give her a gift that would ease the practicalities of her life?

With renewed purpose he straightened his shoulders, picked up his hat in the hall, thrust it over his sleek dark hair and set off at speed for St James's and White's, his venerable club, the den of indulgence and refuge of the noble ruling classes. Here he would find that swaggering whipster Davenport gambling away his newly acquired fortune. Lord Purfoy had a plan that astounded even him and would demand every ounce of skill and courage. Risking his own fortune, he would win back at hazard Miss Gray's rightful inheritance. It was the least he could do for her, to offer her her freedom, then his conscience would be clear.

He walked through Grosvenor Square, resplendent in the sunshine, and was gratified by the thought that most of the grand mansions were occupied for the Season, and by people whom he knew. Raven Purfoy was happy in the knowledge that he existed at the centre of this small acreage of London where more wealth, intelligence, beauty, wit and enterprise were concentrated than anywhere else in the world. After all, he had escaped his family's fortress of gloom with only his title, his wealth and his self-protective pride; why would he trade that freedom to return to the emotional turmoil that had almost destroyed him? Why add the complications of love when he had so many advantages already?

But as he walked on, the clouds obscured the sun and his mood darkened. His comfortable self-satisfaction began to ebb away. How empty his heart was without Miss Gray at its centre; how it ached in an unfamiliar way. His unruly spirit was clamouring that life would never seem as full again because he would not allow himself to love her. Lord Purfoy wondered if in fact he could only be truly himself by accepting this dangerous, unpredictable life of the heart, embracing more than gambling, horses, and unsentimental liaisons with grateful widows or discreet divorcées?

He was soon outside the impressive pillared façade of his club, the famous bow window to his left. Lord Alvanley, the great dandy and buck-about-Town, was not yet ensconced there in his habitual throne amongst the gamesters, surveying the passing beaus, while betting huge sums on improbable wagers. Lord Purfoy hoped he might find him inside. An extravagant man of generous wit and appetite, his company was enjoyed by everyone from the Prince of Wales to Purfoy himself. Lord Purfoy walked up the marble steps, greeted by almost everyone he passed. He was well known and regarded with some awe by his acquaintances who had never got the measure of the man and found his cool sophistication hard to penetrate. True friends were few.

The entrance hall was thronged with men leaving and arriving, some befuddled with drink, a few merry and flushed with their winnings, and one or two white with the shock of having lost a whole ancestral estate or stable of the finest horseflesh in their addiction for the game. Lord Purfoy was one of those rare gamesters whose restraint remained iron-clad throughout, his calculating brain always in control of the baser instincts for risk and excitement, competitiveness and pride.

Suddenly Alvanley was by his side, his large handsome face puffy with excess. 'What's up Purfoy? You look like you've swallowed a wasp. Or you mean business.' Lord Alvanley took him aside and added, 'You know within these walls nothing really matters, so lighten that saturnine countenance, eh?'

'But outside these walls, my lord, some things matter very much indeed.' Lord Purfoy's face remained grim.

'That may be so, but while we're here we cast those cares to the winds, don't you agree? Are you headed for the hazard tables?'

'I am.'

This striking figure led the way. 'Your friend Shilton is in, and that tedious dolt Davenport's been here all day. In his cups and baling lucre like he's a careening ship.' Lord Alvanley had a tall broad body, exquisitely dressed as befitted an intimate of the great and much-missed Beau Brummel. As he walked with Lord Purfoy through the crowd, it parted as if for Moses. They reached the gaming room where tables covered with green baize were laid out for games of hazard, all in full swing.

Lord Purfoy sought out the table where Ferdinand Shilton and Lord Davenport were at play. The pair of dice were customised by White's to prevent any doctored dice being introduced. Raven Purfoy nodded to the caster, then as the other players looked up he greeted them with a curt incline of his head.

Lord Davenport met his glance with blurry eyes and drawled, 'I'm surprised to see you here, Purfoy. Thought you had more diverting sport at home.'

Lord Purfoy ignored the salacious slur and sat in the chair opposite his adversary and next to Mr Shilton who leaned over and said in a low voice, 'They're playing ridiculously deep. Take care, Rav, there are some reckless gamesters here.' He gave a meaningful glance towards Davenport.

'Don't worry, Ferdy, that suits my purposes.'

Ferdinand Shilton looked at his friend askance. Something concerned him about his manner. He knew Purfoy was one of the best mental calculators of odds, but he worried that he seemed set on some form of revenge. Operatic emotion was always dangerous and, when gambling, could be fatal; Mr Shilton eschewed it at all costs.

The caster threw the dice and set the main, and the bets began. Ferdy Shilton was right, Lord Davenport was betting big, but Raven Purfoy eased himself in gradually, winning incrementally, taking more and more of the pot. They had played well past midnight, fortified only by brandy, beef sandwiches and cake and Mr Shilton, pale with exhaustion, stood up and excused himself from play. He put his hand on his friend's shoulder and whispered, 'I'm leaving, Rav, why not come with me? Save it for another day?' Lord Purfoy shook his head and placed a mixture of old guineas and gold sovereigns on the table. His friend knew he intended to remain for some time yet.

* * *

It was early in the morning when only Lord Davenport and Raven Purfoy were left at the table. Davenport was the caster of the dice and Purfoy, white with fatigue, rapped the table. 'Davenport, I suggest we play for the deeds of Bathwick Court and estate, together with Lady Bathwick's jewels.' There was a communal gasp from the onlookers who lounged, brandy in hands, aware that this was one of the biggest games of the club's recent history.

Davenport was deeply in his cups but such a seasoned drinker that it seemed not to impair his judgement greatly. As quick as a whip he replied, 'What do you have to put against such a wager?'

Without hesitation, Lord Purfoy said the words that sent shock waves through the club: 'My whole stable of thoroughbred horses, the teams of two and four and my string of hunters – all – and my brood mares.' Purfoy's eye for bloodstock and his love of his horses was legendary. The quality of the animals in his stables was second to none. He could barely believe he had uttered these profane words and knew Taz would never forgive him; only the lowest form of humanity risked their horses in a wager. Lord Purfoy could barely forgive *himself*. But he knew this was what had to be done to stand a chance of extracting the Bathwick estate from Davenport's destructive grip.

Word had spread fast and most of the other gamesters had broken away from their play to watch this momentous wager. It was the hour before dawn yet everyone was suddenly energised with anticipation and the room went quiet, all eyes fixed on the table before them. There was an intense minute while Lord Davenport considered the wager. He then nodded and picked up the dice, throwing them nervously from hand to hand. 'Just one throw then, winner takes all. Do you agree on your honour, Lord Purfoy?'

'I do.'

The dice were thrown and they rolled to show their faces with three dots each. The crowd murmured, 'The main is six.'

Lord Purfoy had quickly calculated that he had a fractionally increased chance of winning by beating that six. His mission was clear and he could not lose his nerve now. He nodded and the dice were thrown again.

They scattered to the edge of the table and rolled to a stop just by Raven's hand. Both faces showed only one spot. Two aces! The six lost to them.

The onlookers erupted. 'It's an outing. Davenport's thrown out. Purfoy wins!' In that one throw, that one moment in time, an ancestral estate was wagered and lost. Lord Davenport slumped to the table, completely spent. The extent of his drinking finally claimed his wits.

Raven Purfoy felt nothing but plain relief. His head fell to his hands as he was congratulated by the fellow gamesters in the room, slapping him on the back. Unbeknownst to him, Lord Alvanley had also stayed to see the outcome of such a stupendous bet. He pulled him to his feet. 'Congratulations, Purfoy. You've beaten the last record in White's book of wagers.' He then turned to go and took Lord Purfoy by the elbow. 'I saw you arrive on foot. I can take you home in my carriage. It's waiting outside.'

Raven Purfoy's tiredness broke over him like a wave. 'Thank you, my lord, that would be kind. But may I request you don't mention my reckless behaviour to your driver or grooms. Taz cannot be allowed to hear of this wager from anyone.'

Lord Alvanley put an arm around his shoulder. 'I'm afraid you have an icicle's chance in hell of keeping this quiet. The gossip will already be ripping like a gorse fire through Town.' Lord Purfoy groaned.

'Tell me, Purfoy, did you also win that beautiful grey stallion off him?'

'No, how could I? His humiliation was complete. Justice was done. I could not deprive him of the only creature he cares for.' He gave a tired grin. 'Much is the pity.'

Alvanley chuckled. 'Well, he lives to dice another day.'

The handsome Alvanley carriage swayed to a stop in Brook Street. Lord Purfoy climbed down and noticed the blush of dawn already seeping into the London sky with its pale sliver of a moon barely visible to the east, suspended over the spire of St George's Hanover Square. The new day had begun but he was beyond exhaustion. He did not wake his valet so pulled off his boots, discarded his cravat and fell into bed fully clothed. Sleep combined with a deep sense of satisfaction as he slipped into oblivion.

* * *

Eliza was excited to be seeing her half-sister again. Marina Fairley was barely a few minutes' walk away and Eliza stepped out with Polly into the sunny afternoon. Every journey from Brook Street seemed to pass through Grosvenor Square and Eliza recalled with emotion her first experience of a grand Society ball at Lady Bassett's mansion where her life had changed for ever.

As they climbed the front steps of Mrs Fairley's Mount Street house, the front door sprang open. Marina grasped Eliza's hands with delight and pulled her inside. 'How glad I am to see you!' She hesitated for a moment and then threw her arms around her in a spontaneous hug. Polly disappeared down the back stairs to the kitchen and Eliza divested herself of her bonnet and pelisse as Miss Fairley led her into the morning room. 'I've asked Cook for some tea to be brought.'

They sat together on the small sofa by the fire. 'So how was the racing? I'm inordinately relieved to see you well and uninjured. It's the most lethal of sports.' Miss Fairley had been taken into Eliza's confidence about her riding in the celebrated Owners' Race.

Eliza took her hand. 'I so regret my foolishness. I was headstrong and petulant when I first agreed to ride for Mr Flynn, but in honouring my word to him, I ruined my honour and my word in the eyes of the only man I can ever love.'

Marina was struck by a defeated air she had never before seen in Eliza's manner. 'Oh, my dear sister, I feel such sympathy for you. Our passions too easily overwhelm the mind, don't they? I try hard to maintain my reason.'

'This is why I wish to tell you of my practical decision on a way forward for me. Thanks to your help I have discovered who my parents were, but also that I have no inheritance and family, apart from you.'

'Don't forget Lady Dauntsey and her son Davenport.' Marina Fairley smirked.

Eliza met her mischievous eyes with a frown. 'I'd rather forget them. It is you who are my real family.' She straightened her back and took a deep breath. 'I can no longer rely on the kindness of strangers and have decided my only course is to return to Prebbles Flying Circus. Riding is my greatest skill and it's where I belong.'

Marina was suddenly agitated. 'No! No, you cannot! There must be another way. You can't go back to the circus!'

'It has been my home for the last twelve years or so, and I have been happy enough. There is nowhere else for me. I realise it is unrealistic to think of becoming a lady's companion or maid as I'm not practised in any ladylike activity. I cannot become a governess as I'm too ill-educated. I'm not like you, Marina,' she said, her face softening as she looked up at Miss Fairley who was pacing the small room, her expression anxious and perturbed.

'I can't bear you to disappear from my life like this. Come and live with me. As I've said before, my annuity from my grandmother will be enough for us both.'

Eliza had leapt to her feet too and she caught her sister in her arms. 'That means so much to me. To not be entirely orphaned in this world. But I can't live on your charity, just as I can't on the kindness of strangers, like Mr and Mrs Wolfe.'

'But it isn't charity when it's offered with love.' Marina's face was flushed with feeling. 'My affection for you, as a friend, as a sister, has taken me aback. I have tried to live without passion, to make reason supreme; I've sought to be proof against anything, to be invulnerable to disappointment and pain.' She looked deep into Eliza's eyes. 'But meeting you has upended my life. I have realised I cannot live on reason alone. I cannot live without affection too.'

The tray of tea and biscuits was placed on a small table by the sofa and both young women sat down again while Marina poured out two cups. She continued in a faltering voice, gazing down at her lap. 'Forgive my frankness, Eliza, but when I first saw you, sheltering from the rain, I knew I wanted you in my life. I felt your strength and courage, how kind you were, and quick to understand. I recognised then I wished to know you and hoped you would know me too. Nothing would make me happier than to have you live here with my mother and me.' She took her hand. 'Don't go back to the circus, Eliza!'

Eliza was both touched and troubled by the emotion in her sister's voice. It was disconcerting to find her so off-kilter, buffeted by a storm of feelings and a need for kinship as unsettling as her own.

She met Marina's troubled eyes and said, 'I felt the same connection from that first meeting. Since I was seven years old I have lived without a sense of belonging anywhere and then suddenly, there you were. I feel lucky indeed to have found you. But if I lived with your family, what would I do? I have no skills as you have.' She dropped her eyes and in a quiet voice admitted something that seemed foolish even to her. 'You see, I long for a family of my own.'

Marina's face was immediately suffused with understanding and sympathy. She squeezed her hand. 'Of course you do. When you have been deprived of family, then you must make your own, and I will be beside you all the way, offering what encouragement I can.'

For Eliza, to be offered kindness and understanding was a heady thing and she burst out, 'Oh, Marina, thank you! I thought you'd think it foolish and presumptuous when I have so little to offer.'

'I can only wish for what is best for those I love. And you have so much to offer; your bravery, your beauty, your skill and goodness of heart.' They sat together in silence. Then Miss Fairley had a thought. 'What about that American whose horse you rode? He sounds like someone who would be a sensible choice in making a family of your own.'

'He has asked me to marry him.' Eliza paused and met Marina's surprised look with a wry smile. 'It would be more a marriage of convenience for us both. And I'd leave England, and you, my only sister, just as I've found you.' Something made her refrain from adding, *And my heart asks more than such a life can give.*

Miss Fairley's voice cut through Eliza's reverie. 'I've never seen the attraction of marriage. In fact, I don't see the attraction of men. In my experience they just bring disruption and despair in their wake.'

Eliza gave her sister a startled glance. 'How so?' Eliza asked.

'Look at our despicable cousin, for instance. He corrupts every woman who crosses his path.'

Eliza sensed some deeper wound and leaned forward to take Marina's hand. 'He's not harmed you, has he?' she asked, her eyes full of sympathetic feeling.

Marina shrugged. 'When I was too naive to know. But who could I tell? My mother wouldn't have believed me, my father was dead, and his mother would never accept any criticism of her son.'

'Oh, Marina. I'm so sorry. I wish I could have been here to help you. No wonder you have such an aversion to him. I could not dislike him more!'

Marina Fairley squeezed Eliza's hand. 'I have excised him from my heart and mind. I practise my rational philosophy, which helps. But I am gratified beyond measure that after last night's events at his club, he's even brought his doting mother woe. He's just lost half his fortune at hazard!'

'He deserves every ruin.' Eliza was still outraged on her sister's behalf. How unfair that without a fierce parent as protection, a young woman was at the mercy of rich young noblemen like Davenport.

Marina had regained her poise and she continued, 'As you have guessed, it's women who stir my imagination – my grandmother, you, other friends. Our minds are like summer gardens filled with colour, scent and life, while men's are but pavements and railings. How any woman can find romance in that is beyond my understanding.' And she linked her arm through Eliza's.

Eliza laughed. Lord Purfoy certainly liked to cultivate a controlled, civilised manner but she had glimpsed the riot of dangerous emotion and desire that seethed beneath the surface. He had volcanoes under his skin. But it was too painful to contemplate and she put the image from her mind. Turning to Marina, she asked, 'Don't you wish for your own family too?'

Marina shook her head. 'The family I have has brought me enough grief. Apart from my dearest grandmama, the rest think me a disappointment, neither beautiful nor charming enough, too clever for my own good. My mother disdains me and my father never wanted to know me.'

'*Our* father, dear Marina,' Eliza said, eager to share the blood connection for good and ill. 'He cared enough to send you the manuscript you're now translating.'

'He only revealed a flicker of interest in me when I showed some facility in what interested him. Other than that he cared not a jot. I know it's because he did not love my mother, but at least he appears to have loved yours.' She pulled Eliza towards her on the sofa in a brief hug. 'Kindness is an underrated virtue and you have shown me this. I am grateful indeed, Eliza, and selfishly I hope you don't go to America and leave me alone.'

'I think I'd rather return to the circus and with the obstinate unreason of a fool, hope that I will find my path from there.'

Eliza stood up to go and Marina's fervent gaze met her eyes. 'Remember there's always a home for you here. Nothing would make me happier.'

Just at that moment, Mrs Fairley bustled in through the front door with a large striped bandbox. 'Good afternoon.' She hesitated with a distracted look on her face. 'It's Miss Gray, isn't it? My dear, I'm glad you've been entertaining Marina. Such a pity though that it is only shame that unites you.' With that sour remark, she disappeared up the stairs.

As the young women walked to the front door, Miss Fairley whispered, 'Mama is afraid of death, certain that the seduction that preceded my arrival in this world will consign her to the fires of hell. It upsets me that I am her badge of dishonour and sin, and there is nothing I can say or do to console her.'

Eliza took both her hands. 'In that case we are both badges of our parents' sins, but I am very glad that I share this distinction with you, dear sister.' It was suddenly clear to her that Marina Fairley's resistance to emotion was a protection against the maelstrom of blame and guilt at home. Collecting Polly, she set off back to Brook Street to spend her last night under the Wolfes' roof.

* * *

That night Corinna was disconsolate and uncomfortable. The baby was lying against her spine and she had backache. She was also worried about the inhabitants of her house. Things were not going to plan. How much she wished for the ends to be tied in a satisfactory bow, but people were not ribbons and their lives and wills were contrary to order and reason. As she plucked at the coverlet, she thought this was why she loved painting. With her brush she made a pattern of the chaos of life; the lines and colours were all put in their pleasing place.

She wanted to talk to Alick but he was late to bed. She turned restlessly, trying to find a comfortable position in which to lie. The baby was larger than Emma at this stage in her pregnancy and more active, kicking her at inconvenient times and places.

Cook and Polly assured her this was a sign she was carrying a braw boy.

Corinna was just falling asleep when the door opened and her husband entered, his face ghostly in the candlelight.

'Are you still awake?' he whispered as he put the candlestick he was carrying on the table.

Corinna struggled to sit up and said in a cross, sleepy voice, 'Alick! I've been waiting for you. I need to talk.'

He cast off his banyan and clambered into bed. 'I'm sorry, my darling. I stayed drinking with Zadoc. He's off to Ireland tomorrow.'

'Well, Eliza Gray is off tomorrow too, but she goes back to the circus. I'm so concerned for her, but she's even more obstinate than you are! She says she cannot live on the charity of others. But you agree, Alick, we would be very happy for her to live here with us. She could help when the baby comes.'

'Of course. I agree with you on all domestic matters, dearest Corinna.'

He looked pale and tired as he sank back on the pillows and she knew he was hoping she would stop talking and fall asleep, but she had to unburden herself. 'Alick, what did you ascertain about your cousin's marital plans? You know he's asked Miss Gray to marry him?'

'We didn't talk of marriage. He was full of the success of his mare at Epsom. And was excited at tracking down his wider family in Ireland.' He yawned.

'If Miss Gray were to accept him, she'd have a good life. Certainly a comfortable one. There's nothing about his character that gives you pause, is there?'

'No. He's not as interesting as me, of course.' He looked at her mischievously. 'He's a steady but dull dog. Miss Gray's a bit too much of a bright spark.'

'But that's often a good mix, don't you think?'

'Darling, come on now. It's time to sleep. You can't manage other people's lives, you know that. This way madness lies.'

He put out his arms and she settled into them. 'I just want her to be happy. She's such an individual and brave young woman. I recognise my own unpromising beginnings in her story and I want things to work out well in her life, as they have in mine. She knows now she is truly an orphan, with no one to help her. I don't want her to feel alone.'

Alick was almost asleep when he murmured into her hair, 'I wish she'd marry Purfoy.'

This sleepy statement electrified Corinna's tired body and she sat up, propping herself on her arm. 'Why do you say that, Alick? She insists he's the only love for her, but any chance of that having a satisfactory outcome seems to have turned to dust. What do you know that has changed?' Alick's eyes were closed and Corinna shook his shoulder. 'Alick, answer me! This is important.'

He groaned and opened his eyes. 'It's just Rav's so morose. Something's disturbed his spirit. I can only think it's Miss Gray. In my limited opinion, he needs a lively chit like her to take him in hand and lighten his mood. He's no longer much fun to be around.'

Corinna slipped back into his arms again. 'Can't you speak to him about his feelings?'

Alick snorted. 'You should know by now, Rav doesn't talk about feelings. We men certainly don't talk about *his* feelings. We're not women, you know!'

'Well, the least I can do is accompany Miss Gray back to the circus in our chaise. I'll talk to Davey in the morning.' She leaned across her sleeping husband and blew out the candles then gave herself up to wakeful sleep.

* * *

It was past noon when the Wolfe chaise drew up outside the house, Eliza's valise and one of Corinna's portmanteaus filled with her old clothes strapped on the back. Polly had given her a tearful farewell earlier. 'It's been an honour, miss, to help you with your hair and dress, and accompany you on your adventures.' Eliza had hugged her with emotion. It was hard to leave these good, loving people, this warm and comforting place.

In the hall, Alick too was affectionate. When Eliza thanked him for being so welcoming when Lord Purfoy had brought her to his door in the middle of the night nearly two months before, he had taken both her hands in his capacious grasp and kissed them. 'You are more than welcome, and always will be so. You have added such interest and cheer to our lives.' Baby Emma pulled at her skirts and Eliza lifted her up to offer her a kiss.

Zadoc Flynn was getting ready to leave for the next stage of his tour but broke away from his arrangements to take her hand and say with unexpected earnestness, 'You're the finest rider I know and I am privileged that you rode Ohio to such an historic victory. Her illustrious future as a result of your skill will be shared by us both. When I return from Ireland, I will come and see you again, Miss Gray; there may be something I can do that will help and please us both.' With the military formality he had learned from his father, he clicked his booted heels together and bowed over her hand but did not kiss it. 'Farewell, Miss Gray, until we meet again.'

Corinna and Eliza climbed into the chaise and it set off towards the river and Astley's Amphitheatre where the Prebbles Flying Circus was still in residence for the summer. When they were alone, Corinna took Eliza's hand. 'My dear, it has been such a pleasure to get to know you. I recognise so much of my young self in you and want the best for you.'

Eliza's breath caught in her throat. In her young life, so little concern for her happiness or welfare had come her way, and any expressions of such care were irresistible to her. Having been starved of affection, she was overwhelmed when the Wolfes and Miss Fairley offered a liberality of kindness. To sit beside Corinna now and look into her lovely face, full of feeling, and know that someone as she was, with neither family nor wealth, mattered to her, turned Eliza's heart over. 'Mrs Wolfe, I cannot express my gratitude...' Her voice faltered.

'You don't have to. But never forget there is a home with us. You could be a help to me in my confinement. And I would be grateful for a sitter for more of my portraits. You have a particular beauty that is compelling and a challenge to capture in paint.'

Eliza's heart was heavy at her wilful rejection of offers of a life more comfortable than the one to which she was returning. She gazed out of the window as the carriage slowed in the traffic approaching Westminster Bridge. Horsemen, curricles, carriages and countless carts loaded with produce and firewood were jostling for preference. 'I haven't been this far east before,' Corinna said, then pointed at the turreted red-brick edifice beyond the trees. 'That must be Lambeth Palace. I wonder if old Lord Charles is in residence today.'

The Wolfe carriage started up the incline to the bridge and suddenly they were traversing the great grey-green river. Eliza had last passed this way at dead of night, on foot and whipped by a bitter wind. Now in comfort, she gazed out on the wide watery highway filled with a number of stately barges, with one and two sails flapping in the breeze. As they plied their trade up and down the river, small rowing skiffs weaved their way between them. Eliza's eye caught sight of a huge barge that looked like a floating house. 'Look at that! Imagine living on the river!'

Corinna craned her neck too, eager to see the sights. 'All the boatbuilders ranged down this bank of the Thames. Such industry!'

Eliza knew this part of the riverbank well. 'Yes, Astley's is just behind that large boatyard to the right. We're nearly there.' A part of her wished she could stay with Mrs Wolfe in this warm, safe space for ever but she knew she had to make her way in the world. The chaise rolled to a stop outside the impressive building and Eliza leaned across to Corinna and gave her a spontaneous hug. 'Thank you,' was all she could trust herself to say as she hurried out. The coachman carried her bags round the back to the stables and she followed, her heart skipping a beat. There was Percy, gleaming black in the sunshine, his dark lustrous eyes watching for her as his head turned to the left and then right and he snuffled the air.

With a cry Eliza dashed to his stable, wrenched the door open and threw her arms around his neck. She burst into tears. Whinnying softly, Percy bent his noble head and laid it lightly against her cheek. Wherever Percy was, she had a kind of home.

10

VENUS, LIKE FORTUNE, FAVOURS THE BOLD

Rose Bowman came tumbling down the steps from the accommodation above the stables and threw herself into Eliza's arms. 'You're back! How good it is to see you!' She picked up the heaviest of Eliza's portmanteaus and led the way up the steps to their shared room. 'Missed you so.'

Mrs Prebbles bustled out of the office as they passed. When she saw Eliza she stood four-square, her hands on her hips and a look of satisfaction on her rosy face. 'So, Miss Eliza, ye're home. Didn't think yer adventure would last too long.' She was about to return to her work but paused and added, 'We missed ye, the show missed ye. Glad to see ye returned to us, ready to work tonight I 'ope.' This was not a question but a statement, and Eliza nodded.

Rose pulled her into their room and closed the door. 'Well? What made you come back?'

Eliza was weary and overwhelmed with emotion. She did not care to catalogue the complexity of fact and feeling that had propelled her return. Instead, she said, 'I discovered I was truly an orphan and there was no home waiting for me as I had hoped. Through the kindness of a new-found sister and new friends, I was offered somewhere to stay, but I cannot live off others. So here I am. Back to the only work I know I'm good for.'

Rose Bowman was full of high spirits and seemed not to mind the meagre information offered by her friend, she had so much of her own news to impart. 'Saw Mr Flynn last night and he says when he's back from Ireland, he will take me to America with him. There's a job waiting with Flynn's Furs, his father's trading company.' She was bouncing up and down on the bed with excitement at the thought of travel and new horizons beyond her imaginings.

'Rose, do you like and trust him enough to tie your future, at least for a time, with his?' Eliza could not but be affected by her friend's exuberance and had no wish to see her disappointed and betrayed. Thus she felt compelled to raise the question that troubled her. 'You know Mr Flynn also asked me to marry him?'

Rose's enthusiasm was undimmed. 'Oh yes! He said he had mind of you for a wife. Imagine if we both went to the Americas together!'

'But how would that change what he meant to you, Rose?'

Miss Bowman looked at her askance. 'Don't care for him, beyond a rich cove who offers a different game in a new country. Told me once he married, I'd no longer be his girl.'

'And you don't mind?'

Rose scoffed. She was always a realistic young woman who recognised a good opportunity when it arrived. She had no time for the romantic sensibility that fuelled Eliza's life. 'Told you, Eliza, I'm not sweet on him. He's just my key to the door. But if you marry him, he'll be good to you. He's rich, richer than all the coves hanging around Astley's trying for favours.'

Eliza sighed with an intensity of emotion that seemed to

come from the depths of her being. 'I don't want to marry him, Rose.'

'Why not? You couldn't do better. What a fine do we'd have in New York; that's where he lives, ain't it?'

'It is. And at his stud farm in Kentucky.'

Rose whistled through her teeth. 'See what I mean? You love the prancers. Are you dicked in the nob, or what?'

Eliza couldn't prevent a gust of laughter. 'I must be "dicked in the nob" as you so elegantly put it. He offers me everything but love.'

'Pah! The sooner you give up such fancies the better. Girls with nothing must take what they can.'

Eliza changed the subject. 'It's probably time we got ready for tonight's performance. Has anything changed I need to know of?'

'No, it's the same performance. That young girl, Maria, took your place but fell off a few times, and the punters kept on complaining. Wanted you back.'

Eliza's smile was wan as she said, 'Well they've got their way.' She gazed around the room and thought how stark the contrast with the luxury and comfort of the life she had glimpsed while living with the Wolfes. By some lights she seemed obstinate and fool-headed to turn her back on that to return to a life as modest as this, yet she knew it was degrading to her spirit to accept utter dependency on friends, even the kindest. By returning to her work, she earned her own meagre wages and perhaps, with her share of Ohio's winnings and fees, could save for her own home one day.

Eliza fortified herself with these certain facts; she had her freedom, she was no longer adrift and alone now she had found a sister and some friends; against the odds her adventure had worked out well for she had found who her parents were, been shown the golden liquor of life, and offered a dram. But while she concentrated on the propitious, she could not erase the longing that weighed like lead in her chest. Her heart ached with missing him.

She had loved Lord Byron for his poetry but it was Lord Purfoy who had taught her what the words meant. For his own reasons he had rejected her, yet against all good sense, she knew that he would come. Some day her lord would come for her and she would know his tread upon the stair.

She and Rose once again dressed in their costumes for the night's performance, Rose as a highwaywoman, a saucy moll of the high road, jacketed and overborne with pistols that fired blanks, while Eliza was once again masked and plumed as Clorinda the Winged Venus. They made their way to the stables to collect their horses, suitably accoutred by the stable boy. Rose's was saddled with bags full of stolen loot and Percy arrayed in a feathered harness, with gold leather wings strapped to the fetlocks of his back legs to give the impression he had wings on his heels.

They could hear the roar of the crowd even before they arrived. The clowns were going through their routine and the customers were excited, many riotous with cheap ale. As the two young women rode into the circular arena, the cheers were deafening. Eliza heard shouts of *She's back! Our pretty Venus rides again!* as she stood on Percy's back, holding only his reins, while he cantered steadily in a circle. As she balanced on one leg, then slipped into a handstand, his canter continued as steadily as a metronome. She could trust him with her life and he trusted her in return. She gracefully came down from her handstand to ride him backwards, sitting facing his tail; Eliza was aware she felt the same infinite trust for Lord Purfoy as she felt for this horse, and was ashamed that she had given him no reason to have the same trust in her.

* * *

A week had passed and the old friends who gathered at the Wolfe house for their usual late breakfast had grown increasingly melancholy with the days. 'Dammit, Rav! Since you scared away Miss Gray, and that lummox Mr Flynn has left for the godforsaken isle of the leprechauns, life has turned very dull indeed.' Ferdy Shilton's stance was so languid he seemed to be propped upright by the mantlepiece.

Alick laughed in his good-humoured way. 'Come now, Ferdy, you can't blame it on Purfoy. Cousin Zadoc was always going to complete his tour. And Miss Gray is a law unto herself. We offered her a home here but she said she could not live on the charity of others. I respect her for that.'

Raven Purfoy was reclining in a chair, his legs in dark pantaloons stretched out before him, his black tasselled hessians as shiny as glass. His handsome, fine-boned face was dark, and a wintry expression added to the gloomy air. In his hands was *The Sporting Magazine,* but he did not seem to be reading it. He had neither smiled, nor expostulated, nor turned a page for the last half hour. Alick passed him a jug of ale. 'Rav, why the discontented mien? You look like Prometheus suffering on your rock, your liver ruined. Isn't it time to seek some solace with Mrs Cornford? You've not been seen much at Cavendish Square.'

Lord Purfoy leapt to his feet, irascible in a way his friends had seldom seen before. 'Mrs Cornford and I have parted ways. Not that it's any of your damned business!' He was white with disdain.

Mr Shilton intervened. 'Calm down, Rav. You've been as cross as a bear these last days. Are you unwell?'

His lordship sank back into his chair. 'No I've just been

wondering what is the point of life. We're born, we live out our short span and then we die. For what?'

'This is too deep for me, Rav.' Ferdy Shilton shook his head, his brow furrowed. 'I find it best to live each day as it comes, grateful I'm an Englishman with a very fine castle. No point inviting the blue devils to feast at your table.'

'That is to live like a dog! My hunting hound cheerfully greets each day with a wagging tail and a lolling tongue. He knows not, nor cares, about the morrow or his place in the grand scheme of things.'

Alick intervened, 'There's no need to abuse Ferdy, Rav. He has a different approach to life, that's all.' Then, in a calm way, he dropped a thunderbolt into the morning by saying, 'I think it's time you married.' Alick Wolfe had always been straight-talking and unafraid of giving offence, but the thunderous look on his friend's face made him wonder if this time he had gone too far.

Purfoy was on his feet again, *The Sporting Magazine* flung to the floor. 'It's fine for you to talk, Alick, oh happily shackled man! You stole Corinna for yourself and have rubbed our noses in your conjugal happiness and cupidity ever since!'

Alick was rarely riled but he had had enough of this version of their story. Colour flamed in his cheeks and he said, 'Rav! Stop this romance. You know this is not how it was. We all loved Corinna, but you had no thought of her as your wife until I asked her to marry me. Your tale of thwarted love is an excuse for continued dalliances and lack of resolve.' He slammed his hand against the wall to relieve his frustration.

Ferdinand Shilton did not care for raised voices and took Alick's arm in a firm grasp. 'Calm down, Al. We all know that you won Corinna's love when you played Sir Galahad, protecting her from that carter's assault. None of us stood a chance after that.' He still had hold of his friend's arm as he looked across at Lord

Purfoy and continued, 'So, if not Corinna, who should Rav marry then?'

Alick's good humour had returned. 'Why, Miss Gray, of course.'

There was a stunned silence in the room as Lord Purfoy strode to the window, his back turned resolutely against his friends.

Alick's voice softened. 'Look at him. He's a wreck of a man. In her company he became almost human.'

His lordship whirled round, his face haughty, eyes blazing. 'What do you know of the anguish of loving someone you cannot trust? You have given your heart to a woman who's as honourable as a man. Miss Gray showed no such honour. Without a thought she betrayed me on a whim! How can I ever trust her with my love, my life?'

Ferdy Shilton said with a sly smile, 'The clubs are abuzz with your reckless play the other night, staking your horses to win the Bathwick estate off Davenport. Risking your prancers, Rav! Nothing's worth such a loss. Why risk so much, except for love of the chit?'

Without a word Lord Purfoy turned on his heel and swept out of the room. Ferdy Shilton and Alick looked at each other in silence as they heard the front door slam shut behind him.

* * *

Lord Purfoy's spirit was so agitated he needed some remedy for a state of mind he abhorred. He could either return to his mansion next door to drink, or go to his club to play hazard, lose money and drink. Then the thought came to him how good it was for him to exhaust himself with hard physical activity; he turned and walked rapidly east down Brook Street towards Bond Street. The best thing would be to spar in Gentleman Jackson's boxing establishment or, if that was too busy, then to fence with the fencing masters in the academy next door. As usual Jackson's had a throng of fashionable young noblemen round its door. They hailed Lord Purfoy and parted to let him through.

As he entered the building, Lord Purfoy was pleased to see the great man in attendance. Gentleman Jackson was stripped to the waist, his magnificent physique glistening with sweat as he sparred with a portly young baronet, Sir Tufton Warren, who was lurching rather leadenly round the ring. Both men's hands were muffled with linen bandages to protect the noble flesh and knuckles from more brutal contact. When he saw Raven Purfoy, Mr Jackson lifted a beefy arm in salutation. 'How goes, my lord?' Purfoy nodded in greeting and walked through to the changing room to strip off his coat, cravat, shirt and boots, until he too was naked to the waist and in his stockinged feet. He emerged to have his hands bound by one of the young assistants and was shown to the chair by the ringside, named Lord Byron's Seat now that the noble poet and aficionado of the manly art of boxing had left for Italy.

When Mr Jackson eventually ushered the gasping, red-faced Sir Tufton to the bar, Raven Purfoy stood up to greet the Prince of the Ring. They touched fists and stood together, talking, drawing all eyes. Remarkably well-matched physically, each was narrow-hipped with long athletic legs and an impressively broad set of shoulders from which the power of their right and left hooks derived. 'How do, my lord? You ready for a bout?'

As they began to spar, other men collected ringside in twos and threes to watch and applaud any particularly good moves. These were two men in the peak of fitness, their light footed muscularity clear for all to see. Occasional cheers and a few claps arose from the sidelines as spectators appreciated the grace of the dance, followed by the lightning strikes of jabbing, parrying punches, the ducking and weaving. After half an hour of intense activity in the ring, both men held up each other's right arms then stepped out to be offered towels by the assistants, and a tankard each of ale.

They unwound the linen mufflers from their knuckles and Gentleman Jackson said, 'You know, my lord, if ever you needed a job as a prizefighter, I'd be honoured to add you to my stable.'

They both laughed, towelling the sweat from their chests and foreheads. This was a rare accolade from the master of the pugilist art, but it was an offer both knew Lord Purfoy was unlikely to take up. 'You're in fine fettle yourself, sir.' Purfoy stood back to survey Jackson, already in his late forties but still muscled and elegant in his proportions, so much so that he was the subject of many an heroic painting when artists needed to portray the perfect physical specimen of manhood.

'It's what the love of a good woman can do. I recommend it, my lord.'

Lord Purfoy snorted. 'Don't you snare me too! My friends suggested the same thing this morning, but women and love just complicate things, don't you think?'

Jackson's meaty paw came down on his shoulder like a hammer blow as the pugilist chuckled. 'Sure they do. But the rewards are worth every penny of pain. 'Tis the same with boxing, my lord, exertion and pain promise the pleasure. And how sweet that is.' He kissed his fingertips and raised them to the boxing gods above.

'Each to his own, Jackson. I'll have to believe you, but do not intend to find out. I'll see you back here next week.'

Fully dressed and stepping back onto the street, Raven Purfoy felt his mind clarified and his spirit consoled. As he walked, he planned how he could regain control of his life. In a fit of unusual recklessness, he had won back Miss Gray's Bathwick inheritance and at least could now present her with it, thus quietening his conscience. Then to forget her and batten down his heart again; in this way he would have done more than his duty by her.

* * *

The crowds at Astley's Amphitheatre were known for their boisterous good humour. Much ale was drunk, and even the young noblemen, out for an evening's entertainment away from their clubs in St James's, or escaping the Season's soirées and balls to carouse in the theatre's boxes, were rowdy and drunk. Ordinary Londoners had congregated in an exuberant mass in the pit and upper terraces, intent on a good time for not much expense, with their picnics and cheap alcohol to eat and drink throughout the show.

Into this chaotic melee of shouts, jostling and laughter, Marina Fairley led her mother who was accompanying her as chaperone. She was excited to see her sister again, particularly performing on horseback, and she pushed through the crowd to find their box. It was with some dismay she realised they were sharing the space with a crowd of young men, already half-cut before the performance had even begun. 'Mama, here's a seat by the door. Pay them no mind.'

Mrs Fairley looked with some alarm at these bleary-eyed youths who, from their bluster, seemed just down from Oxford determined on merriment, and finding it amusing to spill the dregs of their tankards over the common crowd below. Marina Fairley leaned across to say to her mother, in hope rather than expectation, 'Everyone will calm down once the show begins.' One of the young men had brought a bag of rock cakes and was lobbing them randomly into the pit, hitting people on the head or shoulder, occasionally having them lobbed back accompanied by swearing threats.

A more responsible youth in their party said sharply, 'Say, Tufton, take care, you'll start a riot!'

The red-faced young baronet laughed in a way that made Marina certain he was full of liquor, then slurring his words he said, 'That would liven things up a bit. Like a chance to practice my right hook. Just come from Jackson's Academy this afternoon.' He was boastful and belligerent.

Across the roiling crowd came the clarion of a hunting horn as the horses entered the ring. Rather than silencing the audience, this merely increased the cheering and catcalls, particularly when the evening's star, Eliza as Clorinda the Winged Venus, entered standing on the back of her magnificent black horse.

'Look, Mama, that's Miss Gray!'

'Looks very dangerous, my dear. She hasn't got many clothes on! Thank goodness she's masked so no one will recognise her.' Both women gazed in some wonder at Eliza, dressed in blue silk pantaloons and an embroidered green jacket, tightly braided across her chest, a jewelled mask on her face. Small silver wings were attached at her shoulders from which ribbons of diaphanous blue silk fluttered as she rode.

'She couldn't manage in long skirts, Mama. I think she looks magnificent and so graceful.'

'And she and the horse have wings!'

The young men were leaning out of their box to see better. Sir Tufton Warren turned to his companions to say in an over-loud voice, 'It's the only place outside a bordello or a museum of classical statues where you can actually see what a woman looks like.' He leered and looked across at Miss Fairley who wished she were a man and could wipe that salacious look off his face.

After the show was over, Marina took her mother firmly by

the arm and propelled her through the crowds to the back of the building where the stables were situated. She was determined to talk to Eliza. Again there was a turbulence of fashionable young men mixed up with the ostlers who looked after the horses. Eliza was nowhere to be seen. Marina hoped they had not missed her and hovered uncertainly on the edge of the crowd. Suddenly Eliza appeared, dressed in her respectable yet rather dull clothes, and not immediately recognizable to the drink-befuddled admirers gathered in the hopes of waylaying her. Catching sight of Marina, Eliza was quickly by her side and said in a quiet voice, 'How wonderful to see you. And Mrs Fairley too. Come with me, then we avoid the fuss,' and she drew them into the hay barn to the left of the stables.

Finding themselves lit only by the moon and surrounded by the green sweet smell of sheaves of hay, Marina Fairley threw her arms around Eliza. 'Oh, dear sister. You were wonderful, but I had no idea you had to run that gauntlet of such rudeness and lechery!'

Eliza laughed. 'I've known it most of my life, and it's not as bad as it may appear. Those young blades are all swagger and little doing. They're showing off to their friends. And I have a certain anonymity because of the mask. Unlike Rose, who is fully recognisable.'

'That young miss seems to like it that way,' Mrs Fairley said sourly.

Eliza sprang to her friend's defence. 'Well, much to her and my delight, Rose will soon be going to the Americas. She's been offered work in a business in New York.'

Mrs Fairley sniffed in disapproval. 'Business! So common, my dear. I hope neither of you girls, of noble if irregular blood, will consider *business*.'

Eliza was uncowed. 'Well, Mrs Fairley, I suppose being in

business is less reprehensible than performing as I do for the means to live?'

Marina had always been irritated by her mother's social airs and disapproval of those she considered beneath her. In a sharp voice she said, 'You know Mama, we are fortunate indeed that Grandmama has enough inheritance to allow us to live without consideration or concern for shelter, food or every other convenience. Very few women are as lucky.'

'Oh, Marina. You're such a revolutionary! I cry to God each night: *what did I do to deserve such a daughter?* I don't know where you got your contrary nature from.' Marina and Eliza shared a conspiratorial smile while Mrs Fairley continued, 'It is entirely scandalous that you, Miss Gray, perform in the circus. If I were your mother I would forbid it, and cast you out if you persisted in your rebellion.'

Eliza was taken aback by Mrs Fairley's vehemence, but Marina understood her mother's quixotic nature and ignored the outburst. 'Mama, I have offered Miss Gray a home with me, with us, to share my annuity, but she has preferred not to be beholden to friends – or family. For that she should be commended, not scolded.'

Eliza was aware of the unfamiliar emotion of sisterly sympathy flowing between them; to have someone always think the best of you, to love and protect you come what may, it touched her unexpectedly and her eyes pricked with tears. The young women took each other's hands. Marina said, 'Our carriage awaits us. But come and see me next time you can get away. I miss you so much.' She and Mrs Fairley turned and walked back to where their carriage was parked with others by the Amphitheatre's portico.

As Eliza emerged from the barn, a man stepped out from the shadows. The stable boys had bedded down the horses and retired to their cots above the stables and Eliza realised she was alone. She walked quickly towards the steps that led to her quarters and to Rose but the man was quicker. He grasped her arm and she turned to see his face caught in a shaft of moonlight. 'Lord Davenport!' she said in a shocked voice.

He pulled her roughly to him, his face so close she could smell his breath as he hissed, 'I heard you had returned, and here you are.' Her heart began to thump. She couldn't make out if he was drunk – which she felt able to handle – or bent on revenge, which she could not. He continued, his voice low and menacing, 'Purfoy has taken something valuable of mine and I've come to steal something of value to him.'

Eliza tried to shake him off. 'I don't know what you're talking about. Lord Purfoy has nothing to do with me. Take your grievance to him.'

'Oh, but I think he has very much to do with you. I've seen the way he looks at you; your arrogant friend has designs on you and if he hasn't already claimed you, I intend to take you first.' In one deft movement he caught her hands behind her back and, lifting her off her feet, carried her to the barn.

Eliza kicked him vigorously. 'Rose! Help!' she cried out as loud as she could before his hand clamped over her mouth, his rings knocking her teeth. He was so quick and decisive she realised he was not drunk and fear rose, suffocating her breath. In the dark, he tossed her down into a pile of hay, his hand still gripping her mouth, tangy and metallic-tasting, his body pressing hard and heavy against her.

Eliza could not wriggle free from under his weight but she managed to bite his middle finger with as much force as she could muster. He swore, snatching his arm away for a minute while she scrambled to her feet and made for the slither of moonlight by the door. But Lord Davenport was as fast and he grabbed her skirt and dragged her back, slamming her against an oak strut that supported the roof. He was so strong, she felt the horror of powerlessness in the face of a greater force. One of his arms clamped her hard against his hip as he ruffled up her skirts. His hand moved up her thigh then, in a fever, he began to unbutton the front fall of his pantaloons. His voice was hoarse with anger and lust as he said with quiet menace, 'Your rapacious lord has ruined my inheritance, now I will spoil you for him.' He looked down to where she was pressed against his groin and muttered, 'Not that I imagine he would have been the first to tend this garden.'

Eliza recalled what her sister had said: everything Davenport touched he corrupted. Shock, fear and outrage surged in her chest. He had her hands caught in a vice-like grip behind her back so she stamped heavily on his foot, but he was wearing top boots and merely laughed. 'I like a fighting woman.' She noticed with a shudder his teeth gleam as his lips parted.

Knowing the barn would muffle her cry, Eliza summoned all her breath and, propelled by anger and desperation, shouted one last time, 'Rose! Help me!'

'No one will hear you here.' He laughed again and grasping her chin, bent his head to forcibly kiss her when an almighty clang of metal hitting something hard rent the silence of the night. His grip loosened as he fell to the ground. Rose was standing in the dark behind him, a spade in her hand.

Eliza, suddenly released, staggered towards her. 'Oh, Rose, thank you.'

'You done it for me in the past.'

The young women clung together as they looked at Davenport's prone figure. 'You've not killed him, have you?' Eliza asked with some concern.

'Nah! Just knocked him cold.' As Rose spoke, three stable boys clattered into the barn, woken by the commotion.

Eliza gave a wan smile. 'How grateful I am to you all. Can you carry this man out to his carriage? I'm sure it is waiting in the road.' She then turned back to Rose and said in an urgent voice, 'Rose, this is between us. I don't want Mr Flynn or Lord Purfoy, or any of the men who know me to hear of it. I could not bear a duel to be fought and someone I care for killed or hastened into exile.' Rose nodded and Eliza continued, 'I'm so tired I can hardly think or walk. I have to sleep. But thank you again, Rose.'

* * *

Not everyone was abed. Lord Purfoy was returning from his club and, unusually, had allowed Taz to drive his curricle for him. It was a fair night with an almost full moon and Taz and he sat in companionable silence watching the silvery backs of Lord Purfoy's matched greys rise and fall as they trotted in elegant symmetry. Taz of course had heard immediately through the grooms' gossip line that his master had put his finest horses up as a wager. For years, he had emphatically told anyone who would listen that any cove who risked his stable of bloodstock in such a despicable way deserved no mercy for a sin worse than treason. By his book, such a man deserved to fry in Hell.

However, on hearing the shocking news, Taz did not immediately threaten to leave Lord Purfoy's employ. He did not even remonstrate with him, beyond spitting a contemptuous gob into the gutter, for he had approved the prize. Anything that punctured Lord Davenport's arrogance was a cheerful thought to his egalitarian soul. Even more gratifying to him was that the estate Lord Purfoy had won was Miss Gray's rightful inheritance. Women, in Taz's estimation, were an unnecessary complication in life, the spoilers of men's carefree fun. But for him, Miss Gray was a rare specimen, completely bereft of missish airs, with the heart of a lion and the skill to ride like the best of men. Taz turned to his master and said, 'Guv, I know it's not my place to speak out of turn.'

'When has that ever stopped you?' Lord Purfoy drawled.

Taz chuckled. 'Right enough, m'lord.' Then he continued in his rough voice, 'I read ye as well as the prancers. As tricky ye are too. Bin watching ye. Ye're out of sorts.' He expertly weaved the vehicle through a knot of carriages without slowing his speed, hailing the other grooms as he went. 'These past weeks ye be gnarly as a bull who's lost 'is knackers.'

'I do hope not, Taz. I don't like the thought of that at all.'

'Well, ye have. And all I can think is it's because Miss Gray's gone.'

Lord Purfoy's narrow eyes widened but he did not show the jolt that name gave to his heart. Instead, he said in his droll way, 'But Taz, you think women are the cause of every problem and the solution of none.'

'True enough, m'lord, but that's yer usual female. Complicators, complainers, sticklers for troublous rules, quenchers of every lark. But ye know how I rate Miss Corinna; well I ken Miss Gray as fine. Never seen a rummer rider, better even than ye, m'lord, as she proved.' He sneaked a sidelong glance at his master's stony profile.

'Now you really are speaking out of turn, Taz. Don't try my patience.'

Taz laughed at the rebuke. The horses had quickened their pace as they approached Brook Street and home. In a throwaway manner he said, 'Anyhow, guv, I think ye should do summat about 'er.'

'Well, thank you, Taz, for your unsolicited advice. I think you should stick to horses where your instincts and skills are unrivalled and leave matters of my heart to me.'

Taz drew the horses to a halt outside the Purfoy mansion and leapt down to take their heads. He watched his master with knowing eyes. By his weary mien he knew his words had hit their mark.

Raven Purfoy entered his house. A single candelabrum burned in the hall. It was two o'clock in the morning and everyone had gone to bed except for his valet, John. This young man rose sleepily from the chair in the hall to greet his master and taking up the candlestick, lighted the way to his bedchamber. Lord Purfoy had been distinctly out of sorts, as Taz had said, but now he felt even more disturbed. Why was everyone so keen on his marrying this wild young woman who had alighted in their lives from nowhere, and so disrupted his?

John pulled off Lord Purfoy's boots while he sat on the edge of the bed, then divested his master of his pantaloons and whisked off his shirt. His lordship walked through to the dressing room and had a quick wash in the water that remained in the pitcher brought up that morning. He felt his spirits temporarily lift with the astringent chill. 'Thank you, John. You need your sleep, as do I.' He dismissed his valet and walked through to his great four-poster bed dominating the middle of the room.

There he lay, unable to sleep. It was entirely due to his reckless driving that Miss Gray's fate had collided with his own, never to be entirely disentangled. He was alarmed at the emotional turmoil he felt, this longing for her presence, the soft gaze of those extraordinary eyes settling on his face, his hunger for her touch. He was familiar and at ease with the appetites of the body but had long armoured himself against the snares of love. Miss Gray, however, had arrived like a thunderbolt that prised open the iron palisades of his soul. She had stolen in and settled there, embedded in his heart.

He could not bear this old vulnerability of spirit, his whole being hostage to another. The spectre of the death of his sister rose in the dark to torment him. Once more, guilt and despair threatened to eclipse all hope, all comfort, lost as he had been in the labyrinth of grief. Eliza's current favourite reading matter, *The Corsair,* came to mind:

In helpless – hopeless – brokenness of heart.

How well that captured the powerlessness of love, an emotion he never wished to endure again. Now he could only return to the regulated constraints of the time before Miss Gray, to regain control of his life, to steady the ship, to muffle the insistent pulse of his heart.

Lord Purfoy blew out the candles and sank back into his feather bed. He knew sleep would erase the trials of the day, but then replace them with the strange phantasms of dreams, and his dreams were full of her.

* * *

The morning sun had evaded all attempts to keep it out and had slipped through a gap in the curtains, as persistent as love itself, illuminating all in its path with its spangled light. Raven Purfoy awoke in a drowsing half-sleep, still entrapped in the cobwebs of his dream. Miss Gray was in his arms. He knew not how or where but could smell her skin, her hair and feel her soft breasts pressed against his chest. She seemed to be floating with him through space with only the moon and stars for company. His conscious self was still sleeping and he luxuriated in his sense of the rightness of things; this was where he belonged, where she belonged – through the chaos of his doubt she burned a constant flame that lighted his path.

Then, with growing wakefulness, the sorrows that darkness hid began to surface. With a plunge of spirit Raven sat up in bed. He needed company. This melancholic version of himself was so far from the heroic Corinthian he liked to project; he could not countenance the vulnerability that accompanied desire, need or fear of loss. For this reason alone, Miss Gray had to be banished from his life, eradicated from his thoughts. Without even bothering to put on a gown he strode naked to the door and bellowed, 'John!'

Within an hour, Lord Purfoy, immaculately shaven, dressed, cravat tied and booted in the shiniest Hessians, had strolled into the Wolfes' breakfast room next door. His friends were as late rising as he and he was gratified to see Ferdy Shilton's angelic face somewhat blurred with sleep. Alick, always so calm and authoritative, was carving a leg of gammon and laughing at some comment about the previous night's play. Life for Lord Purfoy suddenly seemed to have slotted back into place.

He hailed his friends, took a cup of coffee and picked up *The Sporting Magazine*, as he always did. But the exploits in the field no longer amused him. He read on, looking for something diverting in the reports of games and gambling bets and exploits of gentlemen of the hunt or shooting range. Stories of duels bored him and the fixtures for the illegal boxing matches out of Town barely elicited a ripple of anticipation. He sighed as the paper fell from his listless fingers.

'What's up, Rav? You look a little devil-tossed to me.' Ferdinand Shilton's mood never seemed to change from one of sunny optimism that warmed all in his orbit; he was a gilded youth indeed, gifted by nature with the most fair, blue-eyed beauty and by family, one of the great fortunes based on coal and land. Adored from the cradle, how could he not exude charm and generosity of spirit? Nothing grievous had ever happened to him and probably never would.

'I haven't been sleeping well these last weeks.' Raven Purfoy was disinclined to be more specific about his distemper of mind.

Alick looked up and said, 'Corinna's been having the same broken nights. Now that the baby's grown so big, she can't get comfortable.'

'Well I assure you, that's not my problem.' They all laughed. Then Lord Purfoy asked, 'Where is she?'

'In her studio. She's finishing a portrait of some dandy. Some vain fool, but he's paying her a vast fee.'

'Would she mind my interrupting her?'

'I think she'd be glad of the diversion.' Alick smiled, more than willing to share with his friends his own good fortune in having such a wife.

Raven Purfoy knocked on the studio door and hearing Corinna's voice, entered. The room was lit with a hazy light filtered through the great copper beech tree in the garden. On her easel was a three-quarter length portrait of a smug young man. She looked up, paint on her apron and a smudge across her nose. 'Oh Rav! I'm so pleased to see you. I'm struggling with his hands. Can you come and stand just there.' She pointed to a place on the other side of the north-facing window. 'Now splay your right hand fingers on your left arm. Perfect.'

Raven stood there with this unnatural pose as she squinted at his hands and dabbed paint on the canvas. 'I need your advice, Cory.' He was surprised that he had said the words.

'Of course. Just let me get this finger right first. Yours are much more elegant than his, but perhaps he'll be pleased to have your beautiful hands rather than his bunches of sausages.' She laughed as she added the last brush-stroke of paint. 'Right, the hand's done. You can now relax and talk.'

Lord Purfoy subsided into the chair and crossed his legs, staring towards the window in abstracted thought. Corinna was watching him with an amused expression. 'You know, Rav, you really are almost indecently handsome. If only you'd smile a little. It so elevates the mood.'

He turned his eyes to meet hers and smiled. 'My dear Cory, if I were married to you, I'd be smiling all the time.'

Corinna took off her paint-spattered apron and in exasperation, threw it on the floor. 'You know, Rav, you have to stop this fantasy of what might have been. I think it's been an excuse too long for your not committing yourself to another.' She walked over to her second easel and whisked away the cloth covering the painting. Illuminated in the sparkling morning light was her portrait of Eliza Gray, beautiful, mysterious, full of emotion. Caught unawares, Lord Purfoy could hardly breathe. He was mesmerised once again by those eyes, seeming almost alive in their vivid soulfulness.

'Corinna! I didn't know it was still here. Can I have it?' He was shocked to hear himself asking for such a memento.

'Yes, until Miss Gray has a home for it.'

He had approached to stand before the portrait, meeting Eliza's gaze, and for a moment he was overcome.

Corinna said very quietly, 'You lost me to Alick through procrastination and nicety of feeling, don't lose Eliza Gray to Zadoc Flynn in the same way.'

This electrified him. He whirled round. 'What? What on earth makes you say that?'

'Well, he's asked her to marry him and intends to take her back to America with him. And you'll never see her again.'

Lord Purfoy was pacing to relieve his feelings. 'How dare he! He's nowhere near good enough for her.'

'That may well be, Rav, but what's the saying, *Faint heart ne'er won fair lady?*'

Colour flared into his pale cheeks and he looked dangerous as his eyes blazed. 'My heart is far from faint!' He was almost shouting. 'It's burning like a furnace over which I have lost control.'

Corinna was placidly cleaning her brushes and wrapping them in paper. 'Well, give up control then. What's your family's famous motto?'

He turned to face her and said, '*Audaci Venus ut Fortuna favet.*'

'Remind me of the translation, my lord,' she said sweetly.

'Venus, like Fortune, favours the bold,' he answered through gritted teeth.

'Well, it strikes me the Purfoys knew a thing or two.' And she laughed.

'Where is she now?' He flung out the question as if it were a challenge.

'She's back working as a rider at the circus.'

Again Lord Purfoy was overwhelmed with unaccustomed emotion and burst out, 'What? Why? What made her return to that? I thought she was with her sister.'

'She's a proud woman and did not want to live on charity, having to ask family and friends for funds even to buy herself toiletries or haberdashery to refurbish her clothes. Alick and I offered her a home with us, as did her sister, Miss Fairley. But she said she was not fit to be a lady of leisure and was only trained for one thing.'

Corinna watched his lordship's face change from outrage to sorrow to confusion and horror when she added, 'Mr Flynn returns from Ireland in two days and she may well decide to accept his offer. Her friend at the circus, Rose Bowman, that pretty circus rider Mr Flynn brought to Lady Bassett's ball, well, she's already said she'll travel with him to work in his father's fur export business. So Miss Gray won't be alone.'

'That is a most consoling thought, thank you,' Lord Purfoy said sarcastically. He was back to pacing the room.

'Why do you hesitate? You evidently love the girl. We all do. It seems quite straightforward to me.'

'Of course I love her. There, I've said it. She's become the sun and moon to me, the only person I long to see. I fear there is no peace for me except with her.' He paced away again, back to the window. 'But then perhaps I can have no peace, for how can I trust her? Her first words to me were a lie; she obviously had not lost her memory but she kept up the pretence!'

'Yes! So you wouldn't return her from whence she'd come.'

'Then, more heinously she betrays me, on a whim, to please that American clodpole!'

'Oh Rav, for heaven's sake, get off your high horse! You're just piqued because she beat you.' Corinna tried to suppress a smile. 'She did not betray you on a whim. The decision was hard for her. She had given her word and then could not withdraw.' Corinna, animated with her own emotion, put out her arms to her friend and hugged him. 'Loving anyone is painful and fraught with danger, and I know you know that and have paid the price.' He was so tall she could not meet his eyes but continued talking to his cravat. 'We all have to plunge into the unknown. But I promise you, through struggle, love grows more precious, and the beloved becomes indispensable, etched into our souls.' They separated and she met his gaze, softened now. 'Honour your sister, Rav, and her short, sweet life, by going forward with hope into the future, with another beloved Eliza.'

Lord Purfoy said with a catch in his voice, 'Alick is blessed to have you as a wife, and I am blessed to call you sister and friend. Thank you.' He took her hand with its painted fingertips and kissed it before swinging out of the door.

* * *

That evening Lord Purfoy strolled round to the mews where Taz was preparing the horses and curricle for the night's entertainment. 'I'm not going to St James's but to Astley's.' Taz glanced at him with a knowing look. Lord Purfoy had no intention of letting his tiger congratulate himself on his percipience in any area of his master's life. He swung up into the driving seat and drove his special greys towards the east of the city, with Taz perched behind. The moon hung large and low in the velvet night, spreading its uncanny light over everything. The buildings and trees, the passing horsemen and carriages, were cloaked in a silvery sheen of significance. Tonight was momentous. Lord Purfoy's spirit, for weeks unsettled and sunk in saturnine gloom, was calm and certain. He would offer Miss Gray her inheritance and the freedom to live as she chose. He then could only hope she would choose to share that life with him. His future happiness lay with Fate herself.

Walking up the front steps at the entrance of Astley's Amphitheatre, Lord Purfoy threaded his way through the chattering throng of young blades and dandies surrounded by a flock of fluttering ladies of the night. The working people of London too were there in force. It was years since he had attended and he was rather taken aback at how boisterous the crowd seemed. Miss Gray had to deal with this night after night; he shuddered at the thought. Having paid to have a box to himself he settled into the plush interior, kicking aside two empty bottles and some pie wrappings left by the previous occupants.

The show started with the usual jugglers and clowns to get the audience in the mood. The crowd went wild with delight and Lord Purfoy shifted in his seat, barely able to contain his boredom. Then three blasts of a hunting horn proclaimed the arrival of the horses. He leaned forward to see a beautiful black horse canter proudly into the ring and on his back was a winged nymph, standing with one arm raised. Lord Purfoy's breath caught in his throat. She was masked but unmistakeable to him. Her wonderful flaxen hair fell loose down her back from a feathered cap. It floated behind her as did the silk ribbons attached to wings on her jacket. Lord Purfoy's gaze would always be drawn to the horse, but handsome as Percy was, his lordship could not look away from the rider, so graceful, so strong and brave, so beloved to him.

He was unprepared for the bolt of love and desire that broke through his natural reserve. There she was, separate from him, almost a stranger, her beauty incandescent in the stage lights; her grace of form, her dancer's poise, her courage in riding so recklessly and at such speed, overwhelmed his senses and filled every cell with longing for her.

Rather than subside into attentive quiet, the audience grew rowdier, mixing whistles and catcalls with the general uproar. Lord Purfoy was shocked out of his reverie and grew increasingly outraged at the lack of respect for both riders and horses. He leaned over to the next box to quieten five young bucks who seemed particularly loud and offensive in their comments, and noticed the young baronet who had been sparring with Gentleman Jackson. 'Sir Tufton! Mind your manners.'

The young baronet, furious at being scolded in front of his friends, leaned over and, in a voice that sailed over the hubbub, shouted, 'His High and Mighty, the arrogant Lord Purfoy, thinks he can tell us how to behave! We paid our dues and what we do is our business.' Faces in the audience turned to peer at the commotion, and some added their inflammatory comments, eager for a fight.

* * *

From the moment she entered the ring, Eliza felt the air turn electric. No thunder had been heard but a stormy energy surged above the usual turbulence of the crowd. The thought erupted in her mind: this was the night he had come for her. So great was the import, she could barely allow herself to hope. Concentrating on her own fine balancing act and control of Percy, she could not risk looking out at the crowd to search for the only face she longed to see. But when the young man's shout was heard, she glanced across at the boxes and fleetingly glimpsed Lord Purfoy's dark head, the light from the central chandelier gleaming off his cheekbones, illuminating his fervent gaze. In that second she thought their eyes met, but then she had to look away.

About to enter a complicated equestrian manoeuvre where she stepped across from Percy's back to the pony cantering beside her, she needed all her powers of concentration and balance. As Eliza managed the move and then back again, a cheer went up and the row in the boxes was obliterated by applause. She moved into a graceful handstand that she maintained while her horse cantered the full circumference of the ring. The noise was deafening as she returned to riding astride without a saddle and at full gallop.

Eliza had come to the end of her performance and left the arena while the clowns, jugglers and a noisy drum and cornet returned. She rode Percy round to the stables and knew she had twenty minutes or so before the show ended and her admirers congregated in the yard. But that night she dismounted and found she was not alone. A young drunk took her arm. 'Miss Clorinda.' He smelled of brandy and ale and was unsteady on his feet. 'I've attended every night since you returned, you can surely reward me with a kiss?' His voice was wheedling and Eliza felt herself shrink from his touch.

'Git yer 'ands off me, sir!' she said in her street accent, hoping its roughness added authority, while she struggled to shake his grip from her arm. Lord Davenport's assault had shaken her, but this young man was drunk and less experienced and she found him less menacing, although she was still dressed in her costume and felt exposed and vulnerable. Sir Tufton Warren was a young man who was not used to having a woman refuse him and he pursued her across the yard.

Suddenly a hand fell heavily on his shoulder and Eliza heard the thrilling voice, 'Sir! You heard the lady. You're drunk. Go home.'

The young baronet was too befuddled to recognise the danger he was in. He scoffed, 'She's no lady. And you're just a braggadocio earl!'

Lord Purfoy grasped him by the lapels of his elaborately fashionable coat. He turned to Eliza and said in a quiet voice, 'Miss Gray, I'd be grateful if you'd leave this fool to me.' Eliza nodded and walked quickly to the hay barn where she was out of sight of the small crowd of young men congregating in the hopes of a fight.

Lord Purfoy pulled Sir Tufton Warren very close to his face and said *sotto voce*, 'She is every inch a lady, and even if she were not, I'd expect you to act as a gentleman.'

'Why so prosy, my lord? These doxies who perform in public don't deserve the respect due a true lady.' His eyes were bloodshot as he leered across at his friends.

Lord Purfoy flung him away. His dander was up. 'You are a

swinish sot, sir, not worthy of even your modest barony. Miss Gray is of far greater nobility than you could ever understand. In fact, I intend to make her my countess if she'll have me.'

'You lie! Men like us don't marry harlots like her!' He had barely finished his sentence when he was struck in the jaw by Raven Purfoy's straight right hook. He fell like a tree amongst the straw and horse dung. His friends clustered round him and helped him to his feet and away, as Lord Purfoy strode towards the barn.

Slipping in through the partly opened door, he was met by the sweet smell of hay and enveloped in darkness. For a moment he could not see Eliza, then she stepped into the shaft of moonlight and he walked to her side and took her hands. 'My dear Miss Gray, I'm so sorry you had to endure that lout's attentions. Are you quite well?'

'I am, and much improved by seeing you, my lord. Arriving when I needed you most.' She smiled. The moonlight painted a silvery aureole round her head as her fair hair tumbled in waves down her back. The magical light made her eyes sparkle in a way that Lord Purfoy found irresistible, and he could not look away.

He realised he still had her hands in his and let them go as he said, 'I came to give you some news I hope might restore your rightful future. At hazard I won back from Lord Davenport the deeds to your inheritance. Bathwick Court and estate and your mother's jewels are yours, to do with as you will.'

Eliza's hands flew to her face. So this was what had so enraged Lord Davenport! How hard it was to understand just what this meant for Lord Purfoy, for her. It was beyond imagining that he had sought to gamble, to risk everything, to present her with such an extraordinary, unexpected gift. All she could say was, 'But why, my lord?'

'Because I believe it is your rightful inheritance. I dislike unfairness in an already unfair world, and I think natural justice would consider you Bathwick's heir, if not to his title then at least to his wealth. I think you have been dealt with harshly.'

Her eyes were wide and anxious, watching his face. 'But how did you win? What did you wager for so great a prize?'

Lord Purfoy faltered. He had to tell her the truth and yet it still pained him to say the words. 'I wagered my horses.'

Eliza was aghast. She knew what they meant to him. They were his family, his passion, his life. In an agitated voice, she said, 'No, my lord, not your horses!'

He was amused. 'Don't look so shocked. You should hear what Taz has to say about it. But I have learned these last few days that you have to risk everything to gain what you truly desire.'

'But why for me?'

He took her hands again in his. 'I wished you to have the freedom to marry or not as you pleased. I did not want you to feel you had to accept Mr Flynn's offer in order to have a home and the necessary freedoms.'

Eliza's shock was replaced with a wave of love as she realised the enormity of what he had done. Suddenly she was sheepish. 'I hope you won't withdraw your offer when you learn I never had any intention of marrying Mr Flynn.' She looked up into his eyes, so dark and fathomless in the shadows.

He drew her closer. 'I am inordinately pleased to hear that.' And a deep generous laugh made her realise how seldom his lordship laughed. 'But does this mean you're against the idea of marriage on principle?'

Eliza was standing so close she had to resist resting her head on the expanse of his chest. 'No, not on principle.' She felt unexpectedly shy as she glanced up at him. 'It depends who is offering.'

Lord Purfoy folded her in his arms and muttered into her hair, 'I would be honoured, Miss Gray, if you would accept my hand in marriage.'

She looked up, offering her face like a flower to the sun. 'Did you not know I loved you from the moment I first saw you? I knew one day you would come for me. I would listen for your footfall on the stair and know it was you.' She stood on tiptoe as he cupped her face in his hand and tenderly kissed her on the lips.

The warmth, the feel, the scent of him intoxicated her. The intimacy of that first kiss filled her senses. His skin smelt of leather and woodsmoke and horses and a masculine aroma distinctly his own, for her the most seductive scent in the world. At last Eliza knew the merging for which she had longed all her life, the meeting of bodies, the blending of souls, and she held him close, prolonging the pleasure. 'What can I do with the joy that bubbles up in me?' she whispered in the dark.

'Bring it to our new life.' His arm tightened across her back as he continued, 'A great grief stole my youth – all hope, all happiness fled. But then you arrived in a gust of wind that blew away the ashes of the past. You were cast into my path, my winged goddess, and gave me back my soul.'

'Every winged goddess needs her winged horse. Will your miraculous gift of the Bathwick inheritance allow me to buy Percy from Prebbles?'

'I always knew wherever you go, Percy comes too.' He held her away from him with a serious expression. 'He's a very fine-looking horse, though I couldn't give him the attention he required because I was incapable of dragging my eyes away from the beauty on his back.' Then he dropped his voice and said, 'Having you so close, I'm bewitched by you; all I wish is to peel off those ridiculous clothes that encase you like a chrysalis. You are a butterfly about to emerge. You already have wings!'

Eliza laughed with sheer happiness. She met his eyes with a mischievous gleam. 'Lord Purfoy, do you think you might kiss me again?'

'I think before I do, you probably should call me by my given name. What think you, my Eliza?'

She had imagined him calling her name but when she finally heard his voice, rich and soft, say *Eliza* with a lazy, elongated second syllable, her knees went weak. He caught her by the elbows as she lifted her face and said, 'Lord Purfoy, Raven, Raven, Raven, could you bear to kiss me again?'

'First, you need to answer my question. Eliza, you know I love you. Will you marry me? Will you be happy to be my countess and rule my domain?'

Eliza slipped her arms around his neck and on tiptoe whispered in his ear, 'Oh, my lord, yes, yes, yes!' She turned her head to meet his lips in a kiss she never wanted to end. Then taking his hand, she led him out into the now empty yard, under a heaven full of stars. They both looked up into the eternal night and Raven Purfoy turned to her and said, 'A star burned bright at your birth, brave and fierce and beautiful.' He pulled her closer in the chill air. 'All my world is in your hands; my horses, my land, my heart, my soul, all yours.'

With his arm holding her to him, Eliza felt his life force radiate through her body. Under that canopy of stars they stood in silence, listening to the night, the only two people in the world, absorbed in the timeless mystery of love.

EPILOGUE
MY HOME IS WHERE THE HEART IS

Eliza was awoken by her husband's kiss. She opened her eyes to watch him tousled-haired and naked walk away from her to pour out two glasses of champagne. He carried them back to their bed, the wine sparkling in the slanting morning light. As he crossed the room through shafts of early sun, she thought him as beautiful as Orpheus on his return from the Underworld. She laughed, still amazed at her good fortune in being loved by him. Words bubbled unbidden to her mind: *I love, I am loved, he is mine.*

Raven passed Eliza a glass and she asked, 'What are we celebrating, my lord?'

'Shame on you for not remembering.'

'Well it's ten months since we married, ten months since we made Hartfield Castle our home. Is that what we're marking?'

He had climbed back into bed. 'No! We're celebrating the first time I kissed you, when the world stopped turning and I asked you to marry me. You, of course, were more concerned about bringing your great horse with you. Do you recall, my daring wild countess?'

'I think I might need a reminder,' Eliza said with a giggle as she handed back her champagne.

He put both glasses down and took his wife into his arms. 'Well, madam, you know by now I don't need to be asked twice.' His hand then reached up for Mr Fox, sitting beady-eyed on Eliza's side of the bed, and he stuffed the small creature under the pillow.

'Rav, what are you doing?' Eliza murmured.

Her noble husband chuckled. 'I don't think we need an audience, do you?' and he began to trace her fine collarbone with an increasingly insistent series of kisses.

* * *

Lying later with Eliza in his arms in the blissful warmth of the marital bed, Raven Purfoy idly circled a finger through the pale damp fronds of the hair that framed his wife's face and murmured, 'I'm ashamed to admit how it thrills me to hear you call me *my lord* in circumstances such as this. I have been called so all my life by everyone from the under-gardener to the Prince of Wales. It has meant very little. However, when your sweet voice whispers *my lord* when you're in my arms, it sends a jolt through my blood and quickens my spirit. How say you, my lady?'

Eliza's head was resting on his shoulder and she reached up to further ruffle his hair, already tousled from the night. How much she liked to see him unbuttoned and undone from the immaculate figure he usually presented to the world. But she had not fully exorcised the ghosts. A small tremor went through her body as she said, 'Why does such happiness make me afraid?'

She watched his smiling eyes narrow and grow serious.

'Afraid? My bold, brave countess who can gallop without a saddle and leap from a speeding horse? Surely not?'

'Physical danger does not scare me. There is a beginning and an end to that. But the thought of loss of someone I love more than life threatens pain that does not cease: it fills me with despair.'

'But Eliza, we have each other. We can face anything together.' He pulled her to him, fierce with the force of his feelings.

'But what if I lost you?' Her voice was barely audible, muffled by his embrace.

'You will never lose me. I'm not going anywhere.' He gave her a gentle shake. 'Come on, Lady Purfoy. The day has long begun. We have horses to ride, an estate to run.'

At breakfast, Raven looked at Eliza with a smile, his dark eyes soft and shining in the morning light. 'It seems my whole existence has been in expectation of this. There was a fated pattern, not that I recognised it before you burst into my ordered life. If only I had known that solitary path I trod was just the prelude, that a greater love than I had ever dreamed possible was there for me.'

Eliza reached for his hand. 'I'm so glad, dearest Rav, you eventually realised something I'd always known. I'm afraid once I'd seen you, there was no other possible ending to our story.' She was watching him, her violet-grey and greenish eyes looking all the more witchy in the soft light reflected off the pale sandstone of the castle walls. 'And how strange our fates one late windy night should cross only because you were driving too fast and in your cups.' Her voice was teasing and she lobbed a piece of currant bun at him.

He laughed. 'You never tire of reminding me what a bad horseman I was that night.' Then he turned serious. ''Tis true I resisted the inevitable. I allowed the past to write the present. But then I am but a mere man and have not the wisdom and soul of a woman.'

Eliza got to her feet and settled in his lap. 'You could never be a mere man, my lord.' She gently tweaked his elegant nose. 'And despite a couple of aberrations, you're really a first-rate horseman.'

'Well, I thank you for that lukewarm accolade. At least I'm good at the truly important things, don't you agree?'

'Oh yes! Very good indeed.' Their eyes met, their gazes burning with such an intensity of emotion that Eliza caught her breath as Raven Purfoy's arm tightened round her waist. Their heads were close together, his dark, hers so fair, her mass of hair loosely gathered into a bun; they recognised so well the energy that crackled between them. When he kissed her she murmured, 'Not again, not now, my lord. The sun is up...'

'What's the sun got to do with anything?' he asked just as there was a knock on the door. Eliza climbed out of his lap as Farrow, the Purfoy butler, entered bearing a letter.

'Oh look, it's from America!' She gave a little shriek, sat down and proceeded to read it. Looking up, her face alight, she said, 'Rose is going to marry Mr Flynn! What wonderful news. Oh no! She has been involved in an accident with a runaway cart on a street in New York. But she says Zadoc was excessively attentive and affectionate to her.' Eliza looked up, a triumphant expression on her face. 'You see, some men do marry their mistresses!'

'Well, Flynn's enough of a blockhead to do so, certainly!'

Eliza crumpled her linen napkin into a ball and threw it at him, laughing. 'Shame on you, Rav! I would have been your mistress if it had been the only way to keep you close!'

'Oh! You only tell me now that I could have had all that I desire of you without signing over my horses, my estates, my heart, my soul! Perhaps it's me who is the fool?'

Eliza ignored him as she read further, then looking up, she had tears in her eyes. 'There's going to be a little Flynn.'

'Well, it's the least of what he deserves. A sprig to plague him all his days!'

Eliza frowned and grew serious. 'Rav, you know you say that you have a great deal of sympathy for King Herod. It is a joke, isn't it?'

Lord Purfoy snorted. 'No! It's not a joke. Look how having cubs has ruined Corinna and Alick, the two best, most entertaining friends I have. They are forever listening out for the wailing cry, interrupting the best dinners to rush off to feed the squaller. Really can't see the joy in 'em until they've left school, perhaps, and can be thought of as fully human.'

'Rav! You *are* funning, I know.' She was not as certain as she sounded but continued, 'We have Corinna and Alick due to stay next week, and they're bringing Emma and baby John. Ferdy's coming later in the week. I'm so looking forward to seeing them all again!'

Her husband disappeared behind his newspaper.

Eliza looked at him, wondering if this was the time to raise something that thrilled her so much she was barely able to keep it to herself, but feared it would not be such welcome news to him. 'My lord, I have something more to impart, I hope not distressing to you.'

Raven put down his paper and gave her a quizzical look. 'What now, sweet wife? You've discovered more disreputable relations? Another stolen inheritance that needs to be restored to you? No, wait! A tribe of travelling circus people need a home and you've decided there's space enough here?'

Eliza smiled. 'No, but they're all possible I suppose.'

'What then can be more distressing?'

She took a breath and said with a rueful expression on her

face, 'I know you're not a man who sees himself as a father, but I'm afraid you may have to get used to the idea. I hope this is not too much of a shock?'

Eliza was full of trepidation and closely watched his face. The smile did not fade from his face and eyes; in fact, it became warmer, more delighted. He was on his feet and pulled her up into his arms. 'Is this true? How long have you known?'

'Just a few weeks. So you're not shocked?'

He laughed with amusement and in his drawling voice she loved so well said, 'My darling Eliza, how can I be shocked? I'm man of the world enough to know that when a man and a woman love each other as much and as often as we do, this is the kind of thing that happens.' He held her close in his embrace.

'But all your talk of Herod?'

'Well, 'tis true, I'm not very keen on other people's squallers, but I shall be positively devoted to our own.' He was grinning with happiness as he lifted her face to meet his gaze and said, 'And my estates are not entailed so whether we have a daughter or son, our child will inherit.'

'So no future suitors are going to have to take to the hazard table ever again to right a wrong?'

'I should hope not!'

'I was afraid to tell you because by your talk, the advent of a child was ruination to a marriage.'

'Oh no, Eliza, I just didn't want you to fear I'd only married you as a brood mare, to provide my heir. I wanted you to know that you alone were more than enough for me.' He kissed her and they leaned together, fingers interlaced, absorbing the profound change about to happen in their lives.

Eliza thought she could not love this man more than she did already, but then he said something like that and her heart turned over and felt fit to burst. She brought his hand to her lips.

'You know, Rav, for a man so richly endowed with the heroic qualities befitting your birth, the most precious thing about you is your kindness and imagination. Thank you.'

Her husband laughed. 'You are such a romantic, Eliza, but I am more than glad you are, you forgive me much.' Still amused, he picked up his paper again. 'My vaunted kindness and imagination tell me our matchmaking friends will be very smug at the news.'

Eliza remembered how she had longed to tell Marina about the baby and smiled. 'Oh good! I can write to my sister and inform her she will become an aunt.'

'A very formidable, bluestocking kind of aunt.'

'The very best kind.' Eliza beamed. Having longed for family all her life, the pleasure in creating her own with the man she loved overwhelmed her with joy. The Irish travellers had told her, when a child, of their legend of the pot of Viking gold buried by leprechauns at the end of the rainbow; for all the following years she had trusted that hidden gold was family, the family she would find. And every rainbow she saw gave her hope they were waiting for her. Now, here, in her hands, in her body, was her own pot of gold. The family she would create for herself. She slipped her arm round her husband's waist and felt his warmth, his great heart beating in his veins.

Eliza heard the clock on the tower strike eleven and said, 'My lord, before you start work with your bailiff, can we take Percy and Horatio for a gallop in the park?'

He had paced to the window to gaze out on the ramparts of his thousand-year-old ancestral home. With his back still to her, Earl Purfoy said, 'You have transformed this gloomy, neglected pile of ancient stones into a house of love and fulfilment with roses round the door.' He turned, his face pale and troubled, his voice quiet. 'My darling Eliza, you know my sister was thrown from a galloping horse here, on this land, under my watch, and killed instantly. Now you carry our child. I can't bear to think of you in any danger; I could not survive having my heart broken for a second time.'

Eliza knew immediately how her desire to ride like the wind was of little consequence in the face of the enormity of their love. She flew to his side and wound her arms around him tight. 'Oh Rav! I promise, I promise, I'll never break your heart. It's safe with me. We have met Fate together, there is nothing now for us to fear.'

He dropped a kiss onto the crown of her head. 'I don't want to stop you riding – it's the delight of your life, I know. But just while you're with child can you promise me to ride side-saddle and not risk your life or our child's by jumping walls and hedges?'

Eliza took his hand. 'Of course, while I carry our child I will ride with due decorum.'

She led him to the stables. Taz greeted them with a grunt and Lord Purfoy said, 'Can you dust off my mother's side-saddle and get Percy ready for my lady?'

Taz gave them both a shrewd look, then turned to walk to the stables. He put the old leather saddle on Percy and as he was tightening the girth, he met his master's eyes with a piercing glance. 'Next ye'll be tellin' me to look out to buy a small Shetland pony.'

Lord Purfoy let out a shout of laughter. 'Taz, you are incorrigible! Yes, I will. I had an obstinate little beast when I was young. I've never forgotten him.'

Eliza smiled across at Taz and met his twinkling black eyes. 'How did you know?' Then she laughed. 'What a foolish question; after all, you know everything, even before your master does.'

Taz smiled and nodded. 'There be a bloom about ye, m'lady.'

Pleased but shy that her condition was so obvious, Eliza gave her husband a rueful glance as with great solicitude, he helped her into the saddle.

They rode at a sedate canter towards the Hundred Acre Wood and stopped by the stream. It was late spring and the world seemed to be alive with possibility. A blackbird was pouring forth its liquid song while a flock of goldfinch chattered noisily in the rushes by the water. They dismounted to let their horses crop the springy turf.

Overcome by the beauty of the day and their own happiness, they clung together for a few moments, then Lord Purfoy took both his wife's hands in his. 'Oh, Eliza, you *are* a beautiful winged goddess you know; you've come from another world to show me how to exist in this one, without cynicism and the dread of death. Your bravery in all things has taught me to grasp the very life of life, and *live*.'

Tears sprang to her eyes with the force of feeling. 'You have given me more tenderness and love than I have ever known; my longed-for family is here in you, and at last I know where I belong.' He folded Eliza into his arms. Her lonely search was at an end and finally she was home.

* * *

MORE FROM JANE DUNN

Another book from Jane Dunn, *A Lady's Fortune*, is available to order now here:

www.mybook.to/LadyBackAd

ACKNOWLEDGEMENTS

This is my fifth historical novel and I would not have reached these heady heights without my fantastic readers. It's wonderful to feel I have connected with you, wherever you are, hoping you have enjoyed something that has given me so much joy and pleasure to create. You are never taken for granted; to read your reviews and receive your comments on social media, email and by post is the most encouraging and heart-warming part of the whole process. So please don't stop. You make it all worthwhile.

Of course these novels wouldn't be offered to anyone to read without the remarkable team at Boldwood Books who have made the publishing process of each one a delight from beginning to end. My editors Sarah Ritherdon and Emily Ruston have brought their characteristic commitment and creative flair to my characters and plot, helping me to tighten the bagginess and amplify the sparse. It's a creative pleasure to work with them. The classy literary sense and emotional intelligence of both text editor Candida Bradford and proofreader Christina de Caix-Curtis have streamlined the finished work. These two do more than their briefs, warmly invested as they are in my characters and their story.

The terrific production team make sure these books read and look as professionally perfect as they do. Sales and Marketing departments drive the success of all Boldwood Books and the team of remarkable individuals are too numerous to mention, but huge gratitude to them all.

Perhaps one of the secret weapons of Boldwood's success is how much their authors feel part of a joint enterprise and bond with their fellow writers, offering in person and on social media help, promotion and enthusiastic support along the way. I am really grateful to have met so many at the famous Boldwood Summer Parties and particular thanks are due to Emma Orchard (Alison Bonomi) and Nicola Cornick who have been incredibly generous and stimulating in their invaluable suggestions and frank conversations. Thank you, fellow Boldies.

I would not be able to write these books without the love and support of family and friends. My wonderful sisters, specifically Karen who has championed me all our lives and is one of my first readers, along with her husband Paul; their different strengths offer invaluable reactions to the story. Jennifer Larson is another whose insights on my characters, together with her own writing skills and knowledge of the American readership of Regency historical novels, bring illumination beyond price.

Annette Mercer, wonder horsewoman, tells me if I have the equine elements correct and also responds to my horse-mad characters with enthusiasm and humour. Stef Hill, skilled writer herself and friend since girlhood; Yvonne Kozlowski, friend, neighbour and loyal reader; Sarah Phillips, enthusiastic supporter of all my works; Meaghan Lomenick and Kitty Tomlin – these are but a few of so many wonderful family members and friends who have supported my carefree escapade into the Regency, and I am eternally grateful to them all.

Closest to the action are my beloved children, Ben and Lily, and stepdaughter Sophia who, with their partners and children, have fed me, cheered me, listened patiently as I follow an enthusiasm down a rabbit hole. Thank you especially.

And above all, thanks go to my dear husband, Nick. I interrupt him with requests for latin mottoes, or discussions as to

what might be the best word in a particular situation, and why –
and I make the poor man sit down and read my manuscript, as
my first reader (he likes the horses!).

I have dedicated this book to love; love at first sight,
passionate love, sexual love, conjugal love, love for family and
love for friends, love for animals, buildings and life – and love of
home. The world is in desperate need of more love and our books
hold out a flame against the encroaching dark.

ABOUT THE AUTHOR

Jane Dunn is an historian and biographer and the author of seven acclaimed biographies, including Daphne du Maurier and her Sisters and the Sunday Times and NYT bestseller, Elizabeth & Mary: Cousins, Rivals, Queens. She lives in Berkshire with her husband, the linguist Nicholas Ostler.

Sign up to Jane Dunn's mailing list for news, competitions and updates on future books.

Follow Jane on social media here:

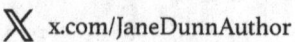 x.com/JaneDunnAuthor

ALSO BY JANE DUNN

Sixpence Stories

Introducing Sixpence Stories!

Discover page-turning historical novels from your favourite authors, meet new friends and be transported back in time.

Join our book club
Facebook group

https://bit.ly/SixpenceGroup

Sign up to our
newsletter

https://bit.ly/SixpenceNews

Boldwood

Boldwood Books is an award-winning fiction publishing company seeking out the best stories from around the world.

Find out more at www.boldwoodbooks.com

Join our reader community for brilliant books, competitions and offers!

Follow us
@BoldwoodBooks
@TheBoldBookClub

Sign up to our weekly deals newsletter

https://bit.ly/BoldwoodBNewsletter